WABASH CARNEGIE P L...
1203 9100 014 187 2

813.0872 Que
Queen, Ellery.
Ellery Queen's crimes and
punishments
   WITHDRAWN
   84162319

WABASH PUBLIC LIBRARY
WABASH, IND. 46992

DEMCO

Ellery Queen's CRIMES AND PUNISHMENTS

ELLERY QUEEN'S CRIMES AND PUNISHMENTS

Edited by Eleanor Sullivan
and Karen A. Prince

Stories collected from issues
of *Ellery Queen's Mystery Magazine*
edited by Ellery Queen

The Dial Press

Davis Publications, Inc.
380 Lexington Avenue
New York, New York 10017

FIRST PRINTING

Copyright © 1984 by Davis Publications, Inc.
All rights reserved.
Library of Congress Catalog Card Number: 59-13341
Printed in the U. S. A.

COPYRIGHT NOTICES AND ACKNOWLEDGMENTS

Grateful acknowledgment is hereby made for permission to include the following:

In the Clear by Patricia McGerr; © 1978 by Patricia McGerr; reprinted by permission of Curtis Brown, Ltd.
Bank Job by Bill Pronzini; © 1978 by Bill Pronzini; reprinted by permission of the author.
Captain Leopold Looks for the Cause by Edward D. Hoch; © 1977 by Edward D. Hoch; reprinted by permission of the author.
The Ehrengraf Method by Lawrence Block; © 1978 by Lawrence Block; reprinted by permission of the author.
A Hint of Danger by William Bankier; © 1978 by William Bankier; reprinted by permission of Curtis Brown, Ltd.
The Wager by Robert L. Fish; © 1973 by Robert L. Fish; originally appeared in PLAYBOY Magazine; reprinted by permission of Robert P. Mills, Ltd.
Tiger in the Night by Eleazar Lipsky; © 1955 by Eleazar Lipsky, renewed; reprinted by permission of the author.
Mrs. Henderson Talks to God by Libby MacCall; © 1978 by Libby MacCall; reprinted by permission of the author.
Two Rolls, No Coffee by Don M. Mankiewicz; copyright 1948 by Popular Publications, Inc., renewed; reprinted by permission of Harold Ober Associates, Inc.
What's on the Telly Tonight? by Mary Braund; © 1972 by Mary Braund; reprinted by permission of McIntosh & Otis, Inc.
The Killer Instinct by Thomas Walsh; © 1977 by Thomas Walsh; reprinted by permission of the author.
A Victim Must Be Found by Henry Slesar; copyright 1956 by Mercury Publications, Inc., renewed; reprinted by permission of the author.
The Tallest Man in the World by Janet Green; copyright 1956 by Janet Green, renewed; reprinted by permission of Curtis Brown, Ltd.
Trust Charlie by Brian Garfield; © 1978 by Brian Garfield; reprinted by permission of the author.
Rough Justice by Michael Gilbert; © 1977 by Michael Gilbert; reprinted by permission of Curtis Brown Associates, Ltd.

The School Bus Caper by Jack Ritchie; © 1978 by Jack Ritchie; reprinted by permission of Larry Sternig Literary Agency.
A Very Small Clue by E. X. Ferrars; © 1977 by E. X. Ferrars; reprinted by permission of Harold Ober Associates, Inc.
Pay-Off Girl by James M. Cain; copyright 1952 by Esquire, Inc., renewed 1980 by Alice M. Piper; reprinted by permission of Harold Ober Associates, Inc.
Tragedy of a Handkerchief by Michael Innes; copyright 1947 by Michael Innes, renewed; reprinted by permission of A. P. Watt, Ltd.
Dangerous Widows by Mignon G. Eberhart; © 1953 by United Newspapers Corp., copyright renewed 1981 by Mignon G. Eberhart; reprinted by permission of Brandt & Brandt Literary Agents, Inc.
The Price of Joy by Ruth Rendell; © 1977 by Ruth Rendell; reprinted by permission of Georges Borchardt, Inc.
The Death of Don Juan by Ellery Queen; copyright © 1962 by Ellery Queen; reprinted by permission of the Estate of Ellery Queen.

CONTENTS

Introduction   8

In the Clear	*Patricia McGerr*	9
Bank Job	*Bill Pronzini*	25
Captain Leopold Looks for the Cause	*Edward D. Hoch*	35
The Ehrengraf Method	*Lawrence Block*	50
A Hint of Danger	*William Bankier*	59
The Wager	*Robert L. Fish*	70
Tiger in the Night	*Eleazar Lipsky*	79
Mrs. Henderson Talks to God	*Libby MacCall*	96
Two Rolls, No Coffee	*Don M. Mankiewicz*	104
What's on the Telly Tonight?	*Mary Braund*	113
The Killer Instinct	*Thomas Walsh*	124
A Victim Must Be Found	*Henry Slesar*	137

The Tallest Man in the World	*Janet Green* 143
Trust Charlie	*Brian Garfield* 167
Rough Justice	*Michael Gilbert* 176
The School Bus Caper	*Jack Ritchie* 185
A Very Small Clue	*E. X. Ferrars* 196
Pay-Off Girl	*James M. Cain* 202
Tragedy of a Handkerchief	*Michael Innes* 210
Dangerous Widows	*Mignon G. Eberhart* 222
The Price of Joy	*Ruth Rendell* 231
The Death of Don Juan	*Ellery Queen* 243

INTRODUCTION

The crimes that take place in this new collection of stories from *Ellery Queen's Mystery Magazine* take a wide variety of forms: murder, bank robbery, blackmail, etc.—even bus theft. The punishments are equally varied, as are the personalities of the criminals.

There are, for instance, Kek Huuygens, Robert L. Fish's master smuggler, Lawrence Block's unscrupulous lawyer, Martin H. Ehrengraf, and Ruth Rendell's hard-nosed businessman, Daniel Derbyshire. On hand to track down the wrongdoers are Jack Ritchie's Henry Turnbuckle, Michael Innes's John Appleby, Michael Gilbert's Patrick Petrella, Edward D. Hoch's Captain Leopold, and others.

Featured is a short novel by Ellery Queen, praised by Anthony Boucher when it was first published in 1962 as the best of the year and a prime specimen of the true whodunit.

Although all 22 stories illustrate the many forms crime and punishment can take, in the end we must admit, with Virgil: "Had I a hundred tongues, a hundred mouths, a voice of iron, and a chest of brass, I could not tell all the forms of crime, could not name all the types of punishment."

Nonetheless, in varied and imaginative ways, mystery writers continue not only to tell the crimes and name the punishments, but to infuse them with meaning and a fitting sense of justice—perhaps taking their cue from the words of W. S. Gilbert in *The Mikado*:

> *"My object all sublime*
> *I shall achieve in time—*
> *To let the punishment fit the crime."*

Patricia McGerr
In the Clear

Frank Crawford was a careful man. Before taking any important action he figured the odds, balanced the gains against the costs, and made detailed plans. Although a moderate gambler, he did not bet more than he could afford to lose, seldom backed a longshot, and never drew to an inside straight. When his marriage at last became intolerable, he studied his alternatives with the same cautious deliberation that he gave a sales campaign for his appliance company.

After nearly twenty years of marriage the only feeling he had for Doris was a kind of mild contempt. The pleasing plumpness of girlhood had become middle-aged obesity. They had few common interests and her striving for intellectual improvement made her, in his eyes, an even greater bore. But she was an adequate housekeeper and put good meals on the table whenever he chose to come home to eat them.

For other satisfactions he looked elsewhere and had a long-standing arrangement with the manicurist in a shop near his office. Inge, though attractive and compliant, was not irreplaceable and he had no wish to make their relationship legal. Doris, on her side, was willing to ignore his infidelity as long as it did not disturb her comfortable existence. Thus there evolved a pattern that made it convenient for them to stay together while leading mainly separate lives. Neither had any reason to seek a change until Julie Casement came to work for the agency that handled Frank's advertising.

Julie was small and slim with shaggily clipped black hair and large trusting brown eyes. Frank took her to dinner and when the evening ended he tried to analyze his odd sense of exaltation. The feelings she stirred in him were different from any he had ever known. Desire was softened by tenderness. He wanted to protect her from all the hurts of the world, even from himself. I'm in love, he decided with astonishment, in love for the first time in my life.

But she turned down his next invitation after one of her co-workers told her he was married. The regret in her tone encouraged him to argue, but it was no use.

"I suppose I sound dreadfully old-fashioned," she admitted, "but it's the way I was raised. I can't go out with you again."

"You must know there's more between us than a casual encounter," Frank persisted. "I care for you, Julie. Last night I thought you felt the same way."

"I do. But there's no point in talking about it. Please don't make it any more painful for me."

"I never want to cause you pain."

"Then say goodbye now. That's all there is to say."

He heard the click of her phone and put his own down more slowly. She was so dear, so good, so defenseless. She needed him to look after her. That evening at dinner he raised for the first time the question of divorce.

"You got some girl in trouble?" Doris asked harshly.

"Of course not."

"Then why the sudden rush to break up our marriage?"

"It's not sudden. Our marriage has been unsatisfactory for many years."

"You may not be satisfied," she countered, "but I am. I don't intend to change my whole way of life just because some bit of fluff has caught your eye."

Leaving the table, he drove across town to Inge's apartment. Responding curtly to her greeting, he strode to the kitchen and poured a generous measure of Scotch.

"What's bugging you?" she asked. "Your old lady giving you a hard time?"

"What's that to you?"

"My, we are in a foul mood. If you don't want to talk to me, why did you come?"

In answer he pulled her toward him and pressed his mouth on hers with a roughness that made her wince. Later, when he left her, his tension was somewhat eased but his spirits were still low. I've got two women, he thought morosely. Two bad bargains. Doris, fat and silly. Inge, hard and greedy. Then there's Julie. Gentle and sweet and unattainable.

Lying awake, he thought about divorce. Doris's opposition might wilt under pressure, but the price would be prohibitive. Living in a community property state, she'd take half of his savings, plus high alimony. He wanted Julie to have a life of luxury, not to scrimp on Doris's leavings. Nor should he make Julie, with her high standards, the cause of a messy divorce. But if Doris should die . . .

In the dark he let his mind play with the picture of himself as widower. Lonely, bereft, turning to Julie for comfort. Ah, yes, that would bring her to him. If only Doris were dead!

It was a concept to which his mind returned again and again in the days that followed. He began to look at his wife with eyes that saw her not as a woman but as a victim. His fantasies showed him a variety of methods—knife and gun, rope and poison. But he knew that when a woman is murdered, her husband is the number-one suspect. And if the investigation shows that the marriage was unhappy and the man had a younger mistress, the police will look no further. Yet if he ruled out both divorce and death, what was left? A long arid stretch of life without Julie.

What he needed was an undetectable poison or a weight that would drop on her head when he was far away. But those were, he knew, impossible dreams. If he killed Doris, he'd go to prison. If he divorced her, he'd be impoverished. He was in a trap with no exit. As a realist, he was learning to live with that fact until one afternoon he saw Julie. She was walking beside a well dressed young man, her face raised to look up at him, absorbed in their conversation. The sight of her with someone else, the thought that he might lose her, was like a stab of physical pain. That was when he thought of Gregor.

Gregor operated a newsstand on a downtown street corner. In addition to papers and magazines, he sold candy, gum, cigarettes, and postcards. He also took bets on numbers and on a variety of sporting events. Through him, according to rumor, one could obtain loans at usurious interest. It was assumed, though no one said it out loud, that he had underworld connections.

Frank waited until evening, after the brisk rush-hour business, then approached to put twenty dollars on a favorite in the next day's races. The transaction completed, he said with a careful casualness, "By the way, a friend of mine has a problem. There's a guy who's—well, in his way, if you know what I mean. You know anybody who might—uh—have him taken care of?"

"Maybe." Without changing expression, Gregor scribbled numbers on a scrap of paper and handed it to Frank. "Ask for Dr. Brill."

"Doctor?"

"If he's looking for a permanent cure."

"Can you tell me what the—uh—doctor charges?"

"Two grand for a routine job with no complications."

"How does—"

"Look, you got the number. Tear it up, give it to your friend, do what you want. But don't tell me any more, don't ask me. You walk away and I forget we ever had this talk. Okay?"

"Right, Gregor."

He was trembling when he left him, the hand that held the phone number thrust deep in his pocket. I can't do it, he told himself. To put out a—what's the word?—a contract on Doris. To hire someone to kill her. It's a crazy notion. But he memorized the number before he burned the paper and he knew, deep within himself, that some day he'd make the call.

For the rest of the week he thought of little else. He must not be rash or hasty. Before he took an irrevocable action, he must study all the angles, make careful preparations. First, there was the money. If Doris died violently, recent large cash withdrawals from his account would be a signal to investigators. Instead he began to squirrel small sums away in a metal box locked in the bottom drawer of his desk. A run of winning hands at his regular Friday-night poker session brought in over three hundred dollars which went into the box intact on Monday morning.

While the fund grew he also gave thought to eliminating, or at least obscuring, his motive. On Doris's birthday he invited another couple to dine with them at the city's best hotel. There he presented her with an expensive amber necklace and was, through the evening, ostentatiously kind and attentive.

"What are you up to?" she asked suspiciously when they were alone. "Buttering me up for something, I can see that."

"We're stuck with each other, old girl," he said with false jollity. "Why not make the best of it? It wasn't bad in the beginning, you know. If we both try a little, maybe we can get back to that."

"I guess it won't hurt to try," she conceded.

As his next move he brought home a packet of travel brochures with the suggestion that they celebrate their wedding anniversary on a Mediterranean cruise. He could count on her to display the folders to her bridge and luncheon partners who would become, if needed, witnesses to his concern for his wife's happiness. If needed—that remained the operative phrase. Several times he came close to calling the number given him by Gregor. Each time he drew back.

What finally decided him was a story in the Monday morning paper linking a series of robberies that had taken place throughout the city and its suburbs during the past few months. The method of operation was, according to police, similar enough to point to a single perpetrator, nicknamed the Bike Bandit because a motorcycle had, in several instances, been heard or seen near the scene of the crime. Seven residents had returned from an evening out to find their homes stripped of money, jewelry, and other small valuable objects. An eighth, surprising the thief in the act, had been struck with a heavy candlestick and left unconscious. She was recovering in a local hospital.

Frank, reading the story a second time, knew that if he was ever going to act, it had to be now. He left his office shortly before noon to make the call from an outdoor booth in an isolated area. When a voice said, "Answering Service" he asked for Dr. Brill.

"Leave your name and number and the doctor will call back."

"This is Mr. Smith," Frank said, and read off the number from the dial. He had about a ten-minute wait.

"Dr. Brill here." The new voice was clear and authoritative. "To whom am I speaking?"

"Mr. Smith. Gregor said you can help me with a—a permanent cure."

"You know the terms?"

"He told me two thousand."

"Right, if it's a standard operation."

"I thought it might be made to look like the Bike Bandit."

"That can be arranged. What's the patient's name and address?"

"Mrs. Frank Crawford, 4100 Rinegold Road."

"Have you set a date?"

"She'll attend a lecture from eight to nine-thirty on Friday evening and get home about ten. If someone can be waiting in the house—"

"We'll handle the details. What about the husband? Will he be with her?"

"No, he has other plans for the evening."

"I assume you have the money ready."

"Yes."

"Then follow these instructions. Put the two grand in a plain brown envelope and leave it in locker number twenty-three at the airport before five P.M. on Wednesday. Got that?"

"Yes. Locker twenty-three on Wednesday. What about the key?"

"We don't need it. Just be sure the case is there on time."

"If you get full payment in advance, how do I know you'll carry out your end of the bargain?"

"How do you know a mechanic puts the parts he charges for in your car? You have to trust us, Mr. Smith. If you don't—well, it's your decision. If the money's in the box on Wednesday, the operation will take place Friday night. If not, the deal is off. No hard feelings either way."

Dr. Brill broke the connection but it was almost a minute before Frank hung up and walked out of the booth. I've done it, he thought. I've hired a killer. His mind veered away from the picture of Doris's dead body. He couldn't go through with it. He wasn't a murderer. He'd take the money from his desk, deposit it in the bank, and that would be the end of it. It would be as if the phone call had never been made.

But on Wednesday, Julie brought over an ad layout for his approval, and seeing her rekindled his desire. As soon as she left he sealed the money in an envelope and drove to the airport. On the way back he dropped the locker key into a roadside trashcan. His decision was irreversible.

On Thursday he stopped at the travel agency to make reservations on the cruise ship Doris had chosen. She was almost childishly pleased when he told her about it that evening. Everything was done. In one more day he'd be free. Then, on Friday morning, there was an unexpected snag. The man at whose house that night's poker session was scheduled came down with flu. Another player phoned to say the game was canceled. "Oh, no!" Frank exclaimed. "We can't call it off now. We'll get a substitute."

"The problem is a place to play. Can you take us in?"

"No, that's not possible. How about Jim?"

"He's having his place painted. What's so bad about missing one week's game? You feeling lucky?"

"No, I just—" He paused, his mind working quickly. He'd overreacted. Mustn't leave the impression that the cancellation was important. "The thing is, my wife's going to an art lecture and if I tell her there's no game, she'll try to drag me along."

"I see your problem, pal." The other man chuckled. "My advice is, don't tell her. See you next week."

Frank sat looking at the silent phone. Damn. Damn. Damn! It was too perfect. I should have known something would go wrong. What do I do now? Call off the operation or postpone it? But the groundwork is all laid. It may be weeks before Doris and I have separate engagements for the same evening. And I'm sure Brill doesn't give refunds.

All right, calm down, think it through. All you've lost is an alibi. You've the rest of the day to set up another. Yet each idea was quickly discarded. Whatever he did must look natural. Any uncharacteristic activity would seem just what it was, an attempt to establish an alibi. He wasn't a moviegoer. He didn't bowl or shoot pool. He met his friends and customers for lunch, not dinner. There was no one with whom he could, without strangeness, arrange to spend the evening. Except Inge.

His lips twisted wryly at the thought. She'd be a natural enough companion. And useless as an alibi. Who would believe a man's mistress if she said he was with her at the time his wife was murdered? And yet— He held onto her name a little longer. To call Inge when his poker game fell through was completely in character. If he took her to a public place and made sure they were visible and identifiable during the crucial time period, he'd be home free. With a lifting of spirits he reached for the phone.

Having made the date, he began to see ways it might serve as more than a simple alibi. Tonight he'd end the relationship, tell her he didn't intend to call her again. Then he could start fresh with Julie, with no old entanglements, no loose ends. More important, it would be one more piece in the mosaic he was building of an improved marriage.

Through the day he pondered his plans until every detail was perfect. He even rehearsed in the washroom the expression of stunned bereavement he would show the police. By the time he left his office he had begun to believe that the game cancellation was, in fact, a stroke of good luck.

He timed his arrival home for a few minutes before the friend with whom Doris was attending the lecture came by to pick her up. He walked with her to the car and helped her in.

"Have a good time," he told them both, "and soak up lots of culture. It will stand us in good stead in those foreign galleries. Did Doris tell you we're planning a cruise?"

"Yes, it sounds wonderful."

"See you later, hon." He patted her hand before closing the door, then watched with satisfaction as the car drove off. A touching farewell for Sue Farrell to describe when the police questioned her.

A short time later he was on his way to Inge's. Parking in an alley, he locked the car doors but left the lights on. Inge lived on the ground floor of an old remodeled house and he was about to knock on her kitchen door when he realized that if she noticed the car headlights on, he'd have to turn them off. Shaken a little by the near error, he walked around to the front.

Over drinks he told her that he'd reserved a table at a restaurant two blocks away.

"That Spanish place?" she protested. "I want to go someplace fancy. You trying to cut expenses?"

"Somebody told me the guitarist is good. I'd like to hear him."

"Yeah? I didn't put on my Sunday best to eat rice and beans at a neighborhood joint."

"It's not that cheap." He cut short the argument. "Anyway, the reservation's made and I'm hungry. If you don't want to go—"

"Oh, all right." Sullenly she gave in. "Some great evening this is going to be."

Inge's shoes were not made for walking and her temper was not improved by Frank's insistence that the restaurant was too close to take his car. Her bad humor too, Frank congratulated himself, is in my favor. When the waiter tells the police we quarreled all through dinner, it will shore up my story of our split. He made no effort to be conciliatory but let her ramble on with her complaints. When the waiter put platters of paella in front of them he said loudly and harshly, "Shut up and eat. I'm sick of your bellyaching."

It was a silent meal. Inge sulked and Frank, secretly rejoicing, maintained an expression of grim displeasure. A mediocre flamenco dancer opened the 9:30 floor show. The guitarist wasn't much better, but Frank applauded with enthusiasm and sent the waiter to request "Adios, muchachas." The guitarist came to their table to lean soulfully over Inge as he sang. Frank thanked him with a five-dollar bill.

"What was that all about?" Inge challenged. "After being so mean all evening, do you think you can get round me with sentimental music?"

"No," he answered. "It's my way of saying goodbye. I won't be seeing you again." He signaled for the check.

"You what?" Smoldering resentment burst into flame. "You think you can brush me off like—like a squeezed lemon? You listen to me, Frank Crawford—"

"There's no need to shout."

"Oh yes, there is." As expected, her voice rose higher. "You think you can pick me up and throw me away whenever you feel like it. Just let me tell you—"

"Hush, everybody's looking at us." He produced a credit card. The waiter took it and went away.

"I've got feelings too, you know." She pushed away from the table and stood up. They were a center of attention for all the nearby diners.

"What do you want?" he asked with deliberate insult. "Severance pay?"

"You'll find out what I want," she said wildly. "You can't treat me like dirt and get away with it."

He signed the check, accepted his card and receipt, and stood. A glance at his watch showed it was 10:10. Right on schedule.

"Come on, let's get out of here." He took her arm. She jerked away and half ran to the door. Passing the maitre d' he mumbled in half apology, "The lady's a little upset."

Following her to the street, he let her stay a few paces ahead of him until she reached her apartment. She darted inside and slammed the door. And that suited him just fine. Inge's part in the program was finished and she had, unwittingly, played it superbly.

He returned to the alley. His car was dark, the headlights no longer burning. He got behind the wheel, turned the key in the ignition, but the engine did not respond. As planned, the battery was dead. He walked through the alley to the next block where there was an all-night drugstore.

"Car trouble," he told the man on duty as he headed for the phone booth at the back.

"You'll have a hard time getting someone to fix it this time of night."

"I'm not going to try. It can stay where it is until morning. I just want to use your phone to call a cab."

In the booth he could not resist dialing his own number. It should be all over by now. He listened, hardly breathing, as the phone began to ring in his house. He counted up to ten. There was no answer. Satisfied, he called the cab company and gave the address of the drugstore. When he stepped out of the booth he was surprised to discover that he was drenched in perspiration. He mopped his face with his handkerchief as he moved to the counter and ordered coffee. When it came his hand was shaking so that half of it slopped over the counter as he tried to raise the cup to his lips.

The cab arrived quickly. Riding home he responded in monosyllables to the driver, discouraging conversation. He had to get his nerves under control, examine the plan for any last-minute flaws. He had left the restaurant at 10:15, entered the drugstore at 10:30. Even with wings he could not have got across town and back in that period.

The house, when the cab pulled up, was dark. The meter registered $2.45. Frank affected embarrassment.

"I'm afraid the smallest I have is a fifty," he said. "Can you change it?"

"You kidding, buddy? I don't carry that kind of cash on late-night calls. Why didn't you break it in the drugstore?"

"I just wasn't thinking. If you'll come to the house with me, I'll get it from my wife."

"Okay, if that's how it's got to be." Grumbling, he accompanied Frank up the sidewalk. "Looks like your old lady's in bed. She won't like being routed out to pay your fare."

"She'll understand."

"Lucky you. Mine'd raise hell."

The driver waited on the porch while Frank unlocked the door and went inside. He took a quick breath, bracing himself, then flipped the switch that lighted the living room. Doris lay in the middle of the rug, arms outflung, eyes staring, mouth twisted in a grimace. Although the sight was expected, his sense of shock was genuine.

"My God! Doris—oh no!" He turned back to the cabman. "Something terrible has happened."

"What's going on, buddy?" The other man followed him in. "Oh, hey! Look at that! Is she dead?"

"I don't know." He dropped to his knees beside her, took her hand. It was cold, lifeless. "Call a doctor. Tell him to hurry."

"What you want is the police."

"Yes, I—you're right. Will you call them? The phone's in the hall."

"Sure thing." He went out.

Frank moved away from the body to a chair at the far end of the room and listened to the driver tell someone, "A lady's been killed." That's no lady, his mind appended with sick humor, that's my wife. All I have to do now is act dazed, broken, and tell the truth about how I spent the evening. When the driver came back he was slumped in the chair, his face buried in his hands.

"They'll be right over," the cabman reported. "He said for me to stay here and nobody should touch anything."
"Yes, fine. Thank you."
"Sorry about your wife, mister." He offered awkward sympathy. "Must be the guy they call the Bike Bandit. If the cops worked as hard chasing crooks as they do handing out tickets, he'd been in jail weeks ago."
His words rolled on but Frank stopped listening. He kept his face covered, his eyes closed, and his thoughts turned inward. At last the doorbell rang, the cabman went to answer it, and the room was suddenly full of men. One of them squatted beside the body. Another crossed the room to Frank who rose to meet him.
"Lieutenant Hamill, Homicide," he identified himself. "This your house?"
"Yes, I—I'm Frank Crawford. And that—" He forced himself to look again at Doris. "That's my wife."
"How about it, Doc?" Hamill asked the man on the floor. "She dead?"
"No doubt of that." He was matter-of-fact. "Offhand, I'd say a blow on the head with a heavy object."
"Okay, boys, you know what to do," Hamill told the others. "Is there someplace we can talk, Mr. Crawford?"
"There's a den."
"What about me?" the driver protested. "I've got to get back on the street. I'm losing a night's work."
"Yeah? What's your part in this?"
"I brought the man home. I was with him when he found the body. I'm the one who called to report the crime."
"I haven't paid your fare," Frank remembered. "I was going to get it from—" He looked at the handbag that lay a few feet from Doris's hand and his voice died away.
"Send a bill," Hamill snapped. "Clancy, get the cabbie's story and let him go. All right, Mr. Crawford, take me to the den."
The smaller room showed signs of disarray. Desk drawers were partly open, a cabinet door swung loose. Nothing obvious, just enough to suggest that a search had been made.
"You keep any cash or valuables in here?" Hamill asked.
"No, I—oh!" A delayed memory struck him.
"Yeah? You notice something missing?"
"Not in here. But I just realized, when I found my wife, I—I took her hand—her left hand—and it was bare."

"Bare?"

"No rings. She always wore a big diamond. Almost a carat." Brill's man, he thought, had helped himself to a nice bonus. It was worth it, though, to add credibility.

"I see. Later I'd like you to go through the house and make an inventory of your losses. But first I want to get a sequence of events. When did you last see your wife?"

"About seven-thirty this evening." He sat down, clasped his hands to stop their trembling. "A friend of hers picked her up to take her to a lecture."

"You know the friend's name and address?"

As he asked the question, the man he'd called Clancy entered unobtrusively and flipped open a small notebook.

"Mrs. George Farrell." Frank watched Clancy write it down. "She lives on Maple Drive. I'm not sure of the number."

"We can find her. After they left what did you do?"

"I had dinner with a friend."

"His name and address?"

"Actually, it was a woman."

"Oh?"

"Inge Ericson, 1421 Grant Street."

Again Clancy's pen moved. He and Hamill exchanged glances.

"I might as well tell you the truth, Lieutenant." Frank did not try to hide his embarrassment. "Inge and I were more than just friends. We've been having—well, I guess you'd call it an affair. But it's over. That's why I went to see her tonight—to break it off."

"Yeah?" The lieutenant's tone was neutral, showing neither belief nor doubt. "How come?"

"To be honest, my wife and I have been through some bad times. I wasn't the best of husbands—you'll hear that from a lot of people. But lately we've made an effort and it was starting to work. We planned to go on a cruise, a sort of second honeymoon. Doris was really looking forward to that. And now—now she'll never—" He broke off, covered his eyes with his hand, and held the pose for several seconds. Then he straightened and made a brave attempt to smile. "Sorry," he said. "Anyway, that's what I had to tell Inge."

"I see." Skepticism broke through. "What you're telling me, Mr. Crawford, is that at the time of your wife's murder you were in your girl friend's apartment saying goodbye forever. I assume that Miss—Ericson, is it?—will tell the same story."

"We didn't stay in her apartment." Frank felt a secret pleasure at the way the detective had swallowed his bait. "Inge's got a temper, and I figured she'd take the news better if there were other people around. So we went to a restaurant near where she lives. La Paloma." Got that, Clancy? he wanted to add.

"And then?"

"We had something to eat, watched the floor show, and I told her what I'd come to say."

"How'd she react?"

"She blew up a little and I took her home."

"How long did you stay in her apartment?"

"I didn't go in. She was still sore and there was nothing more to talk about, so I came home."

"Don't you have a car, Mr. Crawford?"

"Lord, yes, I almost forgot that part. I drove to Inge's but La Paloma is in walking distance. Then when I tried to start my car, I found I had a dead battery. It's still parked there."

"How'd you get the cab?"

"I phoned from a drugstore at the corner of Fifteenth and Stevens. When we got here all I had was a bill too big for him to change. That's why he came into the house with me. I was going to get some money from Doris, but instead—" Again he gave way to emotion, hiding his face.

"That jibe with the hacker's story?" Hamill asked Clancy.

"Yeah. His sheet shows a pickup at ten thirty-five and we got the call at eleven twenty-seven."

"That fits. Get somebody to interview Mrs. Farrell, find out when she brought Mrs. Crawford home, what she saw and heard. Also check the restaurant, the drugstore, and the Ericson girl."

"Will do."

Clancy left. Hamill waited for Frank to recover. When he looked up, the detective's eyes were more sympathetic.

"I know this is a bad time for you, Mr. Crawford, but you've given us a straight story. I'm sure you understand that in a murder case, everything has to be doublechecked."

"You have your job to do." He matched the other's courtesy. "I'll do anything I can to help catch my wife's killer."

"We'll get him," Hamill promised. "The routine's going on while I talk to you."

As if in proof one of his subordinates came to the door. "The doc's finished," he reported. "Okay to take the body away?"

"Got enough pictures?"

"From every angle."

"Okay, let the morgue have her. What else do you know?"

"There are signs of forced entry by the back door. A couple of the neighbors say they heard a sound like a motorcycle being gunned around ten P.M."

Coincidence, Frank wondered, or part of the special Brill service? The younger man left and Hamill turned back to Frank, his manner distinctly more friendly.

"We're getting a pattern," he said. "Maybe you've heard of a string of recent housebreakings?"

"The taxi driver said something about a—was it a Bike Bandit?"

"That's what the newspapers call him. He picks houses with no lights and no television playing and the occupants out for the evening. He steals small things, like money and jewelry, that he can carry on his motorcycle."

"Like my wife's ring."

"Exactly. Let's look around and see what else is missing."

With Hamill behind him Frank went upstairs and into Doris's bedroom. Like the den it gave the impression of a fast search. A jewel box lay open, its contents dumped in the middle of the bed.

"It's mostly costume jewelry," Frank said. "But she had a couple of good pieces—an amber necklace and a bracelet of heavy gold." He poked among the scattered articles. "They're not here."

"So he took the good stuff and left the junk. He knows values."

Continuing the inspection, Frank found that a pair of gold cufflinks had been taken from his bureau. That appeared to be the extent of the burglar's haul. They were in his bedroom when the phone rang. It was for Lieutenant Hamill. He listened for a long time, responding with grunts and short exclamations that apparently expressed satisfaction with what he heard.

"That about covers it," he concluded, "except for Ericson. Get her story and we'll have the whole package. I'll be here for another hour or so." He put down the phone. "Your account is fully corroborated," he told Frank. "The restaurant owner, the waiter, even the guitar player—they all remember you. Your girl friend must have made quite a row."

"She was pretty mad," he agreed.

"The druggist remembers you too. And of course the cab company has a record of your call."

"Has someone talked to Mrs. Farrell?"

"Yes, she said the lecture ended about nine-thirty and she drove your wife right home. The house was dark and everything looked normal."

"That's not much help."

"No, but at least the timing puts you in the clear. If you'll excuse me, I'll get on with my job. We have to go over the whole house for prints, et cetera. The fellow didn't leave any evidence in the other places, but sometimes they get careless and we get lucky. If you want to go to bed—"

"Thank you, no. I couldn't sleep. But I'll stay out of your way."

Frank remained upstairs while the lieutenant rejoined his associates. You're in the clear. In the clear. Hamill's words echoed soothingly in his brain. The tension that had carried him through the evening gave way to euphoria. His alibi was watertight and he was in the clear. Free of Doris. Free of suspicion. Two thousand dollars plus a diamond ring, an amber necklace, a gold bracelet, a pair of gold cufflinks. He couldn't ask for a better bargain.

He was standing by the window gazing into the dark but contemplating a bright future when Hamill returned. Clancy was with him.

"You've found some evidence?" Frank asked them.

"Not here," Hamill answered. "But something else has come up. Tell me, Mr. Crawford, why did you go all the way to the drugstore to call a cab? Why didn't you use your girl friend's phone?"

"We'd had a pretty heavy argument, you know about that. I didn't want to go back to her apartment."

"I'm sure you didn't. The druggist said you seemed very nervous, spilled coffee all over his counter."

"I suppose I was a little on edge. First the quarrel with Inge, then a dead battery."

"The cabdriver called you restless and fidgety."

"I may have been. What are you getting at, Lieutenant? What has all this to do with the murder of my wife?"

"With your wife? Not a thing. You know I sent a man to talk to Miss Ericson?"

"I heard you give the order."

"She didn't answer the doorbell and he couldn't get her on the phone. That worried him. Sometimes when a guy dumps a girl, she gets despondent, takes too many pills, or turns on the gas."

"Are you telling me that something's happened to Inge—"

"I think you know the answer to that as well as I do," Hamill snapped. "When they went in, they found her on the floor. The weapon, a heavy brass bookend, was lying by her side."

"Was she—is she—?"

"She's dead, Crawford."

"Oh, no! No, that can't be—"

"She yelled at you in the restaurant," Hamill said. "She made threats. A dozen or more people heard her. When you were back in her apartment, the fight got hotter. She wasn't willing to be dropped, maybe she had blackmail material. So you picked up the bookend, and crushed her skull. Is that how it happened?"

"No! No, you're wrong. I wasn't in her apartment. I only got as far as the door. She slammed it in my face." He paused, remembering how it had been. Himself on the outside, Inge going alone into the dark house. "He must have already been there. The Bike Bandit. He went in while we were at the restaurant. She caught him robbing the place and he—he killed her."

"That's what we were meant to think," Hamill agreed. "Somebody did a good job of imitating the Biker's m.o. It might even have worked if the Bike Bandit hadn't gone out on his own tonight. But we know he was here in your house at ten o'clock. And a man can't be in two places at once, can he, Mr. Crawford?"

Bill Pronzini

Bank Job

I was standing beside the tellers' cages, in the railed-off section where the branch manager's desk was located, when the knocking began on the bank's rear door.

Frowning, I looked over in that direction. Now who the devil could that be? It was four o'clock and the Fairfield branch of the Midland National Bank had been closed for an hour; it seemed unlikely that a customer would arrive at this late time.

The knocking continued—a rather curious sort of summons, I thought. It was both urgent and hesitant, alternately loud and soft in an odd spasmodic way. I glanced a bit uneasily at the suitcase on the floor beside the desk. But I could not just ignore the rapping. Judging from its insistence, whoever it was seemed to know that the bank was still occupied.

I went out through the gate in the rail divider and walked slowly down the short corridor to the door. The shade was drawn over the glass there—I had drawn it myself earlier—and I could not see out into the private parking area at the rear. The knocking, I realized as I stepped up to the door, was coming from down low on the wood panel, beneath the glass. A child? Still frowning, I drew back the edge of the shade and peered out.

The person out there was a man, not a child—a medium-sized man with a mustache, modishly styled hair, and a business suit and tie. He was down on one knee, with his right hand stretched out to the door. His left hand was pressed against the side of his head, and his temple and the tips of his fingers were stained with what appeared to be blood.

He saw me looking out at about the same time I saw him. We blinked at each other. He made an effort to rise, sank back onto his knee again, and said in a pained voice that barely carried through the door, "Accident—over in the driveway—I need a doctor."

I peered past him. As much of the parking area as I could see was deserted, but from my vantage point I could not make out the driveway on the south side of the bank. I hesitated, but when the man said plaintively, "Please—I need help," I reacted on impulse: I reached down, unlocked the door, and started to pull it open.

The man came upright in one fluid motion, drove a shoulder against the door, and crowded inside. The door edge cracked into my forehead and threw me backward, off-balance. My vision blurred for a moment, and when it cleared and I had my equilibrium again I was looking not at one man but at two.

I was also looking at a gun, held competently in the hand of the first man.

The second one, who seemed to have materialized out of nowhere, closed and relocked the door. Then he too produced a handgun and pointed it at me. He looked enough like the first man to be his brother—medium-size, mustache, modishly styled hair, business suit and tie. The only appreciable difference between them was One was wearing a blue shirt and Two a white shirt.

I stared at them incredulously. "Who are you? What do you want?"

"Unnecessary questions," One said. He had a soft, well modulated voice, calm and reasonable. "It should be obvious who we are and what we want."

"My God," I said, "bank robbers."

"Bingo," Two said. His voice was scratchy, like sand rubbing on glass.

One took a handkerchief from his coat pocket and wiped the blood—or whatever the crimson stuff was—off his fingers and his temple. I realized as he did so that his mustache and hair, and those of the other man, were of the theatrical-makeup variety.

"You just do what you're told," One said, "and everything will be fine. Turn around, walk up the hall."

I did that. By the time I stopped in front of the rail divider, the incredulity had vanished and I had regained my composure. I turned once more to face them.

"I'm afraid you're going to be disappointed," I said.

"Is that right?" One said. "Why?"

"You're not going to be able to rob this bank."

"Why aren't we?"

"Because all the money has been put inside the vault for the weekend," I said. "And I've already set the time locks; the vault doors can't be opened by hand and the time locks won't release until nine o'clock Monday morning."

They exchanged a look. Their faces were expressionless, but their eyes, I saw, were narrowed and cold. One said to Two, "Check out the tellers' cages."

Two nodded and hurried through the divider gate.

One looked at me again. "What's your name?"
"Luther Baysinger," I said.
"You do what here, Luther?"
"I'm the Fairfield branch manager."
"You lock up the money this early every Friday?"
"Yes."
"How come you don't stay open until six o'clock?"
I gestured at the cramped old-fashioned room. "We're a small branch bank in a rural community," I said. "We do a limited business; there has been no need for us to expand our hours."
"Where're the other employees now?"
"I gave them permission to leave early for the weekend."
From inside the second of the two tellers' cages Two called, "Cash drawers are empty!"
One said to me, "Let's go back to the vault."
I pivoted immediately, stepped through the gate, entered the cages, and led the two of them down the walkway to the outer vault door. One examined it, tugged on the wheel. When it failed to yield he turned back to me. "No way to open this door before Monday morning?"
"None at all."
"You're *sure* of that?"
"Of course I'm sure. As I told you, I've set the time locks—here, and on the door to the inner vault as well. The inner vault is where all the bank's assets are kept."
Two said, "Damn. I knew we should have waited when we saw the place closed up. Now what do we do?"
One ignored him. "How much is in that inner vault?" he asked me. "Round numbers."
"A few thousand, that's all," I said carefully.
"Come on, Luther. How much is in there?"
His voice was still calm and reasonable, but he managed nonetheless to imply a threat to the words. If I continued to lie to him, he was saying tacitly, he would do unpleasant things to me.
I sighed. "Around twenty thousand," I said. "We have no need for more than that on hand. We're—"
"I know," One said, "you're a small branch bank in a rural community. How many other people work here?"
"Just two."
"Both tellers?"
"Yes."

"What time do they come in on Monday morning?"
"Nine o'clock."
"Just when the vault locks release."
"Yes. But—"
"Suppose you were to call up those two tellers and tell them to come in at nine-thirty on Monday, instead of nine o'clock—make up some kind of excuse. They wouldn't question that, would they?"

It came to me then, all too clearly, what he was getting at. A coldness settled on my neck and melted down along my back. "It won't work," I said.

He raised an eyebrow. "What won't work?"
"Kidnaping me and holding me for hostage for the weekend."
"No? Why not?"
"The tellers *would* know something was wrong if I asked them to come in late on Monday."
"I doubt that."
"Besides," I lied, "I have a wife, three children, and a mother-in-law living in my house. You couldn't control all of them for an entire weekend."
"So we won't take you to your house. We'll take you somewhere else and have you call your family and tell them you've been called out of town unexpectedly."
"They wouldn't believe it—"
"I think they would. Look, Luther, we don't want to hurt you. All we're interested in is that twenty thousand. We're a little short of cash right now; we need operating capital." He shrugged and looked at Two. "How about it?"
"Sure," Two said. "Okay by me."
"Let's go out front again, Luther."

A bit numbly, I led them away from the vault. When we passed out of the tellers' cages my eyes went to the suitcase beside the desk and lingered on it for a couple of seconds. I pulled my gaze away then—but not soon enough.

One said, "Hold up right there."

I stopped, half turning, and when I saw him looking past me at the suitcase I grimaced.

One noticed that too. "Planning a trip somewhere?" he asked.

"Ah—yes," I said. "A trip, yes. To the state capital—a bankers' convention. I'm expected there tonight and if I don't show up people will know something is wrong—"

"Nuts," One said. He glanced at Two. "Take a look inside that suitcase."
"Wait," I said, "I—"
"Shut up, Luther."
I shut up and watched Two lift the suitcase to the top of the desk next to the nameplate there that read *Luther Baysinger, Branch Manager*. He snapped open the catches and swung up the lid.
Surprise registered on his face. "Hey," he said, "money. It's filled with *money*."
One stepped away from me and went over to stand beside Two, who was rifling through the packets of currency inside the suitcase. A moment later Two hesitated, then said, "What the hell?" and lifted out my .22 Colt Woodsman which was also inside the case.
Both of them looked at me. I stared back defiantly. For several seconds it was very quiet in there; then, because there was nothing else to be done, I lowered my gaze and leaned against the divider.
"All right," I said, "the masquerade is over."
One said, "Masquerade? What's that supposed to mean, Luther?"
"My name isn't Luther," I said.
"What?"
"The real Luther Baysinger is locked inside the vault."
"What?"
"Along with both tellers."
Two said it this time. "What?"
"There's around eight thousand dollars in the suitcase," I said. "I cleaned it out of the cash room in the outer vault not long before you showed up."
"What the hell are you telling us?" One said. "Are you saying you're—"
"The same thing you are, that's right. I'm a bank robber."
They looked at each other. Both of them appeared confused now, no longer quite so sure of themselves.
One said, "I don't believe it."
I shrugged. "It's the truth. We both seem to have picked the same day to knock over the same bank, only I got here first. I've been casing this place for a week; I doubt if you cased it at all. A spur-of-the-moment job, am I right?"
"Hell," Two said to One, "he *is* right. We only just—"
"Be quiet," One said, "let me think." He gave me a long searching look. "What's your name?"
"John Smith."

"Yeah, sure."

"Look," I said, "I'm not going to give you my right name. Why should I? You're not going to tell me yours."

One gestured to Two. "Frisk him," he said. "See if he's carrying any identification."

Two came over to me and ran his hands over my clothing, checked inside all the pockets of my suit. "No wallet," he said.

"Of course not," I said. "I'm a professional, same as you are. I'm not stupid enough to carry identification on a job."

Two went back to where One was standing and they held a whispered conference, giving me sidewise looks all the while. At the end of two minutes One faced me again.

"Let's get this straight," he said. "When did you come in here?"

"Just before three o'clock."

"And then what?"

"I waited until I was the last person in the place except for Baysinger and the two tellers. Then I threw down on them with the Woodsman. The inner vault was already time-locked, so I cleaned out the tellers' drawers and the cash room, and locked them in the outer vault."

"All of that took you an hour, huh?"

"Not quite. It was almost quarter past three before the last customer left, and I spent some time talking to Baysinger about the inner vault before I was convinced he couldn't open it. I was just getting ready to leave when you got here." I gave him a rueful smile. "It was a damned foolish move, going to the door without the gun and then opening up for you. But you caught me off-guard. That accident ploy is pretty clever."

"It's a good thing for you that you didn't have the gun," Two said. "You'd be dead now."

"Or you'd be," I said.

We exchanged more silent stares.

"Anyhow," I said at length, "I thought I could bluff you into leaving by pretending to be Baysinger and telling you about the time locks. But then you started that kidnaping business. I didn't want you to take me out of here because it meant leaving the suitcase; and if you did kidnap me, and I was forced to tell you the truth, you'd dump me somewhere and come back for the money yourselves. Now you've got it anyway—the game's up."

"That's for sure," One said.

I cleared my throat. "Tell you what," I said. "I'll split the eight thousand with you, half and half. That way, we all come out of this with something."

"I've got a better idea."

I knew what was coming, but I said, "What's that?"

"We take the whole boodle."

"Now wait a minute—"

"We've got the guns, and that means we make the rules. You're out of luck, Smith, or whatever your name is. You may have gotten here first, but we got here at the right time."

"Honor among thieves," I said. "Hah."

"Easy come, easy go," Two said. "You know how it is."

"All right, you're taking all the money. What about me?"

"What about you?"

"Do I get to walk out of here?"

"Well, we're sure as hell not going to call the cops on you."

"You did us sort of a favor," One said, "taking care of all the details before we got here. So we'll do you one. We'll tie you up in one of these chairs—not too tight, just tight enough to keep you here for ten or fifteen minutes. When you work yourself loose you're on your own."

"Why can't I just leave when you do?"

One gave me a faint smile. "Because you might get a bright idea to follow us and try to take the money back. We wouldn't like that."

I shook my head resignedly. "Some bank job this turned out to be."

They tied me up in the chair behind the deck, using my necktie and my belt to bind my hands and feet. After which they took the suitcase, and my Colt Woodsman, and went out through the rear door and left me alone.

It took me almost twenty minutes to work my hands loose. When they were free I leaned over to untie my feet and stood up wearily to work the kinks out of my arms and legs. Then I sat down again, pulled the phone over in front of me, and dialed a number.

A moment later a familiar voice said, "Police Chief Roberts speaking."

"This is Luther Baysinger, George," I said. "You'd better get over here to the bank right away. I've just been held up."

Chief Roberts was a tall wiry man in his early sixties, a competent law officer in his own ponderous way; I had known him for nearly thirty years. While his two underlings, Burt Young and Frank

32 BANK JOB

Dawes—the sum total of Fairfield's police force—hurried in and out, making radio calls and looking for fingerprints or clues or whatever, Roberts listened intently to my account of what had happened with the two bank robbers. When I finished he leaned back in the chair across the desk from me and wagged his head in an admiring way.

"Luther," he said, "you always did have more gall than any man in the county. But this business sure does take the cake for pure nerve."

"Am I to take that as a compliment, George?" I said a bit stiffly.

"Sure," he said. "Don't get your back up."

"The fact of the matter is, I had little choice. It was either pretend to be a bank robber myself or spend the weekend at the mercy of those two men. And have them steal all the money inside the vault on Monday morning—approximately forty thousand dollars, not twenty thousand as I told them."

"Lucky thing you had that Woodsman of yours along. That was probably the clincher."

"That, and the fact that I wasn't carrying my wallet. I was in such a hurry this morning that I left it on my dresser at home."

"How come you happened to have the .22?"

"It has been jamming on me in target practice lately," I said. "I intended to drop it off at Ben Ogilvie's gunsmith shop tonight for repairs."

"How'd you know those two hadn't cased the bank beforehand?"

"It was a simple deduction. If they had cased the bank, they would have known who I was; they wouldn't have had to ask."

Roberts wagged his head again. "You're something else, Luther. You really are."

"Mmm," I said. "Do you think you'll be able to apprehend them?"

"Oh, we'll get them, all right. The descriptions you gave us are pretty detailed; Burt's already sent them out to the county and state people and to the F.B.I."

"Fine." I massaged my temples. "I had better begin making an exact count of how much money they got away with. I've called the main branch in the capital and they're sending an official over as soon as possible. I imagine he'll be coming with the local F.B.I. agent."

Roberts rose ponderously. "We'll leave you to it, then." He gathered Young and Dawes and prepared to leave. At the door he paused to grin at me. "Yes, sir," he said, "more damned gall—and more damned luck—than any man in this county . . ."

I returned to my desk after they were gone and allowed myself a cigar. I felt vastly relieved. Fate, for once, had chosen to smile on me; I had, indeed, been lucky.

But for more reasons than Roberts thought.

I recalled his assurance that the bank robbers would soon be apprehended. Unfortunately—or fortunately, depending on the point of view—I did not believe they would be apprehended at all. Mainly because the description of them I had given Roberts was totally inaccurate.

I had also altered my story in a number of other ways. I had told him the outer vault door had not only been unlocked—which was the truth; despite my lie to the two robbers, I had not set any of the time locks—but that it had been open and the money they'd stolen was from the cash room. I had said the robbers brought the suitcase with them, not that it belonged to me, and that the Woodsman had been in my overcoat pocket when they discovered it. I had omitted mention of the fact that I'd purposely called their attention to the suitcase in order to carry out my bank-robber ruse.

And I had also lied about the reasons why I was not carrying my wallet and why I had the Woodsman with me. In truth, I had willfully left the wallet at home and put the gun into the suitcase because of an impulsive, foolish, and half formed idea that, later tonight, I *would* attempt to hold up a business establishment or two somewhere in the next county.

I would almost certainly *not* have gone through with that scheme, but the point was that I had got myself into a rather desperate situation. The bank examiners were due on Monday for their annual audit—a month earlier than usual in a surprise announcement—and I had not been able to replace all of the $14,425.00 I had "borrowed" during the past ten months to support my regrettable penchant for betting on losing horses.

I had, however, managed on short notice to raise $8,370.00 by selling my car and my small boat and disposing of certain semivaluable heirlooms. The very same $8,370.00 which had been in the suitcase, and which I had been about to *put back* into the cash room when the two robbers arrived.

As things had turned out, I no longer had to worry about replacing the money or about the bank examiners discovering my peccadillo. Of course, I would have to be considerably more prudent in the future where my predilection for the Sport of Kings was concerned. And I would be; I am not one to make the same mistake twice. I may have a lot of gall, as Roberts had phrased it, and I may be something of a rogue, but for all that I'm neither a bad nor an unwise fellow. After all, I *had* saved most of the bank's money, hadn't I?

I relaxed with my cigar. Because I had done my "borrowing" from the vault assets without falsifying bank records, I had nothing to do now except to wait patiently for the official and the F.B.I. agent to arrive from the state capital. And when they did, I would tell them the literal truth.

"The exact total of the theft," I would say, "is $14,425.00."

Edward D. Hoch

Captain Leopold Looks for the Cause

Jim Standish awoke that morning feeling good. He'd felt good just about every morning since leaving home and high school and coming to this city on the north shore of Long Island Sound. He glanced out the window at the sun and decided this was the day he'd been waiting for. Slipping into the new T-shirt and jeans he'd bought a week earlier, he took special care to comb his long hair into presentable neatness. When he finished, he decided he was ready to meet and mingle with the squares of the world.

He left his one-room apartment and went down to the lunch counter on the corner for breakfast, as he did every morning. The waitress there, a twenty-year-old blonde named Rita, was a runaway like himself. They'd struck up a friendship and she'd even spent the night with him once last month. But she'd made it clear she wasn't getting permanently involved with a kid two years younger than herself with no money and skimpy prospects. "I'm going to marry a rich man someday," she told him. "They like younger women. Just you wait and see!"

He'd chuckled and said, "Not much chance of a rich man coming by the Sunrise Diner."

The Sunrise was in a part of the city marked for urban renewal—a block of bars and shops and one-room apartments that had been allowed to decay while waiting for the wrecker's ball. It was an area that naturally attracted young runaways like Jim and Rita, who hoped for better things but didn't yet have the means to obtain them.

This day, a warm morning in mid-August, Jim Standish ordered his usual breakfast of orange juice, toast, and coffee. When Rita brought it over, he asked, "Notice anything different today?"

"You're all dandied up, aren't you? Goin' after that job?"

He nodded. "I didn't like the idea of parking cars in the rain, but I guess on a day like this it's okay."

"When you make your first million, come back and see me." She disappeared into the rear after another order.

He scooped some sugar from the bowl on the table and stirred it in his coffee. The taste of Sunrise coffee seemed worse than usual, but it didn't bother him anymore. "I might just do that," he called after her.

He left a dime tip next to his plate to impress her with his new affluence and headed down Bay Street toward the parking lot. On the way he passed Milt Trebbor's surplus-clothing store and Uncle Max's pawnshop. He waved to both men but didn't stop. Uncle Max had already got everything he had to pawn.

At the parking lot Sammy Adams eyed his approach with open disdain. "Well, sunshine—decide you'd take the job after all?"

"If it's still open."

"I work my tail off parkin' cars in the rain yesterday and you come around today when the sun's shinin'!"

"Sorry. I wasn't feeling good yesterday." The lie had barely left his lips when a sudden wave of nausea swept over him. My God, he thought, the power of the mind!

Sammy Adams sighed and motioned him forward. "I'm so hard up for help I'll take what I can get. Now look, I got one rule—no stealin' things from the cars. Understand?"

"I understand."

"Okay, we already talked about pay. You'll get your first check a week from Friday. Now let's park cars."

Jim moved after him, feeling a pain in his abdomen. He hoped he wasn't going to be truly sick. But the pain seemed to pass as he climbed behind the wheel of his first car. He started the motor, shifted into reverse, and then doubled over the steering wheel in a spasm of pain. The car rocketed backward, smashing into the front of a Buick behind it.

Sammy Adams came running up, yanking open the door on the driver's side. "Get outa there, you bum! Who the hell ever taught you how to drive?"

"I'm . . . sick . . ." Jim Standish managed to gasp.

"You'll be a lot sicker when I get through with you! The money for that front end is comin' outa your hide!"

Jim tried to get out of the car, tried to stand up, but he couldn't. His muscles were twitching and he started to throw up. Then he doubled up and collapsed at Sammy's feet.

"I've come to you for help, Captain Leopold," the man across the desk said. His name was Dr. Walter Kersey and he was the city's Director of Public Health. It was not a full-time position in a city this size, and Leopold knew he maintained a small medical practice

on the side. Still, he was serious and conscientious about his job, and Leopold had always liked the man.
"Violent crime in the hospitals, Doctor?" Leopold asked, trying to lighten the man's somber mood.
"It's violent, but I don't know if it's crime or not. Here's the situation—the media will have the story by evening but I wanted you to hear it from me first. We've got six cases of an odd malady in the city—an extremely serious malady that seems to be striking only young people. A sixteen-year-old girl has died and five other young people between the ages of twelve and twenty-three are in hospitals around town with surprisingly similar symptoms."
"You think they were poisoned?"
"It's either that or the beginning of a mystery outbreak like that legionnaire sickness in Philadelphia. Frankly, I don't know which I'd fear more."
"What are their symptoms?" Leopold started to take notes.
"Pallor, rapid heartbeat, irregular breathing, muscle twitches, nausea, diarrhea, vomiting, sharp abdominal pains, all leading to mental confusion and finally coma. Four of the five survivors are comatose now. The other, a boy of eighteen who was just brought in this morning, is still conscious."
"Were they all living at home?"
Dr. Kersey shook his head. "Oddly enough, only the twelve-year-old. Four of the other five, including the dead girl, were runaways living on their own in the inner city. The twenty-three-year-old man is married but living in the same general area."
"Anything racial?"
Dr. Kersey shook his head. "Two of the victims are black, four are white. The only common denominator is youth. If they were poisoned it could be by someone who hates young people."
"Can't your lab turn up traces of the poison?"
"Believe me, we're working on it. But in the meantime we need some good old-fashioned detective work. Who've you got for us?"
Leopold considered it. Connie Trent was on a well-earned vacation in Canada, and Lieutenant Fletcher was investigating a messy case in which a man had hacked to death five members of his family. A couple of the younger detectives were working with Fletcher. "Myself," he answered. "I'm the only one available."

The latest victim of the mystery illness, a young man named Jim Standish, had been brought to the emergency room at Parkside

Hospital from a parking lot near the downtown area where he'd just started working. Leopold stepped through the curtains of the cubicle and looked down at the youth trapped in a maze of wires and tubes.

"What are you doing for him?"

"Their first thought was that he'd had a diabetic seizure," Dr. Kersey explained. "Since that's been ruled out they've been treating him with atropine—one milligram injected intramuscularly every two hours—plus intravenous fluids to replace those he's lost through sweating, salivation, and diarrhea."

Leopold stepped closer to the bed. "Can you hear me, Jim?"

"Yes," the voice answered weakly. "What's the matter with me?"

"That's what we're all trying to find out. I'm a detective, Jim, and I'm checking the possibility you might have been poisoned. There are five other young people sick just like you." He didn't mention that one of them was dead.

"God, I feel terrible . . . I can't think clearly . . ."

"Were you on drugs, Jim?"

"No."

"What did you eat today?"

"Just breakfast, at a lunch counter. The Sunrise."

"Nothing else? No soft drink or beer or candy bar?"

"No."

Leopold could see talking was difficult for him. "All right, rest now. I'll talk to you later."

Outside he asked Dr. Kersey, "Who's running the tests on them?"

"A brilliant young pathologist named Dr. Gaylord. Come on, I think you two should meet."

Dr. Gaylord worked out of Parkside Hospital, so they took the elevator to the floor where the pathology labs were located. When Dr. Kersey introduced him, Leopold tried to hide his surprise at the fact that Dr. Gaylord was a handsome young woman with brown bangs and a friendly smile. "I've heard so much about you, Captain Leopold," she said in a voice at once soft and commanding. "It seems the papers are always full of your cases."

"They give more space to my failures than my successes."

"I hope they won't be giving space to my failures." She glanced back at the microscope and rack of test tubes over which she'd been working when they arrived. He noticed she wore no rings.

"Any luck yet?" Dr. Kersey asked.

"All of it bad. There's a high white-cell count that made me suspect bacillary dysentery, but a microscopic examination of the patients'

CAPTAIN LEOPOLD LOOKS FOR THE CAUSE 39

stool specimens ruled that out. I have one other suspicion and I'm waiting now for the results of plasma cholinesterase tests. They're too elaborate for me to perform here."

Leopold was just a bit awed by the wealth of knowledge she seemed to possess. He'd known pathologists twice her age who knew far less, or at least acted like it. "I'm working on the theory it was some sort of food poisoning," he told her.

She gave him a dimpled smile. "Check back with me in two hours and I may be able to give you a yes or no. My inclination right now is to say no, but we can't be sure."

Outside, Dr. Kersey said, "She's quite a gal. I'd trust her diagnosis more than that of most men."

"I'll call her in two hours," Leopold agreed. "Right now I think I should check out the area where Jim Standish lived—and especially the Sunrise lunch counter."

He knew the block well, as he knew most blocks in the inner city. He knew them from the nightly reports of muggings and stabbings, and the drug busts and porno raids at election time. This block, especially, had figured in the news of late, because of a partisan political battle over whether or not it should be demolished.

Walking along it now, Leopold stuck his head in the doorway of Uncle Max's pawnshop and said hello. "Captain! They got you back pounding a beat, maybe?"

"Not yet, Max. I'm helping the public-health people check out reports of illness."

"The young people—I heard." Max himself was far from old, though his prematurely white hair and beard gave an illusion of both age and wisdom. He'd been robbed three times in the past year—once with a savage beating thrown in for good measure—which was how he'd come to know Leopold.

"Might be the start of an epidemic."

"Like Philadelphia's last year?"

"We hope not. Only six cases so far, and one death." He took out a list of victims and read off the names. "Know any of them?"

"By name? Only one—Jim Standish. I saw him just this morning. The others I might know by their faces."

"Did Standish ever deal with you?"

"Everyone on the block deals with Uncle Max."

"Who told you about the illnesses? It hasn't been in the papers yet."

"The word gets around."

"But how did it get around this time?"

"Rita—the waitress at the Sunrise."

"Thanks," Leopold said, and went on.

He'd stopped in the Sunrise Diner for coffee once or twice, but not often enough to know any of the help. Only one man seemed to be on duty in mid-afternoon, cleaning grease from the griddle.

"Is Rita around?" Leopold asked, sliding onto a stool.

"Off duty. She's in the back changing."

"Ask her if I could have a word with her. It's police business."

The man's eyes widened at the sight of the badge, but he said nothing. He disappeared into the back and returned in a moment to inform Leopold, "I guess you just missed her. She's gone."

Leopold thanked the man and went quickly outside. Circling the short block, he came to an alley that led to a little parking area used by Sunrise employees. A black Chevy was just pulling out when he stopped it.

"Are you Rita?"

"That's my name," she answered.

"You needn't have ducked out the rear door. I just want to ask you about one or two of your customers."

She backed into the parking space and got out of the car. "All right, what's it about?"

Leopold wondered what she had to fear. "I'm a detective captain, but right now I'm working with the public-health director to track down an illness that's stricken six young people in this area. The latest victim, Jim Standish, had breakfast here this morning. Do you know him?"

"I know him. He's a runaway, if that's what you wanted to ask me."

"When they get to be eighteen I stop caring. He can live his own life at that age, if he has any of it left to live."

"What's that mean?"

"He's a pretty sick boy. There are others even worse." He showed her the list of names. "Are any of the others Sunrise customers?"

She scanned it quickly. "That Cathy might be. I know lots of girls named Cathy."

"Did Standish seem ill this morning?"

"Not that I noticed."

"What'd he eat?"

"Orange juice, toast. And coffee."

"Cream and sugar in the coffee?"
"Just sugar, I think. But I didn't pay that close attention."
"Let's go back inside, Rita."
"Look, I gotta hair appointment."
"This won't take a minute."

She stalked back in, acting as if she were under arrest. The man behind the counter glanced up, then busied himself at some task. "What is it you want?" she asked Leopold.

"Which sugar bowl did Standish use?"

"This one on the counter, I suppose. I wasn't watching."

Leopold dipped his finger in and tasted it. Sugar, all right. "This is supposed to be separately packaged," he told the girl. "I'm surprised the Board of Health hasn't got after you."

"I don't own the place."

"Who does?"

"Mr. Hammish. He's only here nights. I don't see much of him and I'm just as happy about that."

"How well did you know Standish?"

She shrugged. "I went out with him once or twice. But he's just a kid—only eighteen."

"Did he have any enemies?"

"No. Everybody liked him."

He asked about enemies because it was hard for him to accept the concept of some unknown disease. He felt more comfortable pursuing a human foe—an unseen poisoner ready to drop pellets into coffee cups.

Leopold was about to question her about others who'd been at the counter with Standish when Uncle Max came in. "There's been another one," he told them. "I thought you'd want to know, Captain."

"Another illness?"

"Looks like it. Fellow who works in Milt Trebbor's surplus store."

Leopold followed him down the street to the store where a small crowd had been attracted by the arrival of an ambulance. Milt Trebbor was out in front, his face ashen with fear. A man wearing a red sweatshirt and jeans was being lifted onto the stretcher by two white-coated attendants.

Leopold introduced himself to the shop owner, a man he knew by sight but had never really met. "What happened here?"

"He had pains and vomiting. Then he just sort of collapsed. I called the ambulance quick!" Trebbor was a little man with an intense expression. Leopold had heard rumors that his stock of surplus goods sometimes included stolen merchandise, but nothing had ever been proved against him.

Glancing down at the man on the stretcher, Leopold observed the lines about his mouth and eyes. "He's no boy!"

"'Course not! Never said he was! Mike Wanamaker's been workin' for me five, six years now. He's in his mid-forties."

The first older victim. Leopold tried to fathom what it meant and decided he needed to call Dr. Gaylord. "Can I use your phone?" he asked Trebbor.

"Sure—in the office."

He dialed the hospital and asked for Dr. Gaylord. When she came on her voice was almost cheerful. "I've got news for you, Captain—good news and bad news. Which do you want first?"

"Give me the bad first."

"One of the teenage boys died. But it's not too surprising. They're all in critical condition and we'll be lucky if even a few pull through."

"What's your good news?"

"The victims' plasma cholinesterase level is only forty percent of normal, and the red-cell level is down to seventeen. I think they're suffering from organic phosphate poisoning."

"That's good news?"

"It's good news that we've identified it. Now it's up to you to find the source."

"Just what is organic phosphate?"

"An insecticide. It used to be widely sprayed from planes over farm areas. But lately the environmentalists have successfully limited its use, because of the dangers to human and animal life. Five drops of it on the skin is a fatal dose."

"It can be absorbed through the skin?"

"That's the commonest danger. Read Rachel Carson's *Silent Spring* if you want to know more about it."

"I don't have too much time for reading right now. We've got another case of it down here." He quickly outlined the circumstances. "This is the first victim over twenty-five. What do you make of it, Doctor?"

"If we're dealing with organic phosphate poisoning, as I'm convinced we are, age is no factor. It's more a matter of exposure. What could those teenagers be doing that the latest victim was also doing?"

"I don't know," Leopold admitted. "But I'm going to find out."

When he came out of the office, Milt Trebbor was back to work, sorting through a pile of blue jeans as if nothing had happened. "Think Mike'll pull through?" he asked Leopold.

"I'm no doctor. I'm more interested in what's causing all these illnesses. Do you know any of the other victims?"

"A couple. Mostly they're from this neighborhood." He motioned toward the counter where the early edition of the afternoon paper lay open to a story on the mysterious illnesses. "Not the twelve-year-old, though. He's from the suburbs."

There were pictures of some of the young people accompanying the article, and Leopold looked them over, trying to see something in their faces that would hint at the cause of their illness. But he could see nothing. "Dr. Gaylord at Parkside Hospital thinks the illness is caused by organic phosphate poisoning," he told Trebbor. "Does that suggest anything to you?"

"Insecticide, isn't it? They sure wouldn't be sprayin' that stuff around the city."

"No, they wouldn't," Leopold agreed. "Well, thanks for your help, anyway."

"Let me know about Mike's condition, will you?"

"I'll do that."

"If it's anything contagious—"

"It's not, as far as we know."

Leopold went back down to the Sunrise Diner, but the waitress Rita was no longer there. Then he retraced Standish's most likely route from the diner to the parking lot where he'd collapsed. The lot's manager, a rat-faced man in his thirties named Sammy Adams, was busy moving cars as the late afternoon rush-hour got under way. "Can't talk now," he told Leopold. "Too busy. All alone since that damned Standish took sick!"

"That's what I want to talk about," Leopold said, showing his badge. "We're investigating his illness."

"Damn kid smashed up a couple of cars! That's enough to make anybody sick."

"Wasn't he ill earlier?"

"Hell, he's been telling me all week he's been sick, but I figured he just didn't feel like parkin' cars in the rain. When the sun came out today he was ready to work."

Leopold showed him the list of other victims. "Know any of them?"

"Not a one, at least not by name."

"None of them parked here?"

"Nope." He hesitated, then added, "But Mike Wanamaker is one of my customers. That's his Ford there. I saw the ambulance taking him away."

"Did he seem sick this morning?"

"Nope. Seemed the same as always to me."

"Okay," Leopold said. "I'll get back to you."

He left Sammy Adams shuffling his cars and walked back along the block of shops and bars. Uncle Max was out again, chatting with a couple of jeans-clad teenagers about an item they wanted to pawn. It looked like a typewriter and Leopold wondered if they'd ripped it off from one of the nearby office buildings. There were more young people farther along, all looking the same, all dressed the same. He decided it was an age of conformity disguised as independence.

Leopold drove out to Parkside Hospital again, as much to see Dr. Gaylord as to pursue the investigation. She was at work in her office adjoining the lab, poring over the questionnaires assembled on the victims of the mystery illness.

"Anything new?" he asked.

"Oh, hello! Not yet, but we're working on the cure." She lifted her glasses to her forehead and leaned back in the chair. "I've suggested an injection of five hundred milligrams of pralidoxime chloride, and it seems to be helping. It's a specific treatment for organic phosphate poisoning."

"Then they'll pull through?"

She shrugged. "It's too soon to tell. All we can do is hope."

"No luck with these?" he asked, gesturing toward the questionnaires fanned out on the desk before her.

"Well, I've just received the one on Mike Wanamaker and it's far from complete because of his condition. As you know, he's the oldest of the seven by far. And I'll admit to not knowing exactly how he fits in with the others."

"He works in Milt Trebbor's surplus store, right in the middle of the block where most of the others congregated."

"That's true of Jim Standish and the two who died and two others," she agreed. "But what about the twelve-year-old from the suburbs?"

"I don't know," Leopold admitted. He drew up a chair and started glancing at the forms. An idea came to him. "Trebbor's something of a shady character. Maybe he wanted to kill Wanamaker and poisoned the others first so that Wanamaker's death wouldn't be noticed."

"But it *is* noticed, Captain," Dr. Gaylord argued logically, "simply because he's so much older than the other six. If this man Trebbor had a scheme like that, he'd have chosen victims closer to Wanamaker's age, wouldn't he?"

"Of course," Leopold agreed with a sigh.

"I think it's a medical mystery and nothing else. Seven people got into something—somehow, somewhere."

He returned to the questionnaires. "Of those able to answer before they went into comas, four had eaten at the Sunrise Diner within a day or two of their illness. Three were connected in some way with Sammy's parking lot—and I can add a fourth. Mike Wanamaker parked his car there. And they were all familiar with Trebbor's surplus store and Uncle Max's pawnshop, except the twelve-year-old."

"You think it's one of those four places?"

"I'm certain of it." He pulled a big yellow pad over to him and drew a straight line on it. "Look, this is Bay Street, with the Sunrise at one end and Sammy's parking lot at the other. Those can be our somewhat arbitrary limits for the moment. Trebbor's store is here, and Max's shop is just three doors away. Now I'll put a small x at the points where the victims got sick, omitting the youngest victim at the moment. We have Standish at the parking lot, and Wanamaker at the surplus store. What about the other four?"

She picked up a pencil to help him with the markings. "Two of them were stricken in other parts of the city, but they live in the Bay Street area. The other two were actually on the street when taken ill. Here's another oddity I've noticed, though I can't explain it. In every case the onset of the illness came in late morning or early afternoon—never in the evening or first thing on arising. That in itself is strange."

"It suggests some exposure around breakfast time, doesn't it? What about the twelve-year-old?"

She consulted one of the questionnaires. "He just doesn't fit with the others. His mother says he hasn't been downtown for weeks, and to her knowledge he's never been on the Bay Street block in his life."

"It's a puzzlement," he admitted. "I'm going to go down and see if I can talk to Standish or one of the other patients. I might learn something."

"I've seen them all, even the ones at the other hospitals, and it hasn't helped me."

"Well, maybe doctors and policemen look for different things. I'll check back with you."

"Good luck."

When she was alone, Dr. Gaylord started in again at her task, poring over the data they'd gathered thus far. She decided to check the tissue samples in the lab once more and went in there, leaving the connecting door open a few inches. The samples were as expected, showing nothing new under the microscope. She sat back, thinking about Captain Leopold and what he'd said—that doctors and policemen look for different things. Was it true?

Was there any difference in a poisoning victim—or a gunshot victim, for that matter—when viewed by a policeman and by a doctor? Certainly doctors were more interested in the effect than in the cause, while the opposite might be true of the police. But was there something else? Was there something the doctor never saw which might be the key to her whole problem?

Something the doctor never saw but the policeman did...

She heard a noise from the adjoining office and realized someone was in there. She walked back through the connecting door and confronted a man she'd never seen before, bent over her desk. "What do you want?" she asked.

He straightened up, surprised.

She saw him grab for a metal bookend on her desk and she tried to scream, but he was too fast.

There was a flash of light as he hit her, then nothing...

It was toward evening before Leopold heard the news, and he hastened to the hospital. The first familiar face he saw belonged to Dr. Kersey. "Hello, Captain. I'm glad you could come."

"How is she?" he asked, surprised at how much it mattered.

"A bad concussion, but she'll pull through. There doesn't seem to be any brain damage."

"Could she say who did it?"

"A man, that's all. She caught a man in her office. Probably a sneak thief. We've had trouble with them before."

"Any description?"

He shook his head. "She's only semiconscious, and rambling."

"Can I see her?"

Dr. Kersey hesitated. "I'll ask the physician in charge." He returned in a moment and motioned Leopold inside. "Just for a minute," he whispered.

Her head was swathed in bandages and she lay back on the pillow with her eyes closed. Leopold bent over and spoke her name.

The eyes opened, and he saw that they were brown like the hair now hidden from view. "I . . ."

"It's Captain Leopold, Doctor."

" . . . close . . ."

"Close?"

The eyes closed and then opened again. "Clothes," she said more distinctly.

"What about clothes?"

" . . . doctors never see them with their clothes on . . ."

Leopold thought about that. "No, I suppose they don't," he said finally.

Her eyes closed and the doctor touched his arm. "You'd better leave now."

Back in the hall he found Dr. Kersey again. "Young Standish is here, isn't he? And some of the others?"

He nodded. "Two of them."

"I want to see the clothes they were wearing when they were brought in."

He already had a pretty good idea of what he would find.

The store lights were already on along Bay Street, bathing the pavement with a mixture of neon and fluorescence that reflected off the puddles where the street flusher had been through. Uncle Max was sweeping the sidewalk in front of his pawnshop and he waved as Leopold approached. But Leopold turned in at Milt Trebbor's surplus store, where the owner was just turning out the lights.

"Hello, Captain. We're closing up."

"No, you're not."

"Oh? How's Mike?"

"Mike's good. The woman you almost killed isn't nearly as good."

"What?" Trebbor tried to move back, out of reach, but Leopold was too fast. He grabbed the man by the front of his shirt. "What in hell is this?"

"It's attempted murder, you skunk—and I'll bet we can dig up at least seven charges of criminal negligence to go with it. Now where's that pile of jeans?"

"What jeans?"

"The ones I saw you looking through this afternoon. They were right here on this counter."

"I—I guess I sold them all."

"Guess again."

"They were dirty. I threw them out."

"Let's go out in back and find them."

"Honest, Captain, I swear to God I didn't know it was the jeans! Not till today when Mike got sick!"

"And then you remembered me mentioning that Dr. Gaylord at Parkside was working on it and you went there to find out what she knew, because you were afraid those people would sue you."

"I didn't mean to hit her, Captain! It was an accident!"

Leopold had his handcuffs out. "Lock the door, Trebbor. You are going to show me where those jeans are and then I'm taking you down to Headquarters. You have a right to consult a lawyer, but anything you say from now on may be used against you."

Dr. Gaylord was sitting up in bed when Leopold came to call.

"Captain! Are those flowers for me?"

"I felt it was the least I could do. I mentioned your name to someone and that caused all this, I'm afraid." He handed the flowers to a nurse and took four pictures from his pocket. "Just for the record I'd like you to look at these."

She pointed to Trebbor's mug shot without hesitation. "That's the man who hit me."

"Fine! You'll get a chance to identify him in a lineup later, though there's a possibility he'll decide to plead guilty to an assault charge."

"How did you find him so quickly?"

Leopold hesitated, a little embarrassed. "You know, I've never even heard your first name. It's hard to go on calling you Dr. Gaylord."

She laughed then, and it was a sunny sound he liked. "My name is Lawn, but please don't make any jokes about it. I went all through school with boys who wanted to mow me."

"Lawn Gaylord. It's a pretty name."

"Never mind my name. Tell me about this man who hit me."

"Milt Trebbor. He runs a surplus store on Bay Street. Apparently he bought a shipment of blue jeans cheap because something had been spilled on them."

"Organic phosphate! Blue jeans—now I remember there was a similar case in California back in 1961 and Berton Roueché wrote about it in his book *The Orange Man*."

"I didn't know about the book," Leopold admitted, "but I should have known about the jeans sooner than I did. I noticed the young people in that block all wore jeans, as so many young people do today, and you'd told me the poison could be absorbed through the skin. I was even there when Wanamaker was carried out, and saw that he was wearing jeans too. In fact, right after that I found Trebbor inspecting the jeans in his store when I went to question him. It had just occurred to him what the trouble was.

"If he'd admitted it then, instead of slugging you and trying to cover up, he'd be in a lot less trouble now. But he was afraid of lawsuits that could ruin him. He knew the jeans were stained when he bought them, but the stains didn't show when they dried and he thought no more about them. Funny thing—he says he sold twenty-two pair during the past two weeks, but only seven people were stricken."

"Some might not have been badly stained," Lawn Gaylord guessed. "Or more likely, the buyers simply washed them before wearing them the first time. I understand girls often do, to shrink them a bit. But those who wore them without washing absorbed the poison into their bodies. After a few hours' wear the symptoms developed."

"Which explains the time element that had us puzzled. But you really gave me the clue when you mumbled about doctors never seeing the victims with their clothes on."

She put a hand to her head. "I don't even remember talking to you. But it's true—for an internal illness like this, the first thing the emergency-room staff does is remove the patient's clothing. The examining doctor would have no way of knowing they were dressed in identical jeans, even if it had been the same doctor—which of course it wasn't."

Leopold nodded. "I checked the clothes Standish and the other Parkside patients were wearing when brought in—new jeans in every case. Then I phoned the mother of the twelve-year-old. She confirmed that she'd bought him a pair of jeans at Trebbor's store. That was all I needed. He still didn't have to be the one who slugged you, but when I remembered telling him your name it seemed a pretty good bet."

He stood up and moved toward the door. "We've talked too much for one day. You need your rest."

She smiled at him, dimpling. "You know, now you have me at a disadvantage."

"How's that?"

"What's *your* first name, Captain Leopold?"

Lawrence Block

The Ehrengraf Method

"And you are Mrs. Culhane," Martin Ehrengraf said. "Do sit down, yes, I think you will find that chair comfortable. And please pardon the disarray. It is the natural condition of my office. Chaos stimulates me. Order stifles me. It is absurd, isn't it, but then so is life itself, eh?"

Dorothy Culhane sat, nodded. She studied the small, trimly built man who remained standing behind his extremely disorderly desk. Her eyes took in the narrow mustache, the thin lips, the deeply set dark eyes. If the man liked clutter in his surroundings, he certainly made up for it in his grooming and attire. He wore a starched white shirt, a perfectly tailored dove-gray three-button suit, a narrow dark-blue necktie.

Oh, but she did not want to think about neckties—

"Of course you are Clark Culhane's mother," Ehrengraf said. "I thought you had already retained an attorney."

"Alan Farrell."

"A good man," Ehrengraf said. "An excellent reputation."

"I dismissed him this morning."

"Ah."

Mrs. Culhane took a deep breath. "He wanted Clark to plead guilty," she said. "Temporary insanity, something of the sort. He wanted my son to admit killing that girl."

"And you did not wish him to do this."

"My son is innocent!" The words came in a rush, uncontrollably. She calmed herself. "My son is innocent," she repeated, levelly now. "He could never kill anyone. He can't admit to a crime he never committed in the first place."

"And when you said as much to Farrell—"

"He told me he was doubtful of his ability to conduct a successful defense based on a plea of innocence." She drew herself up. "So I decided to find someone who could."

"And you came to me."

"Yes."

The little lawyer had seated himself. Now he was doodling idly on a lined yellow legal pad. "Do you know much about me, Mrs. Culhane?"

"Not very much. It's said that your methods are unorthodox—"

"Indeed."

"But that you get results."

"Results. Indeed, results." Martin Ehrengraf made a tent of his fingertips and for the first time since she had entered his office, a smile bloomed briefly on his thin lips. "Indeed I get results. I *must* get results, my dear Mrs. Culhane, or else I do not get my dinner. And while my slimness might indicate otherwise, it is my custom to eat very well indeed. You see, I do something which no other criminal lawyer does, at least not to my knowledge. You have heard what this is?"

"I understand you operate on a contingency basis."

"A contingency basis." Ehrengraf was nodding emphatically. "Yes, that is precisely what I do—operate on a contingency basis. My fees are high, Mrs. Culhane—extremely high. But they are due and payable only in the event that my efforts are crowned with success. If a client of mine is found guilty, then my work on his behalf at least costs him nothing."

The lawyer got to his feet again, stepped out from behind his desk. Light glinted on his highly polished black shoes. "This is common enough in negligence cases. The attorney gets a share in the settlement. If he loses he gets nothing. How much greater is his incentive to perform to the best of his ability, eh? But why limit this practice to negligence suits? Why not have all lawyers paid in this fashion? And doctors, for that matter. If the operation's a failure, why not let the doctor absorb the loss, eh? But such an arrangement will be a long time coming, I'm afraid. Yet I have found it workable in my practice."

"If you can get Clark acquitted—"

"Acquitted?" Ehrengraf rubbed his hands together. "Mrs. Culhane, in my most notable successes it is not even a question of acquittal. It is rather a matter of the case never even coming to trial. New evidence is discovered, the actual miscreant confesses or is brought to justice, and one way or another charges against my client are dropped. Courtroom pyrotechnics, wizardry in cross-examination—ah, I prefer to leave that to the Perry Masons of the world. It is not unfair to say, Mrs. Culhane, that I am more a detective than a lawyer. What is the saying? The best defense is a good offense. Or perhaps it is the other way around, the best offense is a good defense, but it hardly matters. It is also a saying in warfare and in chess, but neither serves as the ideal metaphor for what concerns us. And what does concern us, Mrs. Culhane—" he leaned toward her and his dark eyes flashed "—what concerns us is saving your son's life, securing his freedom, and preserving his reputation. Yes?"

"Yes. Yes, of course."

"The evidence against your son is substantial, Mrs. Culhane. The dead girl, Althea Patton, was his former fiancée. It is said she jilted him—"

"He broke the engagement."

"I don't doubt that for a moment, but the prosecution would have it otherwise. This Patton girl was strangled. Around her throat was found a necktie."

Mrs. Culhane's eyes went involuntarily to the lawyer's own blue tie, then slipped away.

"A *particular* necktie, Mrs. Culhane. A necktie made exclusively for and worn exclusively by members of the Caedmon Society at Oxford University. Your son attended Dartmouth, Mrs. Culhane, and after graduation he spent a year in advanced study in England."

"Yes."

"At Oxford University."

"Yes."

"Where he became a member of the Caedmon Society."

"Yes."

Ehrengraf breathed in through clenched teeth. "He owned a necktie of the Caedmon Society. He appears to be the only member of the society residing in this city and would thus presumably be the only person to own such a tie. He cannot produce that tie, nor can he provide a satisfactory alibi for the night in question."

"Someone must have stolen his tie."

"The murderer, of course."

"To frame my son."

"Of course," Ehrengraf said soothingly. "There could be no other explanation, could there?" He breathed in, breathed out, then set his chin decisively. "I will undertake your son's defense," he announced. "And on my usual terms."

"Oh, thank heavens."

"My fee will be seventy-five thousand dollars. That is a great deal of money, Mrs. Culhane, although you might very well have ended up paying Mr. Farrell that much or more by the time you'd gone through the tortuous processes of trial appeal and so on, and after he'd presented an itemized accounting of his expenses. My fee includes any and all expenses which I might incur. No matter how much time, effort, and money I spend on your son's behalf, the cost to you will be limited to the figure I named. And none of that will be payable unless your son is freed. Does that meet with your approval?"

She hardly had to hesitate but forced herself to take a moment before replying. "Yes," she said. "The terms are satisfactory."

"Another point. If, ten minutes from now, the District Attorney should decide of his own accord to drop all charges against your son, you nevertheless owe me seventy-five thousand dollars. Even though I should have done nothing to earn it."

"I don't see—"

The thin lips smiled. The dark eyes did not participate in the smile. "It is my policy, Mrs. Culhane. Most of my work, as I have said, is more the work of a detective than the work of a lawyer. I operate largely behind the scenes and in the shadows. Perhaps I set currents in motion, or build little fires. Often when the smoke clears it is hard to prove to what extent my client's victory is the fruit of my labor. Thus I do not attempt to prove anything of the sort. I merely share in the victory by collecting my fee in full whether I seem to have earned it or not. You understand? Completely?"

It did seem reasonable, even if the explanation was the slightest bit hazy. Perhaps the little man dabbled in bribery, perhaps he knew the right strings to pull but could scarcely disclose them after the fact. Well, it hardly mattered. All that mattered was Clark's freedom and good name.

"Yes," she said, "I understand. When Clark is released you'll be paid in full."

"Very good."

She frowned. "In the meantime you'll want a retainer, won't you? An advance of some sort?"

"You have a dollar?" She looked in her purse, drew out a dollar bill. "Give it to me, Mrs. Culhane. Very good. An advance of one dollar against a fee of seventy-five thousand dollars. And I assure you, my dear Mrs. Culhane, that should this case not resolve itself in unqualified success I shall even return this dollar to you."

The smile again, and this time there was a twinkle in the eyes. "But that will not happen, Mrs. Culhane, because I do not intend to fail . . ."

It was a little more than a month later when Dorothy Culhane made her second visit to Martin Ehrengraf's office. This time the little lawyer's suit was a navy-blue pinstripe, his necktie maroon with a subdued below-the-knot design. His starched white shirt might have been the same one she had seen on her first visit. The shoes, with black wing tips, were as highly polished as the earlier pair.

His expression was changed slightly. There was something that might have been sorrow in his deepset eyes, a look that suggested his continuing disappointment with human nature.

"It would seem quite clear," Ehrengraf said now. "Your son has been released. All charges have been dropped. He is a free man, free even to the extent that no shadow of suspicion hangs over him in the public mind."

"Yes," Mrs. Culhane said, "and that's wonderful, and I couldn't be happier about it. Of course it's terrible about the girls, I hate to think that Clark's happiness and my own happiness stem from their tragedy, or I suppose it's tragedies, isn't it, but all the same I feel—"

"Mrs. Culhane."

She bit off her words, let her eyes meet his.

"Mrs. Culhane, it's quite cut-and-dried, isn't it? You owe me seventy-five thousand dollars."

"But—"

"We discussed this, Mrs. Culhane. I'm sure you recall our discussion. We went over the matter clearly and at length. On the successful resolution of this matter you were to pay me my fee—seventy-five thousand dollars. Less, of course, the sum of one dollar already paid to me as a retainer."

"But—"

"Even if I did nothing—that was our understanding. Even if the District Attorney elected to drop charges before you'd even departed from these premises. That was the example I gave you at the time."

"Yes."

"And you agreed to those terms."

"Yes, but—"

"But what, Mrs. Culhane?"

She took a deep breath, set herself bravely. "Three girls," she said. "Strangled, all three of them, just like Althea Patton. All the same physical type—slender blondes with high foreheads and prominent front teeth, two of them here in town and one across the river in Montclair, and around each of their throats—"

"A necktie."

"The same necktie."

"A necktie of the Caedmon Society of Oxford University."

"Yes." She drew another breath. "So it was obvious that there's a maniac at large," she went on, "and the last killing was in Montclair, so maybe he's leaving the area, and my God I hope so, it's terrifying, the idea of a man just killing girls at random because they remind him of his mother—"

"I beg your pardon?"

"That's what somebody was saying on television last night. A psychiatrist. It was just a theory."

"Yes," Ehrengraf said. "Theories are interesting, aren't they? Speculation, guesswork, hypotheses, all very interesting."

"But the point is—"

"Yes?"

"I know what we agreed, Mr. Ehrengraf. But on the other hand you made only one visit to Clark in prison, just one brief visit, and then as far as I can see you did nothing at all, and just because the madman happened to strike again while my son was in prison and kill the other girls in exactly the same manner and even use the same kind of tie—well, you have to admit that seventy-five thousand dollars sounds like quite a windfall for you."

"Windfall?"

"So I was discussing this with my own attorney—he's not a criminal lawyer, he handles my personal affairs—and he suggested you might accept a reduced fee by way of settlement."

"He suggested this, eh?"

She avoided the man's eyes. "Yes, he did suggest it, and I must say it seems reasonable to me. Of course I would be glad to reimburse you for any expenses you incurred, although I can't honestly think you could have run up much in the way of expenses, and he suggested that I might give you a fee on top of that of five thousand dollars, but I *am* grateful, Mr. Ehrengraf, and I'd be willing to make that ten thousand dollars, and you have to admit that's not a trifle, don't you? I have money, I'm comfortably set up financially, but no one can afford to pay seventy-five thousand dollars for nothing at all, and—"

"Human beings," Ehrengraf said, and closed his eyes. "And the rich are the worst of all," he added, opening his eyes, fixing them on Dorothy Culhane. "It is an unfortunate fact of life that only the rich can afford to pay high fees. Thus I must make my living acting on their behalf. The poor, *they* do not agree to an arrangement when they are desperate and go back on their word when they are in more reassuring circumstances."

"It's not so much that I'm going back on my word," Mrs. Culhane said. "It's just that—"

"Mrs. Culhane."

"Yes?"

"I am going to tell you something which I doubt will have any effect on you, but at least I shall have tried. The best thing you can do, right at this moment, would be to take out your checkbook and write out a check to me for payment in full. You will probably not do this, and you will ultimately regret it."

"Is that a—are you threatening me?"

A flicker of a smile. "Certainly not. I have given you not a threat but a prediction. You see, if you do not pay my fee, what I shall do is tell you something else which will lead you to pay me my fee after all."

"I don't understand."

"No," Martin Ehrengraf said. "No, I don't suppose you do. Mrs. Culhane, you spoke of expenses. You doubted I could have incurred significant expenses on your son's behalf. There are many things I could say, Mrs. Culhane, but I think it might be best for me to confine myself to a brisk accounting of a small portion of my expenses."

"I don't—"

"Please, my dear lady. If I were listing my expenses, I would begin by jotting down my train fare to New York City. Then taxi fare to John F. Kennedy Airport, which comes to twenty dollars with tip and bridge tolls—"

"Mr. Ehrengraf—"

"*Please.* Then airfare to London and back. I always fly first class—it's an indulgence, but since I pay my own expenses out of my own pocket I feel I have the right to indulge myself. Next a rental car hired from Heathrow Airport and driven to Oxford and back. The price of gasoline is high enough over here, Mrs. Culhane, but in England they call it petrol and charge the earth for it."

She stared at him. His hands were folded on top of his disorderly desk and he went on talking in the calmest possible voice and she felt her jaw dropping but could not seem to raise it back into place.

"In Oxford I had to visit five gentlemen's clothiers, Mrs. Culhane. One shop had no Caedmon Society cravats in stock at the moment.

I purchased one necktie from each of the other shops. I felt it really wouldn't do to buy more than one tie in any one shop. A man prefers not to call attention to himself unnecessarily. The Caedmon Society necktie, Mrs. Culhane, is not unattractive. A navy-blue field with a half-inch stripe of royal blue and two narrower flanking stripes, one of gold, the other of a rather bright green. I don't care for regimental stripes myself, Mrs. Culhane, preferring as I do a more subdued style in neckwear, but the Caedmon tie is a handsome one all the same."

"My God."

"There were other expenses, Mrs. Culhane, but as I pay them myself I don't honestly think there's any need for me to recount them to you, do you?"

"My God. Dear God in heaven."

"Indeed. It would have been better all around, as I said a few moments ago, had you decided to pay my fee without hearing what you've just heard. Ignorance in this case would have been, if not bliss, at least a good deal closer to bliss than what you're undoubtedly feeling at the moment."

"Clark didn't kill that girl."

"Of course he didn't, Mrs. Culhane. I'm sure some rotter stole his tie and framed him. But that would have been an enormous chore to prove and all a lawyer could have done was to persuade a jury that there was room for doubt, and poor Clark would have had a cloud over him all the days of his life. Of course you and I know he's innocent—"

"He *is* innocent," she said.

"Of course, Mrs. Culhane. The killer was a homicidal maniac striking down young women who reminded him of his mother. Or his sister, or God knows whom. You'll want to get out your checkbook, Mrs. Culhane, but don't try to write the check just yet. Your hands are trembling. Just sit there, that's the ticket, and I'll get you a glass of water. Everything's perfectly fine, Mrs. Culhane. That's what you must remember. Everything's perfectly fine and everything will continue to be perfectly fine. Here you are, a couple of ounces of water in a paper cup, just drink it down, *there* you are."

And when it was time to write out the check her hand did not shake a bit. Pay to the order of Martin H. Ehrengraf, seventy-five thousand dollars, signed Dorothy Rodgers Culhane. Signed with a ballpoint pen, no need to blot it dry, and handed across the desk to the impeccably dressed little man.

"Yes, thank you, my dear lady. And here is your dollar, the retainer you gave me. Go ahead and take it, please."

She took the dollar.

"Very good. And you probably won't want to repeat this conversation to anyone. What would be the point?"

"No. No, I won't say anything."

"Of course not."

"Four neckties," she said. He raised his eyebrows a fraction of an inch. "You said you bought four of the neckties. There were only three girls killed."

"Indeed."

"What happened to the fourth necktie?"

"Why, it must be in my bureau drawer, I suppose. And perhaps all four neckties are in my bureau drawer, still in their original wrappings, and purchasing them was just a waste of time and money on my part. Perhaps that homicidal maniac had neckties of his own and the four in my drawer are just an interesting souvenir, a reminder of this case, of what might have been."

"Oh."

"And perhaps I've just told you a story out of the whole cloth, an interesting turn of phrase since we are speaking of silk neckties. Perhaps I never flew to London at all, never motored to Oxford, never purchased a single necktie of the Caedmon Society. Perhaps that was just something I trumped up on the spur of the moment to coax a fee out of you."

"But—"

"Ah, my dear lady," he said, moving to the side of her chair, taking her arm, helping her up out of the chair, turning her, steering her toward the door. "We would do well, Mrs. Culhane, to believe that which it most pleases us to believe. I have my fee. You have your son. The police have another line of inquiry to pursue. It would seem we've all come out of this well, wouldn't you say? Put your mind at rest, dear Mrs. Culhane. There's the elevator down the hall on your left. If you ever need my services you know where I am and how to reach me. And perhaps you'll recommend me to your friends. But discreetly, dear lady. Discretion is everything in matters of this sort."

She walked carefully down the hall to the elevator, rang the bell, and waited. And she did not look back. Not once.

William Bankier
A Hint of Danger

Carter Varley was accustomed to writing mystery stories, having them published, and then hearing no more about them. His friends seldom read one or, if they did, they kept silent about it. Varley considered this to be a kind of passive hostility motivated by envy. As for strangers—the anonymous public who were exposed to his work in various magazines—he supposed they turned the pages, were amused or not, and then went about the business of their lives.

But now, on this drafty November morning with a gray rain sweeping across Wimbledon Common and spattering against the window beside Varley's desk, here was an astonishing letter from America. It had been forwarded to him by the editor of a magazine published in New York, but the postmark was Chattanooga, Tennessee.

"Imagine my surprise," the letter began, "when I read your story entitled 'Forgotten, Not Gone' and discovered it was about me!" The writer went on to identify himself as William Stoke (indeed the name Varley had invented for the villain in his story) and to say that, furthermore, he was a practicing lawyer. This compounded the coincidence almost beyond belief because Varley's fictional Stoke had been a lawyer, too.

With an ethereal feeling Varley cranked paper into his machine and typed an answer. He apologized for any embarrassment and expressed his amazement at the sort of coincidence that happens in real life, too bizarre ever to be written into a story. Varley thanked Stoke for his letter and then, uncharacteristically, invited the American to call if ever he should be in London.

The rain stopped in early afternoon. Varley went out for a walk in the High Street, paid an outrageous price at the grocer's for some salad ingredients, posted his letter to America, and then went to The Dog and Fox for a pint.

Tucked away in a corner, his portly torso wedged into a leather armchair, the mug of brown ale glowing on polished oak easily within reach, Varley stared at the hissing glow of the gas fire and worried about what he had done. He did not want people dropping in on him, not friends, not strangers, certainly not an aggressive American who would think he had a claim on Varley simply because his name had fallen into the author's mind by sheer happenstance.

Varley drank the ale, making up his mind to have another. And perhaps a couple of those Scotch Eggs. The crusty, breaded eggs improved his mood and so did the second pint. He was fretting for nothing. Stoke had written because he was surprised and pleased to see his name in print. Varley's reply was no more than proper, and the invitation was the sort of formality that nobody takes seriously. Chattanooga was a long way from London—nothing more would ever come of it.

Christmas arrived and Varley was forced to recognize that he had not got over the death of his wife two years ago. By burrowing like a mole into mountains of work, he could deceive himself for months at a time into thinking he was self-sufficient and secure. But when he lifted his head at the end of the year he encountered all kinds of ferocious reminders—the scent of oranges, frost in his nostrils on night walks, lights on trees seen through curtained windows, and at his doorway three children singing a carol.

Varley gave them fifty pence and sent them away, then turned out all his lights and sat shivering in the dark, drinking Scotch whisky and facing the past like a martyr submitting to the fire. He saw the old chapel with himself in his twenties, dressed in cassock and surplice on the tenor side of the chancel, holding his hymnbook high and looking across it at Beatrice in the front row of the altos. Midnight service on Christmas Eve.

Those had been the good years, the early days of his life with Beatrice. Time eroded the relationship until it became something no longer worth preserving. But now that he was going it alone, Varley's mind would only deliver up memories of sweet events.

The year finally turned and delivered a cold January followed by a gray wet February, both of which were improvements on the festive season as far as Carter Varley was concerned. Then came a surprisingly sunny March, milder than the month had been in a decade. These were ideal working days and he got his head down and tunneled busily into the material of his experience.

Then the telephone rang.

Varley jumped, barking his knee on the desk and spilling milky coffee on the cherrywood surface. Leaving a paper napkin to absorb the overflow, he limped out of the study and into the bedroom, balancing the clamor of the bell with short angry responses.

"Yes. All right. Hang on."

The voice on the line was, to Varley's ear, almost stage-American. "Hello, this is Mr. Billy Stoke speaking. Is that Mr. Carter Varley?"

"Yes, it is." Said with heart beginning to pound.

"I hope I'm not interrupting your work but we got into London last night and I figured that after the very kind invitation in your letter I had to call and say hello."

"Yes, rather. Very glad you did."

Stoke laughed in a boyish way. "I don't suppose you get telephoned very often by a character in one of your stories."

A few generalities were exchanged during which Stoke mentioned the name Irene. He was not traveling alone and, for some reason, this eased Varley's anxiety. Then the American said, "I know you writers have a schedule to stick to, but I was hoping Irene and I might persuade you to come to London and have a meal with us."

Varley had not ventured beyond the High Street in months. London meant the train to Waterloo, crowds, taxis, a strange hotel lobby. "Yes, very nice. It's a question of time. Perhaps a day next week."

"Afraid we're only in London for a couple of days. We've rented a car and we plan to drive along the south coast."

A momentary silence. Then Varley was astonished to hear himself saying, "Then come out here for dinner. Yes, by all means, come this evening."

The American's pleasure at the invitation was so gratifying that Varley found himself going further. It was as if some hospitable impulse buried long ago had been uncovered. "Look here," he said, "why don't you check out of the hotel? I have a perfectly good guest room here."

That was the end of writing for the day. Varley set aside his current manuscript, took a fresh sheet of paper, and drafted a menu for dinner. Under it he listed the items he would have to buy at the shops, including wine and beer and a bottle of cognac.

By six o'clock the roast of beef, surrounded by potatoes, carrots, and onions, was in the oven, filling the house with its appetizing aroma. A litre of Italian red wine was uncorked and resting on the Jacobean sideboard. Varley admired the table setting—gleaming silver, polished plates, folded linen, four tall candles in antique brass sticks. A long time since he had drawn the oak table away from the wall and raised the drop leaves.

He was placing a few additional lumps of smokeless coal on the open fire when he heard the swing of the iron gate followed by the scrape of footsteps outside the front door. Varley paused at the hall mirror to adjust the knot in his tie and smooth the edges of his graying hair. There was color in his face for the first time in a year and his eyes were clear and alert.

William and Irene Stoke from Chattanooga, Tennessee turned out to be everything Varley could have hoped for and nothing he might have feared. For one thing, they were not dressed in what he considered to be the style of children—no turtleneck sweaters, no peaked caps, no blazers with crests on them. Stoke, tall and heavyset, deeply tanned and handsome, ten years younger than Varley's half century, was wearing a dark suit, white shirt, and modest tie. His shoes had laces and were polished black. Too good to be true.

Irene Stoke could not have been older than thirty. She had a stage beauty, regular features made up immaculately, hair like burnished copper worn in one thick braid over her shoulder, and classic eyes of penetrating green.

They sat with drinks in upholstered chairs drawn close to the fire while rain came out of the darkness and rattled on the windows. Billy Stoke said, "Always wanted to see England but kept putting it off. It was that nice letter of yours that did it."

"What a charming room you've given us," Irene said. She smiled and then raised her eyes to gaze at the rough beams set in the ceiling over two hundred years ago. "I love this house."

The dinner table was small and brought the three of them close together in an intimate circle. Stoke's massive shoulders leaned in and overshadowed the other two and as they turned their heads during conversation they looked into each other's eyes at close range, saw reflected candlelight, and something else they could not identify.

"These people are strangers," Varley said to himself in amazement, wondering how they could be so simpatico.

A possible explanation sprang into his mind over coffee when the huge wine bottle was empty and he was pouring cognac. What if they were professionals? It was a preposterous premise and had he not been half drunk he would have buried it away. But he *was* nicely drunk, happily drunk for the first time in years, so he said, "I've just had a fascinating idea. You're going to laugh."

"What is it?"

"It's more than likely that you aren't really the William Stokes at all. You are American adventurers, a team of con artists if you like, and you wrote that letter simply to gain access to my house, my life, my confidence." Varley spread his arms to encompass the scene. "Done it rather well, too, I should say."

Was he mistaken or did a frown pass between Stoke and his wife? It might have been a trick of the candlelight. The American said, "But what about my letterhead? It identifies me as William Stoke, Attorney at Law, of Chattanooga, Tennessee. And that happens to be who I am."

"Easiest job in the world to have a fake letterhead printed up. First thing you'd do on a scheme like this." Why was he pressing the idea? It might be taken as uncommonly rude unless his guests accepted it as banter. And how could they do that when Varley himself was not sure whether he was serious or not?

But Stoke did laugh. "The author's mind at work," he said. "I guess you've got to see a twist in everything. But why would we go to all this trouble? What's our motive?"

"That's obvious," Varley said. "Financial gain. You get me on good terms, find out where I keep my assets, perhaps persuade me to draw out some money or write a large check. Then you vanish, discarding the false identity as you go."

Had anyone spoken at that moment, Varley might not have felt the hint of danger. But there was silence and he did feel it, a deep thrum like the clong when a tuning fork is struck. It caught him in the chest and buzzed there for seconds, gradually fading away and leaving him feeling cold. He glanced at Stoke, looking for confirmation of the threat, but the big man was tipping back his cognac, lowering the glass and shaking his head, his mouth pursed with amusement.

They sat up till midnight, talking by the fire. The Americans shared the telling of stories about motor trips to New Orleans, to Atlanta, even as far away as California. These distances seemed interstellar to the Englishman who considered the fifty miles to Brighton a long haul.

The visitors acted like a drug on Varley and he found himself opening up about his life, a thing he seldom did. Perhaps the lawyer's subtle questioning led him—he only realized this later; but at the time he rambled on about his solitary state in the world now that he was a widower. No children, no relatives living anywhere; he was a man who could fall off the edge of the earth and never be missed.

"How did your wife...?" Irene began.

Stoke cleared his throat but Varley said, "No, it's all right. An accident. She struck her head while bathing and drowned."

Hours later, waking in darkness, Varley sensed movement on the stairs outside his bedroom door. He got up, stepped into slippers, pulled on a robe, and went out quietly onto the landing. He had left the bathroom light burning for his guests' convenience. It illuminated the stairs to the angle where they turned five steps below. Silence. But a fragrance in the air—a woman's scent. It was some time since Varley had experienced this sensation in his house late at night.

He crept down the stairs into a chilly hallway, found the front door standing open, and passed through it onto the flagstone entrance to the narrow garden running along that side of the cottage. Irene Stoke was standing halfway down the path dressed in a long robe. Her braid was undone, the hair brushed out to shoulder width and halfway down her back. He approached her and they stood together in silence. Then she said, "I couldn't sleep. I'm sorry."

"It's all right."

The moon was full. Its pale illumination flooded the brick wall beside them almost like stage lighting. Not yet in leaf, the dormant vine creeping over the wall seemed a dead thing. Varley could smell moist earth and a flood of ozone from the nearby forest. It occurred to him that he ought to spend a couple of hours outside on every night as fine as this one.

Now the woman put a hand on his shoulder in the sort of companionable contact practiced by old friends. She leaned forward and kissed him, a touch as cool and fragrant as if she had brushed his cheek with a rose.

"Oughtn't to do that," Varley said.

She turned her head and looked up at the silhouette of tiled roof and chimneypots with the white, pocked globe of the moon suspended over it. He saw her mouth form a self-deprecating smile as she said with a note of finality, "I love this house."

After breakfast Varley found himself alone with William Stoke. Irene had insisted on going around to the shops to bring back some food. Stoke toyed with his third cup of coffee. "I guess Irene made a nuisance of herself last night," he said. "Sorry about that."

Having done nothing, Varley felt guilty. "No trouble at all. Difficult to sleep in strange surroundings."

But the American was intent on saying more. "I never expected to tell you this bit of background. But then, I never thought I'd be spending the night in your home." He went on to explain that this was not a holiday trip. The Stokes were preparing to move to England—under some duress. It seemed Irene had been stealing from department stores for years. She had been in police hands more than once and it had reached the point where Stoke's legal influence was wearing thin. They were talking about putting her away.

"Kleptomania," Varley said. "Surely she ought to be seeing a psychiatrist."

"We've tried that. Some people don't respond very well to analysis. Irene is one of them." The American gave his host a troubled smile. "No, I think the only answer is a complete change of scene. Perhaps a small town, a village even, where there's less opportunity for her."

"But how will you practice law?"

"Fortunately we've done well enough. Money is no problem."

The front door closed and Irene came through into the kitchen depositing a laden shopping basket on the counter. She sensed the atmosphere in the room. "My husband has been talking, has he?" Her voice was ultracheerful. "That's Billy's big problem. He never knows when to shut up." Briskly she began unloading the basket.

It was William Stoke's suggestion that they get into the rented sedan and drive down to the south coast. The weather was pleasant enough, the warmest March day on record. As they set out, Stoke said, "We may even see a village we might like to settle in." The truth was now in the open, though nothing more was said.

They took the Brighton road, then bore east through Sussex, touching the coast at Hastings where they got out of the car and walked along the beach for half a mile. Then on past Winchelsea, New Romney, Dymchurch, and Hythe, and thence along the cliffs toward Folkestone and Dover.

"Not too keen on these areas ahead," Stoke said. "Too metropolitan."

"Sandgate is a nice little place," Varley suggested.

Then Irene Stoke said in a bitter tone, "Or we could pitch a tent in a field. Or how about a small cabin, of clay and wattles made."

Varley realized how serious Stoke was when the man stopped by a real-estate office and went in to find out what was for sale and for how much. Irene refused to accompany him, so Varley waited with her in the car. They were silent for a few minutes. From his place in the back seat he had a view of her shoulders and the shiny back of her head, the dark hair tightly braided. The interior of the car

smelled of leather and paint. Finally Irene turned around and said brightly, "He's taken you in completely."
"How do you mean?"
"You believe he's what he says he is."
"I'm still not with you."
She closed her eyes while she said, "You were perceptive last night. Don't be dull now." She opened her eyes and stared at him. "Don't you see? Your writer's instinct was correct. He is *not* William Stoke. I am not his wife. This *is* a confidence trick to relieve you of a lot of money."
"But last night I was only joking." As he said this, he remembered his uncertainty at the time as to whether he was joking or not. And he recalled the hint of danger that came to him from somewhere across the table.
"Joke or not, you had it right. Ted—that's his real name—got this idea and he's been crafty enough to follow it through. It was all as you said, even to having the letterhead printed."
Carter Varley felt the sting behind his eyes, called it pure anger, but was not ready to admit he could weep with disappointment at this betrayal. "Then I'll just have a word with your Ted when he comes back. What's this house hunt, then? Part of the window dressing?"
"Yes. He lives a part one hundred percent."
"But why the story about your kleptomania? Is that true?"
"Of course not. It's all designed to lull you, to make you feel sorry for us." She reached across the seatback and took Varley's hand. "But be careful. Don't say anything to let him know I've told you. He's a psychopath and you'd be in real danger. Just watch him and say nothing."
"Why are you telling me this? It can't be in your interest."
"No. But I think you're a good man." She squeezed his hand and let it go. "Protect yourself and I'll take Ted away tomorrow."
The man who said he was William Stoke came back from the real-estate agent's office with a handful of data sheets on homes for sale. These were passed around and discussed while he drove on. After half an hour the road climbed to a headland with a vast ocean horizon spread out below a high chalk cliff.
"Now there's a view," Stoke said, pulling the car onto a grassy verge. "How'd you like to live with that outside your bedroom window?"
Irene was the first one out of the car, running to the very lip of

the cliff where she stood with fists on hips, owning everything the eye could see.

"Not too close," Stoke called. "It's a lovely fall, but the last couple of feet are murder."

They studied the view from every direction and began to feel the spank of sun and wind on their cheeks. Then Irene noticed a coffee wagon parked far down the slope by the edge of the highway where a cluster of construction huts bordered a building site.

"That's what we need," she said. "Hot coffee."

Varley insisted on going to get three cups. As he walked down the hill, he wondered what he ought to do about the dangerous situation he was in. Morally, he should call the police. If the pseudo-Stoke character was as bad as Irene said he was, then he deserved to be locked up. But it would be a tricky procedure to approach a policeman. No crime had been committed. There would be no reason to hold him. But once the American knew Varley had become suspicious, he might be capable of anything.

Trudging back up the slope with three coffee cartons in a perforated tray, Varley decided to keep silent and ease the strangers out of his house tomorrow. Once alone, he could consider putting the police on their track.

He was crossing the low mound that prevented a person farther down the hill from seeing anyone on the promontory when he heard Irene calling and saw the struggle taking place near the edge of the cliff. Stoke had Irene by the arms but she was fighting hard, out of her shoes, tearing one arm loose and swinging the free hand in a wide arc against the side of his head. It looked like a slap but it was more; she was holding a rock in that hand. Stoke's knees buckled and he sank to the grass.

"He knows that you know," she gasped as Varley ran up and set the coffee aside.

"You told him?"

"He suspected. He hurt me." She showed crimson marks on a pale arm. "I had to tell him."

Carter Varley knelt to look at the ugly wound on the man's head. He was moaning, barely conscious. "You could have killed him."

"I had to act. He was going to throw you over the cliff as soon as you got back." Irene reached out to turn Varley's head so that his eyes met hers. They were wide with shock. "I told you, he's mad."

When Stoke tried to raise his head, Varley whispered, "What do we do?"

"We've got to finish him. No, don't think about it. If he comes round, he'll go crazy. We'll never be able to handle him. If we run away, he'll come back to the house. If you call the police, he'll stay out of sight, but you'll never be safe. Believe me, I know him."

"But what—?"

"Over the edge. Quickly. We'll both say he fell. The head wound will be part of the fall."

"I can't do that."

But Irene had Stoke by the arm, his torso half off the ground. She was surprisingly strong. "Take my word," she gasped. "He deserves to die. The things he's done to so many people. You'll be serving justice."

Stoke's bloodied head was coming up, the whites of his eyes showing, his mouth hanging open. It was a terrifying sight and suddenly Varley wanted an end to it. His heart pounding, he seized the other arm and, together, he and Irene walked the man to the cliff edge. Two steps away they let him go and he tottered forward, stepped crazily into space, and was gone.

The first thing was to wipe away a few traces of blood from the grass, the next to drive to the nearest town for the police. It took some time but by sundown the accident was confirmed, William Stoke was well and truly dead, and Carter Varley was at the wheel of the car driving home.

Irene turned on the radio to a commercial music station. This seemed wrong, so he snapped it off.

"Well!" she said petulantly.

Something else was wrong. "His papers all tallied with the identification of William Stoke from Chattanooga," Varley said. "Driver's license, social security card, and so on. If he wasn't Stoke, and this was a temporary con game, why had he gone to all that trouble?"

"That's easy. Because he *was* William Stoke. Everything he told you was true. I'm the one who has been lying."

Varley's creative imagination prevented him from being too surprised. He remembered the hint of danger at the dinner table last night and understood why Stoke had appeared oblivious. The hint of danger had come from Irene.

"Why have you done this?" he asked.

"Because he made my life a hell. He kept sending me to psychiatrists and now he was trying to bury me in some remote village. Away from temptation." She said this last word contemptuously. "That's a laugh."

"Then you've just murdered your husband."

"*We've* murdered him," she said. "Never forget that. I could tell a story to the authorities that would put us both away for a long time. I hope there'll never be a need."

Varley drove on in outraged, frightened silence. The next time Irene spoke was when he parked the car outside the cottage and went to unlock the front door. She took the key from his hand and turned it in the lock. "I love this house," she said.

That night and the next one had their compensations. Varley had almost forgotten what it was to have a woman in his bed. But still he was shocked by the recent events and deeply angry at the way she had manipulated him. He felt she could not be allowed to get away with it. His mind was made up for him when he went into the market a couple of days later and was approached by the manager holding a slip of paper.

"Sorry to trouble you, Mr. Varley, but the American lady, staying with you I understand, took a few items and forgot to check them through. Only a small amount, but I thought you'd want me to mention it."

Varley paid and walked home, his chest rising and falling. He went upstairs and sat at his desk, looking out of the window, thinking. The fine weather had changed and a more seasonal cold wind was blowing across the common.

Yes, he would have to take care of her. A simple household accident was the best way. But not the fall in the bath and the drowning that had done for poor Beatrice. This would have to be something else, perhaps a broken neck at the bottom of those twisting stairs. They were dangerous till you got used to them.

The office door opened and Irene came in without knocking. She was carrying a glass of whiskey—he frowned at his watch—at eleven in the morning. "What are you up to all alone in here?" she asked, sounding bright and self-satisfied.

Carter Varley picked up a pen and added a few words to a paragraph of recent scrawl. "Oh, just busy with my plotting," he said.

It was her second drink, so Irene did not catch the hint of danger in his voice.

"Q"

Robert L. Fish
The Wager

I suppose if I were watching television coverage of the return of a lunar mission and Kek Huuygens climbed out of the command module after splashdown, I shouldn't be greatly surprised. I'd be even less surprised to see Kek hustled aboard the aircraft carrier and given a thorough search by a suspicious Customs official. Kek, you see, is one of those men who turn up at very odd times in unexpected places. Also, he is rated by the customs services of nearly every nation in the world as the most talented smuggler alive.

Polish by birth, Dutch by adopted name, the holder of a valid U.S. passport, multilingual, a born sleight-of-hand artist, Kek is an elusive target for the stolid bureaucrat who thinks in terms of hollow shoe heels and suitcases with false bottoms. Now and then over the years, Kek has allowed me to publish a little of his lore in my column. When I came across him last, however, he was doing something very ordinary in a commonplace setting. Under the critical eye of a waiter he was nursing a beer at a table in that little sunken-garden affair in Rockefeller Center.

Before I got to his table, I tried to read the clues. Kek had a good tan and he looked healthy. But his suit had a shine that came from wear rather than from silk thread. A neat scissors trim didn't quite conceal the fact that his cuffs were frayed. He was not wearing his usual boutonniere.

"I owe you three cognacs from last time—Vaduz, wasn't it?—and I'm buying," I said as I sat down.

"You are a man of honor," he said and called to the waiter, naming the most expensive cognac. Then he gave me his wide friendly smile. "Yes, you have read the signs and they are true—but not for any reasons you might imagine. Sitting before you, you can observe the impoverishment that comes from total success. Failure can be managed, but success can be a most difficult thing to control."

Hidden inside every Kek Huuygens aphorism there is a story. But if you want it produced, you must pretend complete indifference. "Ah, yes," I said, "failure is something you know in your heart. Success is something that lies in the eye of the beholder. I think—"

"Do you want to hear the story or don't you?" Kek said. "You can't use it in your column, though, I warn you."

"Perhaps in time?"

"Perhaps in time all barbarous customs regulations will be repealed," he said. "Perhaps the angels will come down to rule the earth. Until then you and I alone will share this story." That was Kek's way of saying "Wait until things have cooled off."

It all began in Las Vegas (Huuygens said) and was primarily caused by two unfortunate factors: one, that I spoke the word banco aloud and, two, that it was heard. I am still not convinced that the player against me wasn't the world's best card manipulator, but at any rate I found myself looking at a jack and a nine, while the best I could manage for myself was a six. So I watched my money disappear, got up politely to allow the next standee to take my place, and started for the exit.

I had enough money in the hotel safe to pay my bill and buy me a ticket back to New York—a simple precaution I recommend to all who never learn to keep quiet in a baccarat game—and a few dollars in my pocket; but my financial position was not one any sensible banker would have lent money against. I was sure something would turn up, as it usually did, and in this case it turned up even faster than usual because I hadn't even reached the door before I was stopped.

The man who put his hand on my arm did so in a completely friendly manner, and I recalled him as being one of the group standing around the table during the play. There was something faintly familiar about him, but even quite famous faces are disregarded at a baccarat table; one is not there to collect autographs. The man holding my arm was short, heavy, swarthy, and of a type to cause instant distaste on the part of any discerning observer.

What caught and held my attention was that he addressed me by name—and in French. "M'sieu Huuygens?" he said. To my absolute amazement he pronounced it correctly. I acknowledged that I was, indeed, M'sieu Kek Huuygens. "I should like to talk with you a moment and to buy you a drink," he said.

"I could use one," I admitted, and I allowed him to lead me into the bar. As we went, I noticed two men who had been standing to one side studying their fingernails; they now moved with us and took up new positions to each side, still studying their nails. One would think that fingernails were a subject that could quickly bore, but apparently not to those two. As I sat down beside my chubby host, I looked at him once more, and suddenly recognition came.

He saw the light come on in the little circle over my head and smiled, showing a dazzling collection of white teeth, a tribute to the art of the dental laboratory.

"Yes," he said, "I am Antoine Duvivier," and waved over a waiter. We ordered and I returned my attention to him. Duvivier, as you must know—even newspapermen listen to the radio, I assume—was the president of the island of St. Michel in the Caribbean, or had been until his loyal subjects decided that presidents should be elected, after which he departed in the middle of the night, taking with him most of his country's treasury.

He could see the wheels turning in my head as I tried to see how I could use this information to my advantage, and I must say he waited politely enough while I was forced to give up on the problem. Then he said, "I have watched you play at baccarat."

We received our drinks and I sipped, waiting for him to go on.

"You are quite a gambler, M'sieu Huuygens," he said, "but, of course, you would have to be, in your line of work." He saw my eyebrows go up and added quite coolly, "Yes, M'sieu Huuygens, I have had you investigated, and thoroughly. But please permit me to explain that it was not done from idle curiosity. I am interested in making you a proposition."

I find, in situations like this, the less said the better, so I said nothing.

"Yes," he went on, "I should like to offer you—" He paused, as if reconsidering his words, actually looking embarrassed, as if he were guilty of a gaffe. "Let me rephrase that," he said and searched for a better approach. At last he found it. "What I meant was, I should like to make a *wager* with you, a wager I am sure should be most interesting to a gambler such as yourself."

This time, of course, I had to answer, so I said, "Oh?"

"Yes," he said, pleased at my instant understanding. "I should like to wager twenty thousand dollars of my money, against two dollars of yours, that you will *not* bring a certain object from the Caribbean through United States Customs and deliver it to me in New York City."

I must admit that I admire bluntness, and that the approach was unique.

"The odds are reasonable," I admitted. "One might even say generous. What type of object are we speaking of?"

THE WAGER

He lowered his voice. "It is a carving," he said. "A Tien Tse Huwai, dating back to eight centuries before Christ. It is of ivory and is not particularly large; I imagine it could fit into your coat pocket, although, admittedly, it would be bulky. It depicts a village scene—but you, I understand, are an art connoisseur; you may have heard of it. In translation, its name is *The Village Dance*."

Normally I can control my features, but my surprise must have shown, for Duvivier went on in the same soft voice. "Yes, I have it. The carving behind that glass case in the St. Michel National Gallery is a copy—a plastic casting, excellently done, but a copy. The original is at the home of a friend in Barbados. I could get it that far, but I was afraid to attempt bringing it the rest of the way; to have lost it would have been tragic. Since then I have been looking for a man clever enough to get it into the States without being stopped by Customs." He suddenly grinned, those white blocks of teeth almost blinding me. "I am offering ten-thousand-to-one odds that that clever man is *not* you."

It was a cute ploy, but that was not what interested me at the moment.

"M'sieu," I said simply, "permit me a question: I am familiar with the Tien *Village Dance*. I have never seen it, but it received quite a bit of publicity when your National Gallery purchased it, since it was felt—if you will pardon me—that the money could have been used better elsewhere. However, my surprise a moment ago was not that you have the carving; it was at your offer. The Tien, many years in the future, may indeed command a large price, but the figure your museum paid when you bought it was, as I recall, not much more than the twenty thousand dollars you are willing to—ah—wager to get it into this country. And that value could only be realized at a legitimate sale, which would be difficult, it seems to me, under the circumstances."

Duvivier's smile had been slowly disappearing as I spoke. Now he was looking at me in disappointment.

"You do not understand, M'sieu," he said, and there was a genuine touch of sadness in his voice. "To you, especially after your losses tonight, I am sure the sum of twenty thousand dollars seems a fortune, but, in all honesty, to me it is not. I am not interested in the monetary value of the carving; I have no intention of selling it. I simply wish to own it."

He looked at me with an expression I have seen many times before—the look of a fanatic, a zealot, a Collector, with a capital C.

"You cannot possibly comprehend," he repeated, shaking his head. "It is such an incredibly lovely thing..."

Well, of course, he was quite wrong about my understanding, or lack of it; I understood perfectly. For a moment I almost found myself liking the man; but only for a moment. And a wager is a wager, and I had to admit I had never been offered such attractive odds before in my life.

As for the means of getting the carving into the United States, especially from Barbados, I had a thought on that, too. I was examining my idea in greater detail when his voice broke in on me.

"Well?" he asked, a bit impatiently.

"You have just made yourself a bet," I said. "But it will require a little time."

"How much time?" Now that I was committed, the false friendliness was gone from both voice and visage; for all practical purposes I was now merely an employee.

I thought a moment. "It's hard to say. Less than two months but probably more than one."

He frowned. "Why so long?" I merely shrugged and reached for my glass. "All right," he said grudgingly. "And how do you plan on getting it through Customs?" My response to this was to smile at him gently, so he gave up. "I shall give you a card to my friend in Barbados, which will release the carving into your care. After that—" he smiled again, but this time it was a bit wolfish for my liking "—our wager will be in effect. We will meet at my apartment in New York."

He gave me his address, together with his telephone number, and then handed me a second card with a scrawl on it to a name in Barbados, and that was that. We drank up, shook hands, and I left the bar, pleased to be working again and equally pleased to be quit of Duvivier, if only for a while.

Huuygens paused and looked at me with his satanic eyebrows tilted sharply. I recognized the expression and made a circular gesture over our glasses, which was instantly interpreted by our waiter. Kek waited until we were served, thanked me gravely, and drank. I settled back to listen, sipping. When next Huuygens spoke, however, I thought at first he was changing the subject, but I soon learned this was not the case.

Anyone who says the day of travel by ship has passed (Huuygens went on) has never made an examination of the brochures for Caribbean cruises that fill and overflow the racks of travel agencies. It appears that between sailings from New York and sailings from Port Everglades—not to mention Miami, Baltimore, Norfolk, and others—almost everything afloat must be pressed into service to transport those Americans with credit cards and a little free time to the balmy breezes and shimmering sands of the islands.

They have trips for all seasons, as well as for every taste and pocketbook. There are bridge cruises to St. Lucia, canasta cruises to Trinidad, golf cruises to St. Croix. There are seven-day cruises to the Bahamas, eight-day cruises to Jamaica, thirteen-day cruises to Martinique; there are even—I was not surprised to see—three-day cruises to nowhere. And it struck me that even though it was approaching summer, a cruise would be an ideal way to travel; it had been one of my principal reasons for requiring so much time to consummate the deal.

So I went to the travel agency in the hotel lobby and was instantly inundated with schedules and pamphlets. I managed to get the reams of propaganda to my room without a bellboy, sat down on the bed, and carefully made my selection. When I had my trip laid out to my satisfaction, I descended once again to the hotel lobby and presented my program to the travel agent.

He must have thought I was insane, but I explained I suffered from Widget Syndrome and required a lot of salt air, after which he shrugged and picked up the phone to confirm my reservations through New York. They readily accepted my credit card for the bill—which I sincerely hoped to be able to honor by the time it was presented—and two days later I found myself in Miami, boarding the M. V. *Andropolis* for a joyous sixteen-day cruise. It was longer than I might have chosen, but it was the only one that fit my schedule and I felt that I would shortly earn the rest.

I might as well tell you right now that it was a delightful trip. I should have preferred to have taken along my own feminine companionship, but my finances would not permit it; there are, after all, such hard-cash outlays as bar bills and tips. However, there was no lack of unattached women aboard, some even presentable, and the days—as they say—fairly flew. We had the required rum punch in Ocho Rios, fought off the beggars in Port-au-Prince, visited Bluebeard's Castle in Charlotte Amalie, and eventually made it to Barbados.

Barbados is a lovely island, with narrow winding roads that skirt the ocean and cross between the Caribbean and Atlantic shores through high stands of sugar cane that quite efficiently hide any view of approaching traffic; but my rented car managed to get me to the address I had been given without brushing death more than three or four times. The man to whom I presented the ex-president's card was not in the least perturbed to be giving up the carving; if anything, he seemed relieved to be rid of its responsibility. It was neatly packaged in straw, wrapped in brown paper, and tied with twine, and I left it exactly that way as I drove back to the dock through the friendly islanders, all of whom demonstrated their happy, carefree insouciance by walking in the middle of the road.

There was no problem about carrying the package aboard. Other passengers from the M. V. *Andropolis* were forming a constant line, like ants, to and from the ship, leaving empty-handed to return burdened with Wedgwood, Hummel figures, camera lenses, and weirdly woven straw hats that did not fit. I gave up my boarding pass at the gangplank, climbed to my deck, and locked myself in my stateroom, interested in seeing this carving on which M'sieu Antoine Duvivier was willing to wager the princely sum of $20,000.

The paper came away easily enough. I eased the delicate carving from its bed of straw and took it to the light of my desk lamp. At first I was so interested in studying the piece for its authenticity that the true beauty of the carving didn't strike me; but when I finally came to concede that I was, indeed, holding a genuine Tien Tse Huwai in my hands and got down to looking at the piece itself, I had to admit that M'sieu Duvivier, whatever his other failings, was a man of excellent taste.

I relished the delicate nuances with which Tien had managed his intricate subject, the warmth he had been able to impart to his cold medium, the humor he had been genius enough to instill in the ivory scene. Each figure in the relaxed yet ritualistic village dance had his own posture, and although there were easily forty or fifty men and women involved, carved with infinite detail on a plaque no larger than six by eight inches and possibly three inches in thickness, there was no sense of crowding. One could allow himself to be drawn into the carving, to almost imagine movement or hear the flutes.

I enjoyed the study of the masterpiece for another few minutes, then carefully rewrapped it and tucked it into the air-conditioning duct of my stateroom, pleased that the first portion of my assignment had been completed with such ease. I replaced the grillwork and went upstairs to the bar, prepared to enjoy the remaining three or four days of balmy breezes—if not shimmering sands, since Barbados had been our final port.

The trip back to Miami was enjoyable but uneventful. I lost in the shuffleboard tournament, largely due to a nearsighted partner, but in compensation I picked up a record number of spoons from the bottom of the swimming pool and received in reward, at the captain's party, a crystal ashtray engraved with a design of Triton either coming up or going down for the third time. What I am trying to say is that, all in all, I enjoyed myself completely and the trip was almost compensation for the thorough—and humiliating—search I had to suffer when I finally went through Customs in Miami.

As usual, they did everything but disintegrate my luggage, but at last I was free of Customs—to their obvious chagrin—and I found myself in the street in one piece. So I took myself and my luggage to a hotel for the night.

And the next morning I reboarded the M. V. *Andropolis* for its next trip—in the same cabin—a restful three-day cruise to nowhere . . .

I see (Kek went on, his eyes twinkling) that intelligence has finally forced its presence on you. I should have thought it was rather obvious. These Caribbean cruise ships vary their schedules, mixing trips to the islands with these short cruises to nowhere, where they merely wander aimlessly upon the sea and eventually find their way back—some say with considerable luck—to their home port. Since they touch no foreign shore, and since the ship's shops are closed during these cruises, one is not faced with the delay or embarrassment of facing a Customs agent on one's return.

Therefore, if one were to take a cruise *preceding* a cruise to nowhere and were to be so careless as to inadvertently leave a small object—in the air-conditioning duct of his stateroom, for example—during the turnaround, he could easily retrieve it on the second cruise and walk off the ship with it in his pocket, with no fear of discovery.

Which, of course, is what I did.

The flight to New York was slightly anticlimatic, and I called M'sieu Duvivier as soon as I landed at Kennedy. He was most pleasantly surprised, since less than a month had actually elapsed, and said he would expect me as fast as I could get there by cab.

The ex-president of St. Michel lived in a lovely apartment on

Central Park South, and as I rode up in the elevator I thought of how pleasant it must be to have endless amounts of money at one's disposal; but before I had a chance to dwell on that thought too much, we had arrived and I found myself pushing what I still think was a lapis-lazuli doorbell set in a solid-gold frame. It made one want to weep. At any rate, Duvivier himself answered the door, as anxious as any man I have ever seen. He didn't even wait to ask me in or inquire as to my taste in aperitifs.

"You have it?" he asked, staring at my coat pocket.

"Before we go any further," I said, "I should like you to repeat the exact terms of our wager. The *exact* terms, if you please."

He looked at me in irritation, as if I were being needlessly obstructive.

"All right," he said shortly. "I wagered you twenty thousand dollars of my money against two dollars of yours that you would *not* bring me a small carving from Barbados through United States Customs and deliver it to me in New York. Correct?"

I sighed. "Perfectly correct," I said and reached into my pocket. "You are a lucky man. You won." And I handed him his two dollars.

I stared across the table at Huuygens. I'm afraid my jaw had gone slack. He shook his head at me, a bit sad at my lack of comprehension.

"You can't possibly understand," he said, almost petulantly. "It is so incredibly lovely . . ."

Eleazar Lipsky
Tiger in the Night

"Somebody please help me!" The hoarse animal sounds were over, and the boy stood swaying in the center of the room, both hands clasped to his face. His striped trousers were pegged into yellow shoes, a mocha jacket swept almost to his knees, a flowered tie was resplendent. A flow of blood trickled down his left wrist, staining his sleeve below the elbow, and this blood, oozing through trembling fingers, dropped to the carpet.

"*Please* help me," he begged. "Joe?"

A man answered, "Joe ain't here."

"I need help," the colored boy repeated dully. Something that had jellied and clotted with blood dropped from his hand, and a woman's voice of disgust broke the spell. The roomful of men and women stirred.

"We need an ambulance and the police," the woman stated imperiously. "Clarence! Go down the street and call the station! Give 'em your name, and you tell 'em, this is one time the stickup man got stuck!"

"Yes, Ma!" A weedy youth ducked his head and went clattering down the tenement stairs, flinging explanations to the neighbors, racing through the street to the police call-box. In the apartment, a sharp babble broke out, men and women grabbed hats and began to leave, while the wounded boy stared, moaning softly, unseeing, feeling only the warm blood welling in an empty eye socket, tasting the smell of gunsmoke and boiled meats until the tread of authority filled the room . . .

Some days followed—or was it weeks? It was on the whole not too bad—dark and light and pain deadened with morphine and the good indifferent treatment of the city hospital's prison ward. His leg lay in a plaster cast, and this was a surprise because he had been unaware that a bullet had struck near the knee. After a time he was told that his right eye would be saved. The bullet had gone splashing through his left eye, and his nose had been fractured, but in time the great purpled bruises subsided and he was allowed visitors.

He was a good patient and the nurses liked his cheerful manner.

On a sunny day in September the orderlies put up partitions and set a chair beside his bed. The boy took this jokingly, and with some wonder, and then a well dressed colored man with a briefcase entered and sat facing him. He spoke pleasantly enough.

"Eddie Dickinson?"

The boy nodded. "That's me, sir."

"I'm your lawyer." With a trace of friendly self-importance, he added, "Mister Phillips."

"Sir?"

"I've been appointed by the Court. Is that all right with you?"

The boy frowned. "I don't get it, sir. What for do I need a lawyer? I didn't do nothing. I beg your pardon, sir. I don't want to offend you."

Phillips was a tall man with grave eyes and tapering, sensitive fingers. His manner was precise, almost fussy. He considered the information, and tapped out a cork-tipped cigarette.

"In that case how did you get that eye shot out? And that bullet in your leg? Those things don't generally happen."

"Oh, that?" The boy pressed his thick lips together with a resigned air. "Don't nobody believe me? I told the police, and then I told Mr. Wiley, the district attorney, I don't know how many times."

"Suppose you tell it one more time for me."

"Why would you believe me?"

Phillips smoked comfortably. "I want to know your side. After all, they've got you for murder—felony murder. If they make it stick, you'll get the chair, boy."

Eddie Dickinson smiled incredulously.

"Oh, no, sir!"

"Oh, *yes,* sir!" said Phillips pleasantly. "Hard to believe, isn't it?"

"Sure beats me!" the boy muttered. "All I know, there was a party, this place they call Mrs. Hillegas. I understand she's been running these parties a long time—chitlings and greens, beer and coleslaw, hot dogs, and dancing. I came there with sixty-five dollars sitting in my pocket, and I was stupid enough to tell somebody I met up there."

"Who was that?"

"A girl."

"Do you know that girl's name?"

"No, sir."

They stared at each other before Phillips resumed smoking.

"Go on," he said. "Why did you tell her about the money?"

The boy grinned widely. "I admit that was my mistake. Guess I wanted to show I was a hotshot. I work in the meat market on Twelfth Avenue and I make good pay. You can ask my boss, Mr. Rowe, the Sky High Packing Company, where I'm learning to be a butcher. I had this money saved up, and I can prove that. Ask the savings bank."

"Then what?"

"About two o'clock I was messing with this girl in the hallway when one of them, man they called Choatey—"

Phillips made an encouraging sound. "The one that got killed?"

"That's right, Choatey. He was getting drunk and mean. He stuck a gun in my belly and told me he was going to blow it off if I messed around with this girl. So I tried to argue. Then a little guy named Slope—"

"Lou Slope?"

"Sam or Lou, which I never knew, this Slope yells I got a roll of bills and to take it off of me. So I told Choatey he could have my money, only not to hurt me, and I gave him the money and we sat around talking, but I did *not* like the look in his eye one bit. Then I danced some more with this girl—"

"What was her name?"

The boy lowered his eyes. "Emmalou, I guess. Something like that," he said reluctantly. "But she was a nice girl."

"What does she do?"

"Works in a beauty parlor. I think she does manicures. Anyhow, I got to thinking how it was my money and by what right did Choatey take it from me? I kept watching how he was getting drunk on this beer, and I figured I might snake back my wallet—"

"Did you have a gun?"

"Me?" The boy's voice went falsetto. "I never had no gun in my life! Maybe a knife now and then, only for protection. But gun? Don't know nothing about no gun! No, *sir!* This Choatey had a gun, but not me! What makes you talk like that?"

The lawyer's smile was disconcerting as he polished his glasses with a folded piece of silicon paper. "Come down to the shooting."

"Nothing to tell," said the boy. "I made a grab for the wallet, then he reached for the gun, and we wrastled, and it went off. Or maybe this Slope had the gun. There was a lot of confusion, and to tell you the truth I don't know exactly which way it went, except—blam! A ton of bricks hit me. I was standing there begging for help and I heard this Mrs. Hillegas yell, 'Choatey's dead!' Then she called me some dirty names."

"What names did she call you?"

"I couldn't tell you, sir. It reflected on my mother. I like to respeck people, and I like them to respeck me and mine."

"Very sound," said the lawyer.

"Then somebody yelled, 'Let's frame this guy, or we all in trouble with the law.'"

"Who said that?"

The boy gingerly touched the dry white pad over his left eye. "I don't know. By that time I had lost this eye, and it sure hurt. I just wasn't asking no names. I couldn't believe it. That's something you can't never believe, that maybe you can lose something like an eye. But it do happen to people, and that's how it happened to me, and that's God's truth. I walked into a joint, and they set to rob me, and now they fix the blame on me. It ain't right, sir. They making me out a criminal, the while I'm a working man. Ask anybody, ask my boss."

They sat staring a long moment. Behind the partitions arose the clatter of trays and the joking of nurses with sick prisoners. Phillips squinted as a shaft of sunlight from the barred window struck his eyes.

"Eddie—?"

"Sir?"

"Do you want to help yourself?"

The boy nodded earnestly. "I got a lot to live for, Mr. Phillips. Tell me what to do."

"That's a good story you've got there, Eddie—" The lawyer paused to dispose of cigarette ash behind the radiator, and went on lightly. "One of the best I ever heard."

"Yes, sir?" A grin of pleasure, somewhat puzzled, appeared and hung, expectant of praise, then faded as the lawyer went on, "There's just one fault."

"Sir?"

"You forgot one thing."

"Such as what?"

"Witnesses, Eddie!" Phillips raised a reproachful finger. "Witnesses! More than a dozen people saw the whole thing."

The boy exclaimed scornfully: "You mean the other side—Choatey's *friends?*"

"Exactly."

The boy blinked his sound eye, bloodshot and ringed with purple bruises, and considered the point. "Well," he said nicely, "what can you expeck? They *Choatey's* friends. A man's friends *got* to stick by."

"But Choatey's dead."

"That makes no difference."

"They've got an entirely different version."

"I am *not* surprised," said the boy severely.

The lawyer had been wearing a tweed topcoat and a pearl fedora, and these suddenly seemed heavy. He folded the coat across the bed and flicked an oily black ash from the creamy perfection of his hat. His voice lowered to a troubled level.

"The district attorney believes that you came in at about one o'clock with two men, older men, who looked like longshoremen. One was heavyset and the other had pockmarks. They answered to 'Fats' and 'Rocky'—"

The boy flapped his hand over. "I don't *know* any Fats or Rocky," he cried wearily.

Phillips seemed not to hear. "You had some beers and there was horseplay and foolery with the girls until two o'clock when Fats turned off the music and called a stickup. You all pulled guns—"

"Including me?" the boy asked with irony.

"Everybody lines up in the parlor with some grumbling," continued the lawyer calmly. "It went quietly until Fats began to search the women. When he got his hand into this woman's blouse, Choatey said, 'If you're going to rob us, then rob us. Go about your business, but try to act like gentlemen and show respect for the ladies.' Do you remember that part?"

"Any reason I should?"

"Because then Fats turned to you and said, 'Kill this man for me, Eddie.'"

The boy rolled his eyes incredulously.

"Then what did I do?"

"You made the high sign and you said, 'Like drinking a cup of coffee, Fats!' You were calm and easy and nobody believed you'd do it, but you crossed the room and you shot Choatey. Slope grabbed for your gun, shots were fired, a fight broke out. You had an eye shot out and got a bullet in your leg. Fats and Rocky held off the crowd with guns, then ran off and left you. Choatey was dead with a bullet in his throat and you were caught. All that adds up to murder, Eddie, and the indictment came down this morning. The Court will appoint me to defend you, and I'm here to do what I can."

"You alone, sir?"

"I've got two law partners, but I'm running the case."

Beyond the partition the sounds had changed. Luncheon had ended, orderlies were removing trays, there was an old man's laughter and a commercial on afternoon television. The boy's face screwed in a puzzled frown, his lower lip hooked in blunt yellow incisors.

"Sir, I don't know what to say," he murmured disquietedly. "How do it look to you?"

"I'll tell you this much." Phillips let his hands smooth the fabric at his knees. "Unless you can answer those witnesses, you'll be put to death."

After a pause, the boy asked slowly: "You mean the chair?"

"Yes."

"How can you be sure?"

"I talked with Mr. Wiley, the district attorney—"

The district attorney! A picture leaped into the boy's mind—a lean, yellow-haired man with cold blue eyes, quietly insistent, agile and quick with a knowledge of one's innermost thoughts, a tongue of irony—and the picture faded. Eddie's lips compressed nervously.

"Beats me," he muttered. "I thought losing this eye was about the worst, and now you tell me they fixing me for the chair?"

The lawyer nodded slowly.

The boy's large head, capped with a scalp of black crinkles, fell back. The eye rolled, yellow and bloodshot, picking out details of the lawyer's dignified dress down to the pocket handkerchief.

"Sir, how can I help myself?"

"I'm sure—" Phillips coughed delicately, clasped his hands, leaned against an inner reluctance. "Fats and Rocky have disappeared, and there's no line on them, only descriptions that might fit a thousand men. Mr. Wiley might trade two for one."

"What do *that* mean?"

"If you turn them in, you can save your life."

A wondering smile rose. "Squeal?"

"Yes."

"And *they* set in the chair?"

"They might—not you."

"Suppose you were in my shoes?"

"My advice," said the lawyer stolidly, "is to think of yourself, because in a case like this it's your only sure way out."

The boy's smile trembled. "But I told Mr. Wiley, and I told you—I don't *know* any Fats or Rocky! These people are making me out a fall guy, and that's the simple truth."

"They've got more than a dozen witnesses against you."

"But if I'm not guilty," the boy cried, "how can I point out two men, answer me that?"

Phillips smoked two cigarettes, shook his head as the nurse looked in, then resumed uneasily.

"Trouble is, Eddie, you've got no possible defense—no alibi, no insanity, no mistaken identity, none of those things—nothing except your own version, not one witness for your side, not unless some friend shows up to swear you had no gun, and even then it's a long shot."

"I appreciate all that."

"Have you got a friend?"

"No, sir."

"Boy, boy," murmured Phillips, shaking his head dubiously, "where'd you ever come from?"

"Stokes Corner."

"What's that?"

"Little country town near Charlotte, just a crossroads."

"Are your folks alive?"

"No, sir."

"Not one?"

"No, sir, not a soul."

"What's your education?"

"Just a bit of reading, and I can write and do sums. My father worked in the fields but he taught me what he knew."

"How about schooling?"

"They couldn't keep me in school. I was too wild, and it weren't worthwhile."

"What made you leave Stokes Corner?"

"I just had nothing to keep me."

"Boy!" said the lawyer sharply.

"Sir?"

"You sure you grasp everything I told you?"

"I got a head on my shoulders, sir. I've been teaching myself things, and I'm fixing to be a butcher, and that's no mean thing."

"Have you got a girl?"

The entire face, broad and big-boned, smiled shyly. "I have not."

"But as I recall, you've got a lot to live for."

"Guess I have."

"What girl did you have in mind?"

"Well—" The boy hesitated. "I guess I was thinking of this Emmalou. She was mighty pleasant—" He trailed off, abashed. "She might be a witness for me," he added hopefully. "I've had her on my mind a lot while lying here."

The lawyer shook his head. "Forget that! She was Choatey's girl, and she'll put the gun right in your hand."

"I can't believe that!"

"She'll be their star witness."

"Oh, my!" After a silent moment the yellow eye welled up with tears, and fat drops trickled into the pillow. The column of throat, helpless and thrown back, worked convulsively.

"Excuse me crying this way," the boy whispered wretchedly. "It's just I'm so worried. Everybody at me, the police and Mr. Wiley, asking me things I can't tell them, and nobody in the world to help me, maybe not even you."

Phillips strode to the barred window and gazed down. In the courtyard a group of convalescents were sunning themselves. "Cry it out," he said patiently, and after a time the boy blew his nose, and said, "Funny thing, sir, the one eye is gone, but under the bandage it still gets wet when the good one cries."

The lawyer turned angrily.

"Tell me about Fats and Rocky!"

"Don't even you believe me?"

"I don't know what to believe."

"I am *not* guilty," said the boy with dignity. "I don't *know* those two men."

"Do you want to think it over?"

"Thinking it over don't change the truth."

"I've heard *that* before."

"Are you mad at me, sir?"

"No." With disquiet, Phillips put on his coat and stood twirling his fedora. "If that's your story, that's how I'll try the case. There's only one point. If these other jailbirds here try to coach you, don't expect to cop a plea. This is felony murder, and the D.A.'s office has a policy—no plea! You go to trial, win or lose. Is that clear?"

"Yes, sir."

The lawyer scowled. "I don't know why I get into this kind of thing, I swear I don't! Goodbye!" With an angered nod, he slipped on gray gloves and left the ward. A burst of senile laughter followed him out...

Phillips was a man of affairs in Harlem, a patron of an uptown art theatre, counsel to a neighborhood Chamber of Commerce, contributor to the local press, deacon of his church, an ardent husband and the good-humored father of three spirited girls—the eldest was the garlanded poetess of the Fielding School. His good dress reflected a sense of success. He felt that the sun was shining on him, and in time, if the cards fell right, he could even expect judicial honors. His office was a model of efficiency, and all this had been achieved by his early forties. His face was smooth and calm.

But as the months passed, he found himself overwhelmed by his assigned case. He neglected his civil work, the backbone of his practice, in frantic preparation for the trial, and the large manila envelope lettered DICKINSON, EDW. ADV. THE PEOPLE ETC., bulged wider each hard day. He scoured the area for ammunition against the Hillegas clientele, engaged friendly police in off-the-record talks, evolved intricate summations before his bathroom mirror, and exasperated wife and daughters with his remoteness of mind. On the eve of the trial his teeth were rattling with tension and fatigue. His associates, Zack Pitkowski and Joe Kerrigan, hardened veterans, were stupefied.

They made the point at a luncheon conference at Guido's, a small restaurant on Mulberry Street patronized by lovers of fine Neapolitan cookery. "We're supposed to defend the boy, not start a crusade. When we do our best, the rest is up to the jury. Stop worrying. You didn't kill the man—the boy did."

Phillips clasped his shaking hands between his knees. "I'm convinced the boy is innocent, but how do we prove it?"

"Sure he's innocent," nodded Pitkowski, tossing the phrase worn smooth with usage, "and I've got a heart condition. Don't expect me to fall dead for the best client in the world."

"I can't believe he's kidding us," said Phillips in his now hesitant voice. "I don't think he's that smart."

Pitkowski sipped from a brandy glass. "I musn't get excited, I mustn't be disturbed," he intoned like an article of faith. "It won't be this case that carries me off to my reward."

"He's a likable boy." Phillips let his thoughts roll back to his most recent prison interview. He saw himself, an older man with eroded emotions, facing with exasperating futility the boy's calm smile. He was inclined almost to agree with Kerrigan's restatement of the ancient rule of thumb.

"You can't help a man who won't help himself . . ."

Emmalou Howard had quit her job at Madame Bertha's, a fancy establishment, so it took the lawyer time and ingenuity to locate her in a barber shop on upper Lenox Avenue. Phillips ordered a manicure and studied her covertly as a hot towel partially covered his face. His eyes swam in the moist heat.

The girl, he decided, was enchanting. She was slender and light-skinned and lovely, with turbulent dark hair floating at her shoulders. Her eyes had an elfin glint and her voice was tart with the accent of Virginia. Her cool touch made his palm tingle. She refused to visit his office and in her lunch hour he took her to a Chinese restaurant. She sipped cup after cup of tea in wary silence.

"I thought he was nice, yes," she admitted. "He had clean nails. I always look to that in a man. When they tell you those big lies, Mr. Phillips, you look at his nails, that's the little thing that counts."

"Did you let him kiss you?"

She nodded seriously.

"Well, he couldn't dance, didn't seem to know how, and Mrs. Hillegas keeps the lights low, so I didn't see any harm in it. He was very respectful, I mean, he didn't feel me up right away like most men would, and I appreciated that. He didn't seem to know the fundamentals, not the simplest things, just kept saying 'Hunh?' to everything with his jaw hanging, a real country jake. All he could talk were his plans to be a butcher. Asked me how would I go about carving twelve steer to serve thirteen companies of soldiers? I had to laugh a little, but he was sweet."

"Did Choatey see this kissing?"

Her fingernail drew a line in the tablecloth. "Choatey was high and mighty. I don't know what he saw."

"If he saw you kissing, would he get jealous?"

"Now why," she asked warily, "would he get jealous?"

"Weren't you his girl?"

"I am nobody's girl."

"The boy likes you," said the lawyer hopefully.

"I know that."

"He thinks you can help him."

Her eyes gravely searched his face. She was half his age, yet in her pity she seemed older. "Mr. Phillips, I'll talk to you like I would to my father," she said softly. "I'd like to help that boy, I really would, but I'm under strict orders not to discuss the case, especially with you. If Mr. Wiley knew I had this lunch, he'd snatch me bald.

TIGER IN THE NIGHT

Don't ask me more, because anything I might say can't do you any good."

Yet his guile was great and in an hour he drew out much of value, and the events of the fateful night grew clear in his mind. They parted on friendly terms. "Think it over," he said urgently.

She squeezed his hand and darted back to the barber shop, leaving a lovely and lonely moment behind in the street.

The prosecutor was adamant.

"He has his way out," said Wiley flatly. He was seated on his desk, arms folded, smoking, somewhat wearied of the argument. "If he'll give me Fats and Rocky, he can save his life. I'll let him plead to murder in the second, and I think that's generous. This case is solid."

He was indeed, as he said, generous. A plea to second-degree murder would allow eventual parole and release from prison, and the offer from Wiley, a cool technician, was a tribute to Phillip's dogged persistence. Wiley went on crisply.

"All I ask is a show of good faith. I admit the boy is young, and seemingly not too bright. I admit he might have been involved by older men."

"Then why not give some weight to his version?" the lawyer urged in a nagging tone. "I know that neighborhood, and I tell you that's a bad element around Mrs. Hillegas. Maybe she runs a respectable party, maybe not, but I say it's a joint with God knows what going on in the back rooms."

Wiley raised his brows. "I've got no information on that."

"I tell you I know what I'm saying and I don't care what story the police bring you! The boy resisted a robbery, and that's the fact."

"The truth remains," said Wiley impatiently, "that more than a dozen witnesses were questioned separately, and their versions match down to the smallest details. I took some of those statements myself."

The lawyer paced about to quell his agitation. "Even so," he urged with despair, "he's just a country boy who got himself involved. Why not give him that plea on compassionate grounds?"

Wiley slowly lit a fresh cigar and stated a fact: "With a gun in his hand he was safe as a tiger in the night."

"Oh, now—!" the lawyer protested.

"City boy or country boy," said Wiley grimly, "we've got to have a policy. He killed a man. He knows what he's up against."

The lawyer's teeth clicked audibly as he stared at the lean-faced prosecutor who sat puffing smoke rings. "Tell me one thing, Wiley," he asked vindictively. "If the jury acquits, will you feel relieved?"

"Why, of course," Wiley responded with surprise. "Why shouldn't I?"

The lawyer left the office and at the elevator burst into tears of fatigue, exasperation, and rage.

Ultimately the boy was removed to the city prison and lodged in a tier with a motley crew of stool pigeons, hardened offenders, and material witnesses. With his sweet smile, he made friends and heeded their warnings against informers, in turn to be warned against those giving the warnings, only to find this too was a stool pigeon's trick. He enjoyed the warmth of the rabbit warren, bantered with new friends, joked with correction officers, ate heartily, and absorbed the sights and sounds of a new way of life. His leg wound ached and his raw eye socket prevented sleep, but nights passed with the soft playing of an ocarina. He never discussed his case, and advice from the jailhouse lawyers went unheeded. He knew that his lawyer would do his best.

The trial proved to be unexpectedly interesting to Eddie Dickinson.

For the first time in his brief life he was the focus of attention in an important matter. Not one but three lawyers were looking after him; the most terrifying man in the world, Judge Matthew Brady, was treating him with polite concern; even that mean man, Mr. Wiley, the chief prosecutor, was fussing the worst way to reconstruct exactly what he, Edward Dickinson, had said and done that fatal night to a total stranger named Rupert Choatey. It was altogether a satisfying business. Eddie sat at polite attention, conscious of his clean collar, crimson tie, pressed blue suit—all supplied by his chief counsel—while his three lawyers took turns pleading for an open mind, and invoked the presumption of innocence, demanded justice, and outlined Eddie's version of the facts to twelve stony-faced jurors. There was repeated reference to someone called the defen*dant.*

"Is that me?" he whispered behind a cupped hand. "Am I a defen*dant?*"

Phillips nodded. "That's right."

"Defen*dant*, defen*dant!*" The boy tested the sound. "Am I against all the *People* of the *State* of *New* York?"

"That's just a way of talking."

"Oh, my!" The boy pressed his lips self-consciously as the judge's stern glance floated past; then Eddie sat at attention once more. The technical witnesses brought a puzzled frown to his face, and he sought to impress the jurors, and thus to help his lawyers, by letting the roll of his eye proclaim innocence, incredulity, and outrage. After a time came Mrs. Hillegas, a big-boned woman with gray hair, brimming with scorn and disgust, and she was followed by a mixed bag of dubious types—nightclub workers and petty gamblers. Eddie muttered protest, whispered excitedly, cast derisive glances at the ceiling.

"They lying, Mr. Phillips," he muttered. "It wasn't that way at all, not one little bit."

He brightened when Emmalou Howard was sworn in. She came in a checkered blouse, a girl with delicate hands, her voice a whisper as she took the oath. With a nervous smile she glanced over and the boy's heart bounded with hope.

Her testimony stunned him.

For the rest of the trial he gazed at his hands, sullen and morose, and when he took the stand his manner was dogged and resentful, as though he expected disbelief. The lawyers led him mumbling through his simple story, and under Wiley's cross-examination he replied with a pugnacious thrust of his lower lip.

"Naturally they sticking up for Choatey," he spat with irritation, as though to a dull-witted child. "They are his *friends*. It's what they *got* to do! Still and all, they made up this Fats and Rocky, they robbed me for sure, and they all lying!"

He received the verdict with calm, and his boyish smile was a blow to the lawyer's heart.

There was no recommendation for mercy.

In due course—swifter, it seems, than it takes to tell—judgment was affirmed in the higher court of appeal, and a date was fixed for execution.

On the day before execution, the lawyer arrived at the death house in Sing Sing Prison. Heavy blue clouds were driving across the river and a damp chill was everywhere, but the building was heated and comfortable. A mood of unease hovered in the outer rooms. When Eddie came shambling out to the final interview, throat bobbing at an open shirt, his heavy features were placid. He was stroking a newborn kitten.

"Got any news, Mr. Phillips?"

The lawyer put aside his fedora with a shaking hand. "How are you, Eddie?"

"They feed me all right, and they doctor me," the boy admitted, working his tongue around his teeth. "Only this last week my appetite is bad, since I've got this looseness. It seems to mean I'm getting nervous. I just hope I don't spoil things for the Warden. I'm supposed to eat a hearty last meal." He chuckled with hollow mischief. "Well, not exactly eat it, that's not necessary, but at least order it. That's supposed to show we all friends, that there's nothing personal, so I'm ordering fried chicken, string potatoes, and vanilla ice cream with chocolate syrup. Then the Warden will know I had nothing against him. It's all been explained to me."

Phillips said, "That's a good idea."

The kitten clawed feebly at the boy's hands. "You going to be here tomorrow, Mr. Phillips? I'm asking, because otherwise there is nobody."

"I don't think I'll be able to come," Phillips said.

The boy nodded. "Well, that's all right. You've been better to me than my own father, and don't think I feel reproachful. All this has been an experience." The throat bobbed twice with humor. "You might say, it has taught me a lesson."

"Son—" said the lawyer dolefully.

"Sir?"

"What good was my best? Nothing can save you but those two men, Fats and Rocky. Mr. Wiley swears you must know them."

"When did he say that?"

"Just yesterday. You can still get out of it if you'll give them up."

The boy placed the kitten against his cheek.

"Mr. Phillips, I remember how you told the judge how I had *got* to be innocent, because if I was guilty, why didn't I betray my friends? You said it was unthinkable I could do otherwise. Isn't that what you said?"

"Yes."

"So if I don't give them up, I must be innocent," the boy argued earnestly. "Is that true, or isn't that *not* true?"

"Yes."

"Then what can I say?"

The lawyer rose with a sigh, braced himself against the trembling of his knees, smiled feebly, and shook hands with Eddie. The boy added, "I couldn't fake two men, Mr. Phillips. I thought of that, and I decided it wouldn't be right."

"Good luck," said the lawyer. "If you change your mind, just tell the Warden and he'll hold things up, even at the last minute. You ought to appreciate that Mr. Wiley wouldn't do that for just anyone. He'd still like to help you."

"Isn't that sweet?" said the boy sarcastically.

"Goodbye," responded the lawyer through tight lips.

The boy reassured him: "Now don't you worry, not about one thing, because I'm all right. I'd just like you to let that girl Emmalou know that I'm not mad at her one bit."

"I'll tell her that."

Shaking his head, the lawyer left the death house, skipping heavily in his haste to put prison behind him. Like a blind man he took the train at Ossining and saw nothing until he got off at 125th Street in Manhattan. He found his way to a bar where he drank himself into forgetfulness.

Phillips was standing in his storage room, about to consign the tattered manila envelope to a dead-files cabinet when the telephone rang. It was from Wiley with an invitation to luncheon.

"Drinks are on me," said Wiley.

The lawyer demurred. "I'm busy catching up," he said shakily, "and I'm not drinking." But of course he gave in at the hint of an interesting development. He found drinks waiting at Guido's, and so too was the chaplain of the prison, a young man with an inviting pleasant smile.

Wiley said, "You know Father Dunn?"

"Of course." Phillips studied the menu and settled for a fruit cup and black coffee. He said little while Father Dunn animatedly discussed the progress of various prisoners in whom Wiley was interested. He had regards and good wishes from many, and a few curses which he kept to himself.

Abruptly Wiley said, "Father, tell our friend about Eddie Dickinson."

Phillips gazed up sharply. "Did you know him?"

"Not too well," said the priest. "Except for a pleasant word now and then, I had no official connection with him, and neither did any other chaplain. I saw to it that he had cigarettes and chocolate bars, and that pleased him. The day before he was executed he called for me."

"Did he strike you as a killer?" asked Phillips bitterly, "the kind to whom murder is like drinking a cup of coffee?"

An odd glance flickered between the priest and the district attorney.

Father Dunn said, "His last thought, Mr. Phillips, was for you. He asked me to convey his gratitude. I think he grew to love you. He had no one else in the world, except that he seemed to daydream about this girl in the case—"

He paused, and Wiley supplied the name: "Emmalou Howard."

"That's a boy's heart, I suppose," the priest went on. "It's got to attach itself to something to love, and I gathered that the girl was, or is, a charmer. He was well behaved in the execution chamber. He shook hands with the guards and assured the Warden of his high regard." Father Dunn squeezed his eyes briefly. "Just before he left his cell, he gave me a letter for you."

Skillets were banging somewhere and a voluble argument in dialect broke out at the rotisserie.

"Let's see." Phillips smoothed out the blue-lined prison paper on the tablecloth. The writing was illiterate, the boy had leaned heavily on a stubby pencil, but the message was clear enough. The lawyer studied it through, then read aloud:

"Dear Mr. Phillips. This is my last day and I am writing to you because I am sorry for the way I treated you, only I did not mean to fool you, not at the end. Fats and Rocky were names we made up when we bought the guns, that is why nobody was able to find them through those names. That was Fats idea like most of the ideas were his. If Fats tells you to do something you will do it. I would not have shot Choatey except Fats said so. Please tell Miss Howard that I am sorry about Choatey, only he would be all right if he kept his mouth shut, so he has his self to blame because he asked for it.

"I wanted to tell you about this but you would have made me tell Mister Wiley how to catch the real Fats and Rocky and I could not do a thing like that. Now it is all right, I guess. I want you to know that you did not really lose the case because I killed Choatey all right.

"I know I could of saved my life but I do not think it is right to squeal on your friends. I guess that is all. Your friend. Edward Dickinson."

The lawyer finished and was silent. He had no feeling except—what? The emotion to govern the situation was not there. He had fought a cause, and it was no cause. Only—

The bitterness was strong.

"It's not possible!" he muttered. "He was just a boy—"

"That's just it," said Wiley crisply. "He was too simple entirely. It got him into murder, and when we gave him his chance he didn't take the way out. I don't see what else we could have done."

Phillips turned to the priest.

"Oh, don't ask me," said Father Dunn grimly. "I can't account for it. He could kill a man for nothing, because someone told him to—but he couldn't save his own life." He put aside his coffee irritably. "I hate the whole dirty business of putting a man to death. I don't care *what* he's done—it's the butcher's way."

Phillips abruptly stood up and put on his coat and hat. A curious hard smile hovered on his face.

"Oh, no, you don't understand at all," he said in a low voice. "Mr. Wiley explained it so clearly in court. The boy was guilty. He killed a man, and the law says he deserved to die, because when he went out with a gun he was like a tiger in the night. Isn't that what you told the jury, Mr. Wiley?"

"That was the courtroom," the prosecutor retorted. "I had a case to try."

Phillips seemed not to hear. "I can't defend what that boy did, but there was something human in him, something worth saving. If we had gotten to him first—ahead of those others, ahead of the Fats and the Rockys of this world—who knows, Eddie might be alive today."

Phillips threw some coins on the table and left, his shoulder square, his head high.

It was a clear day with a wintery sun melting the recent snow. He walked the distance far uptown to his office.

He completed his task with the tattered manila envelope, binding it firmly with a faded red ribbon, making sure the boy's letter lay inside, on top of the other papers.

Then he closed the file cabinet and went home.

Libby MacCall

Mrs. Henderson Talks to God

Old Mrs. Henderson had talked to God about her trouble innumerable times before, but there was no harm in having another try. Although she was well aware that He was omniscient and knew everything, she thought it a good idea to remind Him of what had been happening—or, to be more accurate, what had not been happening. After all, He did have more important things to think about than how her life had dwindled down.

When old Mrs. Henderson talked to God, she sat in her low armchair, comfortably certain that He would not have wished her to kneel on her arthritic knees. You know, God, she told Him, it isn't as if I'd ever had a very exciting life. With me, my family, the church, a few friends, and an exciting detective story were always enough. After Arthur (Senior) passed on—may his soul rest in peace—You know I did my best to accept Your will. Everyone said I made a good adjustment to being a widow. It wasn't easy, but I tried hard to count my blessings and be content with what I had. And in those days I still had a lot of blessings to count.

The blessings to which old Mrs. Henderson referred were the daily phone call from her daughter to which she could look forward every morning, and the weekly family Sunday dinner, including the drive in her son-in-law's car, first to church, then to dinner, at which bright, cheerful young people made interesting conversation. During the week, her grandchildren had dropped in frequently to tell her of the bad things that happened to them, as well as the good. They knew they could count on her to be always and uncritically on their side. Young Arthur had always said that she was the only one who really understood him. His parents weren't fair; they were much too hard on him, he told her.

The old lady was sure none of the grandchildren realized that she had a favorite. She had never had a son, and her feeling for Arthur, the youngest grandchild, could only be characterized as overindulgent. A charming boy with huge gray eyes rimmed in incredible lashes, he had progressed from conning her out of too many cookies to graciously worded requests for small loans, "just till I get my allowance." Loans that were never repaid.

"Mother! You spoil them!" her daughter used to protest. With a complacent chuckle old Mrs. Henderson had replied, "That's what grandmothers are for!"

Old Mrs. Henderson massaged her aching knees with hands distorted by arthritis. If only the two granddaughters hadn't moved so far away when they got married, she continued. It isn't that I don't appreciate the pictures of the great-grandchildren. But pictures can't sit on my lap. And You know, God, that most of my old friends have passed away. Those who are left write from Florida, listing their newest ailments.

When her daughter and son-in-law perished in that hideous accident, old Mrs. Henderson would have collapsed if it hadn't been for Arthur. For his sake she forced herself to keep going. Arthur was actually accused of having something to do with his parents' death. "Held on suspicion as a material witness" was the way the newspapers put it. They had to let him go, of course, since there wasn't the least bit of proof. He was suspected only because he had been badly in need of money and stood to inherit a good deal. Not that the money had done him much good. He had lost it all. But that had been entirely his partner's fault.

The dear boy hasn't quite found himself, old Mrs. Henderson told God. He'd be much better off in a business of his own, but it's so hard to get hold of the capital to start one. I'd be glad to give him the money, but the little I can spare isn't enough. What he needs is the principal, which of course he'll have when I die.

And that's what I want to talk to You about. It's past time for me to do just that. I'm too old. My knees ache and my fingers ache, and all I do is sit here waiting for You to call me. But You don't call! If it weren't a sin to take one's own life, I'd hurry things along. I know I mustn't do that, but it can't be a sin to wish that my life would end.

She did wish it, with all her heart. Old Mrs. Henderson wasn't afraid of dying. After all, she was on very good terms with God, and comfortably certain that, whatever heaven was like, there would be no arthritis there, and no loneliness.

Couldn't You just reach down and stop my heart? she asked. I'd be very grateful.

Her heart gave no sign of faltering. She sighed, and returned to the detective novel she was reading. In crime books people were constantly being poisoned, stabbed, shot, disposed of in all sorts of exotic ways. It was too bad that there wasn't a single person who wished to dispose of her. How do you go about getting yourself murdered when you haven't an enemy in the world?

Most old women who were helped into their graves met their fate because someone needed the inheritance and couldn't wait for a natural death. Her own will had been made years ago, leaving one-quarter of her stocks and bonds to each of the two granddaughters, and one half to Arthur. She rationalized this favoritism by reminding herself that the girls would have all the family silver and pictures. No use looking to her grandchildren to help her out of this world. Arthur often said, "I don't know what I'd do without you, Gran!" And they were the only ones who stood to gain by her death.

Well, God, she said, concluding the talk, people are always saying the Lord helps those who help themselves. If You won't help me, then I must help myself.

But how?

Old Mrs. Henderson decided that there was only one way. She must manufacture an executioner, someone who had reason to think he or she would inherit under the terms of her will. (She wouldn't actually change the will, just lead the designated murderer to believe she had done so.)

But who?

After thinking it over for several days, discarding several ideas as too farfetched, she found a solution that pleased her. She would hire a companion. Later, feigning devotion and gratitude, she would tell the woman that she was being generously remembered in her will.

She realized that the average companion did not have it in her to commit murder. The woman would have to be very carefully chosen.

That very day old Mrs. Henderson telephoned her ad to the newspaper. "Companion for elderly widow. Live in. Own room. TV. Limited cooking."

The next few days were eventful ones, so much so that by evening old Mrs. Henderson was utterly spent. More than a dozen of the many women who telephoned seemed worth interviewing in person. Most proved to be elderly widows themselves, gentle, kindly women, who would think twice before treading on a cockroach.

And then came Ludmilla Wiskidensky. Old Mrs. Henderson took

an instant dislike to the grossly fat woman, whose face reminded the old lady of a bowl of yeast dough left to rise in a dusty room. Its color was a sooty gray, and the features embedded in the doughy mass looked like things dropped into the bowl by a careless cook, the eyes a couple of oversized raisins, the nose a swollen candied cherry.

No, said the applicant, not Mrs. *Miss* Wiskidensky. Just call her Millie. Their hair-raising escape from Poland had ruined her mother's health, she went on, so she had devoted her life to caring for her mother and had never married. (Old Mrs. Henderson was sure no one had ever asked her.) Millie sketched a few highlights of the escape, then moved on to her mother's lengthy final illness. Her eyes filled with tears as she explained that, without her mother's Social Security checks, she couldn't keep their apartment, and so she must find a live-in job. Burying her mother suitably had used up all her savings.

That was all the old lady needed to hear. Here was the woman she'd been seeking: badly in need of money, and ruthless. (The escape from Poland had included some quite bloody deeds.) She knew the next few months would be unpleasant. She'd have to allow time to pretend to grow fond of the woman before she could announce her intention of leaving her money, but it would be worth it. Life was insupportable. And Arthur needed the capital. He'd miss her dreadfully, of course, but once he had made his place in the business world, he was sure to find a nice girl.

Had it not been for her little talks with God, old Mrs. Henderson wouldn't have been able to bear up under the new regime. She'd like me to be a complete invalid, she told Him. I do need help tying my shoes these days, but I'm still able to decide which dress to wear. Millie must have made her mother's life a misery!

It's not just her bossiness I mind, You know, she went on. I could stand that, if only she and Arthur got along.

During the week, when old Mrs. Henderson and Millie were alone, they dined together, but the antagonism between her and Arthur soon developed to a point where her presence at Sunday dinner could no longer be tolerated. When Millie served herself lavishly to third helpings of her good Polish dishes, Arthur talked of the high cost of food these days. (Millie had explained to old Mrs. Henderson that her huge appetite and consequent vast bulk—which she referred to as overweight—was due to the years of semi-starvation she had endured.)

Millie monopolized the conversation, relating gory episodes from the saga of her escape. Arthur had turned pale as she described how she had strangled an innocent boy she thought *might* be going to report her. When he urged Millie to be quiet, saying she was spoiling his appetite, she replied that at least she had done no harm to her own flesh and blood. At this point the old lady had had no choice but to banish her from the table.

After she had lumbered out of the room, Arthur urged his grandmother to find a new companion. "Honestly, Gran," he had said, "I worry about you, alone with that monster. She's dangerous! Promise me you'll get rid of her."

When the old lady asked him to lower his voice, lest Millie hear him in the kitchen, he replied, "Good! Maybe she'll quit. Then we can go back to eating in peace. I don't mind TV dinners." (Old Mrs. Henderson had once served him delicious repasts, for she had been a good cook until her arthritis became disabling and she had had to resort to frozen meals.)

It was impossible to explain to Arthur why she continued to employ Millie. But he was right that the situation had become unbearable. She decided the time had come to tell the woman of the mythical legacy she was to receive. Only last Sunday, Arthur had described to her a remarkable opportunity he'd been offered to buy a franchise in the vending-machine business, in which a fortune was to be made if only he could raise the capital for the initial investment. At least she was able to assuage his immediate financial difficulty by "lending" him $200 to save him from being evicted from his apartment.

During the week the old lady spiced her conversation with descriptions of the various ways of murdering old ladies with which she was familiar from the many detective stories she had read. Millie pretended to disapprove, but old Mrs. Henderson felt satisfied that she had taken it all in. Millie was a poor actress. She had also pretended to have no particular interest in the promised legacy, but the old lady had not been fooled.

That same week an old friend who had moved to Florida dropped in for a visit. The friend, unused to northern winters, had contracted a nasty cold, which old Mrs. Henderson proceeded to catch. When Arthur arrived for his Sunday visit, he found her in bed, propped up on three pillows, wheezing and gasping. He had been pounding the pavements, he said, trying to get together enough money to secure the franchise.

"But I mustn't worry you when you're sick." He smiled his bewitching smile and patted her hand. "Has the fat slob been taking good care of you?"

When Millie brought the old lady a steaming cup of chicken soup, Arthur took it out of her hand, insisting that he was in charge of the sickroom for the day. His dinner, Millie protested, was waiting for him in the dining room. It would wait for him, Arthur replied, herding her toward the door.

"The fat slob is jealous of me!" he laughed, coming back to sit on the edge of the bed. "Gran, promise me you'll fire her as soon as you're over this cold."

"Ssh! She heard you," whispered Mrs. Henderson. She knew the woman must still be standing just outside the half open door: one couldn't miss hearing her heavy tread going back to the kitchen.

"Who cares?" Arthur began to feed his grandmother the soup, coaxing her to take "just one more spoonful! Come on, now!" The old lady gazed up into his beautiful eyes, admiring the long dark lashes for the thousandth time.

"This is quite a switch," Arthur said. "Remember when you used to feed me strained soup?"

"Serve you right if I blew chicken soup in your face," she wheezed. "That's what you used to do to me."

"Stop laughing at once!" he commanded. "It's making you cough."

When she finally managed to get her breath, she lay back on her pillows, exhausted. "Oh, Arthur," she whispered, "I'm so useless. If only I could die! Why doesn't the Lord call me?"

Millie came hurrying in, to scold Arthur for tiring her patient. He must leave at once, she said.

"Okay, okay! I'm going!" Arthur stooped to kiss his grandmother. "I'll eat her old Pole-ski mess-ski and then take off," he said, not bothering to lower his voice. "Call you tomorrow."

Old Mrs. Henderson woke to find something soft being pressed gently but firmly over her face.

Her lungs were clamoring for air. She put up her hands to push away whatever it was that interfered with her breathing, then dropped them back to her sides as understanding flooded in on her.

Her plot was now working as she had intended. She was being murdered!

Old Mrs. Henderson began a final prayer. Soon it would all be over. In her weakened condition it couldn't take more than a few moments.

Suddenly the pillow was snatched away. She drew in her breath with a harsh, rasping sound. So she was not going to die, after all. What could have happened to make Millie change her mind? Curiosity overwhelmed all other emotions; she opened her eyes.

Arthur, clutching a pillow, lay on the floor beside the bed, with Millie standing over him. Old Mrs. Henderson gasped. And fainted. So she did not hear Millie telling Arthur what she thought of him. "If I hadn't come back for the empty soup plate, you would most certainly have succeeded," she concluded. "Let's hope she is too sick to understand what you tried to do. I will say nothing. But be sure you will never be left alone with her again."

As Arthur stumbled his way out of the room, she called after him that the leftovers from dinner were in a foil package on the hall table, as usual. He must not forget them, or his grandmother would be upset.

When the old lady recovered consciousness, she had no recollection of what had happened. She awaited Arthur's promised telephone call with her usual eager anticipation, but Arthur did not phone.

On Friday old Mrs. Henderson was amazed to receive a visit from her granddaughters, neither of whom had been in town for months. But her joy lasted only as long as it took them to break the terrible news that had brought them. Arthur had been found dead in his apartment. He had been seized with food poisoning, had collapsed in the bathroom, and must have been too weak to get to the phone to summon help.

After a few moments during which the old lady was too stunned to speak, she began to babble. God had punished her for her wickedness ... It had all gone wrong ... She was the one who was meant to be murdered. She demanded that the police be called, insisting that Arthur had not died a natural death—he had been poisoned! Probably with one of Millie's highly spiced Polish sausages.

Why would Millie want to do that? one of the girls asked, humoring her.

Because Arthur tried to get her fired—because she was jealous of him ...

Her granddaughters exchanged glances and shook their heads sadly. Poor Gran! Obviously she had grown senile. They patted her hand and told her she read too many detective stories.

After Arthur's funeral they kissed her goodbye and went away, having arranged for her affairs to be handled by her lawyer, since the old lady was clearly incapable of managing them herself.

While Millie was seeing them to the door, old Mrs. Henderson addressed God for what she knew would be the last time until she met Him face to face. Don't You think I've been punished enough? she whispered. What I'm going to do isn't a sin, so You shouldn't mind.

Millie came back into the room, plumped up the pillows, and stroked old Mrs. Henderson's shoulder. The old lady pulled away from the caress.

"You can't fool me," she said. "I know you killed Arthur."

"He tried to send me away," Millie replied calmly. "I had to do it."

So! She admitted it! With pounding heart, old Mrs. Henderson waited for the heavy hands to close around her throat.

When nothing happened, she opened her eyes. Millie was smiling happily. "Now I have you all to myself," she said. "Don't worry. I will take good care of you, as good as I did of my mother. No reason you shouldn't live to be a hundred."

Don M. Mankiewicz
Two Rolls, No Coffee

Now that you mention it, chum, it is kind of an odd decoration at that. Not the kind of thing you'd expect to find hanging on the wall back of a bar, particularly in a high-class place like this. Looks like a kid's cane to you, huh? I guess you've led a sheltered life, son. That's a dice stick. Every house-run crap game in the world has a stickman, and just about every stickman uses a curved stick like that to return the dice to the shooter between rolls. Most of them are a little tricky, too, like that one there. They don't always return the same dice they pick up—if you get what I mean.

That stick was given to me by my old man. He'd carried it all over the world with him, like a good mechanic might carry a set of fine end-wrenches or a special pair of calipers that he liked. My dad was a pro, same as I was. He'd handled the sticks at dice tables in Caliente, Reno, Saratoga, Florida, Hot Springs, and even at some of the famous European gambling houses along the Riviera. He had a reputation for honesty that would get him a job with any gambling joint in the world. That may sound a little odd to you, Mac, but a guy who wants to work at a dice table had better be honest, even if his job is switching the dice back and forth so the house doesn't get hit. What I mean by that is, the boss has to know that his employees are all working for him; it'd be awfully easy for a stickman to get tied up with somebody from the outside and make a mistake on purpose with those dice sometime. Once, that is. Never twice.

I don't know why I should be telling you the story of my life like this, mister, but you asked about the stick, and I guess you'll stop me if I'm boring you. Well, when Dad got along in years to the point where it hurt him to stand up all night, he wasn't like most stickmen. He'd saved his money. And he quit. You know, like those fellows you read about in the insurance ads in the magazines, that go off to some cabin in the mountains and spend all their time fishing. Well, that's what my old man did; just quit and bought a shack out near Pike's Peak and, except for a Christmas card every year, I haven't heard from him since. At the time he quit, we were both working as stickmen at Rocco's up the street. You ever been there? Well, don't bother. If you ever feel like going there for an evening's pleasure, as the fellow says, just mail Rocco your money. That way you won't be pushed around and have to smell all the cigar smoke. And you got just as good a chance to win.

What I mean by that is, Rocco's joint is just as crooked as he is, which is the same as to say nothing is left to chance. I have an idea that was one of the things that got my old man to quit, Rocco's being such a crooked house, and him being too old to go traipsing around the country looking for a better job. When he quit, Dad gave me that stick and before he left for the mountains he gave me a quick course in how to operate it.

There wasn't anything I couldn't do with that stick. The way it worked is this: a fellow would come in and start shooting. At the start of his roll he got a whole basket of Rocco's dice, every one of them honest, to pick from. Any two dice in the basket that he liked, those were the dice he used. Well, as long as he kept shooting for reasonable stakes, he'd keep those dice. Every time he'd shoot, I'd slide the dice back to him with the stick, and he'd roll them out again. The house would be taking its percentage out of the side bets, the guy would win-a-little-lose-a-little, and everybody would be happy, particularly Rocco.

That's the way things usually go at any crap table. The bets fairly even, no arguments, honest dice, pass, miss, pass, and the percentage gradually dragging all the money out of everybody's pockets.

But there are emergencies that do come up every now and then. Some guy will get hot and start letting his bets ride—which means he doubles his money with every pass he makes. When somebody starts doing that, that's when Rocco gets glad I've got my stick and know how to use it. You see, if a guy does let his money ride, and if he only gets fairly hot, let's say he makes eleven passes. Now, on that twelfth roll he's shooting two thousand and some dollars *for every dollar he started with*. What we do when this happens is pretty simple, and, while it's not foolproof, it very rarely goes wrong.

We give the guy his perfectly honest dice that he's been shooting with all along for his first throw. If he comes out right there on one roll—if he sevens or elevens, that is—he's a winner and we've got to hope he tries it again. He may crap out on that one roll, too—that is, he may hit two, three, or twelve, and lose right there; but most likely he'll catch a point—that is, he'll roll four, five, six, eight, nine, or ten. And then he's got to make his point, roll it again before he rolls a seven, and the percentages say he's not likely to do it. That's why even an honest crap table (if there is such a thing) would make money.

But percentage doesn't say he can't make or he won't do it, just that he's not *likely* to do it. That stick up on the wall there, Mac, that's what says he *can't* do it. To put it as simply as I can, that stick has a little slot in it, a kind of panel, and when I grab my end of the stick a little tighter than usual, that panel gets all loose and wobbly. When I push the dice with the stick they just wander in back of the panel and some other dice come out about a quarter inch farther up the stick.

Sure it's tough to make a stick like that, but it's tough to make a car, or a watch, or a hat that rabbits can hide in. It's hard to operate a stick like that and not get caught at it, too, and that's why Rocco was paying me one-fifty a week to push the dice back and forth on his table—and this was some years ago when one-fifty was pretty good money. I won't bore you with a lot of details about those other dice, chum. They were made in Minneapolis and, to put it very, very simply, they couldn't come up anything but seven.

You get the picture now, don't you, friend? I mean, here's this sucker, all set to try to make his eight or nine or whatever for a couple of thousand bucks, and here he is shaking these dice that can't come up anything but seven. Of course, real smart gamblers used to notice that nobody ever seemed to make a good score on the crap table, and most of the big-money boys stayed off it. But that didn't bother Rocco; there were plenty of guys in town that figured they could beat that table, and they used to contribute enough to pay my wages and leave the house with a handsome profit.

Every time a guy would miss out on his big roll, whether he did it because his luck was lousy or with some help from my old man's stick, Rocco would look at him real sad and say: "Looks like you lose your dough, son. Two rolls, no coffee." "Two rolls, no coffee" always struck me as a pretty terrible pun, but guys who are winning in crap games all over the world think it's about the wittiest remark ever made.

The guy Rocco said "Two rolls, no coffee" to oftenest was a fellow named Perino. "Patsy" Perino, they used to call him. Rocco made that nickname up because he said Perino was the biggest Patsy that ever was, and the tag sort of stuck. As far as I know, nobody ever called Patsy by his right name; in fact, nobody seemed to know what his square name might be. But everybody used to just call him Patsy and it made him furious.

Patsy was convinced of two things in this world. First of all, he was convinced that he was the unluckiest gambler that ever drew breath, and I must say I can see where he got that idea, because he bucked Rocco's crap table every payday and I don't think he went away winner more than once. That once was close to Christmas, and I knew Patsy hadn't saved anything out of his pay up at the mill and I figured he'd have to buy his girl a present, so I sort of let him win one hundred and forty bucks figuring we'd get it back after the holidays. Rocco gave me hell for it and told me if it ever happened again it would come out of my pay, and, believe me, mister, it never happened again. The other thing Patsy believed was that someday his luck would turn and that when that happened he'd beat that crap table out of every cent he'd poured into it, and more.

Well, like I said, Patsy dropped every cent he could get his hands on into that crap game, and when he stopped coming around, Rocco was worried about him. Not that Rocco gave a damn about Patsy, really. He just thought of Patsy as a kind of agent who had to work all week at a heavy machine and then bring his money to Rocco, and he was sore when Patsy didn't show up.

The upshot of it all was that he sent me up to Patsy's end of town to look around for him and I went wandering up to the bunch of little houses back of the mill where I figured Patsy must live. It's funny, but I'd never been up that way before; working late nights, I'd always had a room near Rocco's place, and when I wasn't working or sleeping I'd usually drop down here for a drink. Well, the first person I ran into was Patsy's girl. Real pretty she was, too, which is kind of surprising when you figure Patsy wasn't much of a catch, being just another guy who worked in the mill, and not even one of the steady ones who'd bring home a full envelope every Friday, but a born gambler who'd never have a nickel. But everybody's always known that Louise was Patsy's girl and that was that. I guess she started going with him in high school, before he'd really begun gambling, and when the dice bug bit him she figured she ought to stick with him, same as if he was sick or something, which, in a manner of speaking, he was.

Well, I gave Louise a big smile and an extra cheerful hello, and she just sort of froze up and went on up the street without a word. I followed her, and finally she went into a grocery store, and so did I. Once I'd told her that we were just curious about why Patsy hadn't been around to Rocco's in so long, that he didn't owe us any money or anything, she unfroze a little, and told me that Patsy was in the

Army and that he wouldn't be back for a year; not, she was quick to add, that it was any of my business.

Well, having nothing better to do, I walked her home, and when we got there she asked me in, just out of politeness, I guess. Louise is about the politest girl there is. We talked of this and that, mostly about Patsy, and I could see that she didn't hold Patsy's failings against me, which was only right after all. She told me about how Patsy had quit the dice time and time again, and how they were always figuring on getting married as soon as he'd saved up enough money, but how he'd always break down as soon as he got his hands on his pay chit and go down to Rocco's and blow it in. Of course, like I said, it wasn't any of my fault, the whole thing, but listening to her tell it, I was almost ashamed of myself. I got Patsy's address from her, which was Camp Carson, Colorado, and wished her luck, and went back to Rocco's.

Well, Patsy turned out to be only the first of a lot of guys to go into the Army from our town, and eventually it got so the place was mainly populated by overage bankers, school kids, and women. The guys who weren't drafted, it seems they all took off for the other towns chasing after the war plants and the big money. Maybe for a lot of guys the war was a time for big money, but not for Rocco and me. We kept the house going as long as we could, even put in slot machines and let the women in, but it was no use. We started booking horses, and the horses stopped running. So what we wound up doing was the best we could, like the fellow says, and take my word for it, mister, it was no good. We like to starve to death before the war was over.

Well, when it finally did end, the boys started coming back, and the dice started to roll again. Not just small-time stuff like before, real big time, big money games. The boys were all loaded from the shipyards and the airplane factories, and wages were way up at the mill, and what with one thing and another we raised the minimum bet at the crap table from half a buck to half a pound, and Rocco raised me from one-fifty to two and a half. Things were really great; only one more thing we needed: Patsy. He didn't show up with the rest of the boys, and I was beginning to think that maybe he was as unhandy a soldier as he was a dice-shooter, and in that case he sure never would be back.

Then one night, after closing time at Rocco's, I was sitting right in here having a drink, not behind the bar like now, but over there at one of those little tables, when who should come strolling through the front door? That's right, chum, Patsy himself.

"Hiya, Patsy!" I said. I was really glad to see him—not just because of business, you know. He was like an old friend, even if I never knew him except as another guy to slide the dice to.

He looked at me kind of funny. "Name's John, Tony," he said. "Not Patsy. I learned a lot in the Army, Tony."

He came over and sat down and started to talk. He told me how he'd been overseas, in Italy with the ski troops, and how he'd seen a lot of killing and done a little himself. But he'd been careful. Real careful. "You know why I was so careful, Tony?" he asked me. I just looked at him. "I was careful, Tony, because I wanted to get back to this town. I wanted to go up to Rocco's and get hunk with that damn dice game of his. When you see him, Tony, you tell him I'm in town and I've got money and I'm coming up tomorrow night—" he glanced at his watch "—make that tonight, and give his dice game a real going-over."

Well, when he said that, I knew he hadn't learned as much in the Army as he thought. A man going duck hunting doesn't tell the ducks. It gives them a chance to get set.

Rocco and I got set, O.K. We checked over our board and our dice, and we went over to the bank and got a great big stack of crisp, fresh-looking hundreds, because in a big game it helps if the house has a lot of cash money to flash around.

When we opened for business that night, I could tell something was up. All the boys from the mill were there, and we figured Patsy had been telling them his big plans. Some of the lads came over to the dice table and started shooting, five bucks at a time, but you could tell they were just killing time. Rocco was walking around between the roulette wheel and the craps setup with an expression on his face like a cat that figures to eat a canary.

About ten o'clock Patsy walked in, and the whole crowd, as if it was a signal, moved over to the dice table. They were standing about four deep around it. The boy who was shooting made his point and picked his saw off the pass line. Then, instead of putting down some more money and shooting again, he set the dice down on the edge of the table. In any language in the world that means the shooter passes the dice.

"Whose dice?" I said.

Patsy shoved his way through the crowd just to the right of the boy who'd passed the dice and said, "I'll take 'em, Tony. O.K.?"

"Well, Patsy—" I began.

"John." He still didn't sound mad. Just firm.

"John," I said. "You're supposed to let the dice come around to you once, but unless there's some objection, they're yours."

Nobody objected. Patsy picked up the dice. Rocco came over and stood beside me to watch. There was an awful dead silence while Patsy rolled out. Every once in a while I'd say, "Pay the line" or "Pay the field," but there weren't any other bettors. Just Patsy. He was betting twenty bucks at a time, and Rocco and I just stood there and watched him make five points in a row, which put him a hundred ahead and was a little unusual, but nothing shocking. He was shooting with perfectly honest dice, of course; any time a man shoots only twenty bobs in Rocco's he'll get honest dice, the way I told you. I was starting to relax a little when it happened.

Patsy slapped down another twenty bucks and rolled two fours. Then, while the dice—perfectly honest dice, you understand—were still lying there on the table, down at my end, way out of his reach, he turned to Rocco.

"Lay the odds, Rocco?" he asked very quietly, like you might ask someone the time of day. This meant he wanted to bet some more that he'd make his eight before he rolled a seven, and that he wanted Rocco to give him the odds, which are six to five he won't.

"For how much?" Rocco sounded disinterested, and his voice let everybody know he'd handle any bet a punk like Patsy could make.

"A thousand," said Patsy.

"Laying twelve hundred to a thou," said Rocco, looking down at my stick.

I tightened my fist around the head of my stick and spun the dice back to Patsy. He didn't look at them, just picked them up in his right hand and shook them back and forth in his fist, holding them way over his head. He slipped his left hand into his pants pocket, hauled out his wallet, and tossed it on the table.

"Tony," he said, "get a thousand out of there and put it on the line." I reached over, picked up the wallet, and glanced inside. There was a lot more than a thousand in there—at least a hundred C-notes, it looked like. I picked ten of them out and tossed them on the line. Rocco peeled twelve of his bills off the house stack and added them to the pile.

"Like to see what you're shooting for," Rocco said with that oily grin of his. I suddenly decided I didn't care much for Rocco. For a second, I wished I could get another chance at stick-handling those dice so I could give Patsy the honest ones back again.

Patsy started shaking the dice again, and then brought his hand towards the table. Everybody craned to get a better look. Then, before he turned the dice loose, he stopped again, and put his hand, dice and all, back over his head, like a football player about to toss a pass. He looked over at Rocco like he'd just had an idea.

"Hey, Rocco," he said, very casual, "how much money in that stack?"

"Come on, come on, fire your pistol!" Rocco came back, getting a little impatient. "You going to take all night for your lousy grand? There's enough down there to cover any bet you want to make, Patsy." He said "Patsy" like it was an insult, not like a nickname.

"Good," said Patsy. Then he looked at me. "Tony," he said, "would you please take ten thousand out of that wallet and put it on the *Come*."

Like the fellow says, my life started to flash through my head a little bit at a time and I started to get dizzy. What Patsy was doing was, well, he was betting he'd come. *Come* in a crap game means to make your point—*starting* when you make your bet. I guess you've never shot craps, Mac, so I won't try and explain it to you. The important thing is, if you roll a seven, you've come, and you win. And Patsy was betting ten grand he'd win. And I'd just sticked him two dice that couldn't come up any way *but* seven!

I just stood there, and the guys from the mills started to mutter and chatter among themselves. "What's holding you back? You going to take all night for a lousy ten grand?" One of the mill guys gave a sort of nervous laugh. I looked at Rocco. He was just standing there with his mouth part ways open, like he was seeing what was happening but didn't quite believe it.

Well, what could I do? I tossed Patsy's ten grand over on the little kidney-shaped part of the layout marked *Come*. I closed my eyes while he threw the dice, and when I opened them up again, all the mill guys were cheering, and Patsy was helping himself to ten grand out of Rocco's dough. When he had it all counted up and put away in his poke he turned to me and said: "I guess I lose my other bet, Tony. Two rolls, no coffee. Too bad."

Then he turned away and walked out of Rocco's place and you could tell he wasn't coming back. The original bet, of course, was still on the table, and, like I was dreaming, I picked it up and put it in what was left of Rocco's stack.

That wound up the crap shooting for that night, and I walked down here from Rocco's not seeing where I was going or who I bumped into. It was all a kind of bad dream, like I said.

Well, I'd got a week's salary out of Rocco just the day before all this happened, and I had a kind of hunch it was going to be the last I'd ever get from him, so I sat down in here and drank a good hunk of it up. There was something in what Patsy'd done that was familiar, vaguely familiar to me, like I'd been through it all before.

About halfway through my ninth bourbon, or maybe my tenth, it came to me. A story my old man used to tell me, about a sucker who'd cleaned out a crap game he knew was crooked, just the same way Patsy did. It had happened to my old man years ago. I put down what was left of my drink and started some heavy thinking, or as heavy as you can think on eight bourbons. Then I remembered that Camp Carson, where the ski troops had trained, is not so very far from Pike's Peak. A guy like Patsy, on a pass, might easily have gone into some gambling joint in, say, Colorado Springs, and maybe . . .

Say, I hope I haven't been boring you, chum, but you know, bartenders are supposed to be a little gabby, and I've been a bartender ever since that night.

What's that, bub? What did Patsy do with his winnings? Well, I don't know if I should tell you that. Your cigar's gone out, though. Here, have a light. Keep 'em. They're on the house—courtesy of Patsy's Bar and Grill.

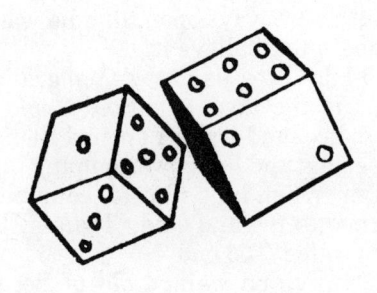

Mary Braund

What's on the Telly Tonight?

Aggie Williams was a witch. At any rate, Uncle Charlie thought so and he ought to know—he had to live with her. He sat by the grate stirring the few incombustible pieces of coal with the black iron poker and wished he could bash Aggie over the head with it. Maybe not actually bring it down on that stringy gray hair, but just wave the poker around in the air a bit, threatening like, so that she would cringe and beg for mercy.

Aha! That was the stuff! Show her that he was a man after all, even if he *had* to live in her crummy little house because his only choice was between that and the workhouse. Not that they called it the workhouse any more, of course. Too mealymouthed these days to call anything by its proper name. But he knew what a workhouse was all right, no matter if it was fancied up with names like "Retirement Home for the Elderly."

Though there were days when he wondered if he might not be a sight better off there than in this miserable hole, having to put up with Aggie and her stinking cooking. Why her mother had never taught her to do anything with food except fry it—but then, no one could teach Aggie Williams anything. He liked a nice plate of chips as well as the next man, but there were limits to a man's endurance—and to his stomach, as well. His stomach wasn't feeling too good these days—it had that great lump sitting inside most of the time, and soda bicarbonate hardly eased the pain these days.

Uncle Charlie jabbed viciously at the smoldering fire.

The food in the workhouse really couldn't be any worse than Aggie's. But then that old battle-ax down at the insurance place had told him, "There just isn't any room in the Old People's Home, Mr. James, and after all, you are very nicely situated with your niece, aren't you? You are really very lucky, Mr. James, to have someone in the family willing and able to look after you. There are far too many old people nowadays, Mr. James, who have no one, just no one at all, to take care of them. Think yourself lucky, Mr. James, that you have a roof over your head and your meals cooked for you."

Uncle Charlie spat into the fire.

All right for her, the old bag, she didn't have to sit and look at Aggie's fat white face every day. Or eat her greasy, indigestible food either. What he'd do if Aggie didn't go out to work most nights, he couldn't imagine. Slaving, Aggie called it. Peace and quiet, that's what he called it.

Crash with the poker on the hard coals again.

She did all right out of him anyway. Handed over most of his pension to her, he did, just kept a few shillings for his packs of Woodbines and a drop of beer down at the Lion when he could make it, and that was getting more and more difficult these days with his rheumatics. What with his rheumatics and his stomach, life was hardly worth living anymore.

Still, there was always television. Thank God for the telly! Once Aggie went off to work at six o'clock, he could pull up the old chair and settle himself down for a nice quiet evening's viewing. Of course, half the stuff wasn't worth watching, but if there was nothing good on one channel there was always hope for better on another. Yes, the telly saved his life all right.

He heard the front door slam. Oh, oh! There she was, back from her afternoon at the Bingo. Maybe today she had won something—that night brighten things up a bit. If ever she won the jackpot they might get steak for supper. Even then it would be fried, of course.

Aggie Williams clumped her way into the little back room.

There he was, the old slob, hunched in front of the fire as usual. Why couldn't men find something useful to do with themselves all day long instead of expecting you to wait on them hand, foot, and finger? There'd be dirty dishes in the sink, left over from dinner, and it wouldn't have even occurred to the lazy old buzzard to wash them up.

Oh, no, just sit there in front of the fire, waiting for her to come in and get his tea, and then complain because it wasn't what his lordship liked. Men! Dirty layabouts, that's what they were.

Well, she'd shape things up a bit round here now that she'd got this new job. No more hogging the television to himself in the evenings, she'd see to that.

"Win anything, Aggie?" Uncle Charlie asked, grinning at her hopefully.

Look at that filthy shirt! She had to drag the clothes off his back before she could get them down to the launderette. Dirty old pigs, that's what men were.

"Not a sausage," she said, thumping her shopping bag on the table. "That Mrs. Green from Spring Street, she won twenty pounds. Twenty pounds, imagine."

Their two pairs of eyes gleamed avariciously at the thought.

"You know what she'll do with it, don't you? Spend it all down at the boozer, if I know her, and them kids running around with their toes sticking out of their shoes. Wasters, that's what some people are, never putting a thing aside for when they might need it."

Uncle Charlie got the message. Boozers and wasters. He flourished the poker secretly.

"What you got for tea then, Aggie?"

"Nice bit of plaice." She sighed heavily. "I suppose I'll have to go and start the chips."

Uncle Charlie's stomach groaned.

There was a strong smell of frying fat and fish when she dumped the plates, knives, and forks on the table. You'd think it would strike him once in a while that he could set the table. She pushed an old pair of his socks to one side, placed a teacup back on its saucer, and brushed a sprinkling of biscuit crumbs onto the floor. When the food was ready she took the evening paper from her shopping bag and they ate in their customary silence. Uncle Charlie scraped the flesh off the gray spotted skin and picked a few bones out of his mouth. As soon as he was finished he went out to the scullery for the soda bicarbonate.

The marble clock on the mantelpiece said 5:45. Soon time to switch on the news.

"Hadn't you better be moving, Aggie?" She was deep in the paper. "Don't want to be late, you know."

"Just looking to see what's on the telly tonight," she answered, without looking up. "There are one or two things I fancy."

Uncle Charlie shifted uneasily on his rheumaticky hip.

"Not working tonight, or something?" he asked anxiously.

Aggie folded the paper deliberately.

"You're not sick are you, Aggie? Or got laid off or anything?"

"Didn't I tell you?" Aggie's surprise was manifestly false. "There was a vacancy on the morning shift. I got it. I won't have to go off to work nights any more, Uncle Charlie. I'll be able to sit and watch the telly with you every evening."

Uncle Charlie choked on his soda bicarbonate.

"There's lots of things I want to see," Aggie went on. "Like this program about antiques at seven. Yes, I think I'll watch that. Some people say it's very good."

"Antiques?" Uncle Charlie howled. Seven o'clock was when he watched *Coronation Street*. "What do *you* know about antiques?"

"There's a lot I'd like to know," said Aggie firmly. "We'll watch it."

His evening ruined, Uncle Charlie left for the Lion at 6:45. But that didn't turn out any better; he had only enough money for half a pint, and though he made it last as long as he could, it wasn't quite 8:30 when he got back to the house.

There was Aggie, her feet up on the pouffe, a cup of tea by her side, a cigarette dangling from her mouth, enjoying some program about starving children in Africa. He ached to switch over to the special about George Best that he had been looking forward to all week.

He sat glumly in the hard brown chair with the wooden arms. Aggie had even taken his comfortable seat. He watched scenes of emaciated children, thatched huts, and pouring rain. That was followed by an earnest discussion between some interviewer and several worried-looking geysers from the Red Cross or something. It was all very sad and it made Uncle Charlie's indigestion much worse.

"You're not really liking this, are you, Aggie?"

"It's not a matter of liking," she said, without taking her eyes from the screen. "It's good for us to know what's going on in the other half of the world. Makes us feel happier with our own lot, don't you think?"

Uncle Charlie grunted. "Any tea left in the pot?" he asked pathetically.

"I made this in the cup. Wouldn't have thought you'd need any after swigging beer all evening."

Uncle Charlie sucked his teeth for a few minutes. "What time is this over?"

Aggie picked up the paper, held it at arm's length, and perused the TV programs. "Well, there's the news next and then there's *Play of the Week*. After that there's *Twenty-Four Hours*, and then there's some concert. I like a bit of serious music now and then."

"You're going to watch all them things?" Uncle Charlie sank to the depths of depression. He cleared his throat tentatively. "There's a special about George Best on the I.T.V."

"George Best? Who's he?"

"He's a footballer. Plays for United. Everyone knows George Best."

"A footballer?" Aggie snorted. "Those fellows have got too much money and not enough sense. I'm not watching any program about long-haired footballers."

"How do you know he's got long hair if you don't know him?" Uncle Charlie asked slyly.

"Everyone's got long hair these days. In any case, I'm watching this."

Even the news didn't cheer Uncle Charlie up. It was all about riots and demonstrations and there was a speech by some Minister about the need to work harder to improve productivity—the sort of stuff he'd heard and seen a hundred times. No nice murders or plane crashes or anything like that.

He sat uneasily through the first few minutes of *Play of the Week*. It seemed to be about a family who didn't understand each other. Well, he knew all about that!

"This isn't very exciting," he said, after making a great effort to keep quiet for several minutes. "Why don't we switch over?"

"I want to watch it," said Aggie sharply. "It's educational and we can all do with a bit of education."

Uncle Charlie took himself off to bed. He lay miserably under the shiny green blanket, listening to the sound of the telly downstairs and thought longingly of his quiet evenings of freedom to turn the knob at will. Then he heard the drone of voices from the play change abruptly to music and laughter and he knew Aggie had switched channels. The old bitch. She had driven him off to bed with her education claptrap, then changed programs as soon as he was out of the way.

He struggled out of bed, wrapped his ancient flannel dressing gown around himself, and crept down the narrow stairs in his bare feet. He tried to sidle in through the door without Aggie hearing him. There she was, cackling her silly head off at some comedian, that fellow with the big mustache. Uncle Charlie liked him, too. The door of the room creaked as he tried to push it a bit wider and Aggie turned round.

"Thought you'd gone to bed," she said, swiveling her black beady eyes between him and the television set.

"I was just going," Uncle Charlie wheedled, "then I heard that show starting and I thought I might watch it, too."

"Well, it's no good," and Aggie heaved her bulk from the chair to turn back to the drama. She settled down again, firmly.

All right, Aggie Williams, thought Uncle Charlie, as he made his way back up the cold stairs. All right, I'll get even with you somehow. Coming in ruining an old man's last vestige of enjoyment, spoiling the only thing left in his life. I'll get even with you somehow.

But how? That was the trouble. In the ensuing weeks Uncle Charlie was made to suffer every night of the week and he couldn't think of a thing to do about it. After all, it *was* Aggie's telly and it *was* her house. He went down to the rental place to see if he could get one of his own. He could sit in the front room and see his own programs and to hell with her, but they wanted six months' rent in advance and he just didn't have that much money.

He and Aggie argued and wrangled, he pleaded and begged for a bit of relief, but it was as if she knew exactly what he wanted to watch and deliberately chose something else. It made Uncle Charlie's indigestion even worse.

In fact, it became so bad that he decided to go to see the doctor. He went down one morning to the doctor's office on the main road and sat on one of the hard wooden chairs, staring at the table in the middle of the room on which were scattered ancient copies of *Punch* and signs that told of the dangers of smoking.

The waiting room was full of old people like himself, and he listened to the coughing and spluttering and grumbling and moved his left arm uneasily. There was his rheumatics and the indigestion and now this heaviness that went all the way down from the back of his chest to his left elbow. He couldn't decide which he should tell the doctor about first. Getting old was no joke.

The doctor listened patiently to the story of the greasy food and Aggie, and the Insurance and the Old People's Home. He sighed deeply, and really Uncle Charlie felt quite sorry for him. The poor old doc looked so tired himself and that dingy office of his was enough to depress anyone.

The doctor took out his stethoscope and bent his ear to Uncle Charlie's ribs. He wrapped the faded blue cloth around Uncle Charlie's thin arm and puffed on the little black bulb. He shook his head.

"Blood pressure's up, Mr. James," he said, writing on the small pad in front of him. "I can't be sure, but I think you may have some trouble with your heart. All this discomfort you've been getting—well, I don't think it's your stomach so much as your heart." He scribbled away on the pad. "But I don't want to alarm you before we give you a thorough checkup. You'd better go along to the hospital. We'll get an appointment set up for you in the next few days. In the meantime take things easy and don't let yourself get excited."

"You mean it's not that rotten food I have to eat?" Uncle Charlie was quite put out that Aggie was not to blame.

"I think the food might have something to do with it, but I'm afraid it's to do with getting old, Mr. James. That and maybe the general tension of life."

You can bet the tension of life, Uncle Charlie thought as he made his way back through the rain-drenched, sooty streets. I should have told him about Aggie and the telly. He began to feel triumphant. She was upsetting his heart, that's what she was doing. He should have got a note from the doctor telling her to let him watch whatever he wanted to, not to upset him by going on all the time about his clothes and the dishes and his bedroom. Bloody old witch.

He sat in the comfy chair all afternoon waiting for her to come home. He got it all planned out—what he was going to watch this evening. *Softly, Softly* and *The Good Old Days*. He liked a bit of nostalgia now and then. He rustled at the coals with the black poker and grinned to himself. She'd listen to him now all right.

They were eating their supper—kidney pie and chips—in silence as usual, when Uncle Charlie remarked casually, dropping it in between mouthfuls, "Went to the doctor's today. He said there might be something wrong with me ticker."

Aggie poked some chips into her mouth, looking at him without expression.

"Yes," Uncle Charlie went on, "he's getting me an appointment at the hospital, with a specialist. A specialist in hearts, you know."

Aggie scraped the remains of the gravy up with her knife and slid it into her mouth. Her black eyes looked past Uncle Charlie to the television set.

"He says I'm not to get myself excited."

Aggie put her hands on the sides of her plate and snorted. "What do you mean, not get yourself excited? What does he think you do all day? Race horses? Win and lose millions on the stock market? Does he know you just sit in a chair and vegetate?"

She stood up from the table with a grunt and started to walk around it. Uncle Charlie knew she was going to switch on the television.

"He means," said Uncle Charlie, waving his arms around, "he means I'm to have my own way a bit in this house. After all, I pay my way. I'm an old man. I don't see why I can't have a few pleasures in life, too. I can see what *I* want to once in a while. It shouldn't be you all the time and never me."

Now he was on his feet and shouting. Aggie put her hands on her hips and faced him coolly. "Oh, the doctor said all that, did he? All for free on the National Health?"

She switched on the television.

"I want to watch *Softly, Softly,*" bellowed Uncle Charlie. Damn, his indigestion was getting worse.

"*Softly, Softly,*" mimicked Aggie. "Remember what the doctor said. Don't get excited."

"*And* I want to see *The Good Old Days,*" Uncle Charlie roared.

"The Gay Nineties, eh? Just your style. Well, *I* want to watch something about South Africa. So that's that, see."

Uncle Charlie was convulsed with rage. All his frustration and anger screamed in him to be released. The blood rushed around in his head. He literally frothed at the mouth, spluttering incoherently. He wanted to do something violent, really violent.

His suffused eyes rolled from Aggie to the television set, to the table, to the fireplace—to the poker. The poker! He leaped for it, grasped it firmly in his skinny hand, and started to straighten up, the poker clenched in his fist, half raised above his head.

Then, oh God, the pain in his chest. A great crushing, gripping, overwhelming pain. The poker fell to the floor. Uncle Charlie stood for a moment, his fingers clutching his chest. He managed to gasp, "I'll get you yet, Aggie Williams, I'll get you yet"—and then he, too, fell to the floor.

The funeral was on Saturday. Aggie went, of course, large and somber in her gray coat and black felt hat, and there were a couple of the neighbors who went for the ride in the limousine—"to keep Aggie company." There was a small bunch of lilies inscribed "From Your Devoted Niece," and that was all. It was over very quickly.

Afterward, the neighbors and Aggie had a Guinness and a pasty in the Lion. Alice Smithers from next door suggested, "Come to our house this afternoon, Aggie. You shouldn't be alone, you know. We can watch *Grandstand* by the fire and have a nice chat."

Aggie was very pious. "Thanks all the same," she said, "but I think I'll go home. I've got to get used to being alone, haven't I?"

"Well, at least you've got nothing to blame yourself for, Aggie," said Alice Smithers, draining her glass. "You gave him a good home, you did. You were a real good companion to him. You can rest assured you'll get your reward, Aggie Williams. You'll get your reward."

WHAT'S ON THE TELLY TONIGHT? 121

When she got home Aggie settled herself in the comfy chair, her feet up on the pouffe, cigarettes to hand and a cup of tea by her side. She stirred the fire contentedly. This was the life—a bit of privacy at last.

The familiar face of David Coleman loomed on the screen at 1:45 P.M. "Lots of good things this afternoon," his cheerful voice declared. "Racing from Newmarket, Rubgy International between Wales and Scotland at the Arms Park, motor cross from Birdlip..."

Aggie's head nodded. Only for a moment... When she opened her eyes again, the horses were being paraded around the ring before the first race at Newmarket. The camera dwelt lovingly on the shining flanks, the jockeys, the trainers, the owners. It scanned the interested spectators leaning idly on the rails—sheepskin-coated women with silk scarves around their heads, large men in tweed overcoats and porkpie hats.

Suddenly Aggie sat upright. Arms folded on the rails, just like one of the gentry, cloth cap flat on his head, grinning widely at the camera was Uncle Charlie! There was no mistaking that scrawny figure. The camera stopped on him for a moment and he even lifted one hand in greeting.

Aggie sat with thumping heart and open mouth, immobile in her chair.

Then the horses were on again, stalking elegantly in their blankets. Then the jockeys were mounting and they were cantering down to the start, into the mist and out of range of the camera.

Gradually the sound of her charging heart subsided. She took a large swig of lukewarm tea and lit a cigarette with a shaking hand. Silly sod! Her imagination was working overtime—must have been that Guinness at lunchtime.

Still, she was relieved when the program moved to the Arms Park for the International.

The singing had started, the full-throated harmony of sixty thousand Welshmen. Aggie liked a bit of community singing. She settled back in her chair. The camera scanned the packed stands, the serried ranks of Welshmen singing lustily for the motherland, and there, right in the middle of Sospan Fach, was Uncle Charlie, his head back, his chest out, his voice raised to the gray Welsh skies.

Mother of God! Aggie moved this time. She leaped to her feet and switched off the television. She made another cup of tea, lit another cigarette. Alice Smithers was right. She shouldn't be alone. She sipped at the scalding tea, then hurried out to the hall, dragged her coat from the hall stand, and left, slamming the front door behind her.

"My, Aggie, you're looking a bit shaky," Alice remarked as she led her into the back room. "Finding it a bit of a strain after all, are you? Never mind, dear, you're bound to grieve for a while. Sit yourself down here. I'm watching the game all by myself, so I'm glad you've come round. The others have gone to see United."

Aggie glanced fearfully at the flickering set, but comforted herself. She'd be all right here with Alice.

All was well until Wales scored the first try, then the ground erupted with cheering, flag-waving Welshmen. Back went the camera over the crowd and Aggie cringed in her seat. Yes, there he was, the old devil, waving a great Welsh dragon, his face wreathed in a thousand smiling creases. He waved the flag enthusiastically at the camera.

"There," Aggie gasped, "there, did you see that? Did you see *that?*"

Alice was busy sorting out her knitting. "What, dear? What's the matter?"

"I thought I saw . . ."Aggie's voice trailed off. "Oh, nothing. It's nothing."

She sweated it out for another hour. Uncle Charlie was all over the place—in the stands at the Arms Park, on the rails in Newmarket, by the finishing line at the motorcycle racing. And Alice didn't even notice anything. Aggie waited and waited for her to say something, but Alice chatted on, clicking her needles just as though everything was quite normal.

Aggie just had to go home in the end. She knew Alice thought she was being a bit odd, but there was no help for that. She just had to go home and lie down for a bit.

She didn't put the television on again that night. She lay in her bed in the little front bedroom, the blankets up round her, trying to fall asleep, thinking about Uncle Charlie. It wouldn't be so bad if he hadn't looked as though he was enjoying himself all the time. It was hours before she eventually dropped off.

It was late Sunday evening before she dared put the telly on again. She sat and thought about it for a long time, working out that she had only seen Uncle Charlie on those outdoors broadcasts, around the country. It was obvious that he couldn't possibly be on anything like a film.

There was some old Western on the I.T.V. She had him at last.

But believe it or not, there, right in the middle of a barroom brawl, guns at his hips, a day-old bristle on his face—there was Uncle Charlie. His face loomed sardonic and somehow American, but it was still unmistakably Uncle Charlie's face.

Aggie was both frightened and enraged. "Rotten old bum," she screamed. "Can't leave a body in peace. Ruining me comfort and quiet."

Uncle Charlie grinned and twirled his guns. Aggie snarled and sobbed. "Dirty old slob," she raged, and whirling, she aimed a kick at the television, missed and lost her balance. Steadying herself on the fender, the poker was right by her nose, and without a second thought, half blinded by terror and fury, Aggie seized the poker and swung a mighty blow at Uncle Charlie's face. There was a tremendous shattering of glass, and smoke and sparks flew from the television set. Then there was silence.

Aggie stood, breathing heavily, the poker still in her hand, surveying the ruin of her television set. Uncle Charlie was gone, but so was her lovely telly.

"Oh, you dirty, filthy, stinking old man," she groaned.

A long while later Aggie still stood in the middle of the floor, surrounded by glass and trailing wires and the empty staring hole in the metal box. The silence became unbearable. She could never stand silence. Like a zombie she moved across the room and switched on the radio. It must have been years since she had last listened to the radio.

There was a great deal of crackling and static, then the waves cleared and faintly but clearly through the ether came the old man's quavering voice.

"I said I'd get you, Aggie Williams. I said I'd get you."

Thomas Walsh

The Killer Instinct

One moment it was not anywhere within Harry McCormick's sight. The next, without a sound, as if magically, it had appeared over on the other side of the trail. In the gloom there he could make out the warm reddish-brown color, the placidly flowing steam from its nostrils, and the magnificently upraised antlers. It was not excited or alarmed, apparently. It could not have sensed him.

Slowly and quite calmly it gazed around from that vantage point. Then in the same manner—or even, McCormick thought, with an air of gracefully elegant nobility—it came down toward him, toward the path, through the thin November snow that had fallen a bit earlier that afternoon.

McCormick was waiting where Art Jelinek had told him to wait. "Sometimes, late in the afternoon, they come back," Jelinek had said. "In the morning they part company, Harry, the doe going one way, the buck another. But a lot of times when it gets dark, he'll come back and pick up her trail again. They want a little company for the night, I suppose. So you wait right here behind these bushes. Don't smoke, don't move around, don't make a sound. I'll go around the next turn in the path and do the same thing. We might as well try our luck today right here."

So the moment had arrived, and Harry McCormick had assumed he would be ready for it. But there was one problem—that he did not feel, not in any way, what he had thought he would. All at once there was something new and entirely unexpected in him, and he did not move so much as a finger. The thing was impossible to do. What he looked at—perfect in function, in appearance, and in the perfect place that someone or other had created for it—was the most beautiful creature he had ever seen.

Now it paused no more than thirty feet away, bending its head to sniff delicately at the doe's footprints. McCormick could hear that. Then, after gazing calmly right and left into the woods, it moved off toward the turn in the path, toward Jelinek—and McCormick still sat with the hunting rifle across his knees, as if frozen there by the sudden realization that this was the buck's place, after all, and not his.

He had not even the thought to fire at it. He could not have explained why. Long shadows darkened the woods, and there was no sound but the desolate whisper of a lonely autumn wind in the tree branches. But what McCormick had begun to feel, if he could have put it into words, was that to use his rifle here was a profane act he must not commit. He could have placed his shot. In the department he had a rating as sharpshooter. But all he actually did was to sit motionless on the rock under him, his unlit pipe in one hand, and remain that way for another few seconds.

What he felt was not buck fever. He was not jumpy in any way. He was held, rather, by a new and queer impression—that Harry McCormick was the savage, the intruder here, that he was in a place not made or intended for him, and that, knowing it now and beyond question, he must not do anything to harm or even harass. My God, he was thinking numbly. Magnificent. Who could ever think of—

There was a mad yell from around the turn, a shot, and a second shot. A slight painful grin twisted McCormick's lips and he got up slowly, rifle under his arm, barrel down. Even more slowly he walked to the turn in the path, not wanting to, and saw Jelinek and the buck before him.

"What the hell was the matter?" Jelinek shouted jubilantly at him. "It came right down the trail to me. Didn't you see it, Harry? Where were you?"

"Right there," McCormick said. "Right where you told me. I saw it."

But of course there was nothing to be done then, nothing at all. The buck was down in the snow, in some broken bushes. It was still alive, Art Jelinek not being the shot that McCormick was, and jerked its head around to them with blind effort, breathing stertorously. There was just a little light in the Adirondack woods now, a dark gray light; but McCormick could see the eyes as it attempted to thrash itself up onto its feet. They fixed on him. It seemed to McCormick that they accused him, in some manner. They were bright, agonized, bewildered, and despairing.

McCormick, after that first glance and not looking back, walked by carefully. He was thinking of one or two minutes ago, and of now. His muscles were vibrating delicately, and he knew that if he spoke so much as another word he would have hit Jelinek. He went on, doing the sensible thing. He walked back through the November silence and dimness, through the heavy lion smell of the woods in autumn, to where Jelinek's car was parked just off the state highway.

"But you've got to expect that," Jelinek attempted to comfort him that night at the motel with condescending superiority. "Your first time up here—so what the hell. Might happen to anybody. A little buck fever, that's all. You kind of froze up, Harry."

"No, it wasn't that," McCormick said, beginning to sip irritably at his bourbon and water. "I just felt that we don't belong up here, Art, or at least for this reason. He did."

"Don't know exactly what you're trying to say," Jelinek protested. "Way the world goes, Harry—dog eat dog."

"Only we're not supposed to be dogs," McCormick said, even more irritably pushing his glass to one side. "We're supposed to be human beings, aren't we? There's the difference."

"What difference?" Jelinek said, again peering out happily at the dead buck strapped onto his car radiator. "The way I figure, if you ain't got the old killer instinct in you, at least when you need it, you ain't even a man. Look at Hitler. Look at them Japs. What do you figure would have happened to you and me thirty-five years ago if nobody had the guts to go out after them and shove it right down their throats?"

"I don't know," McCormick had to admit, "and I've often wondered, with the lovely world we seem to have made out of things. Justice and friendship all over, eh? Universal brotherhood, the beginning of the millennium, whatever the hell that is. But maybe, just maybe, Art, if every one of us didn't have that old killer instinct, we might do a lot better."

"Boy," Jelinek said, shaking his head humorously at such nonsense. "Do you ever have crazy ideas. But what the hell. Guess I got mine, Harry. How about starting back home in the morning?"

So they did. Jelinek was still proud of the dead buck, and when they stopped for gas he explained about it in full detail to the serviceman, meanwhile resting a proprietary hand on one of the antlers. At about eleven o'clock, on a lonely stretch of road just before the Northway, they came upon a big imported limousine drawn up on the grass, with its hood lifted and a uniformed chauffeur bent in over the motor. When he heard them coming, the chauffeur stepped out into the road and waved them down.

"I don't know what's the trouble," he said. "I think it's the ignition—it just keeps stalling on me. How about a ride to the next town, fellows? I'll have to get someone to service it."

"Why not?" Jelinek said. "Glad to oblige, Jack. Hop in."

"Thanks a million," the chauffeur said. He was a big man, McCormick noticed—arms, legs, shoulders, torso. His hands were enormous. He was so big that the whipcord uniform looked as if it was ready to split open on him. And yet, McCormick saw—the first odd thing—it was immaculately new. "Just wait till I leave my car in back of these trees. I wouldn't want some smart kid to come along and strip it down while I'm gone. The boss wouldn't like that at all. He's got a lot of stuff there in back."

Which was the second odd thing. His car started up like a charm. He circled it in back of the trees, where it was out of sight from the road, then opened the door on the passenger side and jerked his thumb. McCormick did not know much about the manners of uniformed chauffeurs, but it seemed to him a rather peculiar way for one to behave. A small boy got out of the car and the chauffeur took his hand.

"Had to pick him up at school this morning," the chauffeur explained affably. "The boss's kid. They want him at home for something. Him and me will just sit in back, huh? Better not leave him here all alone."

McCormick glanced down at a blue cap, a blue coat with six brass buttons, navy style, and a narrow tightly frozen face. The boy got in back, the chauffeur pushing him along with one of those enormous hands, and when Jelinek said, "Hi, Johnny. How are you?" the boy did not answer him.

There was something not quite right about the boy's expression. It seemed to be all drawn in on itself, every inch of it, as if he was called upon to confront an adult world which he did not understand yet and had no idea how to handle properly. He kept his two hands in his lap, clasped tightly. Only after they had started off again did it come to McCormick what the attitude and expression might mean in a six- or seven-year-old child—blind, almost overwhelming terror.

Jelinek had not noticed anything. Jelinek was the driver. But when McCormick turned his head for another look at the boy he found the chauffeur staring back at him with a shiny, mirthlessly sardonic gleam in the gray eyes, as if he might be just a little amused by something. "Yeah?" he said.

"Well, nothing," McCormick said. "Kind of funny, though, isn't it?"

"What's funny?" the chauffeur asked. "Just speak right up, pal. What strikes you?"

"Your car," McCormick said. "Ran like a top when you drove it back of those trees, I thought."

"Yeah, didn't it?" the chauffeur said. "Way it's been acting all morning, pal—off and on. What are you staring at the kid for?"

"I don't really know," McCormick said. "But he's kind of quiet, isn't he? What's the matter with him?"

The chauffeur rubbed his nose with one hand, grinning.

"Ask him yourself," he said. "But yes, sir, and no, sir—that's about all you can get out of him. Knows his manners, all right. Real polite, I'd call him. How about it, kid?"

"Yes, sir," the boy whispered. His hands were still clasped tightly. "But you're not—you're not Martin."

The chauffeur slipped an arm about him, still watching McCormick, and slapped the boy's face as if playfully.

"Now there," the chauffeur said. "What did I tell you? See? Who shot that big buck up front?"

"So who would you think?" Jelinek chortled, still exuberantly boisterous about his triumph over McCormick. "My friend here was dumb enough to let it walk right by him yesterday afternoon. Buck fever, I guess—but that's the way it hits them sometimes. No killer instinct."

"What's that?" the chauffeur inquired lazily. He was still watching McCormick, and McCormick, not sure yet, but with the beginnings of a slow icy crawl up the back, was watching him.

"What's what?" Jelinek said.

"Well, what you were just talking about," the chauffeur said. "Killer instinct. So your friend ain't got it, huh? How about you?"

"Just look up ahead," Jelinek chortled again. "The second I see him—pam! Just about shot the damn head off his shoulders. While all Harry could do—"

"Wow!" the chauffeur said. Eye to eye still, he and McCormick; the child turned blindly away from them to the car window; Jelinek grinning happily to himself. "I guess you got it all right, pal—the old killer instinct. Ever try it with a man, though? That's the big kick."

"With a man?" Jelinek said. He caught then what McCormick had caught. His eyes, wide and startled, jumped up to the rearview mirror to examine the chauffeur. "What's the angle, Jack? What are you talking about?"

"Knew a guy," the chauffeur said, never once taking his eyes from McCormick. But he had slipped one hand in under the whipcord jacket, in position for something; and McCormick, an instant too late, had a sudden and sickening idea as to what the position might be. McCormick was carrying a revolver too—department regulations, even when off duty; but it was up in a shoulder holster under his thick windbreaker, and it came to him that he and Jelinek were as helpless here as the child, even with two against one. The cold panic in him then was so sudden that he let it show, and the chauffeur, to let McCormick know that he had seen and understood, chuckled aloud.

"But that was years ago," he said, again drawling deliberately. "Hated all cops, this guy did. Just couldn't stand them. So they tell me that when he'd knocked off about a quart of old bourbon, he liked to get into his car and take a little ride for himself. Soon as he saw a cop, though, he'd pull over like he was asking for directions. 'Hey, officer,' he'd say, and when the dumb flatfoot came over and stuck his head in the window—pam, like you just put it yourself. Ran up quite a score like that, I heard. Detroit, Los Angeles, K.C.—all over. So how about that, pal? Killer instinct, you figure?"

Jelinek's eyes had narrowed.

"What I figure," he said, his heavy jaw showing itself, "is that maybe you ain't so damned funny as you seem to imagine, Jack. It just so happens that you're talking to a couple of New York City cops right here, and that Harry and I might decide to pull over at the next rest area for about five minutes and show you how funny you are. Want us to try?"

"Maybe later," the chauffeur said, the sly grin still lurking. "But not in a rest area, pal. Don't stop now until I tell you to stop. My lucky day, though. A couple of New York cops, huh?"

Jelinek shot a quick glance over at McCormick, but McCormick could only moisten his lips. It was too late then. The chauffeur, whistling softly through his teeth, slid his hand out from under his whipcord jacket, and showed them a .45 revolver.

"Well, well, well," he went on, as if now vastly amused. "Glad to meet up with you fellows. Really enjoying the company. Enjoying it so much that I guess we won't turn off at the next gas station, after all. You know what? I guess we just better push along nice and quiet now till we hit around Albany. Okay with you?"

McCormick had been on the force thirteen years, and Jelinek seventeen. They each knew what they faced. In their rookie years they had heard many stories about psychopathic police killers—the kind of criminal who could not endure even the thought of authority but had to react against it at every opportunity with blind and insane violence.

This time they did not glance at each other. Jelinek, tightening his hands on the steering wheel, wet his lips quickly. McCormick stared straight ahead at the road. He was trying not to change his expression. The only thing to do now, he realized, was to drag the thing on and on as long as possible—and perhaps in the end, seizing on the first opportunity that offered itself, to turn the tables.

"Whatever you want," McCormick got out. "No argument at all, Jack. Whatever you tell us. Until we hit Albany then."

The chauffeur liked that. Jovially he slapped one of his big hands against the back of McCormick's head, knocking it forward like a rubber ball, and apparently with no effort.

"Tell you something," he went on then. "You seem like you got a good head on your shoulders, pal. You can size up the score right away. How about your killer friend, though? How about him?"

"Who, me?" Jelinek said. His thoughts must have followed McCormick's. He even managed to grin cockily, to show how tough, unafraid, and altogether unworried he was. "Why, sure. Anything you say, Jack. You just tell us."

"Thought I did already," the chauffeur said. "But what I want you to do, fellows, is to behave yourselves like the kid here. Yes, sir, and no, sir. That's all. Got that?"

"Sure have." Jelinek nodded hurriedly. "But take it easy, will you? Just don't get excited, Jack. No sweat."

"Excited about what?" the chauffeur said, and McCormick heard the sly chuckle again. "No, no. Wouldn't even think of it. You fellows ain't nothing to me, not a thing. I have to blow a hole in each of you—well, I have to, that's all. Probably wouldn't even remember your faces afterward. You want to keep that in mind?"

"Right on," Jelinek nodded, returning a grin. But it was stupid of him. It turned his whole face into a mélange of wet paste.

And the chauffeur liked that. It offered him, McCormick understood, exactly what he wanted, what he had to have—the sense of a venomous and complete triumph over them. Jelinek was doing this the wrong way. Whatever he felt, the panic must not be permitted to show. Once it showed, the chauffeur would have achieved his end. So McCormick managed to keep his expression exactly what it was, even when the big hand slapped his head forward a second time.

"Now you," the chauffeur said. "What do you think, pal? You want to start practicing how to say yes, sir, and no, sir, just like the kid here? You remember how it goes, kid?"

The boy, turning his head, stared numbly at McCormick.

"Yes, sir," he whispered.

"Like I said," McCormick murmured. "Anything you say, Jack. Yes, sir."

"There now—" the chauffeur said, and the chuckle was once more behind them. "See how easy it is? You're beginning to learn almost as quick as the kid, fellows. My lucky day, all right. I didn't even have any trouble at the school."

"Oh?" McCormick said. Keep him going, he remembered; the longer the better; wait your chance and then—"What school are you talking about?"

"Mount Marcy School," the chauffeur said. "Where all the rich kids go up here. I had it figured, all right. What would I need? The old man's limousine and the chauffeur's uniform, and I'd have it boxed. So I go up to the house this morning and tell the Limey butler I'm from the service station, to put the snow tires on—and he says go ahead and take the car then, they won't need it today.

"Then down the road I put on the chauffeur's uniform, and they're just as dumb at the school. I tell them the old man wants him home, Robert Rossiter Parkman, Junior, and as soon as they see the car waiting they don't even call back to the Limey butler. Nothing to it, actually. The kid had more brains than any of them. The kid tries to pull back. 'You ain't Martin,' he says. 'Who are you?' And I says—but I kind of forget. How did I put it, kid?"

"You shoved me inside and twisted my arm," the child whispered. "Then you slapped me twice in the mouth, sir—to keep me quiet."

"Yeah, I did, didn't I?" the chauffeur said. "That's right. Kind of slipped my mind for a minute. So I ditched the car then quick as I could—had to, of course, to get out of this part of the country—and flagged down a couple of dumb New York flatfeet that came along. But you know what, fellows? The kid ain't due home until four o'clock, and by that time I ought to be down around New York City, where I got a couple of friends waiting. So what's to worry about?"

"Maybe plenty," Jelinek gritted. "They're going to find the old man's car back there and when they do it won't take five minutes for them to figure out the whole story."

"Might be," the chauffeur admitted. "Why I drove it in like that off the road, pal. Remember? But I think it will be all right. I think it will be a hundred percent fine, even. Three hundred thousand bucks for the kid, right on the nail—that's what we're asking. How can we miss?"

"Maybe," Jelinek said grimly, "when you come to the real tricky part, Jack. The collection."

"No problem there," the chauffeur drawled. "Thought it all out, fellows. Toss a kid five dollars to pick up a package for me, then tail him all the way there and back. If nobody follows him, and believe me I'm going to make damned sure about that, then we're safe home. If they do—well, might have to even it up with little buster here. Breach of faith, they call it. But of course we might do that, anyway. Safest way out. He could remember me."

At that Jelinek could contain himself no longer.

"Damn murdering swine," McCormick heard breathlessly. "Telling us the whole thing, eh? Even sounds like you're proud of it."

But McCormick said nothing. The chauffeur wanted them to know, he understood. Only in that way would he enjoy a full and complete triumph over them. And the bad thing was that he had explained it. They could do nothing at all, which was exactly what the chauffeur wanted them to feel. They were absolutely helpless—and they were dead men. Because now that they *did* know—

Jelinek tried something. Little by little, mile by mile, he began inching up the speedometer. The Northway limit was fifty-five miles an hour, but soon Jelinek was twenty miles over that. He was hoping for a state trooper to spot them, to pull them over. Then, maybe—

But now Jelinek's head was slapped and bounced forward the way McCormick's had been.

"Just slow down," the chauffeur ordered. "You're the law, fellows—so nice and easy now, just as a favor to me. And turn off at the next exit, huh? The sign there says it's one mile ahead."

Jelinek cleared his throat, again being just a little behind McCormick.

"What do you want us to turn off for?" he said. "I thought we were going to hit all the way down to Albany, Jack. You'll have to make time."

"Next exit," the chauffeur repeated softly.

Because now, McCormick felt, the chauffeur had got about everything he wanted from them. The next exit was going to be the end of the road for Jelinek and McCormick. There was no question about it. They knew; they could do nothing; and Jelinek showed a few beads of heavy sweat on his cheeks. He had them knowing now, afraid, inferior, helpless. Then why waste any more time on them? The game was over. They had served their usefulness by providing him with a car. And so now—

Jelinek had to slow up for the turn, and two or three other cars went by them—a young fellow and girl, sitting close together in the front seat of an old Chevy; an elegant young man with long hair and a brown beard racing by in a midget sports car; and a family group—Papa, Mama, kids, Grandma—chugging past in a battered station wagon. Then they were off on the exit road, McCormick seeming to float along on thin air, and without any kind of workable idea in his head. No chance yet, unfortunately, no chance at all. His ears rang. His heart pumped in a slow labored manner. It was Jelinek who tried something.

"You hear that?" Jelinek demanded, clearing his throat first. "Sounds like I'm getting a flat in that front left tire, Harry—the one we had all the trouble with coming up. Get out and take a look at it, will you?"

But no. A round cold circle pressed into the center of McCormick's skull. He braced himself, one hand already out to the car door.

"I wouldn't," the chauffeur said. "Let's keep on going and take a chance, fellows. What I mean to do, soon as we come to a nice quiet place along here, is handcuff you back to back around a tree—so don't get too worried. See that dirt road up there? Good as anyplace else, I guess. Turn in, pal. Take it."

Jelinek took it. Like McCormick, Jelinek had no choice. Off the highway there was a cluster of shabby mobile homes, but after that there were only the woods. McCormick could see a smattering of snow under the trees, and then after a couple of low hills a rough circular turnaround where the road ended.

"I guess right here," the chauffeur said as Jelinek began to brake helplessly. "And you—" McCormick again was nudged gently by the revolver "—out. You walk five slow steps away from the car. Then you stand there. You don't move even a finger. You don't so much as look around, pal. You just stand there."

McCormick again floated. But they would not be handcuffed around a tree, he knew. Why should the man take a chance like that? They might be found and released, and if they were, the alarm would be out. Much better the other way. How had the chauffeur put it? He would not even remember their faces afterward.

So as ordered he took the five steps and halted. Before him there was a downward slope of the woods and at the bottom a small lake.

"All right," the chauffeur said behind him. "Your turn, pal—" obviously to Jelinek "—but don't get out on your side of the car. Slide over the seat and get out on his. Both together, huh?"

"Why?" Jelinek said. There was nothing to try, but he was still trying. "You don't want to lose your head, Jack. Look. Harry and I are good guys. There's no reason to—"

He must have been hit then. There was a sound behind McCormick, and he heard Jelinek stumble. "Hell," Jelinek groaned softly. Now the back of McCormick's legs felt iron-hard, but the back of his head wax-soft. Suddenly and desperately—nothing else for it now—he plunged down the embankment before him in a headlong mad dive, twisting and turning himself at the same time.

Snow stung his face. Bushes whipped and tore at his clothes. But even while rolling over and over he had got his hand in under his sweater and it closed thankfully around the butt of his big police revolver. Sky, earth, sky, earth, sky, earth danced around and over him, but when he came to rest at the bottom of the slope it was on his left arm and his left side, his revolver out.

It did him no good. Snow had dashed into his eyes, and agony tore at his right leg, kicking it sideways. Then there was another shot, not at him, and he saw Jelinek's tall burly figure crumple down on the brow of the road. At the same moment the chauffeur started after McCormick in great lunging strides, and McCormick fired at him, and fired again.

They were bad shots for Harry McCormick. They were, of course, hurried and panicky, and it seemed to him that the sky was still whirling. But they did one thing—they induced caution. The chauffeur ducked low, sheltering himself behind a big rock, and suddenly it became quiet—not a sound anywhere, it seemed to McCormick. But the child? At last he got a little sense into his head. He began shouting.

"Run," he heard himself yell. "Get out of that car, kid. Run!"

And now the chauffeur was between two horns. The child or McCormick? Which? But first things first, he must have decided—and so, just as McCormick had done a moment ago, he came down over the rock in a headlong dive. McCormick had just time for three more quick shots. Again he was wild. Then the chauffeur had landed on him, crushing him into the snow with all the impact of his 230 pounds.

Something happened to time at that moment. After quite a lot of it had gone by, or so McCormick thought, he found himself lying flat on his back, dazedly wiping blood from his face. Where was his gun?

He got up groggily to one knee, groping for the gun, and crashed forward to roll end over end once more. This time when he came to rest he was facing the lake.

Far out on it, and running ahead desperately, was a small figure in a blue cap and a blue sailor's coat with brass buttons. Behind him, gaining with every step, was the chauffeur. But it was still only November, not yet full winter, and the lake ice could not have been frozen solidly. It carried the child easily enough. It could not carry the chauffeur.

So the next thing McCormick heard was a thin tearing crackle of sound, like the rip of cloth. And after it, all around the chauffeur, was not thin immaculate-white snow anymore, but a rippling dark circle with the chauffeur's two arms pawing madly at it. He got to the edge of the circle, but then it crumpled under him for the second time. He went down, came up again, and now had sense enough to support himself on the edge of the broken ice.

"Kid!" McCormick heard. "Shove that pole out, kid. It's right on the shore by you. Help me!"

The child had stopped on the shore. He had raised his hands and now they kept pushing back at the man, to fend him off. Never in his life would McCormick forget the small white face, twisted, the hands pushing, the terrified look in the boy's eyes.

In another moment the boy had turned away from the chauffeur and had begun to run again. What the chauffeur had wanted and perhaps enjoyed in the boy—the blind panic—was the only thing to which the boy could now react. Probably he did not even hear the chauffeur. He ran on and on. He fell. He got up and ran again.

Then McCormick heard one desolate wild cry like that of an animal as the chauffeur tried foolishly to drag himself up and free. He did not succeed. Once his arm showed up to the elbow. The next time, groping futilely, it showed only as far as the wrist. McCormick ran and sprawled, ran and sprawled, but by the time he got around to the pole it was all over.

Then far out on the lake, still virgin and unspotted, was the white snow—and in the middle of it, placidly smooth and undisturbed now, a circle of dark water ...

Weeks later, when Art Jelinek and Harry McCormick were fit for duty again, they discussed the thing one night in the squad room.

"All I hope," McCormick said devoutly, "is that you got your fill of the old killer instinct at last, Art. I admit I have. He was really something, wasn't he?"

"Don't even remind me," Jelinek groaned. "That fellow had the killer instinct all the way up to the top of his head. He would have killed us both, Harry. He *wanted* to kill us—and maybe the kid too. He would have enjoyed it, got his bangs. How in hell can anybody ever handle a psycho like that? Explain it to me, will you? What can you do with a man like that?"

"Not very much," McCormick had to agree. "There's only one thing in our favor, Art. It doesn't always work out for them. It didn't up there on the lake."

Henry Slesar

A Victim Must Be Found

The looks hurt most, the quizzical one from Dennis, the Account Supervisor. The knowing, falsely sympathetic one from Hargrove, the head Art Director. The amused, poor-henpecked-slob look from Mead, Research man of the advertising agency.

Bill Hendricks looked disapprovingly at his secretary. "I told you not to interrupt me," he said. "Tell Mrs. Hendricks I'll call her back."

"She said it was very important, Mr. Hendricks." Her own face registered neither approval or disapproval.

Hendricks scraped back his chair. Dennis waved permission to leave. "It's all right, Bill," he said emotionlessly. "We're almost through here anyway."

"I'll be right back," Hendricks promised.

He went to his office. The receiver was lying on the blotter, and when he picked it up he could almost feel the presence of his wife quivering inside the instrument.

"Karen? For God's sake!" he snapped. "I was in a meeting. I've told you a thousand times—"

"Don't shout at me." The metallic reply was automatic. "It's almost four o'clock and I've just *got* to know—"

"Know what?"

"About dinner—what do you suppose? You said you'd call me at three. What do you think I am, a mindreader?"

Hendricks squeezed the telephone receiver. He pulled out the tangled wire and inched his way around the desk and into his swivel chair. With his free hand he reached absently for a pencil and stabbed at a memo pad, the point breaking and rolling off the desk.

"Now listen to me, Karen," he said in a controlled tone, looking at the open doorway. "You've got to stop yanking me out of meetings this way. A million dinners aren't worth it, do you understand?"

"I'm not going to argue with you over the phone." Karen spaced the words carefully, in that annoying way she had. Hendricks gritted his teeth.

"I'm not arguing," he said. "I'm telling you. You're making me look like a complete fool—"

"Darling, you give me too much credit."

Hendricks started to hang up. But he jerked the telephone back from its cradle just in time.

"I'm not coming home tonight," he said.

"Goodbye," said Karen.

"Goodbye!"

He slammed the receiver down too loudly, and looked up guiltily at the doorway. His hands were shaking, so he shoved them into the pockets of his jacket and leaned back in the chair. There were low muttered sounds in the hallway outside and he realized that the meeting had broken up. He was glad of it.

Mead popped his head into the office.

"Get your call okay?" he smiled.

"Yeah," said Hendricks.

"Nothing much happened after you left. The old man read over the decisions of the plans board—that's about all. You took notes, I expect."

"I made a list," said Hendricks. "Must have left it in the conference room—"

Mead held up a yellow pad with ruled blue lines. "This it?" he grinned.

"Yes, that's it," said Hendricks. He caught the pad from Mead's easy toss. "Thanks a lot, Ralph."

"Nice-looking notes," said Mead, hanging around. Hendricks pretended that he was immersed in the long lines of script on the pad. "Nice and neat," said Mead. "You ought to be in Research, Bill."

"I have to take notes. Got a lousy memory."

"Yeah," Mead said. There was a vacant sort of satisfaction in his round face, and he stood in the doorway, rolling back and forth on the balls of his feet. What was he waiting for? Hendricks thought angrily.

"Drink tonight, Bill?" Mead said finally. "Harry, Lew, and I are going downstairs. Join us?"

Hendricks shook his head. "No, thanks. Got some things to clear up before I go home. This bakery account of mine is in one hell of a mess."

"Sure," said Mead. "Okay, Bill. See you Monday, right?"

"Right," said Hendricks.

He sighed when the Research man was out of sight and then, as if to justify the refusal he had given him, buried himself in his notes.

The minutes ticked past five, and the office sounds slowly diminished. The secretaries bustled into their going-home costumes, their laughter shriller and gayer than usual, for this was Friday afternoon. There was the inevitable jocularity at the elevators, and the isolated laughter of a small after-hours group in some cubicle on the floor. Then they too went their way and the cushioned silence so peculiar to a deserted skyscraper office surrounded Bill Hendricks as he sat in his chair, staring blankly at his own tight scrawls on the yellow pad.

He mused that way for some ten minutes, then snapped out of it with a start. He looked at the pad again, and the detailed instructions he had noted during the conference now seemed strangely meaningless and unimportant. He dropped the pad and pushed it away from him loathingly. Then he took a key from the top drawer and unlocked the deep file drawer to the bottom left of his desk.

A thin manila folder was all that was in the drawer, and its contents were still another kind of notes.

Bill Hendricks read them over with grim pleasure.

1. Nagging at me every damn night.
2. Spending $500 on a coat she didn't need.
3. Calling me a liar in front of my friends.
4. Throwing out a good set of golf clubs.
5. Ripping my best sports shirt, deliberately.
6. Keeping the car home so I have to walk or take a taxi from the station.
7. Refusing to go wherever *I* want to go every damn vacation.
8. Making me sleep in the living room whenever she gets mad.
9. Insulting my secretary.
10. Calling Joe Dennis a windbag loud enough for him to hear.
11. Never making my breakfast in the morning.
12. Always hiding the damn ashtrays.
13. Calling my family a bunch of leeches.
14. Slapping me in the face when I told her the truth about herself.
15. Using my toilet things without permission.
16. Never giving a damn about my clothes—too much starch in the shirts, holes in the socks and underwear.
17. Acting like a damn fool at important business parties.

He came to the last notation and his nostrils flared. Then he picked up his ballpoint pen and made an addition to the list.

18. Always calling me up at the worst possible times with phony urgent messages.

He read the list through once more, satisfied at its increasing length. Then he carefully replaced the sheet in the manila folder, returned both to the file drawer, locked it, and put the key back where it belonged.

Then he went home.

"Bill?"

"Later," he said. He went past the living room and up the stairway to the bedroom. There had been a glass in his wife's hand—he had not missed that. Drinking, of course. That was something else. She could really pour that stuff down. He wouldn't be surprised if she lowered the bourbon a good three inches every day he was away at work. That's Number 19, he told himself with sardonic smugness.

He went into the bedroom.

"Twenty," he said aloud, looking around the untidy room. *Her* clothes, mostly; some of his, of course, but whose job was that? It was the least she could do. What else did she have to do all day?

He picked up some kind of lacy underthing from the floor and slammed it onto a chair. He picked up a crumpled covey of facial tissues and threw them into the narrow wastebasket. He lifted up a pair of his trousers, whipped the belt out from the loops, and hung them up in the closet. Then he took off his shirt, rolled it into a ball, and flung it onto the chair that held her lingerie.

He took a heavyweight wool shirt from his drawer and slowly put it on. Then he remembered the gun and dug through the pile of clothing to see if the box was still there. It was there, of course, tightly sealed with strips of Scotch tape.

"I thought you said you weren't coming home," Karen accused as he came down the stairs.

"I changed my mind," he said.

"Don't expect any dinner—I took you at your word."

He dropped heavily into an armchair and picked up the evening paper from the table alongside. "I had a bite at The Shack," he said.

"Fried food?" She put down her glass and it rang on the marble top of the coffee table. "Fried potatoes and gravy and things?"

"Yes, fried potatoes and things!" He rattled the paper in annoyance.

"Well, it's your stomach," she said with a shrug. "I'd offer you a drink, but I suppose that would be more than that colon of yours could stand right now."

"Worry about your own colon," he said savagely over the top of the paper. "I notice you don't spare it any alcohol!"

"Well, well! *Now* what are we getting at?"

"You know damn well what," he said, the words boiling slowly out of his mouth. "You can really knock hell out of a bottle of bourbon these days, can't you? It's the big suburban hobby now, bunch of the girls getting nice and tight while hubby's at work—"

"Bill!"

He dropped the paper to the floor. "Don't give me that outraged innocence routine," he fumed. "Do you think I'm blind? You can tip a jug with the best of 'em, kid, and I know it!"

"Now we're *really* feeling guilty, aren't we?" Karen said. "What's the matter, dear? Had a tough day? Or did you have a fight with that honey-dripping secretary of yours?"

"Damn it to—"

"Oh, don't explode for my benefit!" she said. "Keep it under control, sweetie. If I had only one eye and three pints of bourbon in the bargain I could see what's going on between you and that mealy-mouthed—"

"That's enough!"

"Sure, it's enough!" she shouted. "I think it's enough and plenty! Now you come home and want Faithful Annie to trot out the pipe and slippers and drink her Ovaltine like a good little girl. Well, Faithful Annie's good and sick of it, let me tell you!" She picked up her glass and swallowed the remains of her drink.

Hendricks stood up.

"Where are you going?"

"Upstairs," he said quietly. "I'll be right back."

He went up the stairs deliberately. In the bedroom, he went straight to his shirt drawer and opened it. He lifted out the folded shirts carefully and put them on the bed. Then he took out the tightly wrapped package in the rear of the drawer and brought it with him to Karen's dressing table.

He fumbled with the Scotch tape until he snapped one of his fingernails on the rim of the box. He swore softly, put the box on the table, and went looking for a pair of scissors.

He couldn't locate them, nor anything else with a sharp enough edge. He tried one of his wife's nail files on the box but it didn't do the trick.

"Damn!" he said to himself.

He went through all the drawers now, looking for some sort of tool to get to the weapon cozily nestling in its container. He was careless about the search, strewing the jumbled contents of his wife's bureau and vanity table all around the bedroom. It didn't matter now, he told himself. In fact, it would be helpful when he told the police about the sudden entrance of the burglar, the hoodlum who had held him at bay and killed his poor Karen.

He cursed so loudly at his fruitless hunt that he was afraid his wife would hear him.

Then he spotted Karen's sewing basket, a floral-decorated straw bag he had given her on some long-forgotten occasion. He went to it quickly and turned it upside down, spilling the contents on the rug.

A spool of thread, a thimble, a tape measure, a small revolver, and a piece of folded paper had dropped out and fallen to the floor.

He picked up the paper first, unfolded it, and read:
1. Never talking to me when he gets home at night.
2. Carrying on with his secretary.
3. Never paying any attention to me at parties.
4. Never letting me . . .

Janet Green

The Tallest Man in the World

I gave up the idea of sleep and lay waiting for the dawn. Night showed black through a chink in the heavy hotel curtains. When the black became opaque, I slipped out of bed, crossed to the window, pulled back the curtains, and watched the first light creep over the top of Edinburgh Castle and spread through the railings along Princes Street.

Then I saw it.

The tallest man in the world. Swinging from the lamppost, its coattails dancing in the wind; and in the distance Maxie running. He hardly seemed to touch the ground, he ran so fast.

I pulled trousers on over pajamas, grabbed my topcoat, and raced down the well of the stairs. Round and round and out of the hotel.

I had to catch Maxie.

As I pelted across the tramlines, my mind went back to the beginning. Open at the Music Hall in Birmingham, close at the Alhambra in Edinburgh, and in between a long string of rich dates ...

Big Maxie was flying in from Stockholm with the six Dwarfs. I remembered the morning well. A clear bright day and my heart so light as I drove the big man's Rolls to the airport. The Indian summer we had been so grateful for had tempted Papa Gaudin to keep his circus playing four more weeks and Maxie was booked to open at the Music Hall in Birmingham on the following night without his usual vacation.

I hoped he would like the supporting bill. The dates I knew would please him. All short journeys and top capacities. Maxie was never happy when the Dwarfs spent their Sundays in the car. He liked the little men to be in the new town for lunch so that they could see and be seen. The Dwarfs loved admiration, and Maxie would laugh and encourage them to strut and posture for it wherever they went. He had loved the Dwarfs as if they were his children since he first met them just after the war as he was making his way from Vilna across war-wrecked Europe to Paris, where Papa Gaudin was getting the Big Top out of mothballs.

At Dusseldorf they did not like Maxie's papers and flung him into a DP camp. For three days he tried to bang his way out, but could find nobody with the time to listen to him or the authority to help him. He has told me since that he never felt so frustrated and helpless in all his life.

Coming from one more futile attempt to get some sense out of the overworked officials, he walked beside the barbed wire and looked out on the world that had abandoned him. Suddenly a thick and nauseating smell offended his nostrils and Maxie knew the latrines were near.

Then he saw them. Behind the stinking sheds. Six Dwarfs poised in the shape of a pyramid.

He stood in the noisome shadows and watched. The formation broke and the Dwarfs turned somersaults, handsprings, and cartwheels, until they had placed themselves in the shape of a new pyramid, working all the time with deftness and precision. Maxie knew that he was in the presence of performers akin to himself and felt like the man lost in a strange country who suddenly hears his own language spoken. Not till the Dwarfs stopped and left the place did Maxie's nostrils once again complain.

Each day for a week he came back. The six Dwarfs were always there—a bunch of bedraggled little men rehearsing with an indomitable belief in their future. Maxie knew that as long as he was in that camp of forgotten people, the courage they showed would draw him to their side like a magnet.

On the eighth day Maxie saw an official attempt to move them away and heard the myopic one in the horn-rimmed spectacles whom the others called Spiro protest, saying in French that he had found the only place in the camp where they could rehearse their act without fear of disturbance or interruption. Nobody, the little man insisted, wanted to come to the corner behind the latrines. The harassed, overworked official, tired no doubt of endless questions and complaints in so many different languages, gave Spiro a push and the Dwarf sprawled on the ground; then the official felt himself lifted in the air by a massive hand that held him by the collar of his shirt, while a great blond Giant said in Polish, "They are performers. They must rehearse."

I imagined how, when Maxie released him, the official would go—quickly.

The Dwarfs saw Maxie pick up Spiro and, sitting him on his wide hand to bring him level with his face, look at him carefully, toss him

THE TALLEST MAN IN THE WORLD 145

high in the air, then catch him in his arms like a ball. And the Giant laughed. A deep, warm laugh that told the Dwarfs he was their ally.

Spiro saw the possibilities at once. He was an erudite little man and, of course, he had read Swift. He told Maxie the story of Gulliver's Travels and together they worked out the details of a new act.

Maxie and the Dwarfs rehearsed every day all the hours that it was light until they reached perfection; then they waited for a night without a moon, and went under the barbed wire.

Maxie found Papa Gaudin at Liège.

The old French showman has never tired of telling how they came, walking into the center of the Big Top as he was rehearsing the Liberty horses. Maxie, with all six Dwarfs on his shoulders, in his arms, all over him. Papa Gaudin embraced Maxie, who was the best and bravest Strong Man he knew, and the little men dropped to the ring, where they waited. The Dwarfs knew they were safe. Spiro had told them that Maxie and they were one.

Papa Gaudin had learned to trust his instinct. He knew quality when he saw it. Maxie and the six Dwarfs went into the Circus that night. They were great then, but became greater during the succeeding months.

Maxie was the showman of the outfit. Spiro was the brains. I never saw that Dwarf without an armful of books. When he stood by himself and you shut your eyes to his puniness, he looked like a professor in his well worn Norfolk jacket. He had great knowledge and lost no opportunity to air it. I never trusted Spiro. I was repelled by him the first day we met. I resented the way he always behaved like a full-sized man. I like a Dwarf to stay a Dwarf . . .

As the airport came in sight, I drove past an advertising billboard. A comely blonde testified that somebody's toothpaste could be relied upon to give me that winning smile. I cursed the lady for reminding me of Del Roy and her trapeze act, then quickly put on armor against the thought. I had not forgotten Spiro's ban on acrobats of any kind, but when Frankie Diamond's troupe split up I saw the chance to snatch his magnificent itinerary of dates. I was forced to take his bill as it stood and that included one trapeze performer. I told myself that Spiro would have to swallow Del Roy. That string of plum dates would surely sweeten the mouthful.

I had the photographers waiting when the plane touched down.

Maxie came out onto the steps with the Dwarfs, who hardly had time to see the cameras before they climbed onto his shoulders and from there made a lineup on the fuselage. I hated to see them preen themselves, busily tightening the belts of their camel's-hair coats and fingering the snapbrims of their Tyrolean hats. They dressed like Maxie right down to their pigskin gloves and smart buckskin shoes.

I admitted to myself that it was good showmanship, with Maxie pretending he did not know where they had gone. The big blond Giant made a fool of by the tiny men. The movie cameras took it all in and I was grateful. No act is too big to turn its back on that kind of publicity.

When Maxie saw me he waved and a grin spread over his face. I always found time to meet Maxie myself. In summer's sun, winter's frost, whether it was plane, train, or boat, I was there; yet he never failed to look surprised and grateful because I had come to meet him.

I was happy that day as I walked quickly to greet the big man. To be with Maxie was like standing on a rock in front of the sea getting a good blow after being holed up in a room for a year with no ventilation. I loved the look of Maxie. He was huge and well set in legs, body, and arms. His golden hair grew in tight, defiant curls close to his head. His eyes were gray and laughing. Maxie was full of good ways and had no evil in him. No, not any.

Together we got the six Dwarfs through Customs. The cameras followed all the way. Spiro gave his usual interview in impeccable English. He had a great line—the pocket acrobat who understood Joyce and Bernard Shaw. When Maxie thought that Spiro had said enough, he put his hand gently on the Dwarf's shoulder. Spiro stopped as soon as he felt the kindly pressure. He appeared to be devoted to Maxie, but I was never without the feeling that one day I would find Spiro's knife between those massive shoulder blades.

I was wrong about Spiro. He did love Maxie. Simply and completely.

When we drove out of the airport, Maxie was at the wheel. I sat beside him and the Dwarfs were in the back. As we passed the billboard advertising the blonde's teeth, they almost bit me. I thought of Del Roy and told Maxie at once that the new bill I had taken over for him opened with a trapeze act. I felt Spiro's garlic-laden breath on the back of my neck and hastened to explain why it had been impossible to drop Del Roy. Maxie nodded, satisfied, and

I heard Spiro talking to the Dwarfs in some language they all understood.

I was never without an uncanny feeling about those Dwarfs. They seemed like one entity, with Spiro as the head and the others the body. That was how I always thought of them—Spiro and the Body.

I smelled the garlic again and knew that Spiro was back of my neck. "As long as the act is up to standard, we're happy," he said.

I felt the garlic recede and was happy myself.

As soon as we left Uxbridge behind us, Maxie pulled the Rolls up under the shade of a tree and asked Spiro for the nuts. I never knew what was coming next with Maxie but was prepared for anything.

He put his hand in his pocket and brought out two little furry creatures, placing them on his blue-silk handkerchief. I thought they were moles, till Maxie said softly, "Golden hamsters. Aren't they pretty?"

Spiro dropped a small packet of nuts into Maxie's lap and the big man fed the tiny animals. They filled their little cheeks till they bulged and their bright eyes shone.

Maxie laughed and laughed. The Dwarfs delighted in his happiness.

When the golden hamsters bulged enough, Maxie put them back in his pocket. I turned and looked inquiringly at Spiro.

"Maxie thought their case was too small," he said.

"A nasty fine if you'd been caught smuggling those things through," I told Maxie.

"We'll get a cage for them in the next town." He smiled.

After we bought the cage and the golden hamsters were bedded down, Maxie began to sing a lewd French number that I always thought of as his song. He would render it in all sorts of languages, as the mood took him. The Dwarfs joined in. They knew the tune and the language did not matter to them. The effect was Babel.

The song saw us all the way to Birmingham. As we waited sometimes for the traffic lights to change, I could see how the Dwarfs amused the occupants of other cars. Only once a man and a woman watched gravely, and I knew that someone else felt as I did. Dwarfs should be quiet and never draw attention to themselves—the way a two-tongued man should hide his head.

I buried the thought and became glad that Maxie was having fun. I knew he would be in a high state of nerves by the time he opened on the following night. It was always the same when he brought the act from the tent to the stage; and that year there had been no interim of rest.

It turned out that I was right. Maxie was so nervous that he stayed in his dressing room till Spiro called him.

Spiro never trusted callboys. Come to that, Spiro never trusted anybody.

Once again Maxie and the six Dwarfs were a smash hit. I watched the act from the back of the circle, and listening to the applause and laughter around me felt guilty because I alone seemed to find the Dwarfs repugnant. Spiders and snakes do it to some people; with me it's Dwarfs.

I never told Maxie how I felt about his "children" and would shake hands all round as if they were my oldest and dearest friends. My bonhomie was so convincing that they were very fond of me and liked to touch me. Imagine how it would feel to a man who hated spiders to have one stroke his cheek.

I know my business though. I give the customers what they want. It would be all the same to me if they plumped for a couple of talking pythons.

The mise-en-scène against which Maxie and the Dwarfs performed was enchanting: a Lilliputian town square, with Maxie towering above the rooftops and the Dwarfs popping in and out of windows and doors. Two of the little men, both exactly alike, did an impossible tumbling trick. Actually they were not even related. Born at opposite ends of Europe, I believe. But people loved the idea of twin Dwarfs and would talk about it in the bar afterwards, making all sorts of indecent conjectures. Of course it was Spiro who saw to it that they both dyed their hair the identical shade of fiery red.

The smallest Dwarf was a Spaniard. He played the trumpet, and at times I felt he could have topped the bill on his own. Spiro had him grow a Vandyke beard. Hair grows on their faces just the way it does on a full-sized man.

The one who wore the fez, a squat, swarthy Turk, running a little to fat, had the happy trick of throwing up no less than sixteen balls at one time. They dropped into pockets all over him—on his shoulders, on his heels, and on the inner sides of his sleeves—while the Turk stood quite still and did nothing. What a round of applause he won for himself! But I swear it was no bigger than the round that went to the thin, pale Dwarf from Lithuania who walked the tightrope and danced. He looked like something that came from under a mushroom, and Spiro permitted him a maximum weight. He was not allowed to go half an ounce over. Of course, ounces are pounds with those people. I used to feel sorry for the skinny little beggar when he was dieting. I once slipped him some fudge, but it was back in my briefcase the same night, and I knew that it was Spiro who had put it there.

Spiro made wisecracks and spun ropes that writhed like tiny snakes in his small fat hands. He also recited poetry. His "Once more unto the breach, dear friends" was quite a performance. It stopped the show, even on a Saturday night.

All that made it seem as if Maxie did nothing, but when you added the score it was everything.

The finale of their act was the Gulliver routine—the one they had worked out in the DP camp. It began with Spiro putting the lasso round Maxie; then all the Dwarfs, giggling and chattering, caught him in a net and brought him to the ground. From a diminutive house the Dwarfs brought multicolored staples, hammers, mallets, and tried to fix the big man to the stage. Suddenly there would be a great roll on the kettledrums, and the pinioned man would rise, pulling up the net with him and the Dwarfs with the net. Then Maxie started to turn. As he went faster and faster, the Dwarfs clung to the ends of the net and the mirrors which each held in his hand caught the lights and made a dazzling moving pattern over the house. It looked like an animated carousel at a fair, heightened by the specially orchestrated music which sounded like that of a calliope. The whole picture was breathtaking and the customers cheered. I stood up and cheered with them.

I had plenty to cheer about. I was Maxie's agent. I collected the ten percent.

Sometimes Maxie and the Dwarfs stayed in a hotel, sometimes in digs, but always together. In Birmingham they had wonderful rooms out at Edgbaston. We went back to a fantastic supper with everybody sitting in front of his favorite dish. The Dwarfs traveled with their own cushions which made us all level at the table. I used to think at times that Spiro seemed bigger than me. The Turk was particularly pleased that night for Maxie had found him some rosepetal jam to go with his yogurt. He ate it with enormous relish, till Spiro slapped his elbows off the table. Then he cried. Maxie took the Turk onto his knee, wiped the round black eyes with his own blue-silk handkerchief, and to cheer him up coaxed a song out of the melancholy Dwarf.

The Turk climbed to the top of a bookcase and sang Maxie's lewd

French number. I listened to the sweet, high treble voice and mused upon the cruelty of the Eastern races.

When Maxie was sure that the Turk was happy again, we played poker. The stakes were astronomical and the losses paid with IOUs, which were meticulously carried forward to the next game. Inside that tight little circle, Maxie and the Dwarfs had their own fiscal system. The real money was admirably looked after by Spiro. Their agreed intention was to retire one day to an orange farm in the South.

According to my calculations they could have bought three of those dream farms already, but I never went for that vision of the future. I knew that Maxie and the Dwarfs would go on trouping till the theatre fell in and the Big Top moldered into dust. And that meant forever.

My plan was to catch the midnight to London, but as usual I went on the early morning train at six o'clock.

Maxie sent me upstairs to wash Spiro's cigar smoke out of my hair and I came down to find him waiting for me in the hall, looking as fresh as if he had just awakened from eight hours of solid sleep.

When he put his arm round my shoulders and said, "Your props are in the car," I felt the warmth of his smile enwrap me like a mantle.

As we slipped through the front door, the first light of morning was breaking over the smoke-scarred Birmingham suburb. Outside the gate the Body jumped up and down behind Spiro, calling to Maxie and each other in half a dozen different lingos.

Spiro spoke my name, and I heard him say above the Babel, "Look, a new act for you. The tallest man in the world."

I did as the Dwarf bade me, and looking over the stunted privet hedge saw my coat hanging on a lamppost, its arms stuck through the crossbar and my hat crowning the top of the lamp. In front of the light was a roughly cut mask through which the still-burning bulbs marked the eyes and mouth.

I turned sharply to Maxie, who leaned against the door laughing, intending to say, "This is beyond a joke"; but he took off his own big camel's-hair coat and wrapped it warmly round me, saying, "Send it to me in a parcel—you'll miss another train if we stay to pull down the tallest man in the world." All my anger at the fate of my own brand-new coat evaporated.

In the car I settled myself beside Maxie, while Spiro and the Body climbed in behind us. Through the rear window I saw a diffident morning breeze gently stir the tails of my coat as the tallest man in the world leered after us. We were off to a great accompaniment, for the noise we had made woke every barking dog in the neighborhood.

I made the train as it moved out of the platform. For a while Maxie and the Dwarfs kept pace with my carriage. They pranced round his legs waving their farewells, and I saw that Maxie was enormously delighted with the antics of his children.

I meant to pick Maxie up in a month's time at Nottingham, but this time the week came and went and I could not get away. The few months before Christmas are always a busy time for me and that year I was having one hell of a job persuading my new comedy find to do a new routine.

About nine weeks went by before I saw Maxie again and during the whole time I never gave a thought to Del Roy.

The town was Liverpool. Maxie and the Dwarfs were ready at the airport with their usual boisterous welcome. I shook hands with the Body, pulled the ear of one, tweaked the nose of another, and bowed gravely to Spiro. I thought for a moment, before we all piled into the Rolls, that his myopic eyes behind the horn-rimmed spectacles seemed unusually preoccupied.

As Maxie swung the Rolls out of the airport, he looked at me affectionately and said unnecessarily, "You're in front tonight, of course."

"Yes—but there's an act I want to pick up at the Shakespeare first. But I'll be in for the second show."

"Well, don't run away afterwards. I've got a big surprise for you."

Maxie was smiling as he began to sing his song, but I was conscious at once that something was wrong, out of place. Then I got it. He was singing alone. The Dwarfs were silent.

We all lunched together at the Adelphi Hotel. There was plenty to talk about. I had booked the act with Papa Gaudin in Paris for Christmas and had started negotiations for a European tour in the spring. I was only mildly surprised when Maxie told me not to rush into anything.

"You never know what's going to turn up," he said, grinning across the table.

I saw Spiro watching him and a maggot of worry began to stir in my mind. Every now and then Maxie looked past us like a man searching for a familiar face. Suddenly he stood up and waved. I looked round. I was curious. Del Roy had come into the restaurant and was sitting alone at a table beneath the tall window. When I turned back, Spiro was looking at me. I raised my brows, but the Dwarf's expression remained blank and uninformative.

The hairs on the back of my neck began to tingle. Those hairs act like an alarm bell to me.

I was not surprised when Del Roy joined us for coffee, but I was astonished when Spiro rose at once, said he had a lot of reading to do, and left. The Body, of course, got up and followed him.

As I watched the Dwarfs file out of the restaurant, I put my hand to the back of my neck. The alarm bell was working overtime.

I must talk to Maxie, I noted anxiously. Those Dwarfs need coddling. And quick.

I looked at him. Maxie's whole attention was riveted on Del Roy. I suppose my interest must have penetrated, for he raised his head and invited me to drive to Chester. He accepted my answer without argument when I said I had a lot of sleep to catch up with, and they went for their drive without me.

As the Rolls spun away from the hotel, I heard Maxie's laugh cleanse the petrol-laden air, and saw the sudden flash of his blue-silk handkerchief as he remembered me and waved goodbye.

Then I looked for Spiro.

He was not in the hotel. I went down to the theatre. The dressing rooms were in darkness. I gathered my thoughts together and remembered all that reading he had to do. I knew at once where I would find Spiro.

When I reached the Public Library he was not there, but I did not anticipate a long wait. Spiro had said he wanted to read. I was sure the little man would appear.

Soon I saw his hat just above the counter and heard the librarian's friendly greeting. Spiro had been coming to these places for years and knew everybody by their Christian names. When he made his way toward the shelves marked *Biography,* I fell into step beside him. He did not look surprised to see me.

"What goes on?" I asked.

He put up his hand and took down a copy of the *Life of Napoleon.*

"The Corsican was five-foot-two," I said. "I'll tell you before you tell me."

Spiro smiled.

"I wish you liked me," he said. "I'm very attached to you."

For a moment I felt sorry for the agile mind imprisoned in the Dwarf's body. Then he laughed and the smell of garlic was suddenly strong. My old dislike enveloped me, and I spoke brusquely. "When did Maxie fall for Del Roy? What happened?"

The little man began to talk.

At first his voice was quiet and controlled, but by the time he came to the end of his account the Dwarf was sweating with anger and the smell of garlic was lost in the smell of Spiro.

The first night in Birmingham, Spiro related how he watched the whole bill through and got Maxie down to the wings to see Del Roy at the start of the second show. Maxie agreed with him that it was a trite little act and not up to their standard. He asked Spiro to bring Del Roy to his dressing room. But it was Spiro, sitting on the makeup bench, who spoke for Maxie.

"Your act is not good enough," Spiro said. "We are dropping you tonight. You will be paid as long as the tour lasts."

You'd have to do that, I thought. Del Roy's contract is as watertight as yours—then kicked myself for thinking like an agent. What was Del Roy to me?

Apparently Del Roy had broken down and cried. Spiro said contemptuously that she looked as if she had been standing in the rain.

I knew exactly what he meant. The thin, pretty-faced girl would have stood drooping in front of Maxie with her tatty Japanese kimono swinging open to reveal arms and legs like peach sticks. I envisaged her using every bit of waif appeal she had, straightening her child's shoulders as she looked bravely up at him to ask what she could do to make her act good enough to remain on the bill.

"I showed her the door," Spiro said. "I knew what was coming next. There was a stray dog in Madrid, a barefoot boy in Rome, et cetera, et cetera."

He shrugged wearily, took off his glasses, wiped them, and went on plaintively. "Almost every capital in Europe has a similar memory and some are not easy to clear up."

"What happened to the golden hamsters?" I asked.

"I found a home for them."

"Pity you couldn't have found a home for Del Roy."

Anger showed violently behind Spiro's thick glasses and I went on quickly, "What happened next?"

Spiro's narrative showed me vividly the picture of Del Roy's fragile figure hurrying along the corridor and up the stone dressing-room stairs to the fly floor, with Maxie watching in the open doorway behind her.

When he came back in, Maxie was pensive. Taking up a towel he had quickly rubbed his smooth brown flesh till it shone.

"We were too rough, Spiro," he had said. "That little girl needs help."

I groaned.

Spiro stood with his back against the books and sighed.

From Birmingham they had gone to Manchester. Although her part of the act was out, Del Roy traveled with the Company. She told the stage manager, a sentimental, impressionable guy, that she guessed she would stick around with the Crowd. She hadn't got a home, she couldn't play any other dates the way her contract was, and her rooms were booked everywhere, so what the hell else was she to do? The stage manager found the opportunity to tell Maxie that he was sorry for the kid and asked if it was okay for Del Roy to use the stage sometimes to keep in practice.

I looked at Spiro and realized that he had suddenly become excited. His small, fat hands were trembling and I thought I saw saliva on his pale red lips.

"Now, as you know," he said, his voice curiously high, "it's an understood thing that we have the stage every morning from eleven-thirty on."

I nodded. I knew Maxie's rule.

Spiro became very heated. "Well, when we came on the stage next day, Del Roy's trapeze was up and she was swinging from the bar. I was going to stop her, but Maxie held my arm."

The image of Maxie was clear to me; he was standing on the side of the stage in his rehearsal kit. Tight black gabardine trousers, nothing above, and Spiro beside him reaching only as high as his waistline.

The Dwarf said Del Roy pointed to the stage clock. The hands were at eleven. The stage carpenter came through the pass door.

"Who's been mucking this clock around?" he grumbled and put the hands forward to eleven-thirty.

"Del Roy, of course," I said.

Spiro spat.

Every morning after that, Del Roy was on the stage when they arrived. Directly she saw Maxie, she would call Props and begin to clear her trapeze. I knew without asking that she had persistently ignored the Dwarfs. Then one morning she fell from her top bar. Spiro said the girl was a hell of a way up and would surely have broken her back if Maxie had not been there to catch her. She begged for time to climb again; said it was the only way that she could regain her nerve.

Maxie lifted her to the rope and Del Roy swarmed rapidly up to swing herself into a sitting position on the top bar. Spiro said she looked like a skinny kid in her small silk briefs and vest.

Del Roy swung herself through a few simple exercises, then called suddenly, "Catch!"

Maxie looked up.

That time she fell deliberately and the Dwarfs saw him laugh before he caught and tossed her in the air like a ball. Then he lowered her gently to the stage.

Spiro stopped talking, took out his fine linen handkerchief with its elaborate monogram, and wiped his hands.

"There have been women before," I said, trying to comfort him.

"Not in the act," he answered.

I knew what Spiro meant.

"Now they rehearse every day," he said bitterly.

I was jerked into fresh attention—the Dwarf's voice was nearly a snarl.

"With what result?"

"We shall know tonight," he said crisply. "Maxie is going to show us all."

I whistled. I knew, if Maxie was ready for an exhibition, there must be something to see.

A librarian approached and told me to put out my cigarette. I stared at the fair young girl. I did not even know I had lit it. Spiro was very upset. He said that they liked people to observe the rules in places like the Public Library and added that he was so easily remembered because of his size. I felt that I had let him down and apologized.

"I'll wait for you outside," I said. "I want to smoke." I also wanted to get away from Spiro's smell.

The Dwarf came and stood on the broad top step outside the Public Library. I was two steps lower so that our faces were level. He passed me his morocco-leather cigar case and I helped myself. We lit the cigars slowly, correctly. Spiro had a fine taste in cigars—they were worth the attention. When the Dwarf's cigar was well alight, he took it out of his mouth and slowly savored the smoke.

"We have a good act," he said mildly. "We should not be happy if anything disturbed it."

Spiro then smiled grimly and went off.

I watched the little man cross the square that marks Liverpool's civic center to pass the near-black Ionic-pillared Town Hall, until he was lost in the crowds outside the Empire Theatre. Above his head I saw the week's bill and read the boldly printed words: *Maxie and the Dwarfs*. The title looked very permanent.

I walked toward the Mersey. Perhaps the wind on the top deck of the New Brighton ferryboat would blow the odor of Spiro out of my nostrils. I did not want to think about him anymore or make conjectures on the punishment he would decide to mete out to Del Roy.

Standing by the top rail of the ferryboat I looked across the water and pretended that I was fascinated by the traffic of the gray-green Mersey. I watched the forest of striped funnels staring over the tops of the bond sheds lining the docks, the tugs snorting indignantly at the head of their charges, the clean bright paint of the Isle of Man steamer gleaming in the winter sun, and the dark, dirty hulk of a merchantman slowly steaming to sea. The ferryboat cut across the merchantman's wake and written clearly in yellow letters along the ship's stern I read the name, *Neseta, Barcelona*.

The image of many different colored rats racing across a hotel bedroom in Barcelona filled my mind. I stood quite still and allowed the memory to grow.

Three years before, Maxie and the Dwarfs had made a short spring tour of the main Spanish towns. From Barcelona I received a letter written by a friend of mine who was on the bill, tipping me off that Sam Ellerman, the European end of a big American film agency, had been talking to Spiro. My friend did not know the outcome of their talks. On the principle that what is mine should remain mine, I flew to Barcelona.

The city was empty of Sam. There was a wild rumor around the bars that he had been chased out of his hotel by a plague of rainbow-colored rats—rats that somehow showed themselves only to Sam. I knew Ellerman well. He suffered from our occupational disease—ulcers. This meant that he was permanently on the wagon. I had an idea those rats were real.

I could not persuade Spiro to talk, although I stayed in Barcelona until the end of the week, when the Spanish tour was finished and we all took the train to Paris.

At the frontier the French people made a big business of looking through the luggage. I happened to be next to Spiro and as they searched his cases I saw several tins of luminous paint. I picked up one of them.

"Phosphorescent bills could be very effective," Spiro said blandly. I put down the paint.

I had some chocolate in my pocket. With it, I enticed the thin, pale Dwarf into the corridor of the train. He told me in French, a language that is almost my own, that Sam had made an offer for the Dwarfs to go to the Coast—that means Hollywood in our parlance—to make a series of comedy two-reelers at top pay. It was a long-term contract which did not include Maxie. Spiro had turned it down flat. I asked if Maxie knew why Sam had been in Barcelona, and the thin, pale Dwarf smiled before he shook his head. I thought the smile was very gentle. For a Dwarf.

Sam did not understand loyalty. He just raised the ante. Then Spiro set the rats on him. I asked the pallid little man how it was done and learned that Barcelona was the bearded Spaniard's hometown and he had hordes of relatives, among them an uncle in the rat-catching trade.

I could guess the rest. The Dwarf ate the chocolate, licked his fingers, and went back to the compartment. He was dirty eater and I was not surprised when Spiro brought him along immediately to the washroom, shaking his head reprovingly at me as they rocked past . . .

I turned on the deck of the ferryboat and put my face to the wind. Somehow I thought that it would take more than a troupe of colored rats to frighten Del Roy. Years of experience had taught me that the small slight ones you meet in show business are the toughest.

I got back to the Liverpool side in time to catch the act at the Shakespeare and leave quickly, hoping that the two fellows whose fooling was not good enough would never hear that I had been in front.

I walked round to the Empire and met the first show coming out. As I went through the stage door, Del Roy passed me.

Maxie was in his dressing room. The towel was extra busy and his golden-brown skin shone like satin.

"Anything good at the Shakespeare?" he asked.

I shrugged my disappointment.

"Cheer up," he smiled, "perhaps the next time you put your hand in the hat, you'll bring out the right number."

From the top of Maxie's wardrobe trunk the theatre cat demanded his attention and with cunning understanding he stroked behind her ears. The cat purred and rubbed her head against his hand. Maxie was delighted.

"Take care," I said. "She can scratch as well as purr."
But Maxie shook his head. "They never scratch me." He laughed.
I fortified myself in the bar for the rest of the evening and went to the back of the circle to see Maxie close the bill, with the alarm bell at the back of my neck well drowned in good Scotch whiskey.

When the last satisfied customer left the house, I made my way down to the empty stalls and saw that Maxie meant to do the thing in style. He had kept the full orchestra, the stage staff—the works.

Spiro and the Body filed into the second row of the stalls and I sat down about halfway back. I was irritated when the theatre manager and his wife came to sit just behind me. A nice woman but she had been a performer herself and would lean forward to reminisce.

The conductor came into the pit, raised his baton, and with the downbeat led the orchestra into a rousing overture. The houselights dimmed and I saw the glow of Spiro's cigar. Soon it became the focal point from which I could not look away.

The curtain rose and I was able to shift my gaze.

Draped in black-velvet tabs, the stage was completely blacked out except for a single spot shining on a silver bar twenty feet up. I realized that the borders had been raised as far as they would go and we were seeing a great deal more of the stage than was usually visible.

Maxie made his entrance from center back. Picked up in a pinpoint spot he walked slowly toward the footlights, rolling a silver stick over his shoulders and into his arms. Then he tossed it into the air, caught it on one arm, threw it up again, and caught it on the other. The thing was thick for a stick and gleamed like water in the moonlight.

The drums began to roll and a shaft of light shot across the stage. Maxie started to twirl round and round, holding the silver stick straight out from his body at arm's length. Each time the stick came into the shaft of light it flashed. Suddenly he released his hold and the stick shot across the stage, up the beam of light, and abruptly stopped as if it was suspended in midair. Then slowly it began to rise, twisting like a corkscrew, going higher and higher till it was level with the bar twenty feet up. Almost at once the stick was upright on the bar. The lights were clever—Del Roy must have put out her hands to catch the rope, but I never saw her move. It got me. I was impressed.

I saw the human silver stick shimmering on the bar and Maxie below on the stage. As he moved into the beam of light he was

THE TALLEST MAN IN THE WORLD

smiling. His golden hair shone. The human stick wavered on the bar, then balanced again. I looked up and down. Then up again. The drums stopped. Light poured suddenly from everywhere onto the silver stick.

"She's going to jump," I gasped, and did not know that I had spoken.

"She can't," said the manager's wife behind me. "There's no net."

The words were no sooner spoken than she screamed, for the silver stick had fallen from the bar and, falling, turned over and over.

Maxie was still smiling as he put out his arms and with no apparent effort caught the stick, twirled it round his shoulders, across and round again.

He was laughing when he brought the silver stick forward and bowed over it.

The orchestra went into a long chord and the curtains fell. I swear that all through the performance Del Roy never moved a limb. She *was* the silver stick.

Maxie came through the tabs and took the call. He had his hand on top of the stick as if he was leaning on it, then suddenly took his hand away. Del Roy dropped her arms, moved her legs, and was suddenly alive. They bowed to us and to each other as if the house was packed.

I stood up and shouted, "Well done!" Then I saw the glow of Spiro's cigar and knew that he was looking straight at me. I shrugged. How was I to know that Del Roy had so much to sell? Maxie and the Dwarfs had seemed the tops. Till then.

Maxie was waiting for me on the stage. I noted that even the stage cloth was made of black velvet and the rope up which Del Roy had twisted, of black woven silk. The girl was trying to scratch between her shoulder blades, but without effect since her hands were covered with black-velvet gloves. Maxie turned her round and with obvious familiarity scratched for her. I knew then she was his mistress.

As I stood beside them, I saw that Del Roy's boyish figure was sheathed in fine black velvet, with a wide ribbon of silver sequins running down the center front and back. On her head she wore a spun-glass silver wig. Even standing so close to her and with the harsh light shining above our heads, she bewitched me. I still saw her as the silver stick.

I could see that Maxie was bursting for my approbation. More than all the paying customers in the world he wanted me, his ten-percenter, to say the act was good.

I told Maxie the truth. The act was unique.

As I finished, I smelled garlic and turned to face Spiro with the Body in a row behind him. On behalf of the Dwarfs he offered formal congratulations. Maxie shook hands with all his children, then presented them formally to Del Roy. Spiro bowed and the thin, pretty girl smiled.

As she rubbed her head lightly against Maxie's arm, I thought of the theatre cat. When I heard her say, "If they come up one by one, I'll give all the mannikins a kiss," I looked at her hands to see if the claws were out. Pulling herself tight against Maxie, she added, "It will make each one feel a man for once."

Spiro stiffened and the bell at the back of my neck burst into a noisy carillon.

"We have no need of that act of civility," he said, bowed again, and led the Body off the stage.

Del Roy was quite sure of Maxie; but I saw that he looked troubled and seemed about to reprove her. Then the conductor and the theatre manager's wife interrupted with their effusive congratulations and the moment was lost.

I spoke on the telephone early next morning to London, with the result that Maxie and the Silver Stick were in the bill that very night. They closed the first half, leaving Maxie and the Dwarfs their usual spot.

I was certain that the customers would love the new act, but I must admit I was not quite prepared for the overwhelming reception it got. When the curtains fell on the broad Empire proscenium, there was absolute silence—as if the breath had been knocked right out of their bellies. Then it broke. Round after round of applause, backed by whistles, shouts, the stamping of feet, and here and there a program thrown into the air.

Maxie and the Silver Stick were not just a smash. They were a riot.

I think it was the emanation of sex that did it. The act was packed with the desire they felt for each other and their fulfillment of it. I knew that a gold mine was in my grasp, still I never thought of putting Del Roy under contract. We are an old-fashioned firm. My father always believed that a handshake was more binding than a dozen signatures on a management contract and during the twenty years that I have run the business since my father's retirement, I have never once regretted the old man's ruling.

I stayed with Maxie for a couple more days, then had to hurry over to Leeds before returning to London. When I did get back to my office, the offers had begun to roll in, and I was surprised at what a popular fellow I had become. It looked as if I would not need to buy a lunch for myself for months to come.

I decided to let things ride. There was no hurry. Maxie was booked with the Dwarfs in Paris for Christmas with Papa Gaudin. While he was there I would sift the offers and take the best for the New Year.

I had only been back in London ten days when Spiro called me from Edinburgh. The time was three o'clock in the morning. I knew who it was because the charges were reversed. I started to tell him that I had been watching a new Hungarian girl I had brought over, not bad—when Spiro interrupted urgently.

I listened to two sentences and knew I must catch the first train.

Arriving in Edinburgh at about five o'clock on the afternoon of the following day, I saw Spiro on the platform. He looked pale and by the time we reached the Caledonian Hotel I felt pale.

The first person we saw as we entered the foyer was Sam Ellerman.

"Hello there," he called.

I greeted him politely but did not stay to talk. Spiro and I had a lot of conferring to do and I was anxious to get upstairs where we could do it in peace.

I let the Dwarf talk without a break. This time he had me so worried I did not even smell the garlic.

Sam had come into town the previous afternoon and had made an offer between shows. I waited for Spiro to tell me the gist of it. Sam wanted Maxie to do a coast-to-coast tour in America, starting immediately and ending at the New York Palace. Del Roy, determined to go, was urging Maxie to break his Christmas contract with Papa Gaudin.

I looked at Spiro and raised my brows questioningly.

"The offer does not include us," he said quietly.

I felt cold. I knew the Silver Stick was good, but had never visualized Maxie without the Dwarfs. To me it would be like dropping half of himself if he went to the States and left them behind.

I said, "But Papa Gaudin. Maxie can't let him down."

"It is the woman." Spiro shrugged. "He is bemused."

I knew then that I should have forgotten my father's principles and put them all under contract.

"I'll talk to Maxie," I said.

"Not till after the second show," Spiro ordered. "Maxie is always very nervous with the Stick. She is temperamental."

I believed him. I knew how tricky those skinny little tramps could be once they'd felt the first feather of success.

I saw Maxie at supper. The Dwarfs and Del Roy were all at the table with him.

Sam joined us. I was not sure why till he said, "I'm looking after this little lady's interests from now on." Then he patted Del Roy's knee, and added, "Of course, Maxie's still your boy."

When I looked at Maxie he flushed and stared over the waiter's head.

We got down to brass tacks quickly. I found that Del Roy had only succeeded in part. Maxie was determined to play Paris at Christmas for Papa Gaudin, but had agreed to go to the States afterward. He beamed suddenly as if he had thought of something pleasant, looked at the Dwarfs, and announced that it would be a wonderful holiday for them; then he added that they would be paid just the same as if they were still performing.

The big simpleton was so pleased and happy that I was sure he had no idea of the enormity of the insult he was heaping upon the Dwarfs. Nor had he realized what kind of a payoff it was for Del Roy. But the woman remembered. I could almost hear her purr, "Tit for tat, Mannikins." I looked at her as she sat still and smiling, and knew that she had engineered the whole deal.

"We are not willing for the act to be split up," Spiro said softly.

The ten eyes of the Body watched and waited. They did not understand the language that was being spoken, but Dwarfs are very susceptible to atmosphere and they knew that the air was full of dissension.

Sam moved impatiently in his seat and Maxie leaned across the table to speak to Spiro.

"But I want to give you a holiday," he said earnestly. "You all deserve it. Afterward we will be together again."

The Turk, who had been watching intently, suddenly asked a question in his shrill high voice. Spiro answered in a whisper and the Turk burst into tears as he sobbed out the answer to the other Dwarfs and pointed one of his pudgy fingers at Del Roy.

She looked at the Turk and laughed derisively.

The bearded Spaniard picked up a pitcher of water and flung it hard into Del Roy's face.

Spiro swept the Body out of the restaurant immediately. The Turk was still weeping and the others clustered round him, all trying to touch him. I thought it was because they wanted to comfort him.

Maxie, bewildered and distressed, looked after the Dwarfs and allowed Sam to help Del Roy dry herself.

I just sat and listened to my alarm bell. Then I heard Maxie voicing excuses for the Dwarfs in the manner of an indulgent father.

Del Roy did not say a word.

We had attracted too much attention to remain in the restaurant, so Maxie and I followed Sam, who took Del Roy upstairs. At the top of the stairs she turned and faced us, a few steps below her. When she finally spoke, her voice was very clear.

The issue was a simple one.

From that moment on it was either she or the Dwarfs.

She turned and went into a room a little way down the corridor. I heard the key click in the lock as she shut Maxie out.

He followed to the top of the stairs, then took a large bowl of flowers from a table and smashed it hard upon the floor. Afterward he strode down the wide sweep of stairs and out of the hotel. For the first time since the bearded Spaniard threw the water in Del Roy's face I saw that Maxie looked intensely angry.

As I turned to run after Maxie, I heard a movement and looked up to see the Dwarfs. All six of them. They were standing in a row on the landing above, peering through the balustrade. The Turk was still sniveling.

I raised my hands, then dropped them helplessly. Spiro copied the gesture and I felt a sudden camaraderie between myself and him.

"We shall keep the act together," he said softly. I knew he meant to comfort me.

Spiro led the Body up some more stairs and out of sight. I heard the Turk's high thin voice wailing, then that too died away.

I shrugged and went to find Maxie.

Walking the hard old streets of Edinburgh, I felt cobblestones under my feet and steps and tramlines, and all the time I was conscious of the dark hump of the Castle brooding over me.

I never found Maxie.

Returning wearily to the hotel I observed that all the lights were out except for the half-lit chandelier above the hall. Passing slowly through the shadows I climbed the stairs to my room.

Spiro was sitting on my bed.

Heck, I thought, haven't I earned my ten percent tonight?

"You can sleep now," he said. "I've fixed it. I found a solution."

The Dwarf looked very tired. I picked him up and stood him on the floor. He blinked at me from behind misty glasses, seemed about to say something more, then shook his head and went away.

I knew why Spiro was sad; he was a realist; he understood that the Dwarfs had to give up Maxie.

In spite of the little man's reassurances, sleep avoided me.

I went to Maxie's room once or twice but he had not returned. I passed Del Roy's room and saw that her door was slightly open. I guessed that she had left it that way to let Maxie know he was forgiven.

I finally gave up the idea of sleep and lay waiting for the dawn . . .

By the time I reached the lamppost, Maxie was tearing down the tallest man in the world. The woman's head wobbled on her shoulders and the black-silk rope dangled from her neck.

Maxie was weeping.

He turned and moved with even steps along deserted Princes Street, carrying Del Roy's body carefully in his arms. I kept up with his long strides, but Maxie did not look at me or speak.

At the police station above Waverley he stopped and went in. I followed.

It was not until I sat quietly with Sam much, much later that I was able to put things in their proper order. Sam helped me to talk. Without his kindness I should have gone crazy.

When I had followed Maxie along Edinburgh's famous street I was sure he was crying for the Silver Stick; but it was not so—Maxie's tears were for his children.

He stood in front of the desk in the police station and said quietly, "I did it. I killed her." Then like a temple offering he laid the body before the astonished police sergeant.

Del Roy looked thinner and smaller in death than she ever had in life.

Two policemen came and took Maxie away. They were sure he was mad.

I begged them not to let him speak to anyone until I had found a lawyer; then I went straight back to Spiro.

The Dwarf was asleep. I shook him and woke him and told him what had happened.

He sat up, listened, and gave me instructions. I obeyed at once, pulling the telephone toward me.

While I was locating the best lawyer in Edinburgh, Spiro dressed and went out of the room.

I arranged to meet the lawyer at the police station above Waverley, put down the receiver, and turned.

The Dwarfs were standing in a row before me. They were all washed and dressed, with their pigskin gloves on their hands, their buckskin shoes on their feet, and their camel's-hair coats tightly belted.

Spiro was pale and his skin glistened.

"They did it," he said. "I shall take them down to the police station and we shall confess."

I looked from one small face to the other. When I came to the Turk he pouted and looked at his feet. I stood up and led them out of the hotel. They followed me like a crocodile of obedient children.

The Dwarfs confessed. They confessed in every conceivable language.

The police checked their story. At one point it looked as if it would hold up. Till the night waiter at the hotel remembered seeing Spiro leave my room at the exact time the MO set for Del Roy's death. She was still warm when he examined the body and he was able to place the time within ten minutes.

That ruled out Spiro. And nobody believed the Body could have acted without its Head.

A policeman on his beat saw Maxie outside the stage door of the theatre, gazing fixedly at the bill, three-quarters of an hour before Del Roy was hanged. They found the broken bowl outside her door, his blue-silk handkerchief on the floor of her room, his fingerprints on the locket that hung round her neck; so fact after fact began to lend substance to Maxie's repeated statement that he alone was responsible for Del Roy's death.

I begged the lawyer to arrange for Spiro and me to see him.

Maxie was gentle, friendly, and peaceful—but we could not move him. Spiro pleaded and argued, got down on his pudgy knees; but Maxie only lifted him up and stood him on the table so that their faces were level, then reminded Spiro of his duty to the Body.

"Go back, my friend," he said, his big hand resting gently on Spiro's shoulder. "See that my children are safe. Do not desert them as I did. Remember, they break what they do not understand. Their crime is my sin—I forsook them."

They made us leave and I took Spiro back to the hotel.

He collapsed. I held him in my arms and forgot he was a Dwarf.

I listened as he sobbed out his story of the night's happenings.

Spiro said that when he took the Dwarfs upstairs, he told them that they must let Maxie go without a struggle. He explained to the Body that it would only be for a little while. Maxie would grow tired of the woman—just as he had of the lame dog in Madrid, the barefoot boy in Rome, and the golden hamsters in Birmingham. Then Maxie would come back to them and all would be as it was before.

Spiro was right, of course. Maxie would have come back eventually to his children.

Spiro said over and over again that the Body had agreed with him; otherwise he would not have left them.

"The Turk as well?" I asked.

Then Spiro beat his head with his two small fists. He had overlooked the Turk who was the most destructive child of all.

I imagined how the Turk would have chattered as he led the others to the theatre to drag down the woman's rope, then back to the hotel and up to her room and to put it round her neck and pull it tight.

Spiro described how they carried Del Roy down the fire escape and made a ladder of their own bodies round the lamppost, how they pulled her up to become the tallest man in the world.

Maxie had the best lawyer that Spiro could retain. I hired a leading psychiatrist who fought a two-day battle with the prosecutor and won.

Maxie went to Broadmoor.

Once a year I see him and we talk about the orange farm where the Dwarfs are waiting.

When they let Maxie out, I shall take him South. I hope he will be in time. Dwarfs do not make old bones.

I am sure of Spiro. His love will keep him alive.

I spent two weeks with them last year. I no longer feel any repugnance for the Dwarfs. They are heartbroken children and Spiro is my friend.

"Q"

Brian Garfield
Trust Charlie

I said, "Either cover up that mirror or let's meet somewhere else."

Rice showed me his surprise, then pained impatience. "For Pete's sake, Charlie. It's an ordinary hotel room. Booked at random."

"I'm still alive after all these years because I'm a practicing paranoid, all right?"

"For Pete's sake."

But we went down to the lobby and outside into the African sun, both of us in shirtsleeves against the heat. Rice sneered at me.

We walked past a rank of ten-year-old taxis. At the open stalls vendors were selling passion fruit and mangoes and coconuts and what-have-you, all of it clustered with flies. We crossed the central square, dodging a spotty traffic of cars and trucks and sagging overcrowded buses; an armored personnel carrier growled past carrying a dozen soldiers who held automatic rifles in casual positions. Two of the soldiers were laughing. Rice glanced up at the statue of the country's president and his sneer seemed to droop. Pedestrians moved lazily through the noxious smoke thrown around by the ill-maintained vehicles: it will be quite a while yet before Africa becomes pollution-conscious.

Rice led me through a narrow passage and we emerged at the corner of a stone customs house that one of the colonial powers must have built long ago. It might have been the Germans or the Portuguese or the English—several nations had claimed the colony at various times; the building itself was too drab to identify its architects. Its walls were overgrown with bougainvillea.

We found a wooden bench under a palm tree. The earth sloped down toward a stone retaining wall that held back the sea—we had a good view across the crescent of the harbor. Coastal freighters were anchored out, lighters plying to and from them; there was a fair crowd of Indian Ocean junks, square sails furled. The saltwater smell was rich, pungent with raw sewage. A few people ambled past us (no one moved quickly in that heat), most of them Africans, some in tribal gear and others in burnouses and Western clothes; the occasional Asian, the even rarer European in flowered prints or khakis or department-store poplin safari outfits.

Rice favored me with a sour dry gaze. "Will this suit you?" We seated ourselves.

Then he smiled, putting as many teeth into it as an alligator, and I felt alarm. Rice seldom smiles except when he is anticipating or savoring someone else's misery.

"I see you've enjoyed your vacation. You've put on at least forty pounds—anything less wouldn't be noticeable on you. I really can't afford to let you off the leash this way. You'll eat yourself to death."

I was overweight to be sure, and overage for that matter, but no more so than I'd been last time he'd seen me ten days earlier in Virginia. It was just his way of needling me. He never misses a chance. But that's fair because I loathe him too.

I said, "It was a good holiday until you cut it short. I've still got eleven days coming to me."

"Pull this off and you can have twelve."

"That tough, is it?"

"Tough? No, I wouldn't say it was tough. I'd say it's impossible."

"That's the kind I like." I grinned at him. "Anyway, it's desperate enough to get you out from behind your desk for the first time in I don't remember how long. What's the flap?"

He squirmed. "We're both on the line this time, I'm afraid."

"In other words you've dropped the ball and if I don't pick it up you'll be thrown out of the game. I've expected this, you know. Sooner or later you were destined to foul up. Have you ever considered washing cars for a living? You may just have enough talent for it."

"Let's save the catcalls for another time, Charlie. This is serious. It could mean my job—and you know what that would mean to you."

I did. If he goes I go. It's an agonizing symbiosis. He keeps his division and justifies his budget on the basis of results, and I'm the one who produces the results for him. If the job is too disagreeable for another division to tackle, then it's dropped in Rice's lap, and Rice in turn drops it in mine. Without me he's nothing; but I need the skunk because he's the only Section Chief who's willing to keep me on the payroll.

The computer kids try to retire me every thirty days because I'm too fat, I'm too old, I'm a disgrace to the corps, I don't fit the bright-young-man Ivy-League image the boys would like to project, I'm arrogant and conceited, and I'm a lousy team player. I am old-fashioned. I flatly refuse to kill people. In sum, I would never pass the entrance requirements and the whiz kids consider me an eyesore, a joke and an embarrassment. They want me out. If it weren't for

Rice I wouldn't have a job. I'd probably have to turn to crime to keep the juices flowing.

He said, "The flap is named August Brent. He's white—British parents but he was born here and he's a citizen, one of the few. Under the old colonial regime he had a key job in the colonial exchequer. Educated at the London School of Economics. Since independence he's been something like second-secretary to the Minister of Finance, some title like that—he's a white man, after all, so they couldn't very well give him a cabinet post; but the fact is, he's been running the ministry. Until the terror."

"And then?"

"When they started terrorizing the Asians and whites a few weeks ago he began to think about getting out. His mistake was in talking to too many people. The government got wind of his intentions to depart."

Rice looked out across the harbor. A graceful ketch was leaving under canvas; there was a racket of gulls. Soldiers in fatigues—armed—walked here and there by twos, quietly menacing.

Rice said, "He was packed and ready to leave. He went out to buy something—airsick pills, something innocuous like that. The soldiers hit his house while he was out. On his way home he spotted them and had time to get out of sight, but he knew the alarm was out, of course, and he made for the British Embassy but it was surrounded by troops. He backtracked and ended up on our doorstep. This was a week ago."

"The American Embassy?"

"Right. He demanded asylum. Threw himself on the Ambassador's mercy."

"Then they called you in."

Rice sighed. "I tried to bring him out, Charlie. I didn't want to disturb your vacation."

"Sure."

"I tried. I botched it. Is that blunt enough to satisfy you?"

"I'm tempted to gloat, sure enough."

"He's still there. In the Embassy. An acute embarrassment to everybody—British, Africans, Americans. I can't guess which of them hates him the most."

"Is he worth anything?"

"On the open market? Nothing. The inside secrets of the finances of a two-bit third-world nationlet—who cares? No. Two cents would buy him."

"Well, I guess the Ambassador must be a human being. Didn't want to throw the poor wretch to the wolves and all that. And anyhow we'd lose face if we reneged on the asylum. That it?"

"Acute embarrassment, yes. By protecting him we offend our African hosts; but by turning him loose we'd be welshing on a commitment. The British, of course, are laughing their heads off."

"Why do the Africans want him?"

"He betrayed them and he's getting away with it. They can't have that. They need to prove it's dangerous for anyone to cross them. Charlie, listen—all else aside, there's no doubt in my mind but that if we gave him back to the Africans he'd last forty-eight hours at the outside. An accident, of course."

The ketch dwindled toward the horizon, hoisting more sail. Rice said, "It's a dreary mess. The man's of no value, not even to himself. If we do get him out, what of it? At best he'll find some petty civil-service job in England. At worst he'll end up sleeping off cheap wine in alleys. Nobody cares about him—nobody needs to. He's a drip. But we have to try, don't we? We have to give him a chance."

"I suppose. How did you try to get him out?"

"Laundry van. They searched it with bayonets. Pricked him pretty good. In the arm. We managed to hustle him back inside. A couple of shots were fired—no injuries but the Africans were pretty sore about it. They've quadrupled the guard around the Embassy. It's not rifles now, it's machine guns and riot troops. They're searching every vehicle and pedestrian that comes out of the building. You couldn't get a mosquito out of there now. I confess it's my fault—the laundry truck was my idea. We had a private jet waiting. It's only five minutes' flight across the border."

"Is the plane still available?"

"Yes."

"Then all we have to do is get him to the plane and he's home free."

"Sure. But if we try again and fail we'll be laughingstocks from Johannesburg to Cairo. They'll tie a can to my tail. Yours too."

"Why not just leave him in there until the Africans find something else to occupy them?"

"No good. Every minute he remains in that building he's a thorn in both sides. He could become the flashpoint of a nasty international incident."

"So we have to get him out safely and soon."

"Soonest."

I stood up. "Let's have a look at the Embassy."

It had been Government House in colonial times, built in Cecil Rhodes' time—Empire, the raj, so forth. It had been built to impress. Now it had the slightly gone-to-seed look that creeps up on buildings in the tropics—a symptom of dampness and heat and termites: the lines seemed to sag and things had gone gray in patches and parts of it appeared to be crumbling; possibly it was a trick of the afternoon shadows.

It stood behind a high wrought-iron fence. There were palm trees, flame trees, acacias. Six Doric columns supported the high porte cochere. American flag. Four Marines on duty at the gate.

The African troops slouched at intervals outside the fence. I counted twenty-eight men, a half-track APC, two jeeps, and a radio truck; probably there were more behind the Embassy. I said drily to Rice, "I don't see anything those four Marines shouldn't be able to handle."

"These are hardly the days of the Panay in the Yangtze. But I'll admit there was something to gunboat diplomacy. Tell me, Charlie, did you actually serve under Teddy Roosevelt?"

"Why, I did my boot training under George Armstrong Custer."

"That's what I thought."

A dusty bus drew up and decanted a camera-bedecked crowd of tourists, most of them Japanese, a few Americans and Europeans. The tour guide was a little man in sunglasses with a gray beard that looked as if rats had slept in it. From the color of his nose he was a drinking man. He said in a piping German-accented voice, "This way please, follow me," and led the tourists past the watchful Marines into the Embassy grounds.

I was astonished. "They just come and go like that?"

"Nobody wants to stop them. The country needs tourists desperately and this building's a landmark. Bismarck and Queen Elizabeth slept in it. Not, I assume, on the same night. Actually she was Princess Elizabeth then. They—" he was talking about the tourists now "—only see the public rooms on the ground floor, of course. No access to working Embassy areas. You need a pass, ID, and an armed escort to get past the doors. I think the tour groups visit twice a day. I heard part of the old German's spiel this morning. He's pretty good—an old Africa hand, used to hunt rhino with Selous when he was a boy."

We walked inside and had to clear ourselves with the Marine

guard. The soldiers across the street watched balefully. We went through the main doors and passed through a series of interior checkpoints and finally entered a comfortable but not very large office whose occupant, like the government-green paint, was drab and in need of a touch-up. I knew him vaguely from past acquaintance: Oscar Claiborne, twenty-five-year man, passed over numerous times for promotion, assigned to one backwater job after another. Officially he was some variety of trade attaché; actually he was the Agency's stringer. One look at him and you yawned.

"Oscar, you know Charlie Dark."

We shook hands. Rice said to Oscar, "Sit-rep?" He deludes himself into thinking his clumsy use of jargon phrases will ingratiate him with the men in the field. Sit-rep, some years ago, used to be Agency lingo for Situation Report.

Oscar said, "No change. He's in his room lying on his side, nursing the bad arm. Taking things calmly enough, I'll give him that."

I said, "How bad is the bayonet injury?"

"Superficial. It's healing nicely." Oscar beamed at me. "Hey, old buddy, how're things goin'?"

"I'd like to talk to Brent," I said to Rice.

August Brent was undersized and sharp-featured and had a cockney look. A monk's fringe of limp sandy hair ran around the back of his bald cranium. His speech was rapid and clipped, the English of a man born in Africa. I liked him well enough; he was too ingratiating but I attributed that to his obvious fear. I was glad to see he wasn't sweating unduly. That symptom is almost impossible to disguise.

We talked for a bit—I wanted him to warm to me. I needed his trust because he'd only go through with it if he believed I could be depended on. The scheme had occurred to me immediately and it was considerably less complex than many I'd tried.

Oscar Claiborne interrupted us and took me outside into the hall. "Bad news, I'm afraid. They've issued a fugitive execution warrant on him."

"Meaning?"

"Meaning he can be shot on sight. Legally."

"And they call this a freedom-loving democracy." I went in search of Rice.

In the Embassy cafeteria Rice brooded at me, watching with a sneer while I put away a big meal. All he had was coffee and all he said was, "I'll hand them one thing—it's fantastic coffee."

"They grow it here, dunce. You ever eat a coffee bean fresh off the bush before the packagers have got their hands on it? Sweet and delicious—like a chocolate drop. You used to be an actor, didn't you?"

He was startled and then suspicious. "You've been prowling in the files."

"No. Actually I saw you on stage once. Nineteen thirty-eight, I think. *The Cat and the Canary.* Summer stock—Woods Hole, wasn't it? You weren't too awful."

"My God. I was seventeen years old. How in hell did you—?"

"Do you still remember anything about theatrics?"

"I was a kid. It was forty years ago."

"But you may remember makeup techniques."

"Maybe. A little. I haven't thought about it. You figure to disguise yourself, Charlie?" His lip curled into a disbelieving grin and he surveyed my girth ostentatiously. "Sure, a little pancake here and there and you could pass for Clint Eastwood." He broke into rude laughter.

I gave him time to subside and said calmly, "We'll move him out tomorrow afternoon. Have the plane ready to go any time after two o'clock."

"How?"

"The guided tour."

"You're nuts. They search every one of those tourists as they leave the Embassy."

"I know. I want you to send people out to the hotels. Find every tourist in town who bears any resemblance, no matter how superficial, to our man. Small thin guys. Ask them to join the bus tour tomorrow afternoon. Give them free tickets, invite them to the Ambassador's party, appeal to their patriotism—do anything, just get 'em on that bus. I want six or eight small thin white men in the group."

"It won't work, Charlie. They *know* him."

"It's a black country." I smiled at him. "All whites look alike in the sunshine. Tell 'em to wear hats."

"They've been rolling up sleeves looking for that bayonet scab."

"Trust me."

"Listen, if he gets killed while he's supposed to be under our protection—"

"Just get me the tourists," I said. "And trust me."

I went back to August Brent's room to bolster his spirits with a pep talk. At first he was alarmed when I described the scheme. It took a while to reassure him. "It's the Purloined Letter technique. The one thing to remember is not to be furtive. If you're bold enough they'll never spot you. Just don't act scared, all right?"

Rice and I took turns coaching him most of the evening. In the morning I booked a ticket on the bus tour and rode the entire route, learning more than I needed to know about that steamy corner of the world, and by one o'clock I was back in the cafeteria eating lunch. The beef in Africa is terrible but the fruits are delicious.

I had made a deal with the man whose place Brent would take on the bus tour. It was costing us a sizable chunk of the division's budget but Rice didn't balk; he had more than money on the line. When the German guide led the afternoon group into the Embassy's front hall we were ready. I spirited our volunteer away from the group into a private office; Brent exchanged clothes and documents with him; careful application of makeup and false hair and we were set to go. I hardly recognized Brent myself—wouldn't have, if I hadn't known who he was. We gave him a few words of cheer and sent him out to join the tour.

Rice came outside with me to watch. Sweat stood out on his forehead. The tour filed out toward the bus and Rice tried to suppress a groan. Out of the side of his mouth he said, "It hasn't got a prayer, you damn fool."

The tourists filed past the Marines and then the African soldiers moved in, intercepting the queue. Rice's handkerchief came out and while he scrubbed his face I said, "Look at something else, damn it. Don't look so interested."

The soldiers were examining the first tourist, removing his hat and then tugging at his hair. They tested his mustache and examined his face with belligerent suspicion. He was one of the half-dozen tourists Rice had recruited—roughly Brent's size and build—and the soldiers' eyes were narrowed with cruel determination. They knew what it would mean to them if they should let Brent slip through.

They rolled up both the man's sleeves—apparently they weren't sure whether Brent had been wounded in the right arm or the left.

They passed the man through, finally, and two women and a Japanese, and then they went to work on the next slight-built white tourist. Rice's breathing rasped against the damp silence. At the bus the tour guide helped the two women up the steps and stood aside by the bus door, bored, cleaning his fingernails, smiling with absent politeness as each tourist climbed aboard. The soldiers grudgingly let the second white through, glanced cursorily at an Oriental woman and two adolescents, and zeroed in on our third volunteer tourist.

Rice said under his breath, "I never should have let you talk me into this. We're not going to make it. We'll never get away with it, Charlie. You and I will spend the rest of our miserable careers in a basement decoding signals from Liechtenstein. They're bound to catch him— they can't help but spot him."

"Trust me."

Nine tourists to go; then eight . . .

When we were airborne I unbuckled my seat belt and went jauntily past Rice's sour face to where August Brent sat peeling the phony hair off his cheeks. He beamed up at me and then winced when the spirit gum tugged at his flesh. I said, "Any plans?"

"I've got a job waiting. Writing opinion columns for a chain of newspapers on African affairs."

"Sounds good." Better than I'd expected for him. I went forward and loomed over Rice, knowing it made him uncomfortable to think that one lurch of the plane could capsize my bulk into his lap. I said, "You need to remind yourself of this lesson from time to time. It always pays to trust old Charlie Dark."

"They *had* to tumble to it. I still don't understand it."

"All those look-alike tourists, all Brent's size—they had to assume he was one of those. I knew it wouldn't occur to them to take a close look at a man they'd seen twice a day for years. Magician's trick, you know—you make a quick move that draws the eye to your right hand while the left hand quietly pulls the switch in plain view, but the audience never sees it. Nobody was going to look twice at that gray-bearded German tour guide with the shiny red nose. Simply put chinwhiskers on Brent and paint his nose . . ." I showed him my grin and pretended to lurch toward him. Rice's flinch elicited my laugh. I tweaked his nose and waddled toward the galley to see what they had to eat.

"Q"

Michael Gilbert

Rough Justice

It was a fine morning in early October when Detective Inspector Patrick Petrella became Detective Chief Inspector Petrella. The promotion had been expected for some time, but it was nevertheless agreeable when a copy of District Orders and a friendly note of congratulation from Chief Superintendent Watterson arrived together on Petrella's desk in Patton Street Police Station.

He had been six months in Q Division and had been carrying out a mental stocktaking. A few successes, a lot of routine work done without discredit, one or two undoubted flops. One of the worst had been his failure to secure the conviction of Arthur Bond. If ever anyone should have been found guilty and jailed—

"A Mr. Bond asking for you," said Constable Lampier, projecting his untidy head of hair round the door. Lampier was the newest, youngest, least efficient, and most cheerful of the constables at Patton Street. Repeated orders from Sergeant Gwilliam to smarten himself up generally and for God's sake get his hair cut had had only a superficial effect. Like brushing a puppy which immediately goes out and chases a cat through a thorn bush.

"Mr. *Who?*"

"Bond. He's the geezer who keeps that garage. The one we didn't make it stick with that time—"

"All right, all right," said Petrella. "Don't let's conduct a postmortem. Just show him in."

Mr. Bond was not one of his favorite people. He had a big white face, a lower lip which turned down like the spout of a jug, and a voice which grated more when he tried to be friendly than when he was in his normal mood of oily arrogance. On this occasion he was making no attempt to be agreeable.

He said, "You've got no right to say the things you've been saying about me. I'm telling you, I'm not standing for it."

"If you'd explain what you're talking about."

"I'll explain, all right."

He opened his briefcase and threw a document onto the table. It was a photocopy, and to Petrella's astonishment it was a copy of a report he had himself written the day before.

He said, "Where on earth did you get that?"

"Never mind where I got it. You got no right to say those things."

"I do mind where you got it. And I insist on an explanation."

"If you want an explanation, ask the editor of the *Courier*."

"I certainly will ask him," said Petrella grimly, "and I hope he's got an explanation, because if he hasn't, he's going to be in trouble."

"The person who's going to be in trouble," said Mr. Bond, his lower lip quivering with some indefinable emotion, "is you. This is libelous. I've got my rights. I'm going to take this to court. You can't go around ruining people's characters. You know that."

"If you produce this document in court you realize you'll have to explain exactly how you got hold of it."

"No difficulty. The editor gave it to me."

"Then he'll have to explain."

"You don't seem to realize," snarled Mr. Bond, "it isn't him or me who's in trouble. It's you."

When he had gone Petrella telephoned Sergeant Gwilliam. He said, "Yesterday I sent a batch of confidentials by hand to Central. Find out who took them, and send him up."

Five minutes later the untidy topknot of Constable Lampier made a second appearance round his door.

"So it was you, was it?" said Petrella.

"That's right, sir."

"Then perhaps you'll explain how one of the documents got into the hands of the editor of the local paper."

"Lost the wallet, sir."

"You *lost* it?"

"Had it taken."

"Explain."

"Went up by tube. Victoria Line from Stockwell. The train was very crowded."

Petrella considered the matter. So far there was an element of plausibility in it. Junior constables on routine errands usually traveled by public transport and, as he knew himself, the Victoria Line could be crowded.

He said, "What actually happened?"

"I don't really know," said Lampier unhappily. "The car was full. I was standing near the door. I put the wallet down on the floor, by my foot. When I got to Victoria it was gone. I made a fuss, but it wasn't any use. Someone must have slid out with it the station before."

"Why didn't you report it?"

"I did, sir," Lampier told him. "That afternoon when I got back. To Sergeant Cove."

Petrella was on the point of telephoning for Sergeant Cove when he spotted the report. It was at the bottom of his In tray. He had been so pleased with reading about his own promotion that he hadn't got down to it.

The editor of the Stockwell and Clapham *Courier* was an elderly man with a face like a bloodhound's. Petrella knew him of old as a nurser of grudges and no friend of authority. The editor said, "The papers were dropped in here by hand this morning. We get a crowd of people in and out of the front office. No one noticed this one in particular. If they're yours you'd better have them."

He pushed across a bundle of papers. Petrella picked them up and looked through them.

As far as he could see they were all there. He said, "Was there a covering letter?"

"There was."

"May I see it?"

The editor hesitated. Then he said, "I don't see why not."

The letter was typewritten.

It said: "Dear Editor, I picked these up in a pub in Victoria Street this afternoon. I think they might interest you, particularly the stuff about Mr. Bond."

The note was unsigned.

"These are official documents," said Petrella. "You should have sent them straight back."

"How was I to know? They're not marked 'Top Secret.'"

"They're on official paper."

"Doesn't mean a thing. Anyone can get hold of notepaper."

"If you didn't know, why didn't you ring up and find out?"

"Why should I go out of my way to help the police? What have they ever done to help me?"

It was an outlook Petrella had heard expressed before, though never quite so baldly.

"All right," he said. "I agree there was no actual obligation on your part to do anything. So why did you have one particular document copied and sent to Mr. Bond?"

"Mr. Bond happens to be a friend of mine," said the editor. "I thought he ought to know about it . . ."

"And that's the whole story?" said Commander Abel.

"That's it, sir."

"Tell me about the previous case involving Bond."

"We'd heard a lot of talk about that particular garage. People put their cars in to have a tire changed and when they came to pick up the cars found the engine taken down and half a dozen other things apparently needing to be put right. And straight overcharging for any job that was done. It's difficult to prove.

"Then we thought we had got something that would stand up. This man, Mr. Ferris, put his car in for an M.O.T. test. When he went to fetch it he got a bill for nearly one hundred pounds. The point was, he'd just had the car overhauled by a garage in Southend, where he'd been staying. A complete five-thousand-mile test. He lodged an official complaint. We had to take it up."

"But you couldn't make it stick."

"No, sir."

"Why not?"

"Bond had it all lined up. One of his mechanics gave evidence. A real old villain. Blinded the bench with science. Our Mr. Fairbrother's a good magistrate, but he's not a motorist. Invoices for spare parts, all in order. Work sheets showing time spent on the overhaul. If a car came in for a test it had to be made roadworthy, didn't it? He'd told the gentleman that. The gentleman had agreed. The job had been done. Here was the evidence all in order."

"Then what went wrong?"

"The whole thing went wrong," said Petrella slowly. "The mechanic was in it, of course. He made up his own time sheets. The spare parts were bought for cash, from car breakers throughout the Borough—the sort of people who keep no records. The invoices themselves were dirty little scraps of paper. And I fancy most of them had been altered."

While Commander Abel was considering the matter the third man present spoke.

Mr. Samson was the senior legal adviser to the Metropolitan Police. He said, "I'm afraid there's no doubt about it. If Bond starts an action for libel, you've got something to answer."

"But surely," said Abel, "a report like this is privileged."

"Qualified privilege."

"What does that mean?"

"It can be set aside by proof of malice."

"And just how would they prove that?"

"They'd say that this officer was so annoyed about Bond getting off last time that he made entirely unjustified allegations against him in a report. If the report had never gone outside Scotland Yard, it wouldn't have mattered. But it did. It was published to third parties."

"That's something that wants looking into too," said Abel grimly.

"You're sure you did have that bag stolen?" said Petrella.

"Dead-sure, sir," said Lampier. "It happened just like I told you."

"You didn't leave it in a pub in Victoria Street?"

"Certainly not, sir."

Petrella examined the untidy young man critically. It was a long time since he had walked a beat himself. He tried to think himself back to those days. Lampier would have got to Victoria Station at about one o'clock. He probably hadn't had any lunch before he started. Would he have stopped at a pub for a drink and a sandwich? It was perfectly possible. Was Lampier a liar? That was possible too. Was it any use pressing him further? Petrella thought not. There came a moment when policemen had to believe one another.

Petrella said, "That's all right, Lampier. I just wanted to be clear about it."

Lampier, as he was going, stopped for a moment by the door and said, "Is anyone going to make trouble, sir, about that paper?"

"If they do, we'll get over it," said Petrella.

He managed to say it confidently, but it was a confidence he was far from feeling.

The next three months were not pleasant. Routine work continued. No one said anything. Even the Stockwell and Clapham *Courier* was muted. There was a brief paragraph to the effect that a local businessman, a Mr. Bond, had issued a writ claiming damages against a police officer.

Petrella had two more conferences with the legal Mr. Samson and could feel lapping around him, like the serpents about Laocoon, the strangling coils of the law. He knew enough about the processes of the civil courts that no public servant came entirely clean out of that particular mud bath.

It was toward the end of the third conference that something really alarming occurred. He began to detect, in the measured utterances of the lawyer, a suggestion that the matter might be settled out of court—a payment to solace Mr. Bond's wounded feelings and an apology in open court.

"My client wishes it to be understood that there is no truth whatever in the statements made about the plaintiff. The plaintiff is a man of excellent character." Like hell he was! Bond was a crook. A successful crook, but a crook nonetheless. The thought of crawling to him made Petrella wince.

"We're in a cleft stick," said Mr. Samson. "If we plead fair comment, we've got to show that what you said was fair. And that really means proving the charges against Bond, which was something you couldn't do in court, and certainly couldn't do now. We can run the defense of qualified privilege, but that lets them bring in all the arguments that you were prejudiced against Bond, that you didn't like him, and were angry that he'd got off."

"Which is true," said Petrella. "But it wasn't my reason for writing the report."

"If you're as candid as that when you give evidence," said Mr. Samson drily, "the case is lost before we begin."

It was a few days after this unhappy interview that Constable Lampier brought Nurse Fearing to see Petrella. She was a middle-aged woman with an air of professional competence about her that was explained when he recognized her as the most senior and respected of the local District Nurses. She said, "I rely on my little car, Inspector. If it goes wrong it has to be put right. I've been driving for forty years. I know a lot about cars, and I know that this garage swindled me. The man must be brought to book."

Petrella listened, fascinated. A lifetime of dealing with nervous young mothers and panic-stricken young fathers had endowed her with a calm authority which brooked no argument. He said, "It isn't going to be at all easy, Mrs. Fearing. I hardly think you realize just how awkward it is."

"I've heard about the other case," said Nurse Fearing. "And all the lies this man, Bond, told. How anyone could get up in court and say things like that passes my comprehension, but then, I'm old-fashioned."

"All the same—" said Petrella. And this was all he did manage to say. For the next ten minutes it was Nurse Fearing who did the talking . . .

"I can't stop you," said Chief Superintendent Watterson. He sounded worried. "A member of the public has made a complaint.

We're bound to follow it up. There's *prima facie* evidence. But I need hardly tell you—"

"That's all right," said Petrella. "I understand the position. If we lose this one we're sunk. Another unsuccessful prosecution. Further proof that I'm prejudiced. Right?"

"If you don't get home this time," said Watterson, "we shall have to settle the libel case on their terms. And that won't do your prospects any good at all."

"You're understating the case," said Petrella. "I won't have any prospects left."

"Are you going to handle it yourself?"

"I may be foolish, but I'm not that foolish. I'm getting Mr. Tasker to handle it."

Mr. Tasker was a local solicitor who did a lot of police-court work, appearing both for and against the police.

"Tasker's good," said Watterson. "But he can't fight unless you give him some ammunition."

"We shall do our best," said Petrella.

He sounded, thought Watterson, unaccountably cheerful for a man who has placed his own head on the block.

Counsel for the defense said, "I only propose to call one more witness, sir. You have heard Mr. Bond and seen the documents he produced. In the ordinary way I should have submitted that this evidence was conclusive. The solicitor appearing for the police challenged it—"

Mr. Tasker smiled blandly.

"—but was quite unable to shake it. Mr. Bond told us that he himself had purchased the new distributor—"

"Not new, reconditioned," said Mr. Tasker without troubling to get up.

"I beg your pardon," said Counsel with elaborate politeness, but a slight flush of annoyance. "I should have said the reconditioned distributor and the new set of points. He also supervised the work, which was actually carried out by his mechanic, whom I am now calling. If he corroborates the evidence already given, I think you will agree that this effectively disposes of the charges which the police"—here Counsel swiveled round and stared at Petrella who was seated beside Mr. Tasker—"the police have seen fit to bring for the second time in three months against my client. I hesitate to use the word persecution, but in the circumstances—"

"I think we'd better hear your witness first," said the magistrate mildly.

"If you please. Call Mr. Ardingly. Now, Mr. Ardingly, I will ask you if you recall effecting certain repairs to an Austin 1100 motorcar on December 28 of last year—"

Mr. Ardingly, who looked about 17, had blue eyes, curly hair, and a shy smile, said he certainly remembered fixing a distributor to the car in question. Yes, he had done the work himself. Yes, he had filled in the time sheets which were shown to him. Yes, that was his signature at the bottom. After about five minutes Counsel sat down with a satisfied smile.

Mr. Tasker rose slowly to his feet. He said, "Mr. Ardingly, this time sheet shows a record of six hours of work on this motorcar on December 28 and an additional three hours on December 29. Did you actually do that amount of work?"

"Nine hours to put on a new distributor," said Mr. Ardingly in tones of surprise. "Not likely."

"Then if it didn't take you nine hours," said Mr. Tasker with a look at Mr. Bond, whose white face had turned even whiter, "why did you put down that number of hours on the sheet?"

"I put down what the guv'nor told me to put down."

"It's a lie," screamed Mr. Bond, leaping up.

"I must ask you to warn your client to behave himself," said the magistrate. "If he does not do so, I will have him taken out of the court and held in custody."

Mr. Bond subsided slowly.

"Now, Mr. Ardingly," said Mr. Tasker. "About the distributor. The reconditioned distributor, which Mr. Bond has told us he purchased from Acme Spares—"

"That's quite right. I went and fetched it for him myself. I slipped them a quid."

"One pound!" said Mr. Tasker in beautifully simulated surprise, peering at the paper he held in his hand. "But this invoice for the distributor is for twelve pounds and fifty pence."

"You know how it is," said Mr. Ardingly with an engaging smile. "They always add on a bit."

"Very satisfactory," said Superintendent Watterson grimly. "Guilty as charged. Papers sent to the Director of Public Prosecutions. Charges of perjury pending against Bond. He can hardly continue his libel action against you. Would you mind explaining how you fixed it?"

"Fixed it?" said Petrella.

"You're not in court now. The truth, the whole truth, and nothing but the truth. How much did you pay Ardingly?"

Petrella looked genuinely shocked. "I should never have dreamed of doing such a thing. Besides, it was quite unnecessary. The boy loathed Bond. He's a nasty old man, and had already made a pass at him."

"And how did you find that out?"

"He's Constable Lampier's cousin."

"I see," said Watterson. As, indeed, he was beginning to do. "No relation of Nurse Fearing, I suppose."

"He was one of her babies."

"Quite a coincidence."

"Not really. She's delivered half of the Borough in her time."

"I suppose there's a moral to it."

"The moral," said Petrella smugly, "is always trust your own staff."

Jack Ritchie
The School Bus Caper

I pondered. "Who would want to steal a school bus?"

"Probably some high-school kids," Clarence said. "They sneaked a few beers and then thought it would be fun to take the bus for a ride. More than likely we'll find it parked up some side road when daylight comes."

He turned the patrol car headlights into a long sparsely graveled driveway that wound uphill for a quarter of a mile and ended in front of a farmhouse, a barn, and a cluster of sheds.

It was a few minutes after seven in the morning and still almost a half an hour before official sunrise. The temperature hovered at ten above zero and the wind-chill factor must have been fifteen below.

"How does it happen that the school bus was parked up here in the first place?" I asked.

"Jackson is a school-bus driver, Henry. In the country the drivers usually take their buses home with them at night. Saves a trip all the way into town in the morning to pick them up for their routes. Jackson is a widower and retired farmer. He rents out his fields and barn to neighbors. He drives the school bus for extra cash or maybe just to feel useful."

Clarence parked under the bluish yard light. A face had been watching at the lighted kitchen window of the farmhouse and the back door opened as we reached the stoop.

A tall weathered man in his sixties welcomed us in. "I thought I'd call on you personal instead of to headquarters in Gordonville seeing as how you live just down the road."

Clarence is the sheriff of Green River County. He introduced me. "This is my brother-in-law, Henry Turnbuckle. He's spending the Christmas holidays with me and my wife. Henry's a detective on the Milwaukee police force."

I nodded modestly. "I do the best I can."

Jackson's phone call to Clarence had come ten minutes earlier while we were finishing breakfast and I had decided to come along to see how Clarence and the sheriff's department handled these matters.

"Tell me what happened, Albert," Clarence said.

"Well, I just walked outside this morning and there it wasn't. The bus, I mean. Number 103."

"What is the license number, Albert?"

Jackson rubbed his jaw. "Darn if I remember."

I pointed to a ring of keys on the kitchen table. "If those are the bus keys, the tag on the chain ought to give us the license number."

It did and Clarence put the information in his notebook. "I don't suppose you heard or saw the bus being stolen?"

"I didn't see or hear a thing. My guess is that whoever took the bus just got inside and released the brake. That would get it rolling down the driveway all the way to the highway and he could get it started down there and I wouldn't hear the motor." He turned to me. "Number 103 sometimes gives me trouble trying to get it started on cold mornings, so I park it up here and point it down the driveway. All I have to do is release the emergency brake, put her in neutral, and let her roll. Halfway down the hill I throw out the clutch and she starts. Never failed yet."

"Mr. Jackson," I said, "did you keep the school bus locked?"

"Well, no. I guess maybe I should have, but I never thought anybody would steal her."

I indicated the ignition keys. "Since you still have the keys, how do you suppose the culprit managed to start the motor once he got the bus down the hill?"

"He probably crossed the ignition wires," Clarence said. "Did you phone the bus company, Albert?"

Jackson nodded. "They sent out another driver and a bus to take over my route this morning."

Clarence pocketed his notebook. "We'll radio out the word, Albert. Probably your bus will turn up somewhere as soon as it gets light."

Jackson felt the same way. "I'm not particularly worried. I mean, who would steal a school bus except some kids? I just hope they don't bang it up any."

Clarence and I drove on to Gordonville, the county seat, where the sheriff's department headquarters is located. Clarence supervises some twenty deputies and his department represents the largest single law-enforcement agency in Green River County.

At fifteen minutes after nine o'clock we received word that the bank at Ferrill had been robbed.

Clarence got off his chair. "Well, Henry, we don't get many of those. We might as well go over there and see for ourselves."

We drove fifteen miles to Ferrill and parked among the sheriff's two patrol cars and a Ferrill squad car.

Inside of the bank building one of Clarence's deputies gave us the basic information.

"The bank opens at nine. One of the first people to come in was a man with a full black beard and it was pretty obvious to the bank employees that it was false. He was about medium height and medium weight and he pointed a gun. He got away with about twenty-five thousand dollars.

"A couple of customers in the café across the street noticed a bearded man carrying a satchel running out of the bank and they saw him hop into a late-model blue-and-white sedan. They didn't get the entire license number, but one of them remembers that the last three digits were consecutive—123."

Clarence remained long enough to make certain his department had everything under control and then we drove back to headquarters.

A deputy was waiting for us. "We found the stolen school bus." He indicated a young woman sitting on one of the wooden benches. "She was driving it about four miles west of town. She claims she's a school-bus driver and that the bus is hers."

Clarence approached the woman. "What is your name, please?"

She seemed to be controlling her temper with difficulty. "Mrs. Rebecca McCullen."

"And you claim you're a school-bus driver?"

"Damn right."

"Are you aware that you were driving a stolen bus?"

"Baloney. It's my bus. Number 88. When you drive the same bus for three years, you get to know it even if everybody else thinks they all look alike."

We went outside to the school bus parked in the lot behind headquarters. The black number 88 was painted on both sides of the bus.

I rubbed my finger over the numbers. "There's a thorough coating of road dirt over these numbers, which indicates they have not been tampered with lately." I spoke to Mrs. McCullen. "Are those your license plates on the bus?"

She shrugged. "Who remembers license numbers? But it's my bus."

"Mrs. McCullen," I said, "would you please check the plastic tag on your key chain and compare it to the license plates on your bus?"

She made the comparison and frowned. "They don't match. They're different numbers. But it's still my bus, license plates or not."

I agreed. "I believe you, madam. For some insidious reason the license plates from the stolen school bus were transferred to your vehicle. Where do you keep this bus when you're not driving it?"

"On my husband's farm. Right next to the house."

"Do you know an Albert Jackson?" I asked. "He's the driver of the bus reported stolen."

She considered the name. "It doesn't ring a bell. But I might know him by sight. If he's a school-bus driver I could have seen him at one of the schools in town or maybe at the bus yard where we get our gas and servicing."

"One more question," I said. "Do you own a dog?"

"No. My husband's allergic to them."

Clarence rubbed his chin. "Well, Mrs. McCullen, I guess for the time being you might just as well go home. We'll call you if we need you again."

When Clarence and I returned to his office, there was more information concerning the Ferrill bank robbery.

The blue-and-white getaway car had been found just four blocks from the bank. Inside, on the front seat, the police discovered a false beard. A check of the dealer license plates on the car indicated that it had come from the Hawkins' Used Car Lot in Ferrill. According to Hawkins, the bearded man had approached him at 8:30 that morning and looked over the cars in his lot. He had asked to test-drive the blue-and-white sedan around the block. Hawkins had said okay and that was the last he saw of the man or the car until the police found it.

Clarence reconstructed the robbery. "Our man got into the dealer's car, drove to the bank, robbed it, then drove a few blocks more around the corner, and abandoned the car. Probably he had another vehicle waiting at that point."

After lunch we received the information that Jackson's bus—with the McCullen license plates on it—had been found parked up a dirt road in a place called Murdock's Woods.

Clarence frowned thoughtfully. "That's less than half a mile from Jackson's farm."

We went to his patrol car and took the highway out of town.

I watched the cold landscape as Clarence drove. "There is the matter of the dogs," I said.

"What dogs?"

"The dogs that weren't there. If you sneak into a farmer's yard with the intention of stealing his school bus or switching license plates, what are you most likely to encounter?"

"I don't know. What am I most likely to encounter?"

"A barking dog who would raise the alarm."

"But Jackson doesn't have a dog. Neither does Mrs. McCullen."

"Exactly. That is my point. I'll wager that ninety-eight percent or more of all farms have at least one dog in residence."

Clarence nodded. "Jackson's dog was Old Brownie, but he died of old age about a month ago. Albert just hasn't had the heart to replace him yet."

I smiled. "And who would know that Albert Jackson no longer has a dog on his premises?"

"Neighbors, I suppose."

I agreed. "It's my belief that whoever stole Jackson's bus brought it back almost to the point where he stole it because he still faced the prospect of having to *walk* home. And considering that it is extremely cold today, I would put the walking distance at under a half a mile from Murdock's Woods."

Clarence cogitated. "The nearest teenager that would fit is Lance Meuhlendorfer. He lives between Murdock's Woods and Jackson's farm."

I nodded. "It's obvious that this Meuhlendorfer lad would know that Jackson no longer has a dog, but how did he know that the McCullen farm didn't have one either? There is about twenty miles between the two, but there must be some common bond. Some common denominator."

As we approached Murdock's Woods, Clarence slowed the patrol car and turned into a dirt road. Fifty feet ahead we found another patrol car parked behind a yellow school bus.

A waiting trooper put out his cigarette and approached. "We tried for fingerprints, but there was nothing on the steering wheel. Whoever took the bus probably wore gloves or mittens. Not that it matters too much. We can't go to the high school and ask eight hundred boys to give us their fingerprints for comparison."

He led us to the open bus door. "The ignition wires are all screwed up. I radioed in and the bus company is sending up somebody to patch things up." He looked past us. "There he is now."

A panel truck pulled up behind our car and parked. A medium-sized man in a plaid jacket got out, bringing a toolbox with him.

Clarence nodded. "Afternoon, Jim."

The man returned the nod and moved on to the school bus. We watched him crouch under the hood and shake his head. "Somebody sure made a mess of this."

Clarence and I went back to our patrol car and got in.

"That's Jim Meuhlendorfer," Clarence said.

It took me a moment to grasp the significance of the name. "You mean he's the father of this Lance Meuhlendorfer?"

Clarence nodded again. "Jim is the mechanic over at the bus yard garage."

I closed my eyes.

But, of course. Now everything fell into place. "Clarence, the Meuhlendorfer boy might have known that Jackson did not have a dog, but how did he know that Mrs. McCullen didn't?"

"I don't know, Henry."

"But on the other hand, *Jim* Meuhlendorfer could easily have learned that Mrs. McCullen didn't have a dog. After all, he worked for the bus company, and surely at some time or another when she brought in her bus for servicing or gassing, he could have fallen into conversation with her and learned about her husband's allergy to dogs. Perhaps he even *deliberately* sought out a country bus driver who did not own a dog."

"Henry, I don't see what you're getting at. Do you mean that Jim Meuhlendorfer stole the school bus? Not his son?"

"Precisely."

"Now, Henry, why would a grown man steal a school bus?"

I smiled. "Clarence, just let us suppose the senior Meuhlendorfer sneaked across the field to Jackson's place last night and stole the school bus. And then suppose he drove this bus some twenty miles to the McCullen farm where he knew there was no dog. And suppose he parked at the foot of their driveway, crept into their yard, and switched the license plates."

Clarence was dubious. "I've known Jim as a neighbor for a long time and he never struck me as being a practical joker."

"Ah," I said wisely, "but it was not a practical joke. In fact, it was no joke at all. After he switched the license plates he drove on to Ferrill. When he got there, he parked the school bus on a side street. He walked about a bit until eight-thirty and then stopped at Hawkins' Used Car Lot and borrowed the blue-and-white sedan. He drove to the bank, committed his robbery, and then drove the car to the point where he had left the school bus. There he simply switched

THE SCHOOL BUS CAPER

vehicles and drove back to Murdock's Woods. He parked the bus and walked home, twenty-five thousand dollars richer."

Clarence seemed pained. "Henry, don't you think it's just a little wild to use a school bus for a getaway car?"

"On the contrary, Clarence. That is the most brilliant aspect of this operation. After the bank was robbed, the alarm would of course be sent out immediately, but what patrol-car deputy would so much as glance twice at the driver of a school bus?"

Clarence stared at the parked school bus ahead. "Why did Jim go through the whole routine of switching the license plates? Wouldn't just stealing the McCullen plates and putting them on his own bus have been enough? Why put Jackson's plates on the McCullen bus?"

"Because while people do not as a general rule remember their license-plate number—particularly on school buses, I would imagine—they would be likely to notice something wrong if there was no license plate at all on their vehicle. If Mrs. McCullen herself did not notice the absence when she got into her bus for her morning rounds, surely one of the children she picked up would have and mentioned it to her. In which case she would probably have notified the sheriff immediately and the department would have an eye out for her license-plate number. But our bank robber certainly didn't want that. He needed time, and switching the plates gave that to him. By the time the police straightened out that particular problem, he would have completed his robbery and been home safe."

Clarence was still not a believer. "Henry, you saw how messed up those wires were. Jim is an expert mechanic. If he were going to cross wires, he would know exactly what to do. It would be a neat job."

"Clarence, we are dealing with a clever man here. If he had left a neat job, we might immediately suspect someone who knew a great deal about school buses and their ignition systems. So he cunningly made us think that it was the work of an amateur."

Clarence picked up his radio microphone, made a call to headquarters, and asked that someone be sent to the bus-company garage to determine if Jim Meuhlendorfer had been at work at the time the bank in Ferrill was being robbed.

We received our answer in ten minutes. According to Jim Meuhlendorfer's boss, Meuhlendorfer had punched in at the garage at eight o'clock, as usual, and he had been there until he was sent out to repair the ignition wires on Jackson's bus a half hour ago.

I cleared my throat. "These things are tricky, you know. Meuhlendorfer could have arranged a dummy and shoved it under some school bus needing transmission work. These things have happened before. Anyone glancing into the garage would have seen the dummy and assumed it was Meuhlendorfer himself. When he returned from his crime, he could have changed places with the dummy and no one would be the wiser."

"I'll be sure to check that out sometime tomorrow, Henry," Clarence said. He started the patrol car and carefully backed around Meuhlendorfer's panel truck and onto the highway.

He turned south. "We might as well drop in at Jackson's place and tell him we found his bus."

Clarence drove past his own house set on an acre of land beside the road, past the Meuhlendorfer home, also of ranch-style construction, and turned into Jackson's long driveway.

I closed my eyes.

"Henry," Clarence said, "you're closing your eyes again."

"I know," I said and opened them. "I see it all so clearly now. How could I have missed it in the first place?"

"Missed what?"

"Clarence, who was the person *closest* to Jackson's bus?"

"One of the Meuhlendorfers?"

"No, Clarence. The person nearest to Jackson's bus was Jackson *himself*." I smiled. "It was Jackson all the time. During the darkness of last night he got into his own bus and drove to the McCullen farm and switched license plates."

"How did he know that the McCullens didn't have a dog?"

"Clarence, when you are planning an elaborate bank robbery, you make it your *business* to find out which one of the other bus drivers doesn't have a dog. And after he switched the license plates he drove to Murdock's Woods, where he parked the bus. After which he walked back to his farmhouse and reported his bus had been stolen. When you and I left him, he simply walked back to Murdock's Woods, picked up the bus, drove to Ferrill, and we know the rest of the whole sordid story."

I chuckled slightly. "But like all clever criminals he made at least one mistake. In this case, the ignition keys."

"I don't follow you, Henry."

"When we entered Jackson's house this morning, the ignition keys for the bus lay in plain sight on the kitchen table. When I wondered how the bus thief could have started the vehicle without the keys, Jackson realized he had made a mistake. He should have hidden the keys and claimed that he had accidentally left them in the bus overnight. While he was thinking desperately for some explanation you inadvertently aided him by suggesting that the thief probably crossed the ignition wires. That saved Jackson for the moment.

"But he realized that *after* he committed his robbery and abandoned the bus in Murdock's Woods, he would have to make it *appear* as though the thief had truly crossed the wires. However, while Jackson is a bus driver, he is not a mechanic. He did not *know* which of the wires to cross, so he simply created anarchy under the hood in the hope that an amateur would be blamed."

Clarence pulled the car into Jackson's farmyard. "We have to consider the description of the bank robber, Henry."

"What description? The false beard hid his face."

"I wasn't thinking of the beard, Henry. The bank robber was described as of medium height and medium build. Jackson is rail-thin and six foot three."

"Oh," I said.

We gave Jackson a lift to Murdock's Woods and then continued on to Gordonville.

Clarence stopped the patrol car at the local high school. "Want to come in?"

"No," I said. "Clarence, you are barking up the wrong tree. This is definitely not a kid caper."

Clarence came back in twenty-five minutes. "Well, that takes care of that. I had a private fatherly talk with Lance and he decided to admit the whole thing. It's usually that way with teenagers, Henry. They can't stand the pressure of having to lie more than ten minutes at a time."

I frowned fiercely. "You mean this mere lad stole Jackson's bus, went joyriding, and switched the license plates? How did he know the McCullens didn't have a dog?"

"There were two boys in on this, Henry. Lance Meuhlendorfer and Eddie Frantz. They're buddies here in high school and Eddie lives on a farm near to the McCullens. Last night Eddie stayed over at Lance's house. They sneaked some beer out of the family refrigerator and took them up to Lance's room. After they finished a few bottles they got the idea for the whole thing. They didn't mean any real harm, they just wanted to sit back and watch the fun. They'll both probably get probation."

Clarence checked out of headquarters at five o'clock and we began the drive back to his home.

After a while I smiled.

"Henry, why are you smiling?"

"Clarence, how old are the Muehlendorfer and the Frantz boys?"

"They're both nearly eighteen."

"Ah, and would one, or both of them, by any *remote* chance be of *medium* height and *medium* build?"

"No," Clarence said. "They're well over six feet and weigh close to two-fifty. They're linemen on the football team."

I watched the passing countryside. It was really depressing at this time of year, if you wanted to be honest about it.

When we reached Clarence's house I took off my overcoat and sat down in one of the overstuffed chairs.

My sister Madge appeared in the kitchen doorway. "Have a nice day?"

I sighed. "Madge, do you have any sherry in the house?"

"I'm afraid not, Henry. How about a beer?"

Clarence looked at me. "Sherry?"

Madge nodded. "Whenever Henry is feeling particularly depressed or frustrated, he usually has some sherry."

"Oh," Clarence said. "Do you drink much sherry, Henry?"

Was he being sarcastic?

Clarence smiled. "I'll tell you what I'll do, Henry. I'll drive back to town and get you a bottle of sherry. No trouble at all. I have to get some more beer anyway."

While he was gone, I paged glumly through a family photo album. I paused at a faded snapshot of a man and a woman.

The man sported a full beard. He was probably one of Clarence's grandparents.

I studied him and then rubbed my jaw. I went to the Gordonville area phone book and turned to the yellow pages. I found there was only one liquor store listed and I dialed the number. I left the proprietor a message that when Clarence arrived there, he should phone me immediately.

The return call came in three minutes.

"Clarence," I said, "do you remember that the bank employees in Ferrill *all* agreed that the beard worn by the bank robber was obviously false?"

"Yes, Henry."

"Well, if I were a used-car dealer and a stranger wearing an obviously false beard came to me and asked to take out one of my best cars on a solo run, would I really let him do it? At the very least, wouldn't I go along as a passenger? But Hawkins didn't. You don't suppose that this particular incident never really occurred at all?"

Clarence returned home more than an hour and a half later.

He sighed. "Hawkins is medium height and medium weight and we found the twenty-five thousand dollars in the trunk of an Edsel he had on his lot." He looked at the wrapped bottle in his hands. "Here's your sherry, Henry."

I smiled. "Thank you, but I don't think I'll need any now."

Clarence, however, had two thoughtful glasses of sherry before we sat down to dinner.

E. X. Ferrars
A Very Small Clue

Nobody saw the letter until they moved the dead old man. His head had covered it as he lay sprawled across the desk and while the photographers had taken their photographs and the fingerprint men had done their work, the envelope had remained hidden. But when at last the ambulance men had lifted the body onto the stretcher to take it out of the room, there was the letter, lying on the blood-soaked blotter. Stamped and addressed.

A letter, of course, was to have been expected. It had been the absence of one that had given Chief Superintendent Mellor the itchy feeling that this was not the simple suicide it had appeared at first glance. Suicides almost always leave letters. And the dead man's housekeeper, who had found the body after she had got home from a visit to her sister and had telephoned the police, had told them tearfully that Mr. Crick was the kindest, the most considerate of men. But it was not the act of a kind and considerate man to end his life without leaving behind a letter that said no one but himself was to blame for his death.

And here was the letter on the desk, so perhaps it was suicide after all.

The envelope was slightly splashed with blood and the writing on it was shaky, but it was perfectly legible and it was addressed to Chief Superintendent Mellor.

That took him by surprise.

He had the envelope tested for fingerprints before he opened it and was told there were only smudged prints on it, except for one on the stamp, and that the probability was they had all been made by the dead man. It was the same with the single sheet of paper that Mellor found in the envelope.

The letter was brief.

"Sir: This is to confess to you that I am the murderer of Miss Christine Beddoes, of The Beeches, Grove Avenue. I will not go into my motive for killing her except to say that I had thought we were to be married, but apparently I was mistaken. Now I find that I cannot live with what I have done and am about to take my own life. I am, Yours, A. Crick."

Mellor showed the letter to Sergeant Arkell, who was standing beside him.

Arkell remarked, "Very formal. Signs it as if he was writing to the newspapers."

"He was a solicitor," Mellor said. "Perhaps that made him formal about murder. A. Crick—I wonder what the A stood for."

"Arthur, sir." The housekeeper, a wrinkled little woman who, now that the body was gone from the room, seemed to have lost the fear she had had at first, looked expectantly at Mellor, as if she hoped to be allowed to read the letter too.

He did not show it to her.

"Do you know a Miss Christine Beddoes?" he asked.

"Miss Beddoes who lives next door? Yes, of course I do."

"Did Mr. Crick know her well?"

"I don't know what you mean by well," she said. "He was a neighborly sort of man, always said good morning and that kind of thing, but she wasn't his sort."

"What do you mean, not his sort?"

She shrugged in a way that expressed a certain disapproval of Miss Christine Beddoes.

Mellor put the letter back into its envelope.

"Well, it's time we went next door," he said to Arkell. "I suppose that's where we'll find her. There's no point in trying to conceal a body if you're going to kill yourself right after the murder—though it's true the letter sounds as if he didn't know he'd feel like suicide till after he'd done the job."

"Murder?" the housekeeper cried. "Who's murdered who?"

"That remains to be seen," Mellor said. "But I'm afraid we're going to find Miss Beddoes next door with a bullet through her brain. I hope to God he made a neat job of it. If there's anything I hate, it's a messy shooting."

Mellor strode out of the room and Arkell followed him.

They went next door to The Beeches, a spacious bungalow which was almost hidden from the street by a high beech hedge. But Mellor, as it turned out, had been only partly correct about what they would find there. He had been right in thinking Miss Beddoes would be at home, but when she opened the door to them it was evident she had no bullet in her brain or anywhere else in her well proportioned body.

She was a slender woman of about twenty-eight, with bright greenish eyes touched up with a good deal of eye shadow, heavy straight hair of a not very convincing shade of auburn that fell to her shoulders, and she was wearing a pale green housecoat of some thick, luxurious-looking silk.

Mellor identified himself and the sergeant and asked if they might come in.

"Of course," Miss Beddoes said. "I'm glad you came. I saw the police cars and the ambulance next door and I knew something awful must have happened and I thought of coming over to ask if I could help. But then I thought I'd only be in the way and that if you wanted me you'd come here."

She led them into a big bright sitting room furnished with what Mellor thought were some oddly shaped chairs and low tables and with some strange sculptures standing about that consisted mainly of holes. "Has something happened to poor Mr. Crick?"

"He's dead," Mellor said. "Shot, sitting at his desk. His housekeeper found him."

"Shot? Do you mean he shot himself? Committed suicide?" Her voice went high and shrill. Her voice was the least attractive thing about her. It was thin and nasal. "But why? Why ever should he do a thing like that?"

"His letter said it was suicide," Mellor replied. "But it also said he'd murdered you, which happens not to be true. So perhaps the rest of it isn't true either. What do you think about that, Miss Beddoes? We thought perhaps you could help us sort it out. First, had you ever been engaged to him? His letter implied that you had. Had you broken it off recently?"

She sank into one of the deep armchairs, the skirt of her housecoat flowing out around her.

"I don't understand," she said. "He wrote that he'd *murdered* me? *Me?* Whatever could he have been thinking about? And we were never engaged—certainly not. Well, that's to say . . ."

Her fingers plucked at the silk of her skirt. There was rather more tension in her face than Mellor had noticed at first. "Perhaps it's just possible he misunderstood our friendship. It never occurred to me before, but he was an old-fashioned sort of man, you know. He may have taken me more seriously than I realized. How sad—how terribly sad. Because his mind must have gone at the end, mustn't it, if he believed he'd murdered me? And he was such an intelligent man."

"When did you see him last?" Mellor asked.

"Two or three days ago," she said. "During the weekend. Yes, it was on Sunday. He came in for a drink before lunch, as he quite often did."

"Did you quarrel?"

"Oh, no. No, it was all just as usual. I think we talked mainly about our gardens. We generally did. We hadn't much else in common, and he didn't stay long."

"How long have you known him, Miss Beddoes?"

"About a year. He called on me with a basket of vegetables from his garden soon after I moved in. He was always very kind. He was a widower, you know, and I think he was lonely."

"But on Sunday he seemed to you quite normal? Not depressed, excitable, overwrought?"

She gave a shake of her head. But then she frowned.

"As a matter of fact, I did wonder if he was feeling well. He was more silent than usual. But I didn't give it much thought. He was a quiet sort of man."

"You see, he did a certain rather strange thing this evening," Mellor said. "Apart, I mean, from confessing to a murder that he hadn't got around to committing. He put a stamp on the letter he left on his desk, the envelope addressed to me. I find that distinctly odd."

"A stamp?" she said. "Is there anything strange about putting a stamp on an envelope?"

"Who was going to post that letter?" he asked. "Not Mr. Crick himself. And when his housekeeper found him, as he must have known she would, she called the police in the natural way, by telephone."

Miss Beddoes gave a bewildered shake of her head. "I don't understand. I can only think that if he was in the state of mind to think he'd murdered me, he didn't know what he was doing."

"Of course that's possible," Mellor agreed.

"A stamp's a very small thing," she said.

"Very small. All the same, I'd like to know how you spent the evening, Miss Beddoes. Say from about eight o'clock to ten."

She stiffened in her deep chair. "How *I* spent it? What are you thinking of?"

"I'm thinking," Mellor said, "that Mr. Crick, having a legal sort of mind and wanting to leave everything in proper order, might have written his letter to me earlier in the evening, intending to come here, kill you, then on his way home mail his letter—there's a mail box just outside, I noticed—then go home and kill himself. But something prevented him doing what he intended. Somebody could have known just what he was planning to do and got into his house and shot him before Mr. Crick himself could commit murder."

"Someone?" She pressed a finger against her bosom, pointing at herself. "Me? You're thinking of me?"

"I only asked you how you spent the evening," he answered.

She gave a soft laugh and seemed to relax. "Then I'll tell you. I went to a party given by Mr. and Mrs. Wheeler, who live at Number Twelve Grove Avenue. I got there about eight o'clock and I came home only a little while before you got here. I'd just had time to change out of my evening dress when you arrived."

"Will Mr. and Mrs. Wheeler be able to say that you didn't leave even for a little while during the evening?" he asked. "Number Twelve can't be very far from here."

"Oh, yes, they'll be quite sure," she said. "So will several other people. It was a small party. If I'd left for a time it would certainly have been noticed. I'm not a murderess, Mr. Mellor."

"Then I can think of only one other explanation," Mellor said, "and perhaps you can help me with that. For instance, I'm sure you can tell me whether the man who did the murder is still here, or has he gone without you? You were just going to leave with him, weren't you, when we showed up? You're fully dressed under that handsome housecoat."

Catching Arkell's eye, the Superintendent gave a slight nod and Arkell went quietly out of the room.

"I may as well tell you," Mellor went on, "that if he hasn't gone already, it's too late now, because the house is surrounded."

As he spoke there was the sound of a shot in the garden. It was followed by excited cries, then by a voice shouting orders.

The woman leaped to her feet.

"The fool, the fool, I told him it wouldn't work!" she cried. "But he said after the old man saw him he had to get rid of him, and he said I'd have to go with him, because he was sure if I didn't I'd talk. Oh, the fool! As if I'd ever have talked. But he never trusted anybody."

"And no doubt he said he'd manage it so no one would wonder why you'd disappeared," Mellor said. "We were supposed to be looking for a dead woman, not a live one."

The door was thrown open and Arkell reappeared, accompanied by a constable. They had a man between them who was struggling fiercely as each of them gripped him by an arm. He was a short squat man with crudely shaped features, which in spite of their coarseness bore a resemblance to the delicate features of the woman.

"Nobody hurt," Arkell said. "He tried shooting it out, but Fred here winged him."

"Ah, I see, I see—one of the old familiar faces," Mellor said. "Your brother, Miss Beddoes? Though his name was Hewitt when I heard of him last. How long since you escaped from Parkhurst, Hewitt? Three days? Seems it was hardly worth the effort. And Arthur Crick saw you here this evening, getting ready to leave, and recognised you, didn't he? He'd seen you in court sometime, I suppose.

"But how did you persuade him to write that letter before you killed him? By the threat of a beating up, was it? He knew you were going to kill him anyhow, but in return for that letter you did it painlessly. But as your sister said, he was a very intelligent man. With you standing over him, he quietly put a stamp on the envelope. I expect that seemed to you a quite normal thing to do. But in fact he was leaving me a message that that letter wasn't what it seemed. So even if the two of you had got away in time, we'd have tracked you down sooner or later. Now you can both come along to the police station."

And wearily, because he had had a long day and knew that there was a long night ahead of him, Mellor added the words of the official warning.

James M. Cain

Pay-Off Girl

I met her a month ago at a little café called Mike's Joint, in Cottage City, Maryland, a town just over the District line from Washington, D.C. As to what she was doing in this lovely honkytonk, I'll get to it, all in due time. As to what I was doing there, I'm not at all sure that I know, as it wasn't my kind of place. But even a code clerk gets restless, especially if he used to dream about being a diplomat and he wound up behind a glass partition, unscrambling cables. And on top of that was my father out in San Diego, who kept writing me sarcastic letters telling how an A-1 canned-goods salesman had turned into a Z-99 government punk, and wanting to know when I'd start working for him again, and making some money. And on top of that was Washington, with the suicide climate it has, which to a Californian is the same as death, only worse.

Or it may have been lack of character. But whatever it was, there I sat, at the end of the bar, having a bottle of beer, when from behind me came a voice: "Mike, a light in that phone booth would help. People could see to dial. And that candle in there smells bad."

"Yes, Miss, I'll get a bulb."

"I know, Mike, but when?"

"I'll get one."

She spoke low, but meant business. He tossed some cubes in a glass and made her iced coffee, and she took the next stool to drink it. As soon as I could see her I got a stifled feeling. She was blonde, a bit younger than I am, which is twenty-five, medium size, with quite a shape, and good-looking enough, though maybe no raving beauty. But what cut my wind were the clothes and the way she wore them. She had on a peasant blouse, with big orange beads dipping into the neck, black shoes with high heels and fancy latticework straps and a pleated orange skirt that flickered around her like flame. And to me, born right on the border, that outfit spelled Mexico, but hot Mexico, with chili, castanets, and hat dancing in it, which I love. I looked all the law allowed, and then had to do eyes front, as she began looking at her beads, at her clothes, at her feet, to see what the trouble was.

Soon a guy came in and said the bookies had sent him here to get paid off on a horse. Mike said have a seat, the young lady would take care of him. She said: "At the table in the corner. I'll be there directly."

I sipped my beer and thought it over. If I say I liked that she was pay-off girl for some bookies, I'm not telling the truth, and if I say it made any difference, I'm telling a downright lie. I just didn't care, because my throat had talked to my mouth, which was so dry the beer rasped through it. I watched her while she finished her coffee, went to the table, and opened a leather case she'd been holding in her lap. She took out a tiny adding machine, some typewritten sheets of paper, and a box of little manila envelopes. She handed the guy a pen, had him sign one of the sheets, and gave him one of the envelopes. Then she picked up the pen and made a note on the sheet. He came to the bar and ordered a drink. Mike winked at me. He said: "They make a nice class of business, gamblers do. When they win they want a drink, and when they lose they need one."

More guys came, and also girls, until they formed a line, and when they were done at the table they crowded up to the bar. She gave some of them envelopes, but not all. Quite a few paid her, and she'd tap the adding machine. Then she had a lull. I paid for my beer, counted ten, swallowed three times, and went over to her table. When she looked up I took off my hat and said: "How do I bet on horses?"

"You sure you want to?"

"I think so."

"You know it's against the law?"

"I've heard it is."

"I didn't say it was wrong. It's legal at the tracks, and what's all right one place can't be any howling outrage someplace else, looks like. But you should know how it is."

"Okay, I know."

"Then sit down and I'll explain."

We talked jerky, with breaks between, and she seemed as rattled as I was. When I got camped down, though, it changed. She drew a long trembly breath and said: "It has to be done by telephone. These gentlemen, the ones making the book, can't have a mob around, so it's all done on your word, like in an auction room, where a nod is as good as a bond, and people don't rat on their bids. I take your name, address, and phone, and when you're looked up you'll get a call. They give you a number, and from then on you phone in, and your name will be good for your bets."

"My name is Miles Kearny."

She wrote it on an envelope, with my phone and address, an apartment in southeast Washington. I took the pen from her hand, rubbed ink on my signet ring, and pressed the ring on the envelope, so the little coronet, with the three tulips over it, showed nice and clear. She got some ink off my hand with her blotter, then studied the impression on the envelope. She said: "Are you a prince or something?"

"No, but it's been in the family. And it's one way to get my hand held. And pave the way for me to ask something."

"Which is?"

"Are you from the West?"

"No, I'm not. I'm from Ohio. Why?"

"And you've never lived in Mexico?"

"No, but I love Mexican clothes."

"Then that explains it."

"Explains what?"

"How you come to look that way, and—how I came to fall for you. I'm from the West. Southern California."

She got badly rattled again and after a long break said: "Have you got it straight now? About losses? They have to be paid."

"I generally pay what I owe."

There was a long, queer break then, and she seemed to have something on her mind. At last she blurted out: "And do you really want in?"

"Listen, I'm over twenty-one."

"In's easy. Out's not."

"You mean it's habit-forming?"

"I mean, be careful who you give your name to, or your address, or phone."

"They give theirs, don't they?"

"They give you a number."

"Is that number yours, too?"

"I can be reached there."

"And who do I ask for?"

"Ruth."

"That all the name you got?"

"In this business, yes."

"I want in."

Next day, by the cold gray light of Foggy Bottom, which is what they call the State Department, you'd think that I'd come to my senses and forget her. But I thought of her all day long, and that night I was back, on the same old stool, when she came in, made a call from the booth, came out, squawked about the light and picked up her coffee to drink it. When she saw me she took it to the table. I went over, took off my hat, and said: "I rang in before I came. My apartment house. But they said no calls came in for me."

"It generally takes a while."

That seemed to be all, and I left. Next night it was the same, and for some nights after that. But one night she said, "Sit down," and then: "Until they straighten it out, why don't you bet with me? Unless, of course, you have to wait until post time. But if you're satisfied to pick them the night before, I could take care of it."

"You mean, you didn't give in my name?"

"I told you, it all takes time."

"Why didn't you give it in?"

"Listen, you wanted to bet."

"Okay, let's bet."

I didn't know one horse from another, but she had a racing paper there, and I picked a horse called Fresno, because he reminded me of home and at least I could remember his name. From the weights he looked like a long shot, so I played him to win, place, and show, two dollars each way. He turned out an also-ran, and the next night I kicked in with six dollars more and picked another horse, still trying for openings to get going with her. That went on for some nights, I hoping to break through, she hoping I'd drop out, and both of us getting nowhere. Then one night Fresno was entered again and I played him again, across the board. Next night I put down my six dollars, and she sat staring at me. She said: "But Fresno won."

"Oh. Well say. Good old Fresno."

"He paid sixty-four eighty for two."

I didn't much care, to tell the truth. I didn't want her money. But she seemed quite upset. She went on: "However, the top bookie price, on any horse that wins, is twenty to one. At that I owe you forty dollars win money, twenty-two dollars place and fourteen dollars show, plus of course the six that you bet. That's eighty-two in all. Mr. Kearny, I'll pay you tomorrow. I came away before the last race was run, and I just now got the results when I called in. I'm sorry, but I don't have the money with me, and you'll have to wait."

"Ruth, I told you from the first, my weakness isn't horses. It's you. If six bucks a night is the ante, okay, that's how it is, and dirt cheap.

But if you'll act as a girl ought to act, quit holding out on me, what your name is and how I get in touch, I'll quit giving an imitation of a third-rate gambler, and we'll both quit worrying whether you pay me or not. We'll start over, and—"

"What do you mean, act as a girl ought to act?"

"I mean go out with me."

"On this job how can I?"

"Somebody making you hold it?"

"They might be, at that."

"With a gun to your head, maybe?"

"They got 'em, don't worry."

"There's only one thing wrong with that. Some other girl and a gun, that might be her reason. But not you. You don't say yes to a gun, or to anybody giving you orders, or trying to. If you did, I wouldn't be here."

She sat looking down in her lap, and then, in a very low voice: "I don't say I was forced. I do say, when you're young you can be a fool. Then people can do things to you. And you might try to get back, for spite. Once you start that, you'll be in too deep to pull out."

"Oh, you could pull out, if you tried."

"How, for instance?"

"Marrying me is one way."

"Me, a pay-off girl for a gang of bookies, marry Miles Kearny, a guy with a crown on his ring and a father that owns a big business and a mother—who's your mother, by the way?"

"My mother's dead."

"I'm sorry."

We had dead air for a while, and she said: "Mr. Kearny, men like you don't marry girls like me, at least to live with them and like it. Maybe a wife can have cross-eyes or buckteeth; but she can't have a past."

"Ruth, I told you my first night here, I'm from California, where we've got present and future. There isn't any past. Too many of their grandmothers did what you do, they worked for gambling houses. They dealt so much faro and rolled so many dice and spun so many roulette wheels, in Sacramento and Virginia City and San Francisco, they don't talk about the past. You got to admit they made a good state though, those old ladies and their children. They made the best there is, and that's where I'd be taking you, and that's why we'd be happy."

"It's out."

"Are you married, Ruth?"
"No, but it's out."
"Why is it?"
"I'll pay you tomorrow night."

Next night the place was full, because a lot of them had bet a favorite that came in and they were celebrating their luck. When she'd paid them off she motioned and I went over. She picked up eight tens and two ones and handed them to me, and to get away from the argument I took the bills and put them in my wallet. Then I tried to start where we'd left off the night before, but she held out her hand and said: "Mr. Kearny, it's been wonderful knowing you, especially knowing someone who always takes off his hat. I've wanted to tell you that. But don't come any more. I won't see you any more, or accept bets, or anything. Goodbye, and good luck."
"I'm not letting you go."
"Aren't you taking my hand?"
"We're getting married, tonight."
Tears squirted out of her eyes, and she said: "Where?"
"Elkton. They got day and night service, for license, preacher and witnesses. Maybe not the way we'd want it done, but it's one way. And it's a two-hour drive in my car."
"What about—?" She waved at the bag, equipment, and money.
I said: "I tell you, I'll look it all up to make sure, but I'm under the impression—just a hunch—that they got parcel post now, so we can lock, seal, and mail it. How's that?"
"You sure are a wheedling cowboy."
"Might be, I love you."
"Might be, that does it."
We fixed it up then, whispering fast, how I'd wait outside in the car while she stuck around to pay the last few winners, which she said would make it easier. So I sat there, knowing I could still drive off, and not even for a second wanting to. All I could think about was how sweet she was, how happy the old man would be, and how happy our life would be, all full of love and hope and California sunshine. Some people went in the café, and a whole slew came out. The jukebox started, a tune called *Night and Day,* then played it again and again.

Then it came to me: I'd been there quite a while. I wondered if something was wrong, if maybe *she* had taken a powder. I got up, walked to the café, and peeped. She was still there, at the table. But a guy was standing beside her, with his hat on, and if it was the way he talked or the way he held himself, as to that I couldn't be sure, but I thought he looked kind of mean. I started in. Mike was blocking the door. He said: "Pal, come back later. Just now I'm kind of full."

"Full? Your crowd's leaving."

"Yeah, but the cops are watching me."

"Hey, what is this?"

He'd sort of mumbled, but I roared it, and as he's little and I'm big it took less than a second for him to bounce off me and for me to start past the bar. But the guy heard it, and as I headed for him he headed for me. We met a few feet from her table, and she was white as a sheet. He was tall, thin, and sporty-looking, in a light, double-breasted suit, and I didn't stop until I bumped him and he had to back up. Some girl screamed. I said: "What seems to be the trouble?"

He turned to Mike and said, "Mike, who's your friend?"

"I don't know, Tony. Some jerk."

He said to her: "Ruth, who is he?"

"How would I know?"

"He's not a friend, by chance?"

"I never saw him before."

I bowed to her and waved at Mike. I said: "I'm greatly obliged to you two for your thoughtful if misplaced effort to conceal my identity. You may now relax, as I propose to stand revealed."

I turned to the guy and said: "I am a friend, as it happens, of Ruth's, and in fact considerably more. I'm going to marry her. As for you, you're getting out."

"I am?"

"I'll show you."

I let drive with a nice one-two, and you think he went down on the floor? He just wasn't there. All that was left was perfume, a queer foreign smell, and it seemed to hang on my fist. When I found him in my sights again he was at the end of the bar, looking at me over a gun. He said: "Put 'em up."

I did.

"Mike, get me his money."

"Listen, Tony, I don't pick pockets—"

"Mike!"

"Yes, Tony."

Mike got my wallet, and did what he was told: "Take out that money, and every ten in it, hold it up to the light, here where I can see.... There they are, two pinholes in Hamilton's eyes, right where I put them before passing the jack to a crooked two-timing dame who was playing me double."

He made me follow his gun to where she was. He leaned down to her, said: "I'm going to kill you, but I'm going to kill him first, so you can see him fall, so get over there, right beside him."

She spit in his face.

Where he had me was right in front of the telephone booth, and all the time he was talking I was working the ring off. Now I could slip it up in the empty bulb socket. I pushed, and the fuse blew. The place went dark. The jukebox stopped with a moan, and I started with a yell. I went straight ahead, not with a one-two this time. I gave it all my weight, and when I hit him he toppled over and I heard the breath go out of him. It was dark, but I knew it was him by the smell. First, I got a thumb on his mastoid and heard him scream from the pain. Then I caught his wrist and used my other thumb there. The gun dropped, it hit my foot, it was in my hand. "Mike," I yelled, "the candle! In the booth! I've got his gun! But for Pete's sake, give us some light!"

So after about three years Mike found his matches and lit up. While I was waiting I felt her arms come around me and heard her whisper in my ear: "You've set me free, do you still want me?"

"You bet I do!"

"Let's go to Elkton!"

So we did, and I'm writing this on the train, stringing it out so I can watch her as she watches mesquite, sage, buttes, and the rest of the West rolling by the window. But I can't string it out much longer. Except that we're goof happy, and the old man is throwing handsprings, that's all.

Period.

New paragraph.

California, here we come.

"Q"

Michael Innes

Tragedy of a Handkerchief

The curtain rose on the last scene of Shakespeare's *Othello,* the dreadful scene in which Desdemona is smothered, the scene which Dr. Johnson declared is not to be endured. But by this audience, it seemed to Inspector Appleby, it was going to be endured tolerably well. For one thing, the smothering was apparently to be staged in the reticent way favored by touring companies that depend on the support of organized parties of school children. Not that the school children, probably, would take a thoroughly Elizabethan robustness at all amiss. But headmistresses are different. If their charges must, in the sovereign name of Shakespeare, be taken to see a horrid murder, let it at least be committed in hugger-mugger in a darkened corner of the stage.

But if the audience was not going to be horrified, neither—so far—had it been gripped. Whatever currents of emotion had been liberated behind this proscenium arch, they were not precisely those intended by the dramatist. Or rather, Inspector Appleby thought, it was as if across the main torrent of feeling as Shakespeare had designed it, there were drifting eddies of private passion muddying and confusing the whole.

One was familiar with something of the sort in amateur theatricals, in which the jealousies and spites of rival performers occasionally reveal themselves as absurdly incongruous with the relationships designed by the story. But it is a thing less common on the professional stage, and during the preceding act the audience had been growing increasingly restless and unconvinced. Perhaps only Appleby himself, who had dropped into this dilapidated provincial theater merely to fill an empty evening in a strange town, was giving a steadily more concentrated attention to the matters transacting themselves on the stage.

Around him were the gigglings of bored children and the rustling of stealthily opened paper bags. Appleby, however, studied Desdemona's bedchamber with a contracted brow.

Othello was about to enter with a taper and announce that *"It is the cause, it is the cause, my soul . . ."*

But there was a hitch. For one of those half-minute intervals which can seem an eternity in terms of theatrical time, Othello failed to appear. The stage stood empty, with the sleeping Desdemona scarcely visible in her curtained and shadowy bed at the rear. And this delay was only one of several signs that all was not well behind the scenes.

Most striking had been the blow—that public indignity to which Othello subjects his wife in the fourth act. The crack of an open palm across a face is a thing easily simulated on the stage; the assailant makes his gesture, his victim staggers back, and at the same time someone watching from the wings smartly claps his hands together. But on this occasion there had been the sound of *two* blows—one from the wings and one from the stage itself. And as Desdemona fell back it had been just possible to discern first a cheek unnaturally flushed and then a trickle of blood from a nostril. Almost as if *Othello* were the brutal pot-house tragedy which some unfriendly critics have accused it of being, the hero had given his wife a bloodied nose.

And the ensuing twenty lines had been uncommonly ticklish, with Desdemona playing out her shock and horror while covertly dabbing at her face with a handkerchief. No doubt an actor may be carried away. But an Othello who allowed himself this artistic excess would be decidedly dangerous. What if he permitted himself a similar wholeheartedness when the moment for smothering Desdemona came?

Still staring at the empty stage, Inspector Appleby shook his head. There had been other hints that private passions were percolating through the familiar dramatic story. *Othello* is a tragedy of suspicion, of suspicion concentrated in Othello himself—the hero who, not easily jealous, is yet brought by the triumphant cunning of the villain Iago to kill his wife because of a baseless belief in her adultery. But among the people on this stage, suspicion was not concentrated but diffused. Behind the high dramatic poetry, behind the traditional business of the piece, an obscure and pervasive wariness lurked, as if in every mind were a doubtful speculation as to what other minds knew.

Desdemona, Appleby could have sworn, was more frightened than Shakespeare's heroine need be; Iago was indefinably on the defensive, whereas his nature should know nothing but ruthless if oblique attack; Iago's wife, Emilia, although she played out the honest, impercipient waiting-woman efficiently scene by scene, was perceptibly wishing more than one of her fellow-players to the devil. As for Michael Cassio, he was harassed—which is no doubt what Cassio should chiefly be. But this Cassio was harassed behind the mask as well as across it. Appleby, knowing nothing of these strolling players without name or fame, yet suspected that Cassio was the company's manager, and one despairingly aware that the play was misfiring badly.

On one side of Appleby a small girl massively exhaled an odor of peppermint drops. On the other side an even smaller boy entertained himself by transforming his program into paper pellets and flicking them at the audience in the seats below.

And now here was Othello at last—a really black Othello of the kind fashionable since Paul Robeson triumphed in the part. Only about this fellow there had been a faint flavor of minstrel from the start and it had long been plain that there was nothing approaching great acting in him. Yet the theater fell suddenly silent.

The man stood there, framed in a canvas doorway, the customary lighted taper in his hand. His eyes rolled, fixed themselves, rolled again. His free hand made exaggerated clawing gestures before him. As far as any elevated conception of his role went, he was violating almost every possible canon of the actor's art. And yet the effect was queerly impressive—startling, indeed. The child on Appleby's left gulped and regurgitated, as if all but choked by peppermint going down the wrong way. The boy on the right let his ammunition lie idle before him. From somewhere higher up another child cried out in fright.

Othello stepped forward into a greenish limelight which gave him the appearance of a rather badly decomposed corpse.

Some forty-five seconds behind schedule, the unbearable scene had begun.

"It is the cause, it is the cause, my soul—
Let me not name it to you, you chaste stars!—
It is the cause . . ."

The mysterious words rolled out into the darkness of the auditorium. And, of course, they were indestructible. Not even green limelight, not even an Othello who made damnable faces as he talked, could touch them.

"Yet I'll not shed her blood,
Nor scar that whiter skin of hers than snow . . ."

To the dreadful threat Desdemona awoke. Propped up on the great bed, she edged herself into another limelight which again offended all artistic decorum.

"Will you come to bed, my lord?"

With mounting tension, the scene moved inexorably forward. Othello—who at least had inches—was towering over the woman on the bed.

"That handkerchief which I so loved and gave thee
Thou gavest to Cassio..."

The Tragedy of the Handkerchief, this play had been contemptuously called. And the French translator, Inspector Appleby remembered, had preferred the more elevated word, *bandeau*.

"By heaven, I saw my handkerchief in 's hand.
O perjured woman! thou dost stone my heart,
And makest me call what I intend to do
A murder, which I thought a sacrifice;
I saw the handkerchief..."

The limelights faded, sparing the susceptibilities of the schoolmistresses. It was just possible to discern Othello as taking up a great pillow in his hands. His last words to Desdemona rang out. There followed only horrible and inarticulate sounds. For, as if to give the now appalled children their money's worth after all, the players in their almost invisible alcove were rendering these final moments with ghastly verisimilitude: the panting respirations of the man pressing the pillow home; the muffled groans and supplications of the dying woman. And then from a door hard by the bedhead came the cries of Emilia demanding admission. Othello drew the bed-hangings to, reeled backwards like a drunken man, plunged into rambling speech as Emilia's clamor grew:

"My wife! my wife! what wife? I have no wife."

From despairing realization, his voice swelled in volume, swelled into its vast theatrical rhetoric, and from behind the hangings the dying Desdemona could be heard to moan anew.

"O, insupportable! O heavy hour!
Me thinks it should be now a huge eclipse
Of sun and moon, and that the affrighted globe
Should yawn at alteration..."

Emilia was calling again. Othello drew the hangings closer to, staggered to the door and unlocked it. The woman burst in with her news of disaster and in rapid colloquy Othello learned that his plot for the death of Cassio had failed. Again his voice rang out in despair:

"Not Cassio kill'd! then murder's out of tune,
And sweet revenge grows harsh..."

And suddenly there was absolute silence on the stage. Othello and

Emilia were standing still—waiting. Again, and with a different note of anxiety, Othello cried out:

"And sweet revenge grows harsh . . ."

Inspector Appleby shivered. For again there was silence, the repeated cue producing nothing. It was now that Desdemona should call out, that Emilia should wrench back the hangings upon the heroine's death-agony and her last sublime attempt to free her lord from blame. But only silence held the boards.

With a swift panicky bump, the curtain fell, blotting out the stage.

"Their names?" asked Inspector Appleby. "We'll stick to Shakespeare for the moment and avoid confusion. And I think Cassio is the man who runs the show?"

The sergeant of police nodded. He was uncertain whether to be relieved or annoyed that a Detective-Inspector from Scotland Yard had emerged helpfully but authoritatively from the audience. "That's so, sir. And here he is."

Chill drafts blew across the stage. The great curtain stirred uneasily, and from behind it there could still be heard the tramp and gabble of bewildered children being shepherded out. Here amid the scenes and tawdry properties everything showed shadowy and insubstantial. The dead woman lay on what had seemed a bed and beneath its grease paint her face showed as black as Othello's. The players, still in costumes, wigs, and beards to which theatrical illusion no longer attached, hovered in a half world between fantasy and fact. And Cassio stood in the midst of them, his hand nervously toying with the hilt of a rapier, his weak and handsome face a study in despair. Inspector Appleby nodded to him.

"This is your company?" he asked. "And Desdemona's death means pretty well the end of it?"

Cassio groaned. "That is so. And it is an unimaginable disaster, as well as being"—he glanced fearfully towards the bed—"unspeakably horrible and painful."

"In fact, if somebody wanted to smash you, this would have been a thoroughly effective way of going about it?"

The actor-manager looked startled. "It certainly would. The sort of audience we get will never book a seat with my company again. But I don't think—"

"Quite so. It is a possible motive but not a likely one. Now, please tell me of the relationships existing between your different members."

The man hesitated. "I am myself married to Bianca."

"A fellow," thought Appleby, "almost damned in a fair wife." Aloud he said: "And the dead woman was actually married to Othello?"

"Yes. And so too are Iago and Emilia."

"I see. In fact, your private relations are quite oddly akin to those in the play? And you may be said to be an isolated community, moving from town to town, with the rest of your company not much more than extras?"

Cassio licked his lips. "That is more or less true. We can't afford much."

"You certainly can't afford murder." Appleby's glance swept the players who were now ranged in a semicircle round him. "I suppose you know that your performance this evening was all at sixes and sevens? Even the children were at a loss." His finger shot out at Othello. "Why did you strike your wife?"

"Yes, why did you strike her?" Emilia had stepped forward. Her eyes, though red with weeping, snapped fire. "And why did you murder her, too?"

"Strike her?" Othello, his face a blotched pallor beneath its paint, had been glaring at Iago. Now he swung round upon Iago's wife. "You foul-mouthed—"

"That will do." Appleby's voice, although quiet, echoed in this resonant space. "There were six of you: Othello and Desdemona, Iago and Emilia, Cassio and Bianca. Your emotional relationships were a sordid muddle and tonight they got out of hand. Well, I'm afraid we must have them into the limelight. And if you won't confess to what was troubling you, I expect there are minor members of your company who can be informative enough."

"But this is outrageous!" It was Bianca who spoke—a beautiful girl with every appearance of self-control. "You can't bully us like that, no matter what has happened." She looked defiantly at the still figure on the bed and then turned to her husband. "Isn't that so?"

But it was Iago, not Cassio, who answered. He was a dark man with a constantly shifting eye and a lip which twitched nervously as he spoke. "Certainly it is so. In interrogating possible witnesses in such an affair, the police are bound by the strictest rules. And until a solicitor—"

"Rubbish!" Unexpectedly and with venom, Emilia had turned on her husband. "Let the man go his own way and it will be the sooner over."

"But at least there are the mere physical possibilities to consider first." Cassio was at once agitated and reasonable. "Just when did the thing happen? And is it possible therefore to rule anyone out straight away?"

Inspector Appleby nodded. "Very well. Opportunity first and motive second... At line 83 Desdemona was alive." Appleby glanced up from the text which had been handed to him. "And at line 117 she was dead. Throughout this interval she was invisible, since at first she was lying within heavy shadow and subsequently the bed-hangings were drawn to by Othello. It is clear that Othello himself may simply have smothered her when the action required that he should appear to do so. But there are other possibilities.

"The bed is set in a recess which is accessible not from the main stage alone. Behind the bed-head there is only a light curtain, and it would thus be accessible to anybody behind the scenes who was passing forward towards the wings. Othello ceased to have Desdemona under his observation at about line 85. There are then nearly twenty lines before Emilia enters. These lines are taken up partly by Othello in desperate soliloquy and partly by Emilia calling from 'without.' When Emilia does enter, it is by the door close by the bed-head. And it follows from this that Emilia could have smothered Desdemona during these twenty lines, some five or six of which she had to speak herself. It would be a procedure requiring considerable nerve, but that is no convincing argument against it.

"A third possibility, however, remains. After Emilia has entered, and until the moment that Desdemona cries out that she has been murdered, there are some twelve broken lines, with a certain amount of time-consuming mime increasing the suspense. During this period, any other actor standing near the wings might have slipped to the bed-head and committed the murder. So the position is this: Othello and Emilia are definitely suspects, so far as opportunity goes. And so is anybody else who could have approached the bed-head unobserved during the twelve lines after Emilia's entry."

"Which rules me out." Cassio spoke without any apparent relief and it was clear that with him the disaster which had befallen his company overshadowed everything else. "I was on the opposite side with the electrician when we heard the cue for Emilia's going on. I just couldn't have made it."

"But your wife could." And Emilia, who had broken in, turned with venom on Bianca. "For I saw you not far behind me when I stepped onstage."

"No doubt you did. And I saw your husband." Bianca, still perfectly calm, turned a brief glance of what was surely cold hatred on Iago. "I saw him standing in the wings there and wondered what he was about."

Iago's lip twitched more violently than before. Then he laughed harshly. "This will get the police nowhere. And what about all the other conventional questions, like who last saw the victim alive?"

Suddenly Othello exclaimed. "My God!" he cried, and whirled on Emilia. "*You* know whether I smothered her. Everyone knows what your habit is."

"What do you mean?" Emilia's hand had flown to her bosom and beneath the grease paint she was very pale.

"When waiting to come on, you have always parted the curtain at the bed-head and had a look at her and perhaps whispered a word. I can't tell why, for you weren't all that friendly. But that's what you always did, and you must have done it tonight. Well, how was it? Was she alive or dead?"

"She was alive." It was after a moment's hesitation that Emilia spoke. "She didn't say anything. And of course it was almost dark. But I could see that she—that she was weeping."

"As she very well might be, considering that her husband had actually struck her on the open stage." The police sergeant spoke for the first time. "Now, if you'll—"

But Appleby brusquely interrupted. "Weeping?" he said. "Had she a handkerchief?"

Emilia looked at him with dilated eyes. "But of course."

Appleby strode to the body on the bed and in a moment was back holding a small square of cambric, wringing wet. "Quite true," he said. "And it was right under the body. But this can't be her ordinary handkerchief, which was blood-stained as a result of the blow and will be in her dressing-room now. So perhaps this is—"

Cassio took a stride forward. "Yes!" he said, "it's the love-token—Othello's magic handkerchief which Desdemona loses."

And Inspector Appleby nodded sombrely. " 'Sure,' " he said slowly, " 'there's some wonder in this handkerchief.' "

Remorselessly the investigation went on. Cassio was the last person in whose hand the handkerchief was seen—but on going offstage Cassio had tossed it on a chair from which anyone might have taken it up. And it seemed likely that a Desdemona overcome with grief had done so.

Emilia's story then was plausible, and if believed it exonerated both Othello and herself. What followed from this? It appeared that of the rest of the company only Iago and Bianca had possessed a reasonable opportunity of slipping from the wings to the bed-head and there smothering Desdemona in that twelve-line interval between Emilia's going onstage and the play's coming to its abrupt and disastrous end. But further than this it was hard to press. Appleby turned from opportunity to motive.

Othello and his wife Desdemona, Iago and his wife Emilia, Cassio and his wife Bianca: these were the people concerned. Desdemona had been murdered. Cassio was not the murderer. And upon the stage, just before the fatality, there had been perceptible an obscure interplay of passion and resentment. What situation did these facts suggest?

Not, Appleby thought, a situation which had been common property long. For it was unlikely that the company had been playing night after night in this fashion; either matters would have come to a head or private passions would have been brought under control, at least during the three hours' traffic on the stage. Some more or less abrupt revelation, therefore, must be the background of what had happened tonight.

Three married couples living in a substantially closed group and with the standards of theatrical folk of the seedier sort. The picture was not hard to see. Adultery, or some particularly exacerbating drift taken by a customary promiscuity, was the likely background to this Desdemona's death. And Appleby felt momentarily depressed. He turned abruptly back to them. Detective investigation requires more than the technique of reading fingerprints and cigarette ends. It requires the art of reading minds and hearts. How, then, did these people's emotions stand now?

Othello was horrified and broken; with him as with Cassio—but more obscurely—things had come to an end. Well, his wife had been horribly killed, shortly after he had struck her brutally in the face. In a sense, then, Othello's immediate emotions were accounted for.

What of Iago? Iago was on the defensive still—and defensiveness means a sense of guilt. He was like a man, Appleby thought, before whom there has opened more evil than he intended or knew. And in whatever desperation he stood, he seemed likely to receive small succor or comfort from his wife. Emilia hated him. Was it a settled hate? Appleby judged that it had not that quality. It was a hatred, then, born of shock. Born of whatever abrupt revelation had preluded the catastrophe.

There remained Bianca, Cassio's wife. She, perhaps, was the enigma in the case, for her emotions ran deep. And her husband was out of it. Cassio was the type of chronically worried man; he expended his anxieties on the business of keeping his company financially afloat and emerged from this only to play subsidiary roles. As a husband he would not be very exciting. And Bianca required excitement. That hidden sort did.

The analysis was complete. Appleby thought a little longer and then spoke. "I am going to tell you," he said quietly, "what happened. But only the principal actors need remain."

There was a sigh from the people gathered round. Like shadows they melted into the wings—some with the alacrity of relief, others with the shuffle of fatigue. It had grown very cold. The curtain stirred and swayed, like a great shroud waiting to envelop those who remained.

"It began with Desdemona's seduction, or with the revelation of it. Is that not so?" Appleby looked gravely round. There was absolute silence. "Is that not so?" he repeated gently. But the silence prolonged itself. And Appleby turned to Othello. "You struck her because of that?"

And abruptly Othello wept. His blotched black face crumpled. "Yes," he said, "I struck her because I had discovered that."

Appleby turned to Iago. "You seduced this man's wife. And the result has been wilful murder. But did you know the truth was out? Or was it you yourself who smothered her to prevent confession and disclosure?"

Iago stepped back, snarling. "You've got nothing on me," he said. "And I won't say a word."

"From this time forth I never will speak word . . ." But Appleby was now facing Emilia. "Your husband had betrayed you. You had discovered he was sleeping with this man's wife. Did you, in the frenzy of your jealousy, smother her?"

Emilia's face had hardened. "These accusations mean nothing. Nobody knows who smothered her. And you will never find out."

There was a pause. Appleby turned slowly to Bianca. "And you?" he asked. "For how long had you been Iago's mistress? And what did you do when you found he had cast you off?"

"Nothing! I did nothing! And she's right. Nobody saw. Nobody can tell anything."

"And so the mystery will be unsolved?" Appleby nodded seriously. "It is not impossible that you are right. But we shall know in the morning." He turned to Cassio. "Did Desdemona have a dressing-room of her own? I'll just look in there before I go . . ."

"They probably won't hang her," Appleby said next day to the police sergeant. "It was a crime of sudden impulse, after all. And of course there was provocation in the adultery she had discovered." He paused. "Will it be any consolation to her in prison to know that she has made history in forensic medicine? I suppose not."

The sergeant sighed. "It's been neat enough," he said, "and something quite beyond our range, I must admit. But how did you first tumble to its being Emilia?"

"It was because she changed her mind about whom to blame. At first she had resolved to plant it on Othello, simply as the likeliest person. 'And why did you murder her, too?' she had asked him. But later on she told a story that pointed to either Bianca or her own husband, Iago. Desdemona, she said, had been alive and weeping when she looked through the curtain at the bed-head. And that, of course, let Othello out, as he had no subsequent opportunity for the murder.

"I asked myself what this change of front meant. Was it simply that Emilia had no grudge against Othello and altered her story in order to implicate her unfaithful husband whom she now hated? Somehow, I didn't think it was that. And then I recalled a gesture she had made. Do you remember? It was when Othello revealed that she was accustomed to draw back the curtain behind the bed and speak to Desdemona before going onstage."

The sergeant considered. "I seem to remember her hand going to her bodice. I thought it a bit theatrical—the conventional gesture of an agitated woman."

Appleby shook his head. "It wasn't quite that. What you saw was a hand flying up to where something should be—something that was now lost. And that something was a handkerchief. I saw the truth in a flash. *She had lost a handkerchief—a tear-soaked handkerchief—while smothering Desdemona.* And my guess was confirmed seconds later when she made her change of front and declared that she had seen Desdemona alive and weeping. For of course her change of story came from a sudden feeling that she must somehow account for the presence of the handkerchief beside the corpse."

"I see." The sergeant shook his head. "It was clever enough. But it was dangerous, being an unnecessary lie."

"It was fatal, as it turned out. But first I saw several things come together. A man may weep, but he won't weep into a small cambric handkerchief. Emilia showed signs of weeping, whereas another suspect, Bianca, was entirely self-controlled. So what had happened was pretty clear. Emilia had discovered her husband's infidelity and had been under strong stress of emotion. She had snatched up the handkerchief—Othello's magic handkerchief—perhaps while running to her dressing-room, and there she had wept into it. When her call came, she thrust it into her bodice. Later, when she yielded to an overwhelming impulse and smothered Desdemona, the handkerchief was dropped in the struggle and the body rolled on top of it.

"But how could all this be proved? Perhaps, as those people said, it couldn't be, and we should never get further than suspicion. But there was one chance—one chance of proving that Emilia had lied.

"A substantial proportion of people are what physiologists call secretors. And this means, among other things, that there is something special about their tears. From their tears, just as well as from their blood, you can determine their blood-group. Well, I had Desdemona's blood on one handkerchief and I had tears on another. I went straight to your local Institute of Medical Research. And they told me what I hoped to learn. *Those tears could not have come from a person of Desdemona's blood-group.*"

The sergeant sighed again. "Yes," he said, "it's neat—very neat, indeed."

"And we shall certainly learn, as soon as the law allows us to make a test, that the tears could have been Emilia's. And as Bianca, who has allowed herself to be blood-grouped, is ruled out equally with Desdemona, the case is clear."

Inspector Appleby rose. "Incidentally there is a moral attached to all this."

"A moral?"

"The moral that one savage old critic declared to be all there is to learn from Shakespeare's play. Housewives, he said, should look to their linen. In other words, it's dangerous to drop a handkerchief—and particularly in the neighborhood of a dead body."

"Q"

Mignon G. Eberhart
Dangerous Widows

One of my widows telephoned me at one o'clock Friday, and the other telephoned me at three o'clock Friday, and both of them invited me urgently to spend the weekend at their country place.

Neither, however, was a social invitation; each widow said frankly she was in need of my advice. In fact, it was an invitation to murder.

In literal fact, too, neither woman was my widow in the accepted sense. They were Henry Briggs's widows. Both, however, were very likely to fall within my scope of duty, for I am a banker, elderly enough to be entrusted with the somewhat difficult chore of advising, coaxing, cajoling, and generally acting as nursemaid to widows who seem strangely determined to invest in nonexistent uranium ore deposits and dry oil wells.

The two Mrs. Briggs were Henry's wives; one was his first wife, Frances Briggs, divorced and never remarried; the other, Eloise Briggs, was his second and the official Mrs. Briggs. Henry Briggs was one of my old clients. And the country house each referred to was the same country house, for it had been left to them, jointly, by his will.

Consequently a rather delicate situation was in the making. I took the 5:30 train to Stamford.

While Henry Briggs had been a client of the bank's for a long time, especially during his last illness, and I had had much to do with his affairs, I had never met either of his wives.

I cannot say that I faced the prospect with any pleasure. I do not like strife or emotions, and both were far too likely to develop. As I got out of the train and looked down the long platform I wondered which one would meet me and thus possibly endeavor to get in her claims first.

Neither did. A thickset, red-faced man, done to a turn in flagrantly country clothes, approached me and said with a hearty manner, "Mr. Wickwire?"

I nodded. He put out a large red hand. His face was jovial and friendly; he had shrewd, cold-blue eyes. "I'm Al Muller—friend of Henry's. The station wagon is this way."

I said, "Quite so," and followed him.

He put my bag in the station wagon, and wedged himself, puffing, behind the wheel. "I'm staying at the house. Thought I might be of some service to them." He negotiated a turn amid traffic.

I said, "Indeed."

His blue eyes shot me a rather narrow glance. "Yes. Frances—that's the first wife—arrived Thursday night by train. Henry was buried that afternoon, you'll remember. Eloise—that's the second wife—was here, of course."

I said, perhaps rather dryly, "And when did you arrive, Mr. Muller?"

He paused to examine a road sign rather deliberately. "Oh, I came up later Thursday night. Seemed to me I owed it to Henry. It's an odd situation, leaving the property like that. Do you know either of the Mrs. Briggs?"

Something about his manner went against my grain. I said stiffly that I hadn't had that pleasure.

He chuckled. "They're as like as two peas in a pod—extremely attractive women. You'll see. And there's a fight brewing there, mark my words. Neither is the sort to give up easily. I don't envy you, Mr. Wickwire."

"I am in no sense an arbiter. That is for the lawyers." I spoke coldly enough to penetrate even Mr. Al Muller's hide. We concluded our ride along the winding country roads in silence.

The house and grounds, when we reached them, proved to be on a rather lavish scale, with velvety lawns, swimming pool, tennis court, gardens. It represented, I knew, the whole of Henry Briggs's property; he had had a fairly large income, but had lived up to it. I had arrived at an approximate sum which I thought the property might fetch and was deducting, in my mind, such things as possible capital gains and taxes when we drew up at the white-columned entrance.

Here two women stood, waiting; both advanced to greet me as I got out of the car. And at least in one instance Muller was right; allowing for possibly fifteen years' difference in age they were very much alike. Both slender, fine-featured, blonde, and extremely attractive.

The younger—the offical Mrs. Briggs—spoke to me first, putting out a jeweled hand toward mine; she introduced me to the first Mrs. Briggs, while Al Muller stood watching with a rather stupid grin on his red face and a very watchful look in those shrewd eyes. We went at once into the house.

A maid took my bag upstairs. Cocktails were set out on a tray in the spacious living room. It was an imposing room, full of what might be called objects of art and dominated by a huge portrait of Henry Briggs, done apparently when he was a rather young man, at least twenty years before his death.

Eloise, the younger Mrs. Briggs, in her proper role of hostess, saw to it that I was comfortably seated, and asked me my preference as to cocktails. In the soft light from the table lamps the likeness between the two women diminished. They were the same general type—that was all.

The first Mrs. Briggs, Frances, was thinner and finer-drawn than the second, with darker hair but penetrating blue eyes. She wore a simple, inexpensive white cotton dress and no jewelry beyond her wedding ring.

Eloise was almost beautiful, with a magnolia skin, soft red mouth, and a rather luxuriant figure. Her dress was simple, too, but even my bachelor eyes perceived that it was an expensive simplicity; a diamond bracelet sparkled on her wrist.

It was Eloise who, again assuming her unquestionably correct position of authority, said that, if I agreed, both she and the other Mrs. Briggs preferred to postpone our discussion of business until morning. I agreed, most sincerely. Al Muller helped himself to another drink, at which both Mrs. Briggs looked at him coldly. The maid who had taken my bag announced dinner.

Aside from the fact that Al Muller became talkative in a jovial, rallying way, it was a quiet and merely social dinner. Not a word that was said, not a gesture, suggested potential strife between the two Mrs. Briggs. They were, in short, perfect ladies.

The evening was an early one. Eloise showed me to my room. "I hope you'll not mind coming down to breakfast," she said. "The maid lives in the village and goes home at night."

I assured her that it didn't matter. "By the way, Mrs. Briggs, exactly why did you ask me to come here?"

She hesitated for a second. Then she came close to me; her lovely mouth smiled invitingly. She put both hands appealingly on my arm. "Because I need your help."

Perfume wafted toward me; there was a deep glow in her eyes. I recoiled slightly. "I'm afraid the only help I can give you is to advise you to put the settlement of the estate in the hands of your lawyer."

Her hands, of necessity, dropped. She eyed me for a moment. Then she said, "Of course. Good night, Mr. Wickwire..."

It was all very calm, all very polite. But there was something very wrong in the house. I was obliged to wait, however, until the house was quiet before I went quietly downstairs again and out the door. I took the road to the village. It was a dark night, with scudding clouds.

The village was still lighted, and the drugstore had a pay telephone booth.

There are certain shortcuts to certain kinds of information which a banker knows. Nevertheless, since it was by then rather late, it took some time to accomplish my purpose.

Fortunately, in a way, I was under the interested observation of the young man behind the soda fountain the whole time, and indeed, I bought several magazines and an ice-cream soda from him. He had, however, told me that he'd have to shut up shop in another ten minutes when my New York call came through.

He turned off the lights as I left the drugstore and took my way back to the Briggs house. It seemed a rather short walk for I was thinking deeply, and it was with a sense of surprise that I turned in at the gates.

I stopped there, struck with another kind of surprise. The house was ablaze with lights. And then I heard the thud of automobiles. Indeed, I ducked out of the driveway barely in time as the first one took the curve and shot up to the entrance.

Other cars and motorcycles followed it. By the time I had run across the grass and reached the house the entire village constabulary as well as state troopers were swarming into the house, where Al Muller lay dead of a revolver shot on the rug below Henry's portrait.

I pushed my way in, passing Eloise and Frances, white and frightened, in the hall.

Al Muller's thick body lay apparently as it had fallen. His too-fancy country oxfords were sprawled wide apart. His brightly checked jacket was crumpled. A gun lay near his hand.

It was dawn when the police at last went away. Both Mrs. Briggs, exhausted and tense with strain, went upstairs as the last police car disappeared down the drive. I watched them go. And I wondered which one had murdered him.

Not that the police called it murder. The inquiry had been a long one and their questions had been many; they had taken our fingerprints; they had determined the ownership of the gun, which had belonged to Henry. But they had been guarded and reticent. They had not—as yet—called it murder.

They had listened to my own story, which luckily the young man in the drugstore could substantiate. They had listened to the stories of the two Mrs. Briggs, which were identical. Each had been awakened, she said, by the sound of the shot; each had waited a few moments, questioning it; they had come into the hall at almost the same time and then downstairs together to find Al Muller dead.

They had telephoned for the police. They had tried to arouse me and discovered my absence. They had been afraid that I, too, had been a victim of some robber who might still be about the grounds. When asked if either of them believed that Al Muller had been depressed by Henry's death to the point of suicide both appeared doubtful.

It was not suicide. It was murder.

But I didn't know which one had murdered him. I listened as their light footsteps, the whisper of their movements, died away above. Then I went back to the living room. Al Muller's body had been removed but the room still seemed to hold his presence, and it was not a pleasant one.

The room was in considerable disorder—chairs pushed around, the rug upon which Al Muller had died rolled up into a corner, small tables and lamps shoved aside carelessly; the portrait of Henry Briggs hung slightly askew on the wall.

I preferred not to touch the rug, or even approach it, but being a banker and a bachelor and somewhat finicky in habits of tidiness, I straightened the chairs and tables. No clues of course; I hadn't really expected there would be. I went to Henry's huge portrait with its heavy frame and straightened that, too. It seemed rather oddly out of place. Someone's shoulder must have brushed against it.

I measured, rather absently, my own shoulder height below the portrait. I am not a tall man, but the lower corner of the gilded frame was at least a foot above my own shoulder. So someone's hand had pushed it aside. I stood looking at Henry for a moment. Then I got a chair and climbed on it and looked behind the portrait.

Some time later I straightened the portrait carefully, got down from the chair, restored it to its place, and sat down in it. Something was going to happen, and it would happen soon.

I cannot say it was a pleasant wait. I hoped there was not another gun in the house. Somewhere a clock was ticking with an ominous, warning note as if to remind me of the fleeting quality of time.

It had run out swiftly for Al Muller. I am not a brave man; when I heard the faint rustle of a woman's garment on the stairway, and the very soft whisper of footsteps, I had to force myself to remain—waiting.

She must have seen the light in the room; still she thought it was empty for when she appeared as quietly as a ghost in the doorway and saw me she caught her breath and flung both hands to her throat. It was Frances, the first Mrs. Briggs.

After a moment she came toward me, her negligee gathered around her. Her fine eyes were very bright. "I didn't know you were here. I came to—to look. I had to see if there was anything the police didn't see. Mr. Wickwire—Eloise killed him."

It was, of course, in the cards. One of them would accuse the other; indeed, each might accuse the other of being the murderess—one because she must shield herself with a lie, the other because she must shield herself with the truth.

I said, "Why?"

Her hands moved toward each other. "I don't know. But I think it had something to do with money. Al Muller was simply not the kind of man to come here out of sympathy. He wanted something."

"Mrs. Briggs, why did you send for me?"

Her bright eyes didn't waver. "Because Muller was here. I didn't trust him. I was going to ask you to get rid of him. But I know Eloise killed him because I didn't. And there was no one else."

"I didn't kill him," Eloise said clearly from the doorway. "So it must have been you!" She was wearing a long floating negligee, and she had a gun in her hand.

Violence has never been, so to speak, my dish. I felt a kind of creeping chill up my backbone. But I had to get both women and myself out of the room and, of course, I'd have to get that gun.

I said, "We are all very tired. I suggest that you two ladies—er—dress while I prepare some sort of breakfast for us." I went to Eloise. "Whose gun is that?"

"Mine. Henry got it for me."

"What were you going to do with it?"

She looked at me. "I don't know," she said blankly and, I think, truthfully.

"You'd better give it to me."

She did so at once which both surprised and pleased me. I then said briskly, "Now I'll see to coffee," and went out of the room and through the dining room to the kitchen where I made a great clatter about cupboard doors and pots and pans. I made a mistake, however, when for safety's sake I dropped the gun into the flour bin.

I gave them barely time to dress and to accomplish what one of them had to accomplish in the living room, and consequently burned the toast while I was watching the clock. But as I took it and coffee into the dining room, Frances Briggs came in, charming and fresh in blue linen. After a moment Eloise, lovely and fresh in pink, entered also.

Both seized upon coffee. Neither spoke, and I was rather uneasily aware of stored-up dynamite. A very slight jar was all that was necessary to induce an explosion, and I was not ready for that. So when I spoke I did so cautiously.

"In view of the circumstances I'd like to suggest that we postpone our business talk. But I have a request to make. I was an old friend of Henry's. If neither of you wishes to keep the portrait of him, I wonder if you would be so kind as to give it to me."

Eloise's eyes leaped to me above the rim of her coffee cup. She put the cup down, and put her handkerchief to her eyes. She said from behind it, "Of course. I didn't realize that you felt that way about Henry. I have other pictures of Henry. He—he would want you to have it." She dabbed at her eyes with her handkerchief.

"Thank you," I said and turned to Frances, who had risen.

She said, "I'm sorry. I'll not pretend that I was in love with Henry when he met you, Eloise. I was not heartbroken when he asked me for a divorce; I agreed to it. But once, when Henry and I were young, when that portrait was made, I loved him. I'm sorry, Mr. Wickwire, I want the portrait."

So I knew what I had to know. I said something about understanding it, made an excuse, and left the room.

I let myself out, cautiously, through the back door. A grape arbor ran along there toward the garage, and I took shelter behind it. I reached the garage and was opening the door of the station wagon when Eloise ran into the garage.

"Mr. Wickwire, where are you going?"

"To the state police. Will you drive? I'm not accustomed to this car. Besides, it might be safer."

"Safer! Do you mean she—" She gave a kind of quick gasp and then slid behind the wheel. "Take the back way down to the road," I said. "The trees and shrubbery will shield us from the house."

The sun was up, streaking across shrubbery and lawns and making a bright path of the country road. She knew the way to the state police headquarters. She went in with me, and the young lieutenant who had directed the night's inquiry was at his desk using the telephone when we were shown into his office. He looked pleased and relaxed; his revolver lay on the desk.

"Oh, there you are. I was about to phone you. The fingerprints on the gun are Al Muller's. So it was probably suicide."

Fingerprints of course can be placed on guns after death, but I didn't care to argue with him about that. I gave one longing thought toward the gun in the flour bin and said, "I'm afraid I have evidence to the contrary. If you'll search the Briggs house you'll find a package of notes, given for loans advanced by Al Muller and signed by Henry Briggs. The signatures are forgeries. And in the meantime—" I cleared my throat "—kindly arrest this Mrs. Briggs at once and charge her—"

I couldn't finish because Eloise was too quick; she snatched the officer's revolver. Two shots went wild, a third crashed through the window, and then the young lieutenant had her tight in his arms, but it was not a loverlike embrace.

He released her when other troopers rushed in. I crawled out from under the desk with such dignity as I could summon. The young lieutenant was also very quick. "The notes," he said, panting and blushing deeply, "are probably on her. Get the matron from the village, Sergeant."

He was right. The notes, a rather bulky package, were concealed in her brassiere. I must say I was relieved to see them; she had had neither the time nor the chance to destroy them.

Later, back at the house, I had a conversation with the young lieutenant and with Frances Briggs. "So Muller loaned her all that money," the lieutenant said. "I take it that he thought he was loaning it to Henry during his illness, but she forged Henry's signatures."

I nodded. "Muller probably discovered, or knew from the beginning, that it was forgery. After Henry's death he—er—"

"Put the screws on," the lieutenant said. "He must have demanded quite a price. So she shot him."

"Then she had to get out of the room and up the backstairs in a hurry. She got the notes out of his pocket, shoved them behind the portrait, put his fingerprints on the gun, and ran up the back way. Frances Briggs came into the hall at about that time."

"But how did you know?"

"I found the notes. I didn't know which woman had shot him or which one had forged the notes and thus must get possession of them again. I gave both women time—I was afraid too much time—but, at any rate, I then asked for Henry's portrait.

"I knew that the woman who had shot Muller would not want the portrait: she wouldn't want any association with so strong a reminder of guilt. So a rejection of the portrait would be an indication of guilt—and an indication that the notes were gone.

"Eloise leaped at the chance to get rid of the portrait. Frances did not."

I added, "I must tell you that I made some inquiries by telephone as to Eloise. She was wearing jewelry; she was dressed expensively. In short, I found that she had staggering charge accounts and had spent far more money than Henry—remember, I am in a position to know—could have given her. So where was she getting the money? Why was Al Muller there?"

But the lieutenant said astutely, "You must have more solid evidence—basis for suspicion."

I told the lieutenant, "When anybody urgently wishes to see any banker, he—she—wants to borrow money. Frances Briggs had a different reason which was sound and sensible. But Eloise—"

"She wanted to borrow enough money on the property to pay off Muller!" the lieutenant cried. "Did she ask you for a loan?"

"Not," I said, "precisely."

"Oh, I see. But you weren't having any—I mean to say, you were not—that is, her charm—that is—" He blushed, looked apologetic, and tried to stop grinning.

"Oh, Mr. Wickwire!" Frances Briggs leaned toward me with a lovely smile, her magnificent eyes warm. "You *are* a detective! And a very courageous man."

There are more ways than one in which an attractive widow may be dangerous. I rose rather quickly and said I had to return to town. Indeed, when another widow invited me to her house on Long Island the next weekend I sent a subordinate in my place.

"Q"

Ruth Rendell
The Price of Joy

Daniel Derbyshire had once seen a cartoon in which a thug held a woman captive and bound while his henchman, on the telephone for a ransom, was remarking, "Her husband don't answer. There's just hysterical laughter." For a while he kept the newspaper in which it appeared and thought of cutting out the cartoon and pinning it to his office wall. But it was in deplorable taste, so he threw it away.

He was 50 and rich. The newspapers, when they mentioned him, referred to him as a tycoon. In the past they had been in the habit of mentioning him quite often, for his successes, for his business coups, and for the fact that he had been married four times. His first wife was named Joy. She was the mother of his children, and he had been happy with her until a crescendo of success, building up fast but not too fast for him to cope with it, altered his style of living and made Joy appear to him as suburban and commonplace.

At his request she had divorced him so that he could marry Vivien, who in her turn had divorced him so that he could marry Jane. In common with Henry the Eighth, he had had one wife who had set him free by dying before he could rid himself of her, and his Jane, like Henry's, had died. After her death, when he was 45, he had married Prunella.

At the age they had been—she was six years his junior—men and women are supposed to know their own minds. At last, he thought, he had found someone with whom he could settle down comfortably for the remainder of his life. But her dullness, when the first flush of sexual novelty was over, had nearly driven him mad. What, he sometimes wondered, in her education and her experience, had led her to believe that a man of his sort worth five millions wanted love in a cottage, with cosy, suffocating evenings at home, a quiet society-shirking life? It never occurred to him to answer that it was he who had led her to believe it.

And then he met Joy again.

Of course, they had never entirely lost touch. The upbringing of their children, of whom she'd had custody, had seen to that. But for years they had communicated with each other mostly through their lawyers and by way of messages carried from one to the other by their now grown-up children. Five years after his fourth marriage he met Joy at a party, quite by chance.

It was remarkable what the years had done. As a girl, Joy had been rather plain. At 52 she was statuesque, elegant, her carefully dressed silver hair surmounting a face that was handsome, wise, and sardonic. The alimony she'd had from him had enabled her to travel and buy a mews house in Mayfair. She had met many men, though she had never remarried.

Joy, when young, had never been desired by any man but himself, but now she was surrounded by men—as he learned when he telephoned her as, these days, he often did. And then, after asking him how he was, she would tell him to hold on for a moment, and he would hear her whisper, "Oh, Philip, bring me an ashtray, would you?" or "That's the front doorbell, John. Be an angel and see to it, my dear."

Her attraction for others made her even more attractive to him. He wanted her again. He saw, in what he observed of her lifestyle and her manners and her dress, that she would be a perfect hostess for him, entertaining his friends as Prunella never could.

He wanted her apart from that. Those children of his would have stared in disbelief had they known with what youthful lust he wanted her, as if they had never made love all those years ago, never become parents together, and he had never grown weary of her.

"You really want to marry me again, Dan?"

"You know I do," he said. "We should never have separated."

"It was you who separated us. You broke my heart."

"They say it's never too late to mend, Joy. Let me mend it."

"And what," said Joy, "about Prunella?"

One can get used to anything, and Daniel was used to discarding wives. The cumbersome and frightening machinery of the law which keeps many ill-matched couples together, the crippling payments demanded, held no fear for him. "That won't last, anyway," he said. "I'll get a quiet divorce fixed up, one of those incompatibility jobs."

"Not on my account, you won't," said Joy. "Maybe Vivien didn't care about me when she got hold of you, but I'm thirty years older than she was and I do care. I like Prunella, what I've seen of her, and I won't do to her what Vivien did to me."

"Are you saying you don't want to marry me?"

"No. I'd like to marry you again. I'm still very fond of you, Dan.

If Prunella were in love with someone else and left you, that would be a different story."

"Or if she were to die, I suppose?"

"Of course. But don't have any ideas about getting rid of her, please. I wouldn't put it past you. You're always quite ruthless about getting what you want, and then when you've got it you don't want it any more."

Daniel, however, hadn't the remotest notion of murdering his wife, and Joy's suggestion slightly shocked him. But those failings in Prunella which had always irritated him now fanned his exasperation to fever pitch. He was more than ever impatient with her timidity which made her shy of appearing with him at distinguished functions, frightened to drive her own car in London, and unwilling to make the simple speech required of her when asked to open the fête in the village where they had their weekend home.

He was nearly enraged when she refused an invitation for them to join a party on a peer's yacht on the grounds that they liked to spend their holidays alone together and quietly in the country. And it was particularly annoying that at this time there appeared in a Sunday-paper supplement an effusive feature about his private life, with many colored photographs of himself and Prunella in tweeds, himself and Prunella with bounding dogs, himself and Prunella confronting each other tenderly against the background of a log fire.

The captions and text were even worse. Had he really said those things? Had he truly told that reporter that he had come home to port after a long voyage on stormy seas? Had he claimed to have found the Right Woman at last after so much trial and error? He was obliged to admit that he had. But those feature stories take so long to appear, and he had said all those embarrassing things long before he had re-encountered Joy.

The idea that Prunella might fall in love with someone else and leave him—that was an attractive idea. But he was too hard-headed and too much of a realist to hope seriously for it. Though Prunella was eight years younger than Joy, in his eyes she looked older. And she never met any men except the happily married José who, with his wife, kept house for them, and the elderly driver of the minicab she employed whenever she wanted to cross London to visit her mother. (How profoundly this annoyed Daniel, that she should be driven about in a car belonging to a shabby minicab company, when she could have used his Rolls-Royce and his chauffeur.)

Moreover, despite her total lack of dress sense, her preference for costume jewelry over diamonds and her taste for drinking sparkling champagne cider, Prunella was fond of money. She liked spending it on her mother, her sisters, and her scruffy nephews and nieces. She had a horse, eating its head off and growing fat in the country. The dogs alone—and they were her dogs—cost a thousand pounds a year in food and veterinary care.

If she left him for another man, he would, of course, contribute something toward her support, but that something would be nothing to what she could skin him for if he left her. And she knew it. She had the examples of Joy's and Vivien's alimony before her.

So Daniel did nothing—that is, he did nothing positive. His negative actions took the form of neglecting Prunella thoroughly, seldom going home before midnight, and phoning Joy every day. He saw Joy whenever she allowed him to, but that wasn't often.

"I lead such a hectic life, darling," she said on the phone. "For instance, there's Max's private viewing tonight, and naturally I shall be at the première of Ivan's film tomorrow—hold on a moment, would you? Be an angel and get me a drink, David—I'd like to see you, Dan, but really it's so difficult."

"It wouldn't be difficult if you wanted to," growled Daniel whose desires were greatly inflamed by all these references to the glossy living in which his first wife was taking part, and taking part, no doubt, with grace.

"Not much use wanting, is there, Dan?—thank you, David, that's delicious—I'm afraid you've made your bed, my dear, and you must lie on it. With Prunella."

When they did meet she was affectionate and charming. But, no, she wouldn't have an affair with him. It was marriage or nothing, and she had to admit that, at her age, she did rather incline to the companionship and security of marriage.

"But we can be friends," she said sweetly, adding that things between him and Prunella couldn't be that bad. She too had seen the Sunday supplement in which they looked so cosy and contented with each other. "And they say the camera doesn't lie, Dan dear."

Things went on in this way for another six months. Daniel hung about after Joy like a lovesick adolescent, and Prunella took to spending two or three nights a week at her mother's. Then, one Monday lunchtime, he received a telephone call at work. His secretary was temporarily out of the room, and he took the call himself.

A man's voice said, "We have your wife."

"I beg your pardon?" said Daniel.

"You heard. We have your wife. There've been enough kidnapings lately for me not to have to spell it out. She's quite safe and nothing'll happen to her—if you pay up."

"I shall go straight to the police," said Daniel.

"Don't be so stupid. Good God, I'd have thought a bloke who's made your kind of money'd have had a bit more brains. Don't you read the papers? Haven't you ever read a thriller? You go to the police and we shall know. The moment the police get word of this I'll chop off your wife's right hand and send it to you by first-class mail."

"You must be mad."

"I'll call you at home. Seven sharp. You'd better be there." The phone went dead.

Daniel sent for his secretary, told her he was feeling unwell, and to cancel the conference scheduled for that afternoon. His chauffeur drove him home. The first thing he did was ask José where Mrs. Derbyshire was.

"She left by cab at ten this morning, sir, to see her mother."

But Prunella's mother hadn't seen her since the previous Friday. Daniel told her some reassuring lie, then phoned the minicab company. The boss answered.

"Jim was to pick her up at ten, you say? Hang on. Did you pick up Mrs. Derbyshire this morning, Jim? No? No, he didn't, Mr. Derbyshire. The booking was canceled by phone at nine thirty."

The gang, whoever they were, must have known Prunella's movements thoroughly, canceled her booking, and sent a substitute of their own. He wondered where they were holding her and what sort of ransom they were going to ask. At 7:00 he found out.

"Hallo again," said the same voice. "Sitting comfortably? Good. I suppose you're very fond of your wife, aren't you?"

"Of course I am," said Daniel.

"Of course you are. As a matter of fact, it was all those pictures of domestic bliss in that rag that gave us the idea."

Daniel cursed the Sunday supplement. Nothing but trouble had come of it. First it had set Joy against him, and now there was this. "Get on with it," he snapped.

"Since you're so fond of your wife, you'd pay anything to get her back, wouldn't you? Mrs. Derbyshire has admitted to us—under a little pressure—that you're worth five millions. So two hundred and fifty thousand pounds wouldn't be asking too much, now, would it?"

"A quarter of a million?" said Daniel, aghast.

"Five percent of what you've got. You won't even notice it. Like to talk to your wife?"

Before Daniel could reply, Prunella had come on the line.

"Oh, Dan, you will give them what they want, won't you? I'm sorry I told them you were so rich, but they made me."

"Are you all right, Pru?"

"At the moment, but I'm cold and I'm frightened." She gave a little sob. "I want to go home. I want to get out of here." A shriek followed as if someone had stuck a pin in her.

The man came back on.

"A quarter of a million in twenty-pound notes," he said. "I quite understand it'll take a day or two to get it. It's Monday now, so we'll say Thursday for delivery date, Thursday evening. You can go to your stockbroker in the morning. Go, not phone. We'll have his premises under observation. If you don't go, I'll send you your wife's left little toe in a matchbox. Call you tomorrow, two o'clock. Okay?"

A couple of sleeping pills afforded Daniel a night's rest. He went into the office as usual. Naturally, he must phone the police—it was a citizen's duty to do that, however unpleasant the consequences. If everyone in this kind of trouble went straight to the police, there would be less of this kidnaping nonsense.

On the other hand, the idea of Prunella's being mutilated wasn't agreeable to think of. She had nice hands, though he was obliged to confess he couldn't remember what her toes looked like. His stockbroker would think it very odd to sell shares at this time amounting to £250,000. Presumably, his bank would have to be notified in advance, as they certainly wouldn't have a quarter of a million lying about in twenty-pound notes. By two o'clock he hadn't phoned the police or been to see his stockbroker. The phone rang.

"You didn't go," the voice said, and there came the sound of a woman's scream. Daniel shuddered. He thought of that horrible cartoon which wasn't at all true to life.

"You damn—" he began. "You lowdown filthy swine."

"There's no need to be rude. If her toe doesn't come in the morning, blame the post office. They've not been too reliable lately. Go to your stockbroker. Now."

Daniel went. His stockbroker told him it was a very bad time to sell, and wouldn't Mr. Derbyshire reconsider? Sure that the scream he had heard was made by Prunella while in the process of having her toe amputated, Daniel said no, he wouldn't reconsider. Back home, he drank a lot of brandy. He thought of phoning Joy, and then thought better of it. He told José that Prunella was staying with her mother, and he told her mother that Prunella had gone to the country.

The next two days were extremely unpleasant. The man phoned four times, but Daniel wasn't allowed to speak to Prunella who, he was told, was "feeling too unwell." On Thursday morning the man said, "You'll be collecting the cash today, right? Put it in a suitcase, and at seven sharp take the suitcase to Charing Cross Station. Leave it there in a left-luggage locker, and this is what you're to do with the key. Take it into the Embankment Gardens and push it into the earth on the left-hand side of the statue of Sir Arthur Sullivan. Got that?

"The statue's the one of the old boy with this woman crying and draping herself about. Muse of music or something. As a matter of fact, she reminds me of your wife. Especially at this moment. If you take the police with you or don't bring the cash, I won't be back here by eight thirty. And if I'm not back here by eight thirty, we cut Mrs. Derbyshire's throat. She's had some experience of the knife already, and she doesn't like it."

Trembling, Daniel took the morning papers which his secretary handed him. On the front page of the top one was a photograph of Princess Anne at a charity performance of *Firebird*, and in the background could be seen Joy, holding the arm of a tall handsome man. He let out a groan.

"Are you all right, Mr. Derbyshire?" his secretary asked.

"Yes—that is, no. Never mind. Call me a cab, will you? I have to go to my bank."

The bank provided him with a guard to escort him and his large suitcase back to the Derbyshire Building. Daniel put the suitcase under his desk and stared at it. A quarter of a million. What a price to pay for a woman you don't even want! He had intended, within the next few months, to settle just this amount on his son and the same amount on his daughter. That, now, would be impossible. And they might kill Prunella anyway. It would be a fine thing to lose the money *and* Prunella.

On the other hand, wouldn't it literally be a *fine* thing? Daniel didn't think it would bother him so much to rob his children of part of their patrimony if by parting with that money he could rid himself of Prunella for good.

Immediately he castigated himself for the thought. But it kept returning. What a pity the kidnapers didn't have a keener insight, and had said instead that for a quarter of a million they would kill his wife...

He must be overwrought, he thought, his mind unhinged by all this anxiety.

Five o'clock. He sent his secretary home and then he opened the large suitcase. The notes were new and crisp and pale lilac in color—12,500 of them in packets. It was a great deal of money, a queen's ransom. But he would willingly and happily have parted with it if it could have bought him Joy. Instead, it was going to buy him Prunella.

At this point a terrible thought came to Daniel. Until now he had considered going to the police, considered stalling, but he had never considered simply *not paying*. And yet what a fool he was to think it would have been preferable if the man had asked for money to kill her rather than to save her! To kill her need cost him nothing. All he had to do was not pay. Wasn't this, in fact, the answer to the dilemma by which he had been beset for nearly a year?

But poor Prunella, frightened, lonely, cold, maltreated. She was his wife, and once he had loved her. He owed it to her to try to save her. Having closed the suitcase, he sent for his chauffeur and went home.

"Don't put the car away, George. I shall need you again at six thirty."

He took the suitcase into his study. Prunella would be back with him by—when? Ten? Midnight? Without, very likely, one of her toes. Still, that hadn't been his fault. Not really. It was disagreeable to think of anyone being killed by having her throat cut. But was there any *agreeable* way of being killed?

Suicide was a different matter. Obviously it would be preferable to kill oneself with pills and liquor rather than by hanging. But if one were going to *be* killed, there seemed very little to choose between being strangled or blindfolded and shot or run over by a car. There wasn't a nice way of dying by someone else's violence.

They would kill her anyway, he thought. They wouldn't dare take the risk of her later being able to identify them. And he would have thrown that quarter of a million away just as effectively as if he had sunk it in the Thames. Besides, there was always the chance they wouldn't kill her and the money be lost anyway.

At 6:15 he had another look inside the suitcase. Already, by what he had done, he had lost a couple of days' interest on that money. They would kill Prunella and dump her body by some roadside. The police would see that he'd had the money ready and realize that the gang had killed his wife before he'd had time to pay the ransom. The British public would sympathize with him and understand when, in his grief, he tried to heal his broken heart by remarrying his first wife, the mother of his children.

Six thirty. The Rolls-Royce stood waiting on the driveway. Daniel poured himself a large brandy. He waited till 6:40 and then rang the bell for his chauffeur.

"Put the car away, George. I won't be needing it again tonight."

José served him his solitary dinner at 7:15. Daniel took one mouthful of soup, gagged and rushed to the bathroom where he was sick.

The man phoned at 9:00. Prunella was still alive, minus a hand and a toe. It wasn't very nice for her because they couldn't, under the circumstances, call a doctor to attend her.

The man said, "Follow the prescribed procedure at nine in the morning, Charing Cross Station and the locker key in the earth by the Sullivan statue."

Daniel didn't sleep at all. He kept on throwing up all night, but he didn't take the suitcase to the station in the morning.

All that day there was no sign from the kidnapers. Late that evening the man phoned again. Daniel put the receiver down without speaking, and after that there were no more calls. His body had begun to twitch and jerk, sweat kept breaking out all over him, and his heartbeat was irregular, sometimes pounding and sometimes seeming to stop altogether in a very frightening way.

But on Saturday morning a great peace descended on him. It was over now, it must be. Prunella was dead, and after a decent interval he could go to Joy, a free, ardent wooer.

No work today. Having made up his mind to get in touch with the police during the next few hours—it would be a bit ticklish, thinking of the right things to say—he took Prunella's two Great Danes and the Dalmation out for a walk. When he got back he went straight into the study to plan his phone tactics with the police. The large suitcase was open on the desk, and Prunella was standing over it, examining its contents.

He felt himself turn white. He felt as if all the blood had rushed out of his tissues and charged into his heart to start up that hideous pounding once more.

"Thank God you're all right," he managed to whisper.

She faced him. She looked extremely well, though somewhat disgruntled. It was plain she had all her fingers and toes intact.

"What did you get the money for if you weren't going to pay up?"

"I was," said Daniel. "I was stalling."

"Like hell. You can come in now, Jim." Prunella opened the door to admit the minicab driver who looked much younger and far more strapping than Daniel remembered him. "Jim, this is my loving husband," she said. "Funny, I ought to have known it wouldn't work."

Daniel sat down. "Be kind enough to explain," he said icily.

"I've been in love with Jim for the past six months, but I knew I wouldn't get much out of you if I left you. And Jim's only got his minicab. So we figured this out. Sorry, Jim, I'm afraid this is it. He doesn't think I'm worth a quarter of a million, so I'll have to stay with him."

"Stay!" Daniel shouted. "I wouldn't have you here after what you've done for twice what's in that suitcase! Of all the filthy cruel tricks to play on anyone! You don't know what I've been through. This has probably caused permanent injury to my health. I've lost hundreds in interest on that money." He was choking with rage. "I'll divorce you and name that crook, and God help me, I won't give you a damned penny!"

"You haven't any proof," said Prunella, "and we won't give you any. From what José says, you've told everyone I've been with mother." She sighed. "Jim and I know when we're beaten. We shall part here and now forever."

"What were you going to do?" Daniel growled.

"Well, since you ask, Jim would have hung onto the cash, and after the fuss had died down I'd have left you and joined him. But that's out of the question now. It won't be very nice for me living with a man who doesn't care if I get my throat cut, but I haven't any choice." Prunella took her coat off. "And now I'd better see what José is doing about lunch. I'll try and be a better wife to you now, Dan, to make up for all the trouble I've caused. I won't go out so much and we'll stay in every evening together."

"You're crazy," said Daniel. "I won't stand for it. I'll leave you." But he couldn't. Joy wouldn't have him if he left her. He jumped up. "Don't you understand I don't want you!"

"Only too well," said Prunella, glancing at the suitcase, "but we'll get over that. We'll work at our marriage, we must. Goodbye, Jim. It was a fine idea while it lasted."

Daniel seized the suitcase, frantically fastening its clasps. "Take it," he shouted. "Take it and go."

THE PRICE OF JOY

"D'you mean that?" said the voice of the man on the phone. Jim grinned broadly. "Thanks a lot."

"Thank you, Dan. That's very generous of you. And just one other thing. May I take the dogs too?"

"Take what you like and get out of my house!"

He watched them go off down the street together, Jim carrying the quarter of a million in the suitcase, Prunella, one arm linked with his, the other holding the dogs on their triple leash. A large brandy steadied him. No one would believe that a man's own wife could do a thing like that. Of all the bare-faced abominable treachery! And those disgusting threats of mutilation while, no doubt, she'd been laughing in the background. God, how he'd have liked to smash them both! All he hoped now was that they'd get mugged, maimed for life, for the contents of that suitcase.

And then, as his rage cooled into seething resentment, he realized what had been achieved. He was free. Prunella had left him of her own accord. Within three or four months he could be divorced. He rang for George, got into the car, and told George to drive him to a certain mews in Mayfair.

Leaning back against the cushions, he thought of the price he had paid for Joy. Surely no woman of 52, once discarded, had ever before been purchased for a quarter of a million? One day he would tell her. When they were married. But she was worth it. He longed for her with the passion of a boy of 20, though when he was 20 and courting her for the first time, he had never felt this yearning and this tremulous urgency.

Thirty years ago he had gone to her in her father's house on his old motorbike; now he was going to her in a Rolls-Royce Silver Cloud, having paid a fortune for the privilege of asking her once more to be his wife. His heart raced. He ran up the steps of her house and rang the bell.

She opened the door herself. Daniel thought she looked 20 years younger, perhaps 30 years, yet far more lovely than when he had first seen her. Her silver hair was an anachronism above that youthful flushed face.

"Dan! How lovely. How nice of you to come."

She turned and led him into the living room before he could take her in his arms. There was a man standing by the table. Strange men kept appearing in his life today, but this one wasn't hiding. He was pouring champagne. Daniel observed vaguely that there were other people there too—strange people getting in his way on this day of all days.

He recognized the champagne pourer as Joy's escort in the newspaper photograph. She must get rid of him and all the others, he thought, and he turned to her impulsively, arrogantly. She smiled and took his arm.

"Dan dear," she said, "I want you to meet Paul. We were married this morning."

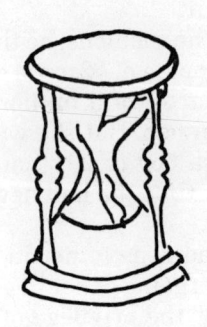

Ellery Queen
The Death of Don Juan

ACT I. Scene 1.

An early account of the death of Don Juan Tenorio, Fourteenth Century Spanish libertine—who, according to his valet, enjoyed the embraces of no fewer than 2,954 mistresses during his lifetime—relates that the great lover was murdered in a monastery by Franciscan monks enraged by his virility. For four hundred years poets and dramatists have passed up this ending to Don Juan's mighty career as too unimaginative. No such charge can be brought against *their* versions.

Don Juan, they tell us, planted the seeds of his own destruction when he harrowed the virtue of a certain noble young lady, daughter of the commander of Sevilla. While this sort of thing was no novelty to the famous gallant, it was to the young lady; and Don Juan found himself fighting a duel with her father, the commander, whom he killed.

Here the poetic imagination soars. Don Juan visits the tomb of the late victim of his sword. A marble statue of the grandee decorates the tomb. Don Juan invites the statue to a feast, an inexplicable gesture under the circumstances. Having failed in the flesh, the ensculptured nobleman leaps at his second chance to avenge his daughter's ruptured honor. The marble guest shows up at the feast, grasps the roué in his stony clutch, and drags him off to hell. Curtain.

This Don Juan changeling counts among its affectionate foster-parents Molière, Mozart's librettist Da Ponte, Dumas *père*, Balzac, Byron, and Shaw. Now to the roster must be added the modest name of Ellery Queen, who has fathered his own. According to Ellery, Don Juan was really murdered in a New England town named Wrightsville, and this is how it came about.

From the days of William S. Hart and Wallace Reid, Wrightsville's dramatic appetite was catered to by the Bijou Theater in High Village. When in the course of human events the movies' fat years turned lean, the Bijou's owner bought up the old scrap-iron dump on Route 478 and on the site built Wright County's first alfresco movie theater, a drive-in that supplanted Pine Grove in the Junction as the favorite smooching place of the young in heart.

This left the two-by-fours nailed over the doors of the abandoned Bijou; and the chairman of the Wrightsville Realty Board, whose office faced the empty building from the other side of Lower Main, vowed at a Board lunch over his fourth old-fashioned that one dark night he was going to sneak over to that eyesore on the fair face of High Village and blow the damn thing up, he was so sick of looking at it.

When, suddenly, Stanley Bluefield bought it.

Stanley Bluefield was a rare specimen in the Wrightsville zoo. Where the young of the first families grew up to work with their money, Stanley played with it. Seven generations of Bluefields had labored and schemed so that Stanley's life might be one grand game.

As Stanley often said, his vocation was hobbies. He collected such unexpected things as chastity belts, Minié balls, and shrunken heads. He financed one expedition to prove the historicity of Atlantis and another to unearth the bones of Homer. He flitted from Yoga to Zen to voodoo, and then came back to the Congregational church. And the old Bluefield mansion on the Hill was usually infested with freeloaders no one in Wrightsville had ever laid eyes on—"my people collection," he called them.

Stanley Bluefield looked like a rabbit about to drop its first litter. But there was a sweet, stubborn innocence in the portly little bachelor that some weedy souls of the region found appealing.

Stanley bought the Bijou because he discovered The Theater. To prepare himself, he lived for two years in New York studying drama, after which he financed a play and watched the professionals spend his money in a lost but educational cause. He hurried home to organize an amateur company.

"No, indeed, no red barns surrounded by hollyhocks for me," he told the *Wrightsville Record* reporter. "My plan is to establish a permanent repertory theater, a year-round project to be staffed by local talent."

"This area hasn't supported professional companies in years, Mr. Bluefield," the reporter said. "What makes you think it will support an amateur one?"

One of the little man's pinkish eyes winked. "You wait and see."

Stanley's secret weapon was Joan Truslow. Joanie was what the boys at the Lions and the Red Men luncheons called "a real stacked little gopher," with natural ash-blonde hair and enormous spring-violet eyes. She had been majoring in drama at Merrimac U. when the arthritis got her father and 'Aphas was forced to resign as town clerk. Joan had had to come home and take a job as receptionist at The Eternal Rest Mortuary on Upper Whistling. She was the first to answer Stanley's call, and her audition awed him.

"*Wonderful*," he had confided to Roger Fowler. "That girl will make us all *proud*."

Rodge was not comforted. A chemical engineer, he had used his cut of Great-uncle Fowler's pie to buy one of the blackened brick plants standing idle along the Willow River in Low Village and convert it to Fowler Chemicals, Inc. His interest in Stanley Bluefield's Playhouse was strictly hormonal; he had been chasing Joan Truslow since their high-school days.

To keep an eye on her, young Fowler had offered his services to Stanley, who was not one to look a gift horse under the crupper. The Playhouse needed a technician-in-charge to be responsible for carpentry, props, lights, and other dreary indispensables. So long as the backstage crew functioned, Stanley did not care how many opportunities Roger seized to corner the stagestruck Miss Truslow and, sotto voce, con amore, try to sell her a bill of household goods.

Stanley did the Bijou over, inside and out, and renamed it The Playhouse. It cost him a fortune, and of course Emmeline DuPré's was the first voice of doom. (Miss DuPré, known to the cruder element as the Town Crier, taught Dancing and Dramatics to the children of the already haut monde of Wrightville.)

"Stanley will never see a penny of his unearned lucre," Miss DuPré announced.

For once the Town Crier seemed to cry true. The Playhouse was a resounding flop, Joanie Truslow notwithstanding. Stanley tried Shaw, Kaufman and Hart, Tennessee Williams, even (these were conceived in desperation and born calamities) Ionesco and Anouilh; comedy, farce, melodrama, tragedy; the square and the offbeat. They continued to play to dwindling houses.

"Of course, we're not very *good* yet," Stanley reflected aloud after a lethal week.

"Joan's colossal, and you know it," Rodge Fowler said in spite of himself.

"Thank you, sir." Joan's dimple drove him crazy. "I thought you were against careers for females."

"Who's against careers for females? I'm just against a career for you," Roger said, hating himself for driving the dimple to cover.

"Look, Stan, how much more of your ancestral dough are you prepared to drop into this cultural tomb we call home?"

Stanley said in his precise, immovable way, "I am *not* giving up yet, Roger."

A *Record* editorial said: "Is local taste so low that our favorite amusements must be TV Westerns and dramatized deodorant commercials, and movies that give our children the willies? At a time when Wrightsville is reflecting the nationwide jump in juvenile delinquency, alcoholism, dope addiction, gambling, and what have you, the community should be supporting Mr. Bluefield's efforts to bring us worthwhile dramatic fare. Why not attend The Playhouse regularly, and bring along your teenagers?"

The empty seats kept spreading like a rash.

A letter to the *Record* signed Cassandra, in a literary style indistinguishable from Emmeline DuPré's, suggested that The Wrightsville Playhouse be renamed The Haunted Playhouse.

When the town's snickers reached the Hill, Stanley's pink eyes turned a murderous red. Very few people in Wrightsville were aware of the paper thinness of Stanley Bluefield's skin.

He flung himself into the Viking throne in his catch-all study, and he thought and he thought.

All at once the name of Archer Dullman flew into his head.

Ten minutes later Wrightville's patron of the performing arts was driving lickety-hop for the airport and the next plane connection to New York.

ACT I. Scene 2.

Ellery checked in at the Hollis, showered and changed, cased the lobby, toured the Square (which was round), and returned to the hotel without having seen a single familiar face.

He was waiting for the maitre d' (also new to him) in a queue of strangers at the entrance to the main dining room, thinking that time was being its usual unkind self, when a voice behind him said, "Mr. Queen, I presume?"

"Roger!" Ellery wrung young Fowler's hand like Dr. Livingstone at Ujiji. The truth was, he had met Rodge Fowler less than half a dozen times during his various visits to Wrightsville. "How are you? What's happened to this town?"

"I'm fine, and it's still here with certain modifications," Roger said, blowing on his hand. "What brings you this-a-way?"

"I'm bound for the Mahoganies—vacation. I hear you're Wrightsville's latest outbreak of industrial genius."

"That's what they tell me, but who told you?"

"I'm a *Record* mail-subscriber from way back. How come you've joined a drama group, Rodge? I thought you got your kicks in a chem lab."

"Love," Roger said hollowly. "Or whatever they're calling it these days."

"Of course. Joan Truslow. But isn't the company folding? That ought to drop Joanie back into your lap."

Roger looked glum. *"The Death of Don Juan."*

"That old stand of corn? Even Wrightsville—"

"You're not getting the message, man. Starring Mark Manson. Complete with doublet, hose, and codpiece. We open tomorrow night."

"Manson." Ellery stared. "Who dug him up?"

"Stanley Bluefield, via some Times Square undertaker named Archer Dullman. Manson's a pretty lively corpse, Ellery. We're sold out for the run."

"So the old boy still packs them in in Squedunk," Ellery said admiringly. *"The Death of Don Juan . . .* This I've got to see."

"There's Stanley at that corner table, with Manson and Dullman. I'm meeting them for dinner. Why not join us?"

Ellery had forgotten how much like a happy rabbit Stanley Bluefield looked. "I'm *delighted* you're here for the opening," Stanley cried. "You will be, Ellery, won't you?"

"If I have to hang from a rafter. I haven't had the pleasure of attending one of Mr. Manson's performances in—" Ellery had been about to say "in a great many years," but he changed it to "in some time."

"How are things at the Embassy, Mr. Green?" the actor asked sadly, tilting his cocktail glass, finding it empty, running his forefinger around the inside of the glass, and licking the finger. "You should have seen me with Booth, sir. John Wilkes, that is. Those were the days. *Serveuse,* may I trouble you for an encore?"

The wavering finger pushed the empty glass into alignment with nine others, whereupon Manson smiled at Ellery and fell asleep. Head thrown back, he resembled a mummy; his gentle, fine-boned face was overlaid with a mesh of wrinkles.

The waitress took their orders. Manson woke up, courteously ordered *Chaud-Froid de Cailles en Belle Vue,* and fell asleep again.

"What's that?" the waitress demanded.

"Never mind, honey. Bring him a rare T-bone."

Stanley looked peevish. "I do hope—"

"Don't worry, Bluefield. He never misses a curtain."

Ellery turned, surprised. The speaker was the man introduced to him as Archer Dullman. He had immediately forgotten Dullman was there. He now saw why. Dullman was not large and not small, neither fat nor thin, ruddy nor pale. Hair, eyes, voice were neutral. It was hard to imagine him excited, angry, amorous, or drunk. Ellery paid close attention to him after that.

"Are you Mr. Manson's manager, Mr. Dullman?"

"It's a buck."

Even so, it was some time before he realized that Dullman had not actually answered his question.

Ellery buttered a roll. "By the way, isn't it an Actors' Equity rule that its members may not perform with amateurs?"

It was Stanley who answered; in rather a hurry, Ellery thought. "Oh, but you can almost always get Equity's permission in special cases. Where no Equity company is playing the area, and provided the amateur group initiates the request, deposits the full amount of the member's salary with them, and so forth. Ah, the soup!" He greeted the return of their waitress with relief. "Best chowder in town. Right, Minnie?"

Ellery wondered what was bugging the little man. Then he remembered.

The "Archer" had fooled him. Around Broadway, Dullman was always called "The Dull Man." It was a typical Broadway quip; Dullman was supposed to be sharper than a columnist's tooth. If Stanley Bluefield had allowed himself to be sucked into a typical Dullman deal . . .

"They've been calling us The Haunted Playhouse and laughing their heads off," Stanley was chortling. "Who's laughing now?"

"Not me," Rodge Fowler growled. "That scene on the couch between Manson and Joan in the first act is an absolute disgrace."

"How would you expect Don Juan to act on a couch?" Dullman asked with a smile.

"You didn't have to direct it that way, Dullman!"

"Oh, you're directing?" Ellery murmured. But nobody heard him.

"Think of the dear old ladies, Fowler."

"I'm thinking of Joan!"

"Now, Rodge," Stanley said.

Manson chose that moment to wake up. He peered around the crowded dining room and staggered to his feet. His hairpiece had come loose and slipped to one side, exposing a hemisphere of dead-white scalp. He stood there like some aged Caesar in his cups, bowing to his people.

"My dear, dear friends," the actor said; and then, with simple confidence, he slid into Dullman's arms.

Stanley and Roger were half out of their chairs. But Ellery was already supporting the actor's other side.

"Manson can walk, Dullman. Just give him some support."

Between them they dragged Manson, graciously smiling, from the dining room. The lobby seethed with people attending a Ladies' Aid ball; a great many were waiting for the elevators.

"We can't maneuver him through that mob, Dullman. What floor is he on?"

"Second."

"Then let's walk him up. Manson, lift your feet. That's it. You're doing nobly."

Ellery and Dullman hustled him up the staircase toward the mezzanine. Dullman was crooning in the actor's ear, "No more martinis, huh, Mark? So tomorrow night you can step out on that stage in those sexy tights of yours and give these Yokelsville ladies a thrill. You're the great Mark Manson, remember?" Manson made small pleased noises.

Stanley and Roger came running up behind them.

"How is he?" Stanley panted.

"Beginning to feel pain, I think," Ellery said. "How about it, Manson?"

"My dear sir," the actor said indulgently. "Anyone would think I am intoxicated. Really, this is undignified and unnecessary."

He achieved the mezzanine landing and paused there to recuperate. Ellery glanced at Dullman, and Dullman nodded. They released him.

Ellery grabbed in vain. *"Catch him!"*

But both Stanley and Roger stood there, stunned. Manson, still smiling, toppled backward between them.

Fascinated, they watched the star of *The Death of Don Juan* bounce his way step after step down the long marble staircase until he landed on the lobby floor and lay still . . .

ACT I. Scene 3.

They went straight from the hospital to Dullman's room at the Hollis. Dullman sat down at the telephone.

"Long distance? New York City. I want to speak to Phil Stone, theatrical agent, West Forty-fourth Street. No, I'll hold on."

"Stone." Stanley was hopping about the room. "I don't know him, Archer."

"So you don't know him," the New Yorker grunted. "Phil? Arch Dullman."

"So what do you want?" Ellery could hear Stone's bass rasp distinctly.

"Philly boy," Dullman said.

"Please, Archie, no routines. It's been an itch of a day, and I was just going home. What's on your mind?"

"Phil, I'm on a spot up here—"

"Up where?"

"Wrightsville. New England."

"Never heard. Can't be a show town. What are you, in a new racket?"

"There's a stock company here just getting started. I made a deal for Mark Manson with this producer to do *The Death of Don Juan*."

"What producer?"

"Stanley Bluefield. Opening's tomorrow night. Tonight Manson falls down a staircase in the hotel and breaks the wrist and a couple fingers of his right hand, besides cracking two ribs."

"Old lushes never die. That's all?"

"It's plenty. There might even be concussion. They're keeping him in the hospital twenty-four hours just in case."

"So what?" The agent sounded remote.

"The thing is, they've taped his ribs and put a cast on his forearm and hand. He won't be able to work for weeks." A drop of perspiration coursed down Dullman's nose and landed on the butt of his cigar. "Phil—how about Foster Benedict?"

Stone's guffaw rattled the telephone.

"Foster Benedict?" Stanley Bluefield looked astounded. He leaped to Dullman's free ear. "You get him, Archer!"

But Ellery was watching Rodge Fowler. At the sound of Benedict's name Roger had gripped the arms of his chair as if a nerve had been jabbed.

Dullman paid no attention to Stanley. "Well, you hyena?"

Stone's voice said dryly, "Might I be so stupid as to ask if this Bluefield and his company are pros?"

Arch Dullman spat his cigar butt, a thing of shining shreds, onto the carpet. "It's an amateur group."

"Look, crook," the agent boomed. "This backwoods Sam Harris wants a replacement for Manson, he's got to contact me, not you. He's got to satisfy Equity, not you. You still there, Archie?"

"I'm still here," Dullman sighed. "Here's Bluefield."

Stanley was at the phone in a flash. Dullman picked up the butt and put it back in his mouth. He remained near the phone.

"Stanley Bluefield here," Stanley said nervously. "Do I understand, Mr. Stone, that Foster Benedict is available for a two-week engagement in *The Death of Don Juan,* to start tomorrow night?"

"Mr. Benedict's resting between engagements. I don't know if I could talk him into going right back to work."

"How well does he know the part?"

"Foster's done that turkey so many times he quacks. That's another reason it might not interest him. He's sick of it."

"How much," Stanley asked, not without humor, "will it take to cure him?"

Stone said carelessly, "Fifteen hundred a week might do it."

"Give me that phone," Dullman said. "Who do you think you're dealing with, Phil? Benedict's washed up in Hollywood, dead on Broadway, and TV's had a bellyful of him. I happen to know he's flat on his tokus. I wouldn't let Mr. Bluefield touch him with a skunk pole if Manson's accident hadn't left us over this barrel. Seven-fifty, Phil, take it or leave it. You taking or leaving?"

After ten seconds the agent said, "I'll call you back." Dullman gave him the numbers of the Hollis phone and his extension and hung up.

"He'll take." Dullman lay down on the bed and stared at the ceiling.

Stanley began to hop around the room again.

"You're asking for it," Roger Fowler said tightly. "Benedict's a bad actor, Stan. And I'm not referring to his professional competence."

"*Please,* Roger," the little man said testily. "Don't I have enough on my mind?"

Twelve minutes later the telephone rang. From the bed Dullman said, "You can take it."

"Yes?" Stanley cried.

"We're taking," Stone's bass said. "But you understand, Mr. Bluefield, you got to clear this deal with Equity yourself before we lift a hoof."

"Yes, yes. First thing in the morning."

"I'll be waiting for Equity's go-ahead. Soon as I get it, Benedict's on his way."

"Hold it," Dullman said.

"Hold it," Stanley said.

Dullman got wearily off the bed, whispered something, and returned to the bed.

Stanley pursed his lips. "According to my information, Mr. Stone, Benedict might start out tomorrow for Wrightsville and wind up in a Montreal hotel room with some girl he picked up en route. Can you guarantee delivery?"

"What's that sucker Dullman want, my blood? I'll put him on the plane. That's the best I can do."

Stanley glanced anxiously at Dullman. Dullman shrugged.

"Well, all right, but please impress on Mr. Benedict..."

"Yeah, yeah."

"He'll have to change planes in Boston, by the way. There's no through flight. I'll have a car waiting at Wrightsville Airport. If he makes an early enough connection we ought to be able to get in a quick run-through."

"That's up to Equity. Like I said, he ain't moving a muscle—"

"Leave Equity to me. You just get Benedict here."

"Up in his lines," Dullman said.

"Up in his lines," Stanley said, and he hung up. "Archer, that was an inspiration!" Dullman grunted. "Roger, would you run across the Square and ask the *Record* to hold the press? I'll phone them the new copy for tomorrow's ad in a few minutes."

"You're dead set on going ahead with this?" Roger said.

"Now, Rodge," Stanley said.

Dullman began to snore.

Ellery thought the whole performance extraordinary.

ACT I. Scene 4.

Ellery made his way around the Square and into Lower Main under a filthy sky.

It had been an exasperating day for Stanley Bluefield. The little man had been on the long-distance phone with Equity since early morning. By the time the details were straightened out to Equity's satisfaction, and Foster Benedict was airborne to Boston, the actor was on a schedule so tight that he could not hope to set down in Wrightsville before 7:55 P.M. This would give Benedict barely enough time to make up, get into costume, and dash onstage for the 8:30 curtain.

Ellery walked into the lobby of the rejuvenated Bijou, pushed through one of the new black patent-leatherette doors, and entered Stanley Bluefield's Playhouse.

The elegantly done-over interior lay under a heavy hush. The cast, already made up and in costume, were sitting about the nakedly lit first-act set either sipping from coffee containers that might have been poisoned or staring into the gloom of the theater in emotional rapport. A pretty blonde girl he recognized as Joan Truslow was stretched out tensely on the set couch where, Ellery surmised, Don Juan Benedict was shortly to seduce her in the service of art. Roger Fowler, in coveralls, was stroking her temples.

Ellery slipped down the last aisle on his right and through the stage door. He found himself in a cramped triangle of space, the stage to his left. To his right a single door displayed a painted star and a placard hastily lettered *MR. BENEDICT*. A narrow iron ladder led to a tiny railed landing above and to another dressing room.

Curious, Ellery opened the starred door and looked in. Stanley had outdone himself here. Brilliant lighting switched on in the windowless room at the opening of the door. Air conditioning hummed softly. The driftwood-paneled walls were hung with theatrical prints. Costumes lay thrown about and the handsome mirrored dressing table was a clutter of wigs, hand props, and pots and boxes of theatrical makeup, evidently as Manson had left them before his accident.

Impressed, Ellery backed out. He edged around an open metal chest marked *Tools* and made his way behind the upstage flat to the other side of the theater. Here there was ample space for the property room, the stage entrance, the lighting board, and a spiral of iron steps leading up to half a dozen additional dressing rooms Beneath them, at stage level, a door announced *Mr. Bluefield. Keep Out*.

Ellery knocked.

Stanley's voice screamed, "I said *nobody!*"

"It's Ellery Queen."

"Oh. Come in."

The office was a little symphony in stainless steel. Stanley sat at his desk, left elbow anchored to the blotter, left fist supporting his cheek, eyes fixed on the telephone. All Ellery could think of was Napoleon after the Battle of Waterloo contemplating what might have been.

Arch Dullman stood at the one window, chewing on a dead cigar. He did not turn around.

Ellery dropped into a chair. "Storm trouble?"

The bunny-nose twitched. "Benedict phoned from the airfield in Boston. All planes grounded."

The window lit up as if an atom bomb had gone off. Dullman jumped back and Stanley shot to his feet. A crash jarred the theatrical photographs on the walls out of alignment. Immediately the heavens opened and the alley below the window became a river.

"This whole damn production is jinxed," Dullman said, glancing at his watch. "They'll be starting to come in soon, Bluefield. We'll have to postpone."

"And give them another chance to laugh at me?" The little Bluefield jaw enlarged. "We're holding that curtain."

"How long do you think we can hold it? Benedict's plane mightn't be able to take off for hours."

"The storm is traveling northwestward, Archer. Boston should clear any minute. It's only a half-hour's flight."

Dullman went out. Ellery heard him order the houselights switched on and the curtain closed. He did not come back.

The phone came to life at 8:25. Stanley pounced on it. "What did I tell you? He's taking off!"

Foster Benedict got to the The Playhouse at eighteen minutes past nine. The rain had stopped, but the alley leading to the stage entrance was dotted with puddles and the actor had to hop and sidestep to avoid them. From his scowl, he took the puddles as a personal affront. Stanley and Dullman hopped and sidestepped along with him, both talking at once.

The company waiting expectantly in the stage entrance pressed back as Benedict approached. He strode past them without a glance, leaving an aroma of whiskey and eau de cologne behind him. If he was drunk, Ellery could detect no evidence of it.

Rodge Fowler was stern-jawed. And Joan Truslow, Ellery noticed, looked as if she had been struck in the face.

Foster Benedict glanced about. "You—Mr. Bluefish, is it? Where's my dressing room?"

"At the other side of the stage, Mr. Benedict," Stanley puffed. "But there's no time—"

"They've been sitting out there for over an hour," Dullman said. The booing and stamping of the audience had been audible in the alley.

"Ah." The actor seated himself in the stage doorman's chair. "The voice of Wrightsburg."

"Wrights*ville,*" Stanley said. "Mr. Benedict, really—"

"And these, I gather," Benedict said, inspecting the silent cast, "are the so-called actors in this misbegotten exercise in theatrical folly?"

"Mr. Benedict," Stanley said again, *"please!"*

Ellery had not seen Benedict for a long time. The face that had once been called the handsomest in the American theater looked like overhandled dough. Sacs bulged under the malicious eyes. The once taut throat was beginning to string. Only the rich and supple voice was the same.

"The little lady there," the actor said, his stare settling on Joan. "An orchid in the vegetable patch. What does she play, Dullman? The heroine, I hope."

"Yes, yes," Dullman said. "But there's no time for introductions or anything, Benedict. You'll have to go on as you are for the first act—"

"My makeup box, Phil." Benedict extended his arm and snapped his fingers, his eyes still on Joan. Her face was chalky. Ellery glanced at Roger's hands. They were fists.

"Phil Stone isn't here," Dullman said. "Remember?"

"Oh, hell, I forgot my makeup. But does it really matter?"

"There's no time to make up, either! Manson's stuff is still in the star dressing room and you can use his when you dress between acts. Look, are you going on or aren't you?"

"Mr. Benedict." Stanley was trembling. "I give you precisely thirty seconds to get out on that stage and take your position for the curtain. Or I prefer charges to Equity."

The actor rose, smiling. "If I recall the stage business, dear heart, and believe me I do," he said to Joan, "we'll have an enchanting opportunity to become better acquainted during the first act. Then perhaps a little champagne supper after the performance? All *right*, Bluefish!" he said crossly. "Just as I am, eh?" He shrugged. "Well,

I've played the idiotic role every other way. It may be amusing at that."

He stalked onstage.

"Places!" Dullman bellowed. Joan drifted away like a ghost in shock. The rest of the cast scurried. "Fowler, Fowler?"

Roger came to life.

"Where's that lights man of yours? Get with it, will you?" As Roger walked away, Dullman froze. "Is that Benedict out there making a *speech?*"

"In the too, too solid flesh," Ellery said with awe, peeping from the wings. Benedict had stepped out on the apron and he was explaining with comical gestures and facial contortions why "this distinguished Wrongsville audience" was about to see the great Foster Benedict perform Act One of *The Death of Don Juan*—"the biggest egg ever laid by a turkey"—in street clothes and sans makeup. The audience was beginning to titter and clap.

Ellery turned at a gurgle behind him. Stanley's nose was twitching again.

"What is he *doing?* Who does he think he *is?*"

"Barrymore in *My Dear Children,* I guess." Dullman was chewing away on his cigar. He seemed fascinated.

They could only watch helplessly while Benedict played the buffoon. His exit was a triumph of extemporization. He bowed gravely, assumed a ballet stance, and then, like Nijinsky in *The Spectre of the Rose,* he took off in a mighty leap for the wings.

ACT I. Scene 5.

Ellery, jammed in with Stanley Bluefield among the standees at the rear of the theater, watched the first act in total disbelief.

Benedict deliberately paraphrased speech after speech. The bewildered amateurs waiting for their cues forgot their lines. Then he would throw the correct cue, winking over the footlights. He capered, struck attitudes, invented business, addressed broad asides to the hilarious audience. He transformed the old melodrama into a slapstick farce.

Ellery glanced down at Stanley. What he saw made him murmur hastily, "He's doing far more damage to himself than to you."

But Stanley said, "It's me they're howling at," in a pink-eyed fury, and he groped his way through the lobby doors and disappeared.

THE DEATH OF DON JUAN 257

The seduction scene was an interminable embarrassment. Once during the scene, in sheer self-defense, Joan did something that made Benedict yelp. But he immediately tossed an ad lib to the audience that Ellery did not catch, and in the ensuing shriek of laughter returned to the attack.

At the scene's conclusion Joan stumbled off the stage like a sleepwalker.

Ellery found that he was grinding his teeth.

The curtain came down at last. Ushers opened the fire-exit doors at both sides of the theater. People, wiping their eyes, pushed into the alleys. Ellery wriggled through the lobby to the street and lit a bitter-tasting cigarette. Long after the warning buzzer sounded, he lingered on the sidewalk.

Finally, he went back in.

The houselights were still on. Surprised, Ellery glanced at his watch. Probably Benedict needed extra time to get into costume and make up for the second act. Or perhaps—the thought pleased him—Roger had punched him in the nose.

The houselights remained on. The audience began to shuffle, murmur, cough.

Ellery edged through the standees to the extreme left aisle and made for the stage door. It was deathly quiet backstage.

Stanley Bluefield's door was open, and Arch Dullman was stamping up and down the office in a cloud of angry smoke. He seized Ellery.

"Seen Bluefield anywhere?"

"No," Ellery said. "What's wrong?"

"I don't give a damn who Benedict thinks he is," Dullman said. "Even a sucker like Bluefield deserves a better shake. First that moldy hunk of ham turns the first act into a low-comedy vaudeville bit, now he won't answer his call! Queen, do me a favor and get him out of there."

"Why me?"

"I don't trust myself. What's more, you tell him for me that if he doesn't play the rest of this show straight I'll personally bust that balloon he calls a head!"

Ellery's built-in alarm was jangling for all it was worth. "You'd better come with me."

They hurried behind the upstage flat to the other side of the theater. Ellery rapped on the starred door. He rapped again. "Mr. Benedict?"

There was no answer.

"Mr. Benedict, you're holding up the curtain."

Silence.

"Benedict?"

Ellery opened the door.

Foster Benedict, his back to the door, was in the chair at the dressing table, half lying among the wigs and makeup boxes.

He was partly dressed in a Don Juan costume. The shirt was of flowing white silk and just below the left shoulder, from the apex of a wet red ragged stain, the handle of a knife protruded.

ACT II. Scene 1.

"This character is clean off his chump," Dullman said, jamming a fresh cigar between his teeth. "Imagine playing around with the trick knife and the goo at a time like this. How about acting your age, Benedict? In fact, how about acting?" He brushed past Ellery. "Come on, snap out of it."

"Don't touch him," Ellery said.

Dullman stared at him. "You're kidding."

"No."

Dullman's mouth opened and the cigar fell out. He stooped and fumbled for it.

Ellery leaned over the dressing table, keeping his hands to himself. The skin was a mud-yellow and the lips were already cyanotic. Benedict's eyes were open. As Ellery's face came within their focus they fluttered and rolled.

He saw now that the stain was spreading.

"Bluefield," Dullman said. "My God, where's Bluefield? I've got to find Bluefield."

"Never mind Bluefield. I saw a doctor I know in the audience—Dr. Farnham. Hurry, Dullman."

Dullman turned blindly to the doorway. It was blocked by the cast and the stagehands. None of them appeared to understand what had happened. Joan Truslow had her hand to her mouth childishly, looking at the blood and the knife. As Dullman broke through he collided with Roger Fowler, coming fast.

"What's going on? Where's Joan?"

"Out of my way, damn you," Dullman said. He stumbled toward the stage.

Ellery shut the door and went quickly back to the dressing table. "Benedict, can you talk?"

The lips trembled a little. The jaws opened and closed and opened again, and a thick sound came out. It was just a sound, meaningless.

"Who knifed you?"

The jaws moved again. They were like the jaws of a fish newly yanked from the water. This time not even the thick sound came out.

"Benedict, do you hear me?" The eyes remained fixed. "If you understand what I'm saying, blink."

The eyelids came down and went up.

"Rest a moment. You're going to be all right." You're going to be dead, Ellery thought. Where the devil was Dr. Farnham? He won't be able to touch the knife, he thought.

The door burst open. Dr. Conklin Farnham hurried in. Dullman ran in after him and shut the door and leaned against it, breathing hard.

"Hello, Conk," Ellery said. "All I want from him is a name."

Dr. Farnham glanced at the knife wound and his mouth thinned out. He took Benedict's dangling arm without raising it and placed his fingertips on the artery. Then he felt the artery in the temple, examined the staring eyes.

"Call an ambulance."

"And the police," Ellery said.

Arch Dullman opened the door once more. The cast and the stagehands were still standing outside, all except Joan and Roger. Dullman said something to someone and shut the door again.

"Can't you at least stop the bleeding, Conk?"

"It's pretty much stopped by itself."

And Ellery saw that the stain was no longer spreading. "I've got to talk to him. Is it all right?"

The doctor nodded. His lips formed the words, *Any minute now.*

"Benedict," Ellery said. "Use the eye signal again. Do you still hear me?"

Benedict blinked.

"Listen. You were sitting here making up. Someone opened your door and crossed the room. You could see who it was in the mirror. Who was it came at you with the knife?"

The bluing lips parted. The tongue fluttered; its sound was like a small bird's wings. Finally a grudging gurgle emerged. Dr. Farnham was feeling for the pulse again.

"He's going, Ellery." This time he said the words aloud.

"You're dying, man," Ellery cried. *"Who knifed you?"*

The struggle was an admirable thing. He was really trying to communicate. But then over the eyes slipped a substance through which they looked far and away. Without warning the dying man raised his head a full inch from the dressing table, and he held it there quite steadily. He made the fish mouth again.

But from it now, in a confiding whisper, came two words.

Then the head fell back to the table with a noise like wood. The actor seemed to clear his throat. His body stiffened in some last instinctive stubbornness and his breath emptied long and gently and he was altogether empty.

"He's dead," Dr. Farnham said after a moment.

Dullman said in a queer voice, "What did he say?"

"He's dead," Ellery said.

"I mean *him*. I didn't hear what he said from here."

"You heard him, Conk."

"Yes," the doctor said. " 'The heroine.' "

"That's what he said." Ellery turned away. He felt as empty as Benedict looked.

"The heroine." Dullman laughed. "Get what you wanted, Queen? Feel like a big man now?"

"He didn't know her name," Ellery said, as if this explained something important.

"I don't understand," Dr. Farnham said.

"Benedict arrived so late tonight there wasn't time for introductions. He could only identify her by her role in the play. The heroine."

"But I took Joan's appendix out when she was fifteen," Dr. Farnham muttered. "My father delivered her."

Someone rapped on the door. Dullman opened it.

"I'm told something's happened to Mr. Benedict—"

"Well, look who's here," Dullman said. "Come on in, Bluefield."

ACT II. Scene 2.

Stanley Bluefield's shoes, the cuffs of his trousers, were soaked.

"I've been walking and walking. You see, I couldn't stand what he was doing to the play. I felt that if I stayed one minute longer .. "

"Stanley," Ellery said.

"And how dreadful," Stanley went on, still looking at the occupied chair. "I mean, he doesn't look human any more, does he?"

"Stanley—"

"But he brought it on himself, wouldn't you say? You can't go about humiliating people that way. People who've never done you any harm. Who killed him?"

Ellery swung the little man around. "You'll have to talk to the audience, Stanley. I think you'd better use the word 'accident.' And tell your ushers privately not to allow anyone to leave the theater until the police get here."

"Who killed him?"

"Will you do that?"

"Yes, of course," Stanley said. He squished out, leaving a damp trail.

Ellery wandered back to the dressing table. All at once he stooped for a closer look at the knife handle.

Dr. Farnham stirred.

"It's a fact they're taking their sweet time," Dullman said. "You want out, Doctor?"

"I left my wife in the audience," Farnham said stiffly.

"Don't worry about Molly, Conk." Ellery dug a small leather case out of his pocket. "And you're my corroborating witness to Benedict's statement."

"That's right," Dullman said. "I didn't hear a thing."

The leather case produced a powerful little lens, and through it Ellery examined the handle of the knife on both sides.

"What," Dullman jeered, "no deerstalker hat?"

Ellery ignored him. The heavy haft had been recently wound in black-plastic friction tape. An eighth of an inch from the edge, the tape showed a straight line of thin, irregular indentations some five-eighths of an inch long. In a corresponding position on the underside there was a line of indentations similar in character and length.

Ellery stowed away his lens. "By the way, Dullman, have you seen this knife before?"

"Any particular reason why I should tell you?"

"Any particular reason why you shouldn't?"

"It's not mine. I don't know whose it is."

"But you have seen it before." When Dullman did not answer, Ellery added, "Believe me, I know how much you wish you were out of this." The way Dullman's glance shifted made Ellery smile faintly. "But you can't wish away Benedict's murder, and in any case you'll have to submit to police questioning. Where have you seen this knife before?"

Dullman said reluctantly, "I don't even know if it's the same one."

"Granted. But where did you see one like it?"

"In that metal toolchest just outside. It was a big-bladed knife with a black-taped handle. From the look of this one I'd say they're the same—but I can't swear to it."

"When did you see it last?"

"I didn't see it 'last.' I saw it once. It was after the first-act curtain. Benedict had weakened one of the legs of the set couch with his damn-fool gymnastics during that scene with the Truslow girl, and even the stagecrew was demoralized. So I decided to fix the leg myself. I went for tools, and that's when I spotted the knife. It was lying on the top tray of the chest in plain sight."

"Did you notice any peculiar-looking indentations in the tape?"

"Indentations?"

"Impressions. Come here, Dullman. But don't touch it."

Dullman looked and shook his head. "I didn't see anything like that. I'm sure I'd have noticed. I remember thinking how shiny and new-looking the tape was."

"How soon after the curtain came down was this?"

"Was what?"

"When you saw the knife in the chest."

"Right after. Benedict was just coming offstage. He went into the dressing room here while I was poking around in the tools."

"He was alone?"

"He was alone."

"Did you talk to him?"

Dullman examined the pulpy end of his cigar. "You might say he talked to me."

"What did he say?"

"Why, he explained—with one of those famous stage leers of his—exactly what his plans were for after the performance. Spelled it out," Dullman said, jamming the cigar back in his mouth.

"And you said to him—?"

"Nothing. Look, Queen, if I went after every bum and slob I've had to deal with in show business I'd have more notches to my account than Dan'l Boone." Dullman grinned. "Anyway, you and the doctor here say you heard who Benedict put the finger on. So why cross-examine me?"

"Who occupies the dressing room just above this one?"

"Joan Truslow."

Ellery went out.

The lid of the chest marked *Tools* was open, as he had seen it on his backstage tour early in the evening. There was no knife in the tray, or anywhere else in the chest. If Dullman was telling the truth, the knife in Foster Benedict's back almost certainly had come from this toolchest.

Ellery heard two sirens coming on fast outside.

He glanced up at the narrow landing. The upper dressing-room door was halfway open.

He sprang to the iron ladder.

ACT II. Scene 3.

He knocked and stepped into Joan Truslow's tiny dressing room at once, shutting the door behind him.

Joan and Roger jumped apart. Tears had left a clownish design in the girl's makeup.

Ellery set his back against the door.

"Do you make a habit of barging into ladies' dressing rooms?" Roger said truculently.

"No one seems to approve of me tonight," Ellery complained. "Rodge, there's not much time."

"For what?"

But Joan put her hand on Roger's arm. "How is he, Mr. Queen?"

"Benedict? Oh, he died."

Ellery studied her reaction carefully. It told him nothing.

"I'm sorry," she said. "Even though he was beastly."

"I saw his lips moving during your speeches in that couch scene. What was he saying to you, Joan?"

"Vile things. I can't repeat them."

"The police just got here."

She betrayed herself by the manner in which she turned away and sat down at her dressing table to begin repairing her makeup. The trivial routine was like a skillful bit of stage business, in which the effect of naturalness was produced by the most carefully thought-out artifice.

"Anyway, what are people supposed to do, go into mourning?" Roger sounded as if he had been following a separate train of thought. "He was a dirty old goat. If ever anyone asked for it, he did."

Ellery kept watching Joan's reflection in the mirror. "You know, Rodge, that's very much like a remark Stanley made a few minutes ago. It rather surprises me. Granted Benedict's outrageous behavior tonight, it was hardly sufficient reason to stick a knife in his back. Wouldn't you say?" The lipstick in Joan's fingers kept flying. "Or—on second thought—does either of you know of a sufficient reason? On the part of anyone?"

"How could we know a thing like that?"

"Speak for yourself, Rodge," Ellery smiled. "How about you, Joan?"

She murmured, "Me?" and shook her head at herself.

"Well." Ellery pushed away from the door. "Oh, Roger, last night in Arch Dullman's room, when Benedict was first mentioned as a substitute for Manson, I got the impression you knew Benedict from somewhere. Was I imagining things?"

"I can't help your impressions."

"Then you never met him before tonight?"

"I knew his smelly reputation."

"That's not what the lawyers call a responsive answer," Ellery said coldly.

Roger glared. "Are you accusing me of Benedict's murder?"

"Are you afraid I may have cause to?"

"You'd better get out of here!"

"Unfortunately, you won't be able to take that attitude with the police."

"Get out!"

Ellery shrugged as part of his own act. He had baited Roger to catch Joan off-guard. And he had caught her. She had continued her elaborate toilet at the mirror as if they were discussing the weather. His hostile exchange with Roger should have made her show some sign of alarm, or anxiety, or at least interest.

He left gloomily.

He was not prepared for the police officer he found in charge below, despite a forewarning of long standing. On the retirement of Wrightsville's perennial Chief of Police, Dakin, the old Yankee had written Ellery about his successor.

"Selectmen brought in this Anselm Newby from Connhaven," Dakin had written, "where he was a police captain with a mighty good record. Newby's young and he's tough and as far as I know he's honest and he does know modern police methods. But he's maybe not as smart as he thinks.

"If you ever get to Wrightsville again, Ellery, better steer clear of him. I once told him about you and he gives me a codfish look and says no New York wiseacre is ever going to mix into *his* department. It's a fact there ain't much to like about Anse."

Ellery had visualized Chief of Police Newby as a large man with muscles, a prominent jaw, and a Marine sergeant's voice. Instead, the man in the Chief's cap who turned to look him over when he was admitted to the dressing room was short and slight, almost delicately built.

"I was just going to send a man for you, Mr. Queen." Chief Newby's quiet voice was another surprise. "Where've you been?"

The quiet voice covered a sting; it was like the swish of a lazily brandished whip. But it was Newby's eyes that brought old Dakin's characterization into focus. They were of an inorganic blue, unfeeling as mineral.

"Talking to members of the company."

"Like Joan Truslow?"

Ellery thought very quickly. "Joan was one of them, Chief. I didn't mention Benedict's talking before he died, of course. But as long as we had to wait for you—"

"Mr. Queen," Newby said. "Let's understand each other right off. In Wrightsville a police investigation is run by one man. Me."

"To my knowledge it's never been run any other way."

"I've heard tell different."

"You've been misinformed. However, I've known and liked this town and its people for a long time. You can't stop me from keeping my eyes open in their interest and reaching my own conclusions. And broadcasting them, if necessary."

Anselm Newby stared at him. Ellery stared back.

"I've already talked to Dr. Franham and Mr. Dullman," Newby said suddenly, and Ellery knew he had won a small victory. "You tell me your version."

Ellery gave him an unembroidered account. Newby listened without comment, interrupting only to acknowledge the arrival of the Coroner and issue orders to uniformed men coming in to report. Throughout Ellery's recital the Chief of Police kept an eye on a young technician who had been going over the room for fingerprints and was now taking photographs. Times had certainly changed in Wrightsville.

"Those words Benedict said, you heard them yourself?" the Chief asked when Ellery stopped. "This wasn't something Farnham heard and repeated to you?"

"We both heard them. I'm positive Dullman did, too, although he pretended he hadn't."

"Why would he do that?"

Ellery could not resist saying, "You want my *opinion,* Chief?"

The blue eyes sparked. But he merely said, "Please."

"Dullman is walking on eggs. This thing is the worst possible break for him. He wants no part of it."

"Why not?"

"Because to admit he heard Benedict's accusation would mean becoming an important witness in a sensational murder case. I don't think Dullman can stand the publicity."

"I thought show people live on publicity."

"Not Dullman. For an Actors' Equity member like Benedict or Manson to work in an amateur company, it has to be a legitimately amateur operation from start to finish. Arch Dullman is an 'operator.' He makes an undercover deal with someone like Stanley Bluefield—desperate to run a successful amateur playhouse—in a setup that otherwise satisfies Equity's strict specifications. Dullman delivers a name actor—one who's passé in the big time and who'll do anything for eating money—in return for taking over behind the scenes, with Bluefield fronting for him."

"What's Dullman get out of it?"

"He pockets most—or all—of the box-office take," Ellery said. "If this deal with Bluefield became a matter of public record, Dullman might never represent a professional actor again."

"I see." Newby was watching his technician. "Well, that's very interesting, Mr. Queen. Now if you'll excuse me—"

Take that, Ellery thought. Aloud, he said, "Mind if I hang around?"

Newby said politely, "Suit yourself," and turned away.

The knife had been removed from Benedict's back and it was lying on the dressing table. It was a long, hefty hunting knife, its bloodstained blade honed to a wicked edge.

The Coroner grunted, "I'm through for now," and opened the door. Two ambulance men came in at his nod and took the body out. "I'll do the post mortem first thing in the morning."

"Could a woman have sunk the knife to the hilt?" Newby asked.

"Far's I can tell without an autopsy, it went into the heart without striking bone. If that's so, a kid could have done it." The Coroner left.

Newby walked over to the table. The technician was packing his gear. "Find any prints on the knife?"

"No, sir. It was either handled with a handkerchief or gloves or wiped off afterward. This plastic tape is pretty slick, Chief, anyway."

"What about prints elsewhere?"

"Some of Benedict's on the dressing table and on the makeup stuff, and a lot of someone else's, a man's."

"Those would be Manson's. No woman's prints?"

"No, sir. But about this knife. There are some queer marks on the handle."

"Marks?" Newby picked up the knife by the tip of the blade and scrutinized the haft. He seemed puzzled.

"There's some on the other side, too."

The Chief turned the knife over. "Any notion what made these, Bill?"

"Well, no, sir."

Newby studied the marks again. Without looking around he said, "Mr. Queen, did you happen to notice these marks?"

"Yes," Ellery said.

The Chief waited, as if for Ellery to go on. But Ellery did not go on. Newby's ears slowly reddened.

"We could send the knife up to the big lab in Connhaven," the young technician suggested.

"I know that, Bill! But suppose first we try to identify them on our own. Right?"

"Yes, sir."

Newby stalked out to the stage. Meekly, Ellery followed.

The little police chief's interrogation of the company was surgical. In short order he established that, between the lowering of the curtain on Act One and the discovery of the dying man, every member of the cast except Joan Truslow had either been in view of someone else or could otherwise prove an alibi. With equal economy he disposed of the stagehands.

He had long since released the audience. Now he sent the cast and the crew home.

On the emptying of the theater the curtain had been raised and the houselights turned off. Stanley Bluefield and Archer Dullman sat in gloom and silence, too. Each man an island, Ellery thought; and he wondered how good an explorer Anselm Newby really was.

For the first time he sensed an impatience, almost an eagerness, in Newby.

"Well, gentlemen, it's getting late—"

"Chief." Stanley was lying back on the set couch, his lips parted, gazing up into the flies and managing to resemble an old lady after an exhausting day. "Are you intending to close me down?"

"No call for that, Mr. Bluefield. We'll just seal off that dressing room."

"Then I can go ahead with, say, rehearsals?"

"Better figure on the day after tomorrow. The Prosecutor's office will be all over the place till then."

Stanley struggled off the couch.

"Oh, one thing before you go, Mr. Bluefield. Did you see or hear anything tonight that might help us out?"

Stanley said, "I wasn't here," and trudged off the stage.

"You, Mr. Dullman?"

"I told you all I know, Chief." Dullman shifted the remains of his cigar to the other side of his mouth. "Is it all right with you if I go see what's with my client before somebody does a carving job on him?"

"Just don't leave town. And Mr. Dullman."

"What?"

"Don't talk about what Benedict said." When Dullman was gone, Newby said, "Well." He got up and made for the stage steps.

"Chief," Ellery said.

Newby paused.

"You don't have much of a case, you know."

The little policeman trotted down into the orchestra. He selected the aisle seat in the third row center and settled himself. Like a critic, Ellery thought. A critic who's already made up his mind.

"Gotch," Chief Newby called.

"Yes, sir."

"Get Miss Truslow."

ACT II. Scene 4.

Joan sailed out of the wings chin up. But all she saw was Ellery straddling a chair far upstage, and she began to look around uncertainly.

Roger yelled, "You down there—Newby!" and ran over to the footlights. "What's the idea keeping Miss Truslow a prisoner in her dressing room all this time?"

"Roger," Joan said.

"If you think you've got something on her, spit it out and I'll have a lawyer down here before it hits the floor!"

"Sit down, Miss Truslow," Newby's soft voice said from below. "You, too, Fowler."

Joan sat down immediately.

Whatever it was that Roger glimpsed in her violet eyes, it silenced him. He joined her on the couch, reached for her hand. She withdrew it.

Newby said, "Miss Truslow, when did you make your last stage exit?"

"At the end of my scene with Foster Benedict on the—on this couch."

"How long before the act ended was that?"

"About ten minutes."

"Did you go right to your dressing room?"

"Yes."

"In doing that, you had to pass by the toolchest. Was it open?"

"The chest? I can't say. I didn't notice much of anything." Joan caught her hands in the act of twisting in her lap, and she stilled them. "I was badly upset. They must have told you what he—the way he carried on during our big scene."

"Yes. I hear he gave you a rough time." The little Chief sounded sympathetic. "But you did notice the toolchest later, Miss Truslow, didn't you?"

She looked up. "Later?"

"During intermission. After Benedict got to his dressing room."

Joan blinked into the lights. "But you don't understand, Chief Newby. I went straight to my dressing room and I stayed there. I was . . . frozen, I suppose is the word. I just sat asking myself how I was going to get through the rest of the play. It was all I could think of."

"While you were up there, did you hear anything going on in the room below? In Benedict's dressing room?"

"I don't remember hearing anything."

"When *did* you leave your dressing room, Miss Truslow?"

"When I heard all the commotion downstairs. After he was found."

"That was the first time, you say?"

"Yes."

Newby said suddenly, "Fowler, Queen found you with this girl. How come?"

"How come?" Roger snapped. "Why, somebody ran into the prop room to tell me something had happened to Benedict. I ran back with him and spotted Joan in the crowd around Benedict's doorway. I hauled her out of there and up to her dressing room so I could put my arms around her in privacy when she broke down, which she promptly did. Wasn't that sneaky of me?"

"Then that was the first time you saw her after she left the stage?"

"I couldn't get to her before, though God knows I wanted to. I was too tied up backstage—" Roger halted. "That was sneaky of *you,* Newby. And damn nasty, too! What are you trying to prove?"

"Miss Truslow, how well did you know Foster Benedict?"

Ellery saw Joan go stiff. "Know him?"

"Were you two acquainted? Ever see him before tonight?"

She said something.

"What? I couldn't hear that."

Joan cleared her throat. "No."

"Logan." A police officer jumped off the apron and darted to his Chief. Newby said something behind his hand. The man hurried up the aisle and out of the theater. "Miss Truslow, a witness says that when Benedict went into his dressing room the toolchest was open and a big knife with a taped handle was lying in the tray. I'll ask you again. Did you or didn't you leave your dressing room, climb down, go to the toolchest—"

"I didn't," Joan cried.

"—go the toolchest, pick up the knife—"

"Hold it." Roger was on his feet. "You really want to know about that knife, Newby?"

"You have some information about it?"

"Definitely."

"What?"

"It's mine."

"Oh?" Newby sat waiting.

"I can prove it," Roger said quickly. "If you'll strip the tape off you'll find my initials machine-stamped into the haft. I've used it on hunting trips for years. I brought it to the theater just today. We'd bought some new guy-rope yesterday and I needed a sharp knife—"

"I know all about your ownership of the knife," Newby smiled. "The question isn't who owned the knife, or even who put it in the toolchest. It's who took it out of the chest and used it on Benedict. Now, Miss Truslow—"

"Excuse me," Ellery said. The Chief was startled into silence. "Roger, when did you tape the handle?"

"Tonight, after the play started. I'd used it in replacing a frayed guy-rope and I hadn't been able to keep a good grip on it because my hands were sweaty from the heat backstage. So I wound some electrician's tape around the haft in case I had to use it again in an emergency during the performance."

"When did you drop it into the chest?"

"Near the end of the act."

"I thought I'd made it clear, Mr. Queen!" The whiplash in the policeman's voice was no longer lazy. "Interrupt once more and out you go. And I mean it."

"Yes, Chief," Ellery murmured. "Sorry."

Newby was quiet. Then he said, "Now I want to be sure I've got this right, Miss Truslow. You claim you went from the stage straight to your dressing room, you stayed there all the time Benedict was being knifed in the room right under yours, you didn't hear a sound, you didn't come down till after Benedict was found dying, and at no time did you touch the knife. Is that it?"

"That's it." Joan jumped up. "No, Roger!" She walked steadily over to the footlights. "Now let me ask you a question, Chief Newby. Why are you treating me as if you've decided I killed Foster Benedict?"

"Didn't you?" Newby asked.

"I did *not* kill him!"

"Somebody said you did."

Joan peered and blinked through the glare in her eyes. "But that's not possible. It isn't true. I can't imagine anyone making up a story like that about me. Who said it?"

"Benedict, in the presence of witnesses, a few seconds before he died."

Joan said something unintelligible. Newby and Ellery sprang to their feet. But Roger was closest, and he caught her just as her legs gave way . . .

ACT III. Scene 1.

Ellery awoke at noon. He leaped for the door and took in the

Record, with its familiar yellow label conveying the compliments of the Hotel Hollis.

For the first time in years the *Record*'s front page ran a two-line banner:

MURDER HITS WRIGHTSVILLE!
FAMOUS STAGE STAR SLAIN!

The account of the crime was wordy and inaccurate. There were publicity photos of Foster Benedict and the cast. The front page was salted with statements by Dr. Farnham, members of the audience, cast, stagecrew, even police. Chief Anselm Newby's contribution was boxed but uninformative.

The *Record* quoted Stanley Bluefield ("The Playhouse must go on"), Archer Dullman ("No comment"), and Ellery Queen ("Any statement I might make about Benedict's death would encroach on the authority of your excellent Chief of Police").

There was a story on Mark Manson under a one-column cut showing him at a bar, uninjured arm holding aloft a cocktail glass. ("Mr. Manson was found at the Hollis bar at a late hour last night on his discharge from Wrightsville General Hospital, in company of his manager, Archer Dullman. Asked to comment on the tragedy, Mr. Manson said, 'Words truly fail me, sir, which is why you discover me saying it with martinis.' With the help of this reporter, Mr. Dullman was finally able to persuade Mr. Manson to retire to his hotel room.")

A choppy review of the first act of *The Death of Don Juan* showed evidences of hasty editing. What the original copy had said Ellery could only imagine.

The sole reference in print to Joan was a cryptic "Miss Joan Truslow and Mr. Roger Fowler of The Playhouse staff could not be located for a statement as we went to press."

Of Foster Benedict's dying words no mention was made.

Ellery ordered breakfast and then hurried his shower.

He was finishing his second cup of coffee when the telephone rang. It was Roger.

"Where the devil did you hide Joan last night?"

"In my Aunt Carrie's house." Roger sounded harassed. "She's in Europe, left me a key. Joan was in no condition to face reporters or yak with the likes of Emmeline DuPré. Her father knows where we are, but that's all."

"Didn't you tell Newby?"

"Tell Newby? It's Newby who smuggled us over to Aunt Carrie's.

Considerate guy, Newby. He has a cop staked out in the backyard and another in plain clothes parked across the street in an unmarked car."

Ellery said nothing.

Roger continued grimly, "I gave Joanie a sleeping pill and stayed up most of the night biting my nails. Far as I know, Newby has no direct evidence against Joan—just those last words of a dying man whose mind, if you ask me, was already in outer space. Just the same, I'll feel better with a lawyer around. Before I call one in, though..." Roger hesitated. "What I mean is, I'm sorry I blew my stack last night. Would you come over here right away?"

"Where is it?" Ellery almost chuckled.

Roger gave him an address on State Street, in the oldest residential quarter of town.

It was an immaculately preserved Eighteenth Century mansion under the protection of the great elms that were the pride of State Street. The black shades were drawn, and from the street the clapboard house looked shut down.

Ellery strolled around to the rear and knocked on the back door, pretending not to notice the policeman lurking inside a latticed summerhouse. Roger admitted him and led the way through a huge kitchen and pantry and along a cool hall to a stately parlor whose furniture was under dust covers.

Joan was waiting in an armchair. She looked tired and withdrawn.

"This is all Roger's idea," she said, managing a smile. "From the way he's been carrying on—"

"Do you want my help, Joan?"

"Well, if Roger's right—"

"I'm afraid he is."

"But it's so stupid, Mr. Queen. Why would Foster Benedict accuse *me*? And even if he had some mysterious reason, how can anyone believe it? I didn't go near him... I've always hated knives," she cried. "I couldn't use a knife on a trout."

"It isn't a trout that was knifed. Joan, look at me."

She raised her head.

"Did you kill Benedict?"

"No! How many times do I have to say it?"

He lit a cigarette while he weighed her anger. She was an actress of talent—her performance the night before in the face of Benedict's coarse horseplay had proved that. It was a difficult decision.

"All right, Rodge," Ellery said suddenly. "Speak your piece."

"It's not mine. It's Joan's."

"I'm all ears, Joan."

Her chest rose and fell. "I lied to Chief Newby when I said I'd never known Foster Benedict before last night. I met Foster six years ago here in Wrightsville. I was still in high school. Roger was home from college for the summer."

"In *Wrightsville?*"

"I know, he acted as if he's never heard of Wrightsville. But then I realized it wasn't an act at all. He'd simply forgotten, Mr. Queen. He was one of Stanley Bluefield's houseguests for a few weeks that summer."

"He didn't even remember Stanley," Roger said bitterly. "Let's face it, the great lover was one step ahead of the butterfly net."

"Then it was a practical lunacy," Ellery remarked. "Every six months out of the past ten or twelve years Benedict practiced houseguesting as a sort of unemployment insurance. Dullman claims he averaged fifteen hosts a year. He must have had a hard time keeping track. Go on, Joan."

"I was sixteen, and Foster Benedict had been my secret crush for years," Joan said in a low voice. "When I read in the *Record* that he was staying at Mr. Bluefield's I did a very silly thing. I phoned him."

She flushed. "You can imagine the conversation—how much I admired his work, my stage ambitions... He must have been having a dull time, because he said he'd like to meet me. I was in seventh heaven. He began to take me out. Drives up to the lake. Moonlight readings... I certainly asked for it."

She sat forward nervously. "I guess it was like one of those oldtime melodramas—the handsome roué, the foolish young girl—the only thing missing was the mortgage. Would you believe that when he promised me a part in his next play I actually fell for it?" Joan laughed. "And then he went away, and I wrote him some desperate love letters he didn't bother to answer, and I didn't see or hear from him again until last night.

"And then when he made his royal entrance into The Playhouse, he not only didn't remember Wrightsville, or Mr. Bluefield, he'd forgotten me, too."

She was staring into the mirror of the time-polished floor. "I was a stranger to him. Just another scalp to add to his collection. I'd meant so little to him that not even my features had registered, let alone my name."

"I warned you six years ago that Benedict was pure poison," Roger shouted, "but would you listen? Ellery, if you knew how many times I've begged her to get off this acting kick and marry me—"

"Let's get to you, Rodge. I take it your evasions last night also covered up a prior acquaintance with Benedict?"

"How could I explain without dragging Joan into it?"

"Then you met him at the same time, six years ago?"

"I knew she was dating him—a high-school kid!—and I'd read of his weakness for the young ones. I was fit to be tied. I collared him one night after he took Joan home and I warned him to lay off. I said I'd kill him, or some such juvenile big talk. He laughed in my face and I knocked him cold. He was sore as hell about it—I'd mussed up his precious profile—and he banged right down to headquarters to prefer charges of assault. That was when Dakin was Chief of Police. But then I guess Benedict had second thoughts—bad publicity, or something. Anyway, he dropped the charges and left town."

"Did the brawl get into the *Record?*"

Roger shrugged. "It was a one-day wonder."

"And was Joan named in the story?"

"Well, yes. Some oaf at headquarters shot his mouth off. Dakin fired him."

Ellery shook his head. "You two are beyond belief. How did you expect to keep all that from Newby? Last night when you denied having known Benedict, Joan, didn't you notice Newby send one of his men on an errand? He's a city-trained policeman—he wouldn't take your word. He'd check the *Record* morgue and his own headquarters files. He may even have phoned the New York City police to search Benedict's apartment—Benedict's bragged often enough in print about his collection of feminine love letters.

"So Newby either knows already, or he'll learn very soon, that you both lied to him on a crucial question, and exactly what happend six years ago, and exactly why. Don't you see what you've handed him? —On a silver platter?"

Joan was mute.

"From Newby's viewpoint there's a strong circumstantial case against you, Joan. Situated in the only other dressing room on that side of the theater, you had the best opportunity to kill Benedict without being seen. The weapon? You wouldn't have had to move a step out of your way en route to Benedict's dressing room to take the knife from the toolchest. What's been holding Newby up is motive."

Joan's lips moved, but nothing came out.

"Newby knows perfectly well that Benedict's conduct onstage last night, rotten as it was, toward a girl who'd never laid eyes on him before would hardly pass muster as a reason for her to run for the nearest knife. But with the background of that romance between you six years ago in this very town, Joan, and your lie about it, and especially if the New York police dig up your letters, Benedict's humiliation of you in public last night takes on an entirely different meaning. It becomes a motive that would convince anybody. And any jury.

"Add to opportunity, weapon, and motive Benedict's dying declaration, and you see how near you are to being formally charged with the murder."

"You're a help," Roger flared. "I thought you'd be on Joan's side."

"And on yours, Roger?"

"Mine?"

"Don't you know you're Newby's ace in the hole? You threatened six years ago to kill Benedict—"

"Are you serious? That was just talk!"

"—and you beat him up. You've admitted the knife that killed Benedict is yours, and you brought it to the theater the day of the murder. You probably can't account for your whereabouts every minute of the short murder period. If not for Benedict's statement, Newby would have a stronger case against you than against Joan. As it is, Rodge, you may be facing an accessory charge."

For once Roger found nothing to say. Joan's hand stole into his.

"However," Ellery said briskly. "Joan, do you still say you didn't kill Benedict?"

"Of course. Because I didn't."

"Would you be willing to take a test that might prove you didn't?"

"You mean a lie-detector test?"

"Something far more direct. On the other hand, I've got to point out that if you did kill Benedict, this test might constitute evidence against you as damning as a fingerprint."

Joan rose. "What do I do, Mr. Queen?"

"Rodge, ask the police officer in the car parked across the street to drive Joan and you to Newby's office. I'll meet you there." He took Joan's hand in both of his. "This is beginning to shape up as quite a girl."

"Never mind her shape," Roger said. "Can't you go with us?"

"I have something to pick up," Ellery said, "at a hardware store."

ACT III. Scene 2.

Ellery walked into Anselm Newby's office with a small package under his arm to find Joan and Roger seated close together under Newby's mineral eye.

A tall thin man in a business suit turned from the window as Ellery came in.

"Fowler's been telling me about some test or other you want to make, Queen," the little police chief said acidly. "I though we'd agreed you were to keep your nose out of this case."

"That was a unilateral agreement, you'll recall," Ellery said, smiling. "However, I'm sure you wouldn't want to make a false arrest, and the Prosecutor of Wright County wouldn't want to try a hopeless case. Isn't that so, Mr. Odham?" he asked the man at the window.

"So you know who I am." The tall man came forward with a grin.

"The *Record* runs your photo with flattering regularity."

Prosecutor Odham pumped Ellery's hand. "Art Chalanski, my predecessor, had told me some fantastic stories about you."

"Apparently Chief Newby doesn't share your enthusiasm for fantasy," Ellery murmured. "By the way, Mr. Odham, you *were* about to charge Joan Truslow with the Benedict murder, weren't you? I haven't dared ask the Chief."

Newby glared and Prosecutor Odham chuckled. But there was no humor in the Prosecutor's frosty gray eyes.

"What have you got, Mr. Queen?"

Ellery said politely to the police chief, "May I see the knife?"

"What for?"

"In a moment. Don't worry, Chief, I won't so much as breathe on it."

Newby opened the safe behind his desk and brought out a shallow box padded with surgical cotton.

The bloodstained knife lay on the cotton. He held on to the box pointedly.

"This thin short line of indentations in the tape of the handle." Ellery made no attempt to touch the knife. "Have you determined yet what made them, Chief?"

"Why?"

"Because they may either blow up your case against Joan or nail it down."

Newby flushed. "You'll have to show me."

"I intend to. But you haven't answered my question. Have you decided what kind of marks these are?"

"I suppose you know!"

"Anse," Odham said. "No, Mr. Queen, we haven't. I take it you have?"

"Yes."

"Well?" Newby said. "What are they marks of?"

"Teeth."

"Teeth?" The Prosecutor looked startled. So did Joan and Roger.

"Maybe they're teethmarks and maybe they're not," Newby said slowly, "though I admit we didn't think of teeth. But even if they are, only two teeth could be involved—"

"Four," Ellery said. "Two upper and two lower—there are corresponding impressions on the other side of the haft. What's more, I'm positive they're front teeth."

"Suppose they are. These could only be edge impressions, and they're certainly not distinctive enough for a positive identification."

"You may be right," Ellery said soberly. "They may not prove to be positive evidence. But they may well prove to be negative evidence."

"What's that supposed to mean?"

"Suppose I can demonstrate that Joan Truslow's front teeth couldn't possibly have left these marks? Or any pairs of her contiguous teeth upper and lower, for that matter? Mind you, I don't know whether they demonstrate any such thing. The only teeth I've experimented with so far are my own. I've explained to Joan the risk she's running. Nevertheless, she's agreed to the test."

"Is that so, Miss Truslow?" the Prosecutor demanded.

Joan nodded. She had a death grip on the sides of her chair seat. As for Roger, he had entangled himself in an impossible combination of arms and legs.

Odham said, "Then Mr. Queen, you go right ahead."

Ellery's package remained intact. "Before I do, let's be sure we agree on the significance of the teethmarks. Last night Roger told us he didn't put the freshly taped knife in the toolchest backstage until Act One was nearly over. Rodge, were those marks in the tape when you dropped the knife in the chest?"

"You've forgotten," Roger said shortly. "I've never seen them."

"My error. Take a look."

Roger untangled himself and took a look. "I don't see how they could have been. The knife wasn't out of my possession until I put it in the chest, and I'm certainly not in the habit of gnawing on knife handles." He went back to Joan's side and entangled himself again.

"What would you expect Fowler to say?" Newby said.

Joan's hand checked Roger just in time.

"Well, if you won't accept Roger's testimony," Ellery said, "consider Arch Dullman's. Last night Dullman said he saw the knife in the chest directly after the curtain came down—as Benedict came offstage, in fact—and he was positive there were no indentations in the tape at that time. Didn't Dullman tell you that, Chief?"

Newby bit his lip.

"By the testimony, then, someone bit into the tape *after* Benedict entered his dressing room and *before* we found him. In other words, *during the murder period.*" Ellery began to unwrap his package. "The one person who we know beyond dispute handled the knife during the murder period was the murderer. It's a reasonable conclusion that the impressions were made by the murderer's teeth."

Chief Newby's teeth were locked. But Odham said, "Go on, Mr. Queen."

Out of the wrappings Ellery took a roll of new black-plastic friction tape and a large hunting knife. He stripped the cellophane from the roll and handed roll and knife to Roger. "You taped the original knife, Rodge. Do a repeat on this one." Roger set to work. "Meanwhile, Joan, I'd like you to take a close look at the original."

Joan got up and walked over to Newby. She seemed calmer than the Chief.

She really has talent, Ellery thought. "Notice the exact position of the marks relative to the edge of the handle."

"About an eighth of an inch from the edge."

"Yes. Oh, thanks." Ellery took the test knife from Roger and gave it to Joan. "I want you to take two bites. First with your front teeth about an eighth of an inch from the edge, as in the other one." He looked at her. "Go ahead, Joan."

But Joan stood painfully still.

"The moment of truth, Joan?" Ellery said with a smile. "Then try the Method. You're a pirate and you're boarding the fat Spanish galleon with a knife in your teeth, like any self-respecting buccaneer." He said sharply, "Do it."

Joan breathed in, placed the haft to her mouth, and bit into it firmly.

Ellery took it from her at once and examined the marks. "Good!

Now I want you to take a second bite—well clear of the first, Joan, so the two bites don't overlap. This time, though, make it a full bite."

When she returned the knife Ellery ran to the window. "May I have the other one, Chief?" He was already studying the test impressions through his lens. Newby, quite pale, brought the murder weapon, Odham at his heels.

Joan and Roger remained where they were, in a dreadful quiet.

"See for yourselves."

The police chief peered, squinted, compared. He went back to his desk for a transparent ruler. He made a great many deliberate measurements. When he was through examining the upper surfaces of the hafts he turned the knives over and did it all again.

Finally he looked up. "I guess, Mr. Odham," he said in a rather hollow voice, "you'd best check these yourself."

The Prosecutor seized knives and lens. Afterward there was a glint of anger in his eyes. "No impressions of any two adjoining teeth, either in the matching bite or the full set, are identical with the impressions on the murder knife. Same sort of marks, all right, but entirely different in detail—not as wide, not the same spacing—there can't be any doubt about it. You have a lot to thank Mr. Queen for, Miss Truslow. And so do we, Anse. I'll be talking to you later."

Not until Odham was gone did Joan's defenses crumble. She sank into Roger's arms, sobbing.

Ellery turned to the window, waiting for Newby's explosion. To his surprise nothing happened, and he turned back. There was the slender little chief, slumped on his tail, feet on desk, looking human.

"I sure had it coming, Queen," he said ruefully. "What gripes me most is having put all my eggs in one basket. Boom."

Ellery grinned. "I've laid my quota of omelets, Chief. Do you know anyone in this business who hasn't?"

Newby got to his feet. "Well, now what? Between Benedict's putting the finger on this girl and your removing it, I'm worse off than when I started. Can you make any sense out of this, Queen?"

"To a certain point."

"What point's that?"

Ellery tucked his lens away. "I know now who killed Benedict and why, if that's any help."

"Thanks, buddy."

"No, I mean it."

"I wish I could appreciate the rib," Newby sighed, "but somehow I'm not in the mood."

"But it's not a rib, Chief. The only thing is, I haven't a particle of proof." Ellery rubbed his nose as Newby gaped. "Though there *is* a notion stirring . . . and if it should work . . ."

ACT III. Scene 3.

The following morning's *Record* shouted:
LOCAL GIRL CLEARED IN KILLING!
The lead story was earmarked "Exclusive" and began:

"Joan Truslow of the Wrightsville Playhouse company was proved innocent yesterday of the Foster Benedict murder by Ellery Queen, the *Record* learned last night from an unusually reliable source.

"Miss Truslow, allegedly Chief Anselm Newby's main suspect in the Broadway star's sensational killing, was cleared by the New York detective in a dramatic session at police headquarters. A secret demonstration took place in the presence of Chief Newby and Prosecutor Loren Odham of Wright County. The exact nature of the test was not disclosed, but it is said to have involved the knife that slew Benedict.

"Chief Newby would neither affirm nor deny the *Record*'s information.

" 'I will say that Miss Truslow is no longer a suspect,' Newby told the *Record*. 'However, we are not satisfied with some of her testimony. She will be questioned further soon.'

"Asked whether he was referring to strong rumors around headquarters last night, Chief Newby admitted that Miss Truslow is believed to be withholding testimony vital to the solution of the murder.

"By press time last night, Miss Truslow had not been located by newsmen. She is said to be hiding out somewhere in town.

"Prosecutor Odham could not be reached," et cetera, et cetera.

The *Record* story's "Exclusive" tag was an understandable brag. Wire service and metropolitan newspaper reporters had invaded Wrightsville at the first flash of Foster Benedict's slaying, and the war for news raged through the town. The *Record* disclosure almost wrecked Stanley Bluefield's plans to take up his personal war with Wrightsville's Philistines where mere murder had broken it off.

Stanley had sent out a call for his entire company. They converged on The Playhouse on the morning the *Record* story broke to find the forces of the press drawn up in battle array. In a moment the surrounded locals were under full-scale attack; and Stanley, purple from shouting, sent to police headquarters for reinforcements.

A wild fifteen minutes later Chief Newby laid down the terms of a truce.

"You people have one hour out here for interviews with Mr. Bluefield's company," the chief snapped. "Nobody gets into the theater after that without a signed pass from me."

As it turned out, the newsmen retired from the field in less than half their allotted time. One of their two main objectives was not present: Ellery had slipped out of the Hollis early in the morning and disappeared.

Their other target, Joan, who showed up at The Playhouse with Roger, had refused to parley. To every question fired at her about "the testimony vital to the solution" that she was reported to be withholding, Joan looked more frightened and shook her head violently. "I have nothing to say, nothing," she kept repeating. Nor would she reveal where she was staying.

On being attacked in his turn, Roger became totally deaf. In the end he had charged into the theater with her, and the press beat a disgusted retreat shortly after, to bivouac at various High Village bars.

Chief Newby stationed police at the stage entrance, fire exits, and in the lobby, and left for an undisclosed destination.

So it was with slightly hysterical laughter that the company greeted Stanley Bluefield's opening words: "Alone at last."

They were assembled onstage under the working lights. Stanley had hopped up on a set chair.

"You'll all be happy to hear that we're going right ahead with *The Death of Don Juan.*" He raised his little paw for silence. "With due respect to the late Foster Benedict, he saw fit to make a farcical joke out of our production. We're going to do it *properly.*"

Someone called out, "But Mr. Bluefield, we don't have a Don Juan."

Stanley showed his teeth. "Ah, but we will have, and a good one, too. I can't disclose his name because I haven't completed the business arrangements. He should be joining us the day after tomorrow.

"I spent most of yesterday making cuts and line changes and revising some of the business, especially in Act One, where I think we've been in danger of wrong audience reactions. Today and tomorrow we'll go over the changes, so we ought to be in good shape when our new Don Juan gets here. Meanwhile, as a favor to me, Mr. Manson has kindly consented to walk through the part for us. Does anyone need a pencil?"

They plunged into the work with relief.

The day passed quickly. Sandwiches and coffee were brought in twice. There was only one interruption, when a tabloid photographer tried to get into the theater by stretching a ladder across the alley between a window in the next building and The Playhouse roof. But he was intercepted, and an extra policeman was assigned to the roof.

It was almost ten o'clock when Stanley called a halt.

The company began to disperse.

"Not you, Miss Truslow!"

Joan stopped in her tracks. It was Chief Newby.

"I haven't wanted to interfere with Mr. Bluefield's working day. But now, Miss Truslow, you and I are going to have a real old-fashioned heart-to-heart talk. Whether it takes five minutes or all night is up to you. I think you know what I'm talking about."

Joan groped for one of the set chairs. "I have nothing to tell you! Why won't you let me alone?"

"She's out on her feet, Chief," Roger protested. "Can't this wait?"

"Not any more," Newby said quietly. "You stay where you are, Miss Truslow, while I get rid of those newspaper men outside. I don't want the papers in on this just yet. I'll come back for you when the street's clear."

The theater emptied. Lights began winking out. One harsh spotlight remained onstage. Joan cowered in its glare.

"Roger, what am I going to do? I don't know what to do."

"You know what to do, Joanie," Roger said gently.

"He won't let go of me till . . ."

"Till what? Till you tell him what you're hiding?" Roger pushed a curl of damp blonde hair back from her forehead. "I know you've been hiding something, darling. I've known it longer than Newby. What is it? Can't you tell even me?"

Joan's hands quivered in her lap.

"He's bound to get it out of you tonight."

"Rodge—I'm afraid."

"That's why I want you to share it with me, baby. Look, Joan, I love you. What good would I be if I didn't share your troubles?"

"Rodge . . ."

"Tell me."

She swallowed twice, hard, looked around nervously. The deep silence of the theater seemed to reassure her.

"All right. All right, Rodge... The other night—during the intermission—when I was in my dressing room feeling so hurt by Foster's not remembering me..."

"Yes?"

"I decided to go down to his dressing room and—and... Oh, Rodge, I don't know why I wanted to! Maybe to tell him what I thought of him..."

"Hurry it up," Roger urged her. "The reason doesn't matter! What happened?"

"I was about to step onto the ladder from the landing when I heard Foster's dressing-room door open below, and... *I saw him.*"

"The murderer?" Roger cried.

Joan nodded, shuddering. "I saw him sneak out... and away."

"Did you recognize him?"

"Yes."

"But my God, Joan, why didn't you tell Newby?"

"Because he'd accuse me of making it up. At that time the Chief was sure I'd done it."

"But now he knows you didn't!"

"Now I'm just plain scared, Roger."

"That Benedict's killer will come after you? He's not getting the chance!" Roger cupped her chin fiercely. "You're ending this nightmare right now, young lady. Let me get out of these work clothes, and then you're going outside to tell Newby who murdered Benedict—and the more reporters that hear it the better. Don't move from here, Joanie, I'm only going as far as the prop room—I'll be right back."

The darkness swallowed him. His rapid footsteps died away.

Joan found herself alone on the stage.

She was perched stiff-backed on the edge of the big Spanish chair at the base of the light cone formed by the spot. There was no other light anywhere. The dark surrounded and held her fast, like walls.

The dark and the silence. The silence that had reassured her before, now made her uneasy.

Joan began to move her head. They were small, jerky movements. She kept probing here and there with furtive glances, over her shoulder, toward the invisible wings, out into the crouching blackness beyond the dead footlights.

"Rodge?" she called.

The quaver of her own voice only brought the silence closer.
"Roger?"
Joan curled up in the chair suddenly, shut her eyes tight.
And as if drawn to the place of her imprisonment by her fear, a bulky blob of something detached itself from the murky upstage formlessness and crept toward the light.
It began to take stealthy shape.
The shape of a man.
Of a man with something gripped at chest level.
A knife.
"*Now!*" Ellery's roar dropped from the catwalk far over the stage like a bomb.
Quick as Chief Newby and his men were, Roger was quicker. He hurtled out of the wings and launched himself at the man with the knife like a swimmer at the start of a race. He hit the man at the knees and the man went over with a crash that rattled the stage. The knife went skittering off somewhere. The man kicked out viciously, and Roger fell on him and there was a sickening *crack!* and the man screamed once. Then he was still.
As soon as he could, Chief Newby hurried to the set chair. "That was as good an act as Broadway ever saw! And it took real guts, Miss Truslow." He bent over the chair, puzzled. "Miss Truslow?"
But Miss Truslow was no longer acting. Miss Truslow had peacefully passed out.

ACT III. Scene 4.

One of the waitresses in the Hollis private dining room was clearing the table as the other poured their coffee.
"I hope you didn't mind my choice of menu, Joan," Ellery was saying.
Under the cloth her fingers were interwoven with Roger's. "How could I mind such a lovely steak?"
"I was commemorating the steak knife he lifted from the Hollis in your honor."
"In case I forgot?" Joan laughed. "That was the longest dream of my life, Ellery. But I'm awake now, and that's even lovelier."
"Queen, where's the dessert you promised?" Chief Newby asked. "I've got a lot to do at headquarters."
"No dessert for me," Joan said dreamily.

"Likewise," Roger said likewise.

"You don't eat this dessert," the Chief explained, "you listen to it. Anyway, *I'm* listening."

"Well, it goes like this," Ellery began. "I kept urging Benedict, as he was dying, to tell me who stabbed him. When he was able to get some words out, seconds before he died, Conk Farnham and I were sure we heard him say, 'The heroine'—an unmistakable accusation of you, Joan. You were heroine of the play, and Benedict didn't know—or, as it turned out, didn't remember—your name.

"But then the toothmark test proved Joan's innocence. Dying men may accuse innocent persons falsely in mystery stories, but in life they show a simple respect for the truth. So Benedict couldn't have meant the heroine of the play. He must have meant a word that sounded like heroine but meant something else. There's only one word that sounds like heroine-with-an-e, and that's heroin-without-an-e.

"The fact was," Ellery continued, "at the very last Benedict wasn't answering my who-did-it question at all. His dying mind had rambled off to another element of the crime. Heroin. The narcotic.

He emptied his coffee cup, and Chief Newby hastily refilled it.

"But no drug was found," Joan protested. "How did drugs come into it?"

"Just what I asked myself. To answer it called for reconstructing the situation.

"When Act One ended, Benedict entered the star dressing room for the first time. He had forgotten to bring along his makeup kit and Arch Dullman had told him to use the makeup in the dressing room. In view of Benedict's dying statement, it is now clear that he must have opened one of the boxes, perhaps labeled makeup powder, and instead of finding powder in it he found heroin."

"Benedict's finding of the drug just pointed to the killer," Newby objected. "You claimed to be dead certain."

"I was. I had another line to him that tied him to the killing hand and foot," Ellery said. "Thusly:

"The killer obviously didn't get to the dressing room until Benedict was already there—if he'd been able to beat Benedict to the room no murder would have been necessary. He'd simply have taken the heroin and walked out.

"So now I had him standing outside the dressing room, with Benedict inside exploring the unfamiliar makeup materials, one box of which contained the heroin.

"Let's take a good look at this killer. He's in a panic. He has to shut Benedict's mouth about the drug before, as it were, Benedict can open it. And there's the toolchest a step or two from the door, the tape-handled knife lying temptingly in the tray.

"Killer therefore grabs knife.

"Now he has the knife clutched in one hand and all he has to do is open the dressing-room door with the other—"

"Which he can't do!" Newby exclaimed.

"Exactly. The haft of the knife showed his teeth marks—he had held the knife in his mouth. A man with two normal hands who must grip a knife in one and open a door with the other has no need to put the knife in his mouth. Plainly, then, he didn't have the use of *both* hands. One must have been incapacitated.

"And that could mean only Mark Manson, one of whose hands was in a cast that extended to the elbow."

Joan made a face. "Really, Roger, was it necessary to break his wrist all over again last night?"

"It was him or me—or you." Roger leaned over and kissed her. Joan blushed.

"Don't mind these two," Newby said. "You sure make it sound easy, Queen!"

"I shouldn't have explained," Ellery sighed. "Well, the rest followed easily. The hospital said they would keep Manson under observation for twenty-four hours. So he must have been discharged too late on opening night to get to the theater before the play started. He must have arrived during intermission.

"With the audience in the alleys and the fire-exit doors open, all Manson had to do was drape his jacket over his injured arm to conceal the cast, mingle with the crowd in the alley, stroll into the theater, and make his way to the backstage door on the side where the star dressing room is. He simply wasn't noticed then or afterward, when he slipped out and parked in the Hollis bar—where Dullman and the *Record* reporter found him."

"But Mark Manson and *dope*," Joan said.

Ellery shrugged. "Manson's an old man, Joan, with no theatrical future except an actors' home and his scrapbooks. But he's still traveling in stock, hitting small towns and big-city suburbs. It's the perfect cover for a narcotics distributor. No glory, but loot galore."

"He did a keen Wrightsville business before he took that tumble. We've already picked up the two local pushers he supplied." Chief Newby folded his napkin grimly. "Middlemen in the dope racket are usually too scared to talk, but I guess the pain of that wrist you broke for him all over again, Fowler, was kind of frazzling. Or maybe he figures it'll help when he comes up on the murder rap. Anyway, Manson got real chatty last night. The Feds are pulling in the big fish now."

Ellery pushed his chair back. "And that, dear hearts, as the late Mr. Benedict might have said, is my cue to go on—on to that vacation waiting for me in the Mahoganies."

"And for yours truly it's back to work," Newby said, pushing his chair back too.

"Wait! Please?" Joan was tugging at Roger's sleeve. "Rodge . . . haven't you always said—?"

"Yes?" Roger said alertly.

"I mean, who wants to be an actress?"

That was how it came about that young Roger Fowler was seen streaking across the Square that afternoon with young Joan Truslow in breathless tow, taking the shortcut to the Town Clerk's office, while far behind puffed the Chief of Police and the visiting Mr. Queen, their two witnesses required by law.